GOD'S BANKER

By Chris Malburg

ALSO BY CHRIS MALBURG

Deadly Acceleration
How Fire Your Boss
Bonds Now!
Surviving the Bond Bear Market: Bondland's
Nuclear Winter
Planning for the Small Business
Small Business Accounting for Decision Makers
The Controller's and Treasurer's Desk Reference
Controller's Business Advisor
The Cash Management Handbook
The Professional Investor's Tax Guide
Business Plans to Manage Day-to-Day Operations
The Property Tax Consultant's Guide

God's Banker

By **Chris** Malburg

Library of Congress Cataloging-in-Publication Data
Malburg, Chris
God'd Banker / Chris Malburg
ISBN-13: 9781499630619
ISBN-10: 1499630611
1. Assassination--Fiction. 2. Pope--Fiction. 3. Catholic Church--Fiction 4. Coup de ta--Fiction 5. Vatican Bank--Fiction 6. Vatican City--Fiction 7. St. Peter's Square--Fiction 8. Barrett sniper rifle

TABLE OF CONTENT

* * *

GOD'S BANKER

BY CHRIS
MALBURG

Prologue

Thump went the oak door. His Eminence Cardinal Angelo Armato leaned his substantial body weight against the timbers, thick as his thigh, and shoved. The door to the room of the *Segnatura* clicked into place as two sets of brass fittings slid from striker to receiver in the equally heavy solid oak doorjamb. Armato shoved home the two iron bolts—each the length of a man's arm with one above and one below the golden door handle. The *Segnatura* was now sealed.

He turned from the door and faced the room before him. Torches lined the Vatican's ancient walls, providing the main illumination. Candelabras of solid gold stood, each bearing multiple candles whose flames danced among the red velvet seat cushions and the oval table. The soft, flickering light made the room—small by Vatican standards—seem warm and cozy. Around the table sat five of the 16th Century Roman Catholic Church's most powerful cardinals. These were the men who advised the Pope on setting Church doctrine and running the world's largest religious organization of its time.

His Holiness, Pope Alexander VI, sat at the head of the table. For this meeting the Pope wore his formal regalia. He looked to the back of the *Segnatura* and nodded permission for Armato take his seat. His Holiness intended to impress his all-powerful manifestation of God's splendor as His personal representative here on earth to the Cardinals. Every part of his papal regalia this evening was symbolic. His Holiness bent his great head slightly to begin. The five-sided *mitre* sitting atop his head was of the finest snow-white satin. From the sharp tip at its highest point on down to its ornate headband it was decorated with solid gold fittings and two rubies—front and back—each weighing in at 20 carats. Above all other components of the papal regalia, the *mitre* established his ultimate authority and signified his accountability only to God. For what he had in mind tonight, this perfectly stated his authority.

He shifted uncomfortably under the weight of the *amice* he wore around his neck—no more than a fancy, stiffened napkin, really—whose function was to prevent chafing from the heavy *cope* that enshrouded his entire body. The *cope's* heavily embroidered eggshell-colored satin shown through the golden thread used to decorate and once again signify the Pope's ultimate power back here on earth. He looked around the table at each of his Cardinals. Their faces were bathed in the flattering candlelight. Each had a look of expectation on his face. It was as the Pontiff intended. Tonight, he thought, their expectations would be rewarded ten times, twenty times over.

He had chosen his venue carefully. His Holiness loved this room. The *Segnatura* was his personal study and library. In this room he convened his most intimate and sensitive meetings. His eyes lifted up to the ceiling—as was his habit. His aides had told him the Cardinals thought this affectation meant His Holiness was seeking some divine inspiration before beginning. The glimmer of a smile crossed his lips at this admission. In truth, Pope Alexander VI was merely admiring Raphael's frescoes that adorned the vaulted ceiling and walls. His Holiness always enjoyed admiring the great artist's works from this particular seat.

The Pope slowly lowered his eyes and briefly held the golden pectoral cross in both hands. It hung from a golden chain around his neck. How will these men, each more loyal to their own causes than to either me or to the Church, receive what I am about to tell them? It was a question that had haunted the Pontiff for months as he pondered what to do with his information. In the end, he concluded it was too momentous for a single man, even the Pope, to hold alone. So, after months of prayer and deliberation, he decided to hold this meeting and tell them what he alone knew. Its very existence had the ability to tear his precious Church asunder if misused. But Alexander VI had a plan.

"Your Eminences," began His Holiness as he formally addressed his Cardinals, "I asked you to the *Segnatura* on this evening to tell you something." Pope Alexander VI paused to look at each of the five Cardinals again. He saw now that each leaned a little closer, edges of their red capes falling onto the tabletop. None had the temerity or impudence to rush His Holiness. These greedy men could not comprehend the secret he had decided to disclose.

The Pope continued. His 82 year-old voice was firm and unwavering. "The Roman Catholic Church in its history has amassed a fortune in property and businesses." His comments were well rehearsed. Begin with something they all know. "What you do not know is the base from which this fortune came. Since Constantine recognized Christianity in the year of our Lord 313, the Church began vesting herself with the raiment of the world. Accumulation of a vast treasure of worldly objects became testimony to her strength and power. This wealth was used over the centuries to build the most prestigious cathedrals the world has seen, to dress Church clergy in vestments of vast opulence. As the Church grows, so does its mounting need for ever more earthly riches."

His Holiness, Pope Alexander VI, knew a pause here would enhance the dramatic effect of what he would say next. He looked at His Eminence Cardinal Angelo Armato seated across the table. Of all his Cardinals, Armato was the one to worry about. Opposite him and across the vast table sat Cardinal Douglusio Esparza. He was the architect and designer of the most beautiful churches and cathedrals throughout his native Spain. Esparza had the smile and look of one eager to get his hands on some of the riches the Pontiff described. But His Holiness knew that in Esparza's case it would be used to build even more churches, ever grander in their opulence.

The Pope continued, "Still, this vast treasure has been growing for hundreds of years. It is stored in a single place. Throughout the Church's history, only the current Pope has known its location. Until tonight." This he said with a firmness of conviction that signified there was no turning back from the decision to share its location.

"Indeed, Your Eminences, I have seen the cavern in which the Church's wealth is stored. Words cannot describe what is buried deep within. There are thick golden ropes as long as tall men. There are solid golden statues of horses, life size in stature. Hand carved alabaster busts of every Pope and his Cardinals since the beginning line the walls. And there is more. Much, much more. A fleet of sailing ships with masts and sails hoisted sit on blocks, ready to carry these riches to safety should the need arise."

The Pontiff glanced around the table. Certainly he had every man's rapt attention, as he knew he would. "I have a map of its location. This is what I want to disclose to you tonight in the *Segnatura*. The map is too important to our Church to leave in the hands of just one man. Tonight I am entrusting each of you with a fragment of the map."

The cardinals sat dumbfounded for only a brief moment. Then they began speaking excitedly among themselves. All but Cardinal Armato, who sat silent as stone.

"Please," said Pope Alexander VI, "this vast treasure is intended for use in the Church's ministries and to further establish and affirm its predominance as God's chosen religion." This stopped the cardinals excited chatter dead. "Yet the incredible value of the Church's possessions is too immense for a single man—even the Pope—to hold by himself." The Pope nodded his head to one of his personal acolytes standing motionless off to the side before an object lying on the floor and covered with a brilliant red velvet spread whose borders were embroidered with golden rope. In its center was the richly embroidered three-bared cross of the 16th Century Catholic Church, also in gold.

"You are a counsel of five—my most trusted advisors. I fear that my health is not what it once was. Before our Lord calls me to Hhis side, I must entrust to each of you five a part of the map locating the Church's secret cavern where it houses these most splendid earthly riches. I caution you not to pool your resources to plunder the cavern. Rather, I ask you to use

4

the best judgment God has bestowed on all of you to allocate it according to our Church's needs."

The Pontiff nodded to the acolyte standing next to the red velvet-draped object. The man pulled the richly adorned covering, revealing the object beneath. The velvet cloth slid effortlessly over the flat, polished granite surface it covered. His Holiness heard a collective intake of breath from around the table. Indeed, he too paused to gaze at the stone tablet now sitting before them on the floor. Though he had seen this tablet many times, the map engraved on its flawless, shiny face along with the complicated writing it contained, he always had to stop and wonder at what his predecessors were thinking when they created this most secret of maps.

Set into the tablet were three iron chisels standing upright in the stone. They were equally spaced along a line that scored the tablet. Hitting any one of the chisels would cleave the tablet into two neat pieces; three chisels, meant six pieces.

His Holiness nodded one final time to the acolyte. The man easily hefted an iron hammer with a one-meter hickory handle. The man's forearms bulged as he brought the hammer up to his shoulder and then paused for the briefest of seconds to glance at the Pope for confirmation. The Pope inclined his head with the ornate *mitre*, giving final permission. Suddenly the hammer came crashing down on the first chisel. He quickly hoisted the hammer again to his shoulder and again brought it crashing down on the second. He repeated this action a third and final time. Now the granite tablet lay on the floor in six neat pieces.

His Holiness nodded again to his acolyte. The man quickly left by the Pope's private door to the *Segnatura*. The Pope rose from his seat slowly, since he was an old man who was weighed down by the gold-decorated cope, *mitre* and the rest of his ornate vestments as well as his immense responsibilities for his Church. He walked to the six pieces of tablet. His hands rose from his sides, palms up in a commanding gesture for the Cardinals to rise and come to him. His Holiness repeated St. Teresa's Bookmark prayer. She was the Carmelite nun from Avila who was also a celebrated mystic. The prayer was called St. Teresa's Bookmark because she had carried it around, stuffed inside her prayer book, where it was found after her death in 1582. The Pontiff picked up a heavy piece of the tablet and handed it to the first of the five Cardinals, repeating St. Teresa's prayer of trust:

> *Let nothing disturb you,*
> *Let nothing frighten you,*
> *All things are passing,*
> *God only is changeless,*
> *Patience gains all things,*
> *Who has God wants nothing,*
> *God alone suffices.*

Once all five pieces of the tablet that pinpointed the Church's treasury cavern were distributed, His Holiness picked up the sixth tablet piece, turned on his heel—feet encased in silk and gold slippers—and left the *Segnatura* through his private door.

* * *

Pope Alexander VI died suddenly within six months of this momentous evening in the Vatican's most exclusive of rooms. In that sense, his fears for his health were prophetic. Within twelve months after that, each of the five Cardinals had also died. Just two died of natural causes for they were also elderly and medicine in the 16th Century was not what it is today. The other three fell victim to accidents that occurred frequently during that time in history. The last of the Cardinals to succumb was His Eminence Cardinal Angelo Armato, the one that Pope Alexander VI distrusted. None of the pieces of tablet that were distributed that evening have surfaced to date. Nor has the vast treasure promised by Pope Alexander VI ever been found. Though many have searched their entire lives, each has come up empty. Existence of an immense treasure cavern containing the Catholic Church's vast wealth accumulated from the beginning to the 16th Century remains nothing but a much talked-about rumor to this day.

Chapter 1

Present day

"Wind?" The Professional spoke the single word softly. It was a question tinged with a slow Louisiana drawl. "Wind?" he asked again only a little more insistently but still maintaining his calm, working professional's demeanor. The Professional's assistant took his eye from the 14X spotter scope and glanced at the unobtrusive wind meter he had set up on the roof of the building next door to the *Castel Sant'Angelo*. It was two stories lower than the Castel and allowed him to look down on its roof. Had someone not known exactly where to look, they would have missed the little meter entirely. But the man was not familiar with such an instrument as the little wind meter. He squinted through his spotting scope at its digital readout. There, now in clear focus were the numbers. He searched briefly for the English equivalent to his native Italian.

"*Vento,*" he said then caught himself. "The wind, she is a still, *approximo* three," he said in badly broken English with a heavy Italian accent.

"*Vento,*" muttered the Professional. Christ. He pulled his right eye off the rifle scope and looked at his spotter. The man was dressed in the drab brown friar's cassock with rope around the waist. On his feet were the traditional sandals. "She-yit," he said more in calm frustration than anger. Truth was he actually liked the guy. He was doing the best he could under the circumstances. No one could fault that. The man, dressed as a friar, had never done this before. Hell, who had? Only a very select few. Less than ten men in the world. And of those few, there was just one who could do what the Professional had been hired to do and he was it.

"Three? Seriously? *Approximo* three? Three what, Greggory? Exactly three what?" He swiveled his own riflescope over at the wind meter. Sure enough it read 3.1 miles per hour. He had already converted the miles per hour into kilometers in his head—5.0 kilometers per hour. He needed metric units of measure since that is what his riflescope used. The reading that Greggory dictated was confirmation. He would just have to be careful they were both communicating the measurements in the metric he was used to rather than the good ol' American English that Greggory thought he wanted.

He looked out of the darkened room in which they had set up shop. He spotted the orange windsock on top of the Vatican offices across St. Pete's Square, then aimed the rifle toward it. He had brought along the Barrett M98-Bravo Long Range because of its accuracy over the distance he would have to cover. It rested atop the ancient but hugely sturdy table on which he lay and was supported with four sand bags under and around its 27-inch barrel.

They were using an empty, locked storage room that was way off the tour routes of the ancient castle that originally served as a mausoleum for the emperor Hadrian before it was converted into a papal fortress in the 6th century. The room offered a small window with no glass so it was open to the air. They were perched eight stories directly above the Castle's entrance on *Piazza di San Pietro* that had an almost unobstructed sight line up the thoroughfare, *Via della Concilliazion,* to *Piazza de Sant Pietro* and next door to the building within that housed his target—the *Basillique de Sant Pietro.* Sure, the Professional thought, there were some trees and that pesky Obelisk to deal with. But from this particular window nothing interfered with his narrow sight line straight to where his target would soon be standing.

The Professional had chosen the room not only for its height and down-angle to St. Peter's balcony, but also for its 13th-century secret passageways in the unlikely event things went wrong. These passageways had provided sanctuary to many popes in times of danger. Indeed, Clemente VII hid here during the 1527 Sack of Rome. Its upper floors attracted tourists for its lavishly decorated Renaissance interiors. The fourth floor held the famous *Sala Paolina* fresco. Two stories above that, Puccini had immortalized the terrace in his opera, *Tosca.* The

Professional was holed up in a nondescript and never used storage room two more stories above that.

At the very top was the restaurant. He had dinner there two nights ago when he was scoping out the place as a possibility. Just another tourist, he thought as he had sat there enjoying a plate of pasta with the view of Rome and its attractions. No wine though. He never consumed alcohol or coffee when he was on assignment. Now as he lay there on the table working on his calculations he could smell the roasting beef, pork, chicken and the delicious sauces that went with them wafting down from above.

Using the riflescope's metered cross hairs, he calculated the angle of the windsock to the rooftop—just 20 degrees. It gave him the wind reading at the target's point some 1,790 yards away. Doing the calculation in his head as he had done thousands of times before, he arrived at the wind speed on target—4.9 miles per hour. *The wind grew stronger as it progressed along his firing lane—by 1.8 miles per hour.* It took him seconds to convert these to metric units. He performed the computations in his head.

"Okay Greggory, enter the rest of the data for me, would ya'," the Professional drawled.

Greggory worked slowly, clumsily. He muttered to himself as he entered and then reentered the data. This should have been easy. All the Italian spotter actually had to do was enter the temperature, humidity and distance from the sea. From there, the laptop computer would execute the actual calculations. Greggory continued to slowly punch the keys, entering the data into the laptop's sighting solution software, taking care to enter only metric units.

"Did ya' remember to get the altitude this room is at?"

"*Si grazie.* We are 60 meters above sea level--"

Fuck. "No Greggory. We are *not* 60 meters above sea level. We are exactly 62.3 meters above sea level." Fuck. The Professional looked at Greggory and saw the horror of his error etched over his face. "No problem man. I caught it. Just put it into the computer correctly at 62.3 meters, okay?"

"*Si grazie.* I also calculate the down angle from here to the target at 62 degrees."

The Professional paused for a moment. Over the last week he had struggled to train his spotter. He removed his eye from the scope again and looked down at St. Peter's Square Balcony where he was pointed. "Sounds about right," he said. "What about the mirage, Greggory? Y'all rememba' to factor that in too? The Professional knew that a shot at 1,790 yards—1636.8 meters—would encounter a mirage effect that needed to be factored into the equation. A temperature difference of 10 degrees required one minute of angle correction to counter the mirage effect. "And what's the temp now Greggory?

"Ah, m-i-r-a-g-e?" the word came out slowly, halting and without comprehension, as if it had never before crossed his lips. "Excuse. What is m-i-r-a-g-e again?"

Christ, the Professional wanted to scream. But he wouldn't allow his pulse to run away from his absolute control. Not at this late stage. Instead he mustered all of his calm and said softly, "Greggory, if ya don't rememba what the mirage factor is, then you could not have entered it into the goddamn computer. Am ah right?" Continuing to breath slowly, his voice maintained its even gait. He spoke calmly, patiently. "Just what the fuck do ya' think we're doing up here, Greggory? I have failed you in your training. Y'all have mah deepest apologies, Suh."

Greggory mistook the Professional's soft, even voice for forgiveness. He smiled and said proudly, "No *Signore*, you have trained me very well. We now do a very great thing in service to our Lord."

She-yit, thought the Professional. A religious zealot. But he already knew this. That's all the fuck I need right now, he thought. Okay. Calm, even breathing. Just talk him through it. With his soft, confident and calm voice he said, "That's fine, Greggory. Now, tell me the current temperature please."

Si. It is now 22.8 degrees Celsius. The temperature is dropping as the sun is a-going down behind the buildings."

Alrighty, then. The Professional knew the answer. Temperature change affected mirage, which affected the shot angle. "Give me minus one degree of down angle, make us at 61 degrees. That is the mirage effect."

Greggory clumsily pressed the numbers into the keyboard. Then he muttered something in Italian. He reentered the numbers yet another time and hit the Return button. Within three seconds the result popped up on his screen.

"What's she say? About one click left and one click up?"

"Close, *Signore*. The computer, she a-says a-two clicks left."

The Professional pulled his right eye off the scope again. He looked out the window and followed the line of colorful flags lining St. Peter's Square right up the wall of the building. His eye then climbed up the four stories to the balcony and watched the two flags on either side of the balcony blow in the gentle breeze. Both were the brilliant half gold and half white flag of Vatican City, the Papal State with the Keys of Saint Peter crossed diagonally over the white half. Each flag consistently blew north, in the gentle breeze. "I still say just one click left."

The Professional reached his right hand to the elevation and windage knobs on the ATN 4-12X80 Day/Night scope and made the adjustment. He had already clicked the parallax control knob to where he wanted it. He reached his thumb and forefinger into the ammo box he had brought and extracted a single cartridge. For this shot he had chosen the .338 Lapua Magnum Long Range Sierra Match King Hollow Point Boat Tail projectile. He would load the Barrett's detachable 10-round magazine with just five of these highly specialized and deadly Finnish-made cartridges. The Professional figured if he couldn't hit what he was aiming for with those, it would all be over anyway.

With the assurance of a trained expert who had done this enough times to fill three sniper's log books, he slowly slid the bolt closed, feeling its smooth action pushing the cartridge into the breach and then clicking precisely closed when it was properly seated. The Barrett was not a new weapon. Indeed, the Professional had used it to fill all of one sniper log book and half of another. Like a favorite hammer that a skilled carpenter used every single day, he knew each crevice and mark on the Barrett. They were entirely of his own making. The Professional had been issued the Barrett when he graduated from SEAL sniper school. The ultra-precise weapon had been in his possession ever since. The Professional kept it cleaned and oiled to the meticulous standards that only a few men in the world with such dedication to his craft would understand.

He laid his finger on the aluminum alloy frame outside the trigger guard and put his eye back into the scope. He took one breath, slowly let it out, relaxed his entire body and began his deadly wait, hoping that he had caught all of Greggory's errors.

* * *

CHAPTER 2

Jim Cramer had seen hundreds of companies go public on the New York Stock Exchange. Still today's initial public offering was special. Historic, really. He shifted his stance on the battered hardwood floor of the NYSE. He had been standing here for the last 45 minutes and his feet hurt. He asked himself again why he didn't wear the Ecco rubber soled walking shoes today instead of the Mezzlan Giotto loafers. The Eccos cost $80 and were his favorite. The Giottos set him back $1,100 and hurt. He shifted his stance, trying again to get comfortable. He had selected a position between the specialist stations of IBM and the newest offering, GOD. He shook his head at this *chutzpa*. GOD, of all the stock symbols the Vatican Bank could have chosen. This one was a no-brainer. Who but the Catholic Church itself would or could call its stock GOD?

"Booyah Maria. What do 'ya think of this one?" Cramer spoke into his lapel microphone, directly to his co-anchor for today's historic first trading day of GOD. Maria Bartaromo was in Rome preparing for her own historic interview of the Pope himself. The interview was to take place in the Pope's personal residence located on the floors occupying the right side of St. Peter's Basilica. The famous balcony where the Pope gives the Angelus, the blessing of the faithful, every Sunday was immediately off of the Pope's personal study where Bartaromo sat impatiently waiting for His Holiness to arrive.

"Should be a wild day," Maria mumbled without taking her eyes from her notes. "Where GOD goes is anybody's guess. How's it going there on the floor?" she asked absently still scanning her list of questions.

Television viewers worldwide would see the two anchors on split screen. Cramer saw in the monitor as she looked up, a look of irritation on her face at being interrupted. This one is big, thought Bartaromo. The stuff of which Pulitzers are made. She wasn't going to screw it up. Her contract was coming up for renewal. A Pulitzer wouldn't hurt the negotiations. They had another two minutes, 30 seconds left in the commercial break.

13

Cramer looked around at the GOD stock specialists. The trading jackets they wore were bright red and looked something like the Cardinal's capes the six real Cardinals wore as they stood up on the balcony ready to ring today's opening bell. The Vatican Bank pulled out all the stops, thought Cramer. Of course he had heard the rumors—uttered only within the confines of the deal's chief underwriter. And even then it was said in *sotto voce* so as not to be overheard. That Cramer knew of the Vatican's management difficulties was testimony to his connections over at Goldman Sachs. It was nothing stated in the notes to GOD's published financial statements. They were pristine as everyone knew. No, thought Cramer, this was something else. Something that could screw over those religious dogmatists who just had to own a piece of the Church.

Cramer knew this was the biggest public offering ever. Bigger than Google. Bigger than Facebook. The Catholic Church was the religious epicenter to 1.2 billion faithful the world over. The only other religion that could lay a glove on the Roman Catholic Church was the Sunni Muslims at around 940 million.

Cramer had begun his two-minute drill before airtime. He started his breathing faster and shallower. He flexed his abdominal muscles to get the blood flowing. He willed his heart rate to ramp up. "Maria, this one is gargantuan. All those Catholics see it as their religious duty to take a position in GOD. Goldman Sachs is managing this issue. They're underwriting it with four other bow-tie firms." Cramer looked up to the balcony and saw Cardinal David Caneman reach to the bell ringer as the clock was about to strike 9:30 a.m. New York time, to start the trading day. "Gotta go."

Jim Cramer looked into the camera facing him and saw the red light glow. His producer's fingers silently counted down 3-2-1.

His voice was ready to screech out the breathless words that were his attention-grabbing trademark, "Jim Cramer, here on the floor of the New York Stock Exchange! Folks this is going to be

14

the biggest day in IPO history." The opening bell clanged for the prescribed five seconds. "The Vatican Bank has just gone public." Cramer made it a point of looking up to the Big Board where the stock prices were listed. He knew the producer in the truck parked outside at the curb would have already cut the picture to the board and that now just his voice boomed out to over 2.2 million television sets tuned to CNBC.

"There are no prices for GOD listed yet folks. As usual the deal runners have allocated the stock they get to sell to their biggest clients—all huge institutional investors—and some of the whales they manage money for. The little guy gets left out. No matter how bad they want this stock—and millions of the religious faithful want it, believe me. None will get any. Word has it that the opening price set during last night's pricing conference call held by Goldman was $80 a share. We'll see where it trades by day's end." Then, Cramer being Cramer, he could not resist editorializing.

"I just gotta say it; can't stand not to. Folks, just steer clear of GOD. Who knows where this stock is going? Even if you could get some, don't. Just don't." Cramer's voice rose to its characteristic squeak when he wanted to make a point. "Let the elephants pound around the stock, taking it wherever they will. Do not let yourself get trampled in the process." He stopped to catch his breath. "Remember Facebook. It started at too high an issue price, then the managers and underwriters drove it up even further to get their clients out at a profit. From there they allowed it to free-fall. I'm not saying that's going to happen here. But hey. Why take the chance? Just sit tight and keep your powder dry. Maria?"

Through the ATN scope, the Professional could clearly see Bartaromo. She was seated on a chair placed in front of the Pope's desk inside the French doors standing open to his office that led out to the famous balcony facing Saint Peter's Square. There were two television cameras—one on each side of her. The Pope's chair was two feet to her left. There were also two standards holding the high intensity lights that were needed for the cameras. He shifted the Barrett's scope so its reticle framed the side of Bartaromo's right temple. With all the light used there, he could see her plain as day. The cross-hairs intersected inside her right ear. He paused for a few seconds not breathing, not moving. Then he shifted his view down to her notes. From just over one mile away he could read the questions she would be asking the Pope when he finally arrived.

Even from the Castle, the Professional could hear the crowd gathering inside Saint Pete's Square. The Pope's scheduled address after the Vatican Bank went public had been announced weeks ago. He had been inside his sniper's nest for over four hours already. Thousands had beaten him into the Square to get the best places to stand. Well boys, thought the Professional, this is one time your faithfulness will be rewarded. You can tell your grandkids that you saw the Pope get killed on a beautiful summer day in Rome.

He saw Bartaromo suddenly stand up as an acolyte opened a door to the office and His Holiness himself walked in. Through the scope he watched her shake his hand. She did not genuflect or take his hand to kiss the ring. The Professional thought that punctilious ceremony would have demeaned her. She was the interviewer. Let the official clergy bow and scrape.

The Professional's contract called for a public execution. Would have been just as easy to get the shot off now while the Pope was sitting in his office. He saw the sight lane was clear as the Pope sat down beside the reporter. Still, may as well give the people a show they'll never forget.

"Greggory?" he asked calmly, "y'all give me the data readings again, please." The Professional would monitor all the data that went into computing the sight adjustments in case anything changed between the last time he adjusted the scope and just before the shot.

"Si, *Signore*," said Greggory. Then he slowly began reciting the numbers from the various instruments. "Temperature, wind, angle of the shot, m-i-r-a-g-e effect, distance." This last measurement would not change. They had agreed that the shot

16

would be targeted at the middle of the Pontiff's forehead as he was standing at his microphone on the balcony overlooking the Square. Shortly after the lectern and microphone were placed on the balcony Greggory had used a laser range finder to precisely measure the distance. He raised his spotting scope and pressed the laser range finder button again. A tiny red dot appeared on the microphone for just an instant and then vanished. He read the numbers inside the image he saw through the eyepiece. "Exactly 1,790..." Greggory paused for a second. "Yards." He heard the Professional release the breath he had just taken in anticipation of asking 1,790 what? Greggory converted the yardage to meters and verified that was what he had entered into the computer.

His Holiness continued chatting amicably with the famous financial reporter. She asked her questions; he answered. They were having a mutually beneficial time. Both were oblivious to the gravely menacing danger lurking just over one mile away in a darkened storage room in the Castel Sant' Angelo.

Back on the NYSE floor Jim Cramer eyed his guest. His Eminence Cardinal David Caneman stood beside him, resplendent in his red and white Cardinal's vestments and snow white Roman collar. Cramer pointed his microphone toward His Eminence. Caneman was answering his second question. The cleric tugged at his red cape and touched a finger to his *pileolus*, the red skull cap.

"...Yes, Jim. But frankly, the Vatican Bank is going public for the same reason all large enterprises do. The Bank needs new capital to grow and to further its business purpose—"

"But Your Eminence," interrupted Cramer as was his style even with Roman Catholic Cardinals who head the largest financial institutions, "this action will now put the American Vatican Bank under the microscope of regulatory oversight. In light of all the allegations against priests with young boys and allegations of financial improprieties over the years, can the Bank really stand such scrutiny?" Cramer saw the shadow of irritation cross the Cardinal's face, then vanish just as quickly.

"Of course, Jim. I completely understand such concerns." The banker-turned-priest-turned-banker responded slowly, deliberately. His slight European accent was utterly charming. He was making his point clearly, for all to hear. What he said in these initial minutes of the Vatican Bank's public offering would define how the stock would perform for months to come. With a market capitalization of over $200 billion, the Vatican Bank's CEO was printing money with his every word. The voice and its inflections lent him a cultured, continental aspect, which he played for all it was worth.

"The Bank's public offering will provide statutory oversight of the Church and its activities by legal authority—the United States Securities and Exchange Commission. This is the most thorough regulatory body in the world. It will prove to itself and everyone that the Church has nothing to hide." His Eminence paused to flash his most trustworthy smile into the cameras. "Indeed, it is about time that the Church came out from behind its antiquated robes and vestments and into the light. Personally, Jim, I welcome the transparency and visibility to public scrutiny that this unprecedented action provides. For decades the Roman Catholic Church has maintained a policy of strict secrecy in everything it does. No more. We act for the betterment of mankind in everything we do. Perhaps this will now put to rest such accusations of impropriety."

Cramer's voice ratcheted up a notch so that his audience could hear the characteristic squeal that signaled he was about to crush his subject with a question from out in left field. "Your Eminence, what about the rumors of a vast treasure the Church has accumulated over the centuries? That would explain the sudden pop GOD is getting in its stock price even in these initial minutes. I mean, investors gotta be thinkin' what if such vast resources actually do exist. The Vatican Bank will be sitting on a pile of assets that would liquefy its balance sheet into the foreseeable future. If the rumors are even half true, then there is no question ever about GOD's financial stability."

18

Cardinal David Caneman placed a slender, manicured finger inside his Roman collar and pulled it slightly away from his neck. He slowly shook his head as would a patient and beloved teacher working with a misguided student. The gentle, engaging smile appeared again to capture the cameras. "I have heard the same stories ever since I was in seminary....that a secret treasure vault exists somewhere and that over the centuries the Popes have handed down its secret location from one to the other. I can tell you, Jim, there is *probably* nothing to it. They are *most likely* just that, rumors. I know His Holiness personally and have since he was a parish priest. If there were any truth to such rumors, he would have told someone—"

"You, perhaps?"

His Eminence paused for a moment at the unexpected impudence. Then he nodded his head as if considering the proposition of being entrusted with such information. "Maybe. Though I would never presume to speak for His Holiness. There are several who have earned His Holiness' trust."

Cramer glanced at the Big Board and saw where GOD was now trading. In just the last few minutes it had risen from 91 to 98. Let's see if such a rumor has legs with this stock, he thought. "Folks, to put this into perspective, the possibility of just $10 billion in hidden assets that the Vatican Bank could tap into would drive up the stock price at least 25 percent. Maybe more, much more, if there's a reason to believe there's even more wealth behind that."

Cardinal David Caneman stepped in, "Jim, if people are buying GOD stock hoping for a sudden discovery of centuries-old, secretly hidden assets, they probably would do better buying T-bills at these inflated yields."

Cramer heard the urgent voice of his producer through his earpiece. "Folks we're going to split screen now with Maria Bartaromo in Rome for an exclusive interview with His Holiness, Pope Julian IV."

The split screen now showed His Holiness with Maria Bartaromo on one side and Jim Cramer with His Eminence Cardinal David Caneman on the other. This Pope's image was pure magic the world over. Without a doubt he was among the most loved of the modern era Popes even though he had been in his office for just five years now. Cardinal Caneman deeply bowed his head as protocol demanded. Because it was just an electronic image he did not genuflect as would have been the custom had they been meeting face-to-face.

Courtesy due his high office required the Pope to speak first. "Ah, David you are looking well this fine morning—it is morning there in New York, is it not?"

Caneman smiled at his boss. "Yes, Your Holiness, it is a magnificent morning here in New York. And thank you. Today is truly a great day for the Church." His smile extinguished just after he saw the camera's red light die away.

Finally, with the niceties out of the way, the road was clear. Maria Bartaromo jumped in with her first question. "Your Holiness, with its public stock offering, the Vatican Bank stands to raise upwards of $200 billion. That is a lot of money, sir. What will you do with it?" Despite her focus on this major interview, Bartaromo could not help looking at the Pope closely as she spoke. She had never seen him in person before. So, it's true, she thought. The Pope's ears are every bit as big and standing out from his head as the cartoonists depict them.

The Pope smiled at Bartaromo. There was a twinkle in his eye. This was part of his self-effacing charm and one of the reasons he was so loved by Catholics and others the world over. He was also skilled in disarming his critics. "Maria, it's okay. My ears are magnificent, are they not?" His Holiness continued smiling at his joke on catching Bartaromo staring. "Really, Maria, I get that a lot. I don't mind. But you *are* right. The $200 billion that Vatican Bank will raise today is a lot of money.

"I am personally grateful to all those who may chose to buy stock in the *Istituto per le Opere di Religione,* The Institute for Works of Religion, or more commonly known as the Vatican Bank. But you know, Maria, the money is not mine to do anything with." He smiled into the camera. "Why, I would not have the first idea of how to manage such vast resources." He opened his hands and lifted his palms upward in as clear a gesture as any pope had ever made that this was the God's honest truth.

"But fortunately, my dear, I have a true banking professional in His Eminence Cardinal David Caneman to run Vatican Bank. Cardinal Caneman reports to a Committee of Cardinals—"

"Excuse me, Your Holiness," interrupted Jim Cramer from his side of the split screen. "But doesn't the Committee of Cardinals report directly to you?"

"Ah is that you, Jim Cramer? I am a big fan. Huge," said the Pope. "Booya, Jim Cramer. I just love it when you bite the heads off of those rubber toy bulls you have on your show and shout, *Buy, Buy, Buy*." With that simple, perfectly timed compliment the Pope sucked out any credibility or relevance Cramer's question might have had as if the air had suddenly escaped fully and completely from a toy balloon. "It is Cardinal Caneman and the Committee of Cardinals who actually run the Vatican Bank."

The Professional watched on his iPhone connected to a wireless earpiece as Bartaromo led the Pope and Caneman through another three minutes of questions. Each minute he lifted his head to check the flags along St. Peter's Square that led up to the balcony on which His Holiness would soon appear.

"Greggory?" The Professional's voice still carried its soft, relaxed intonation that was the stock-in-trade of every marksman the world over when his target was in the crosshairs. "Has there been any change at all in the numbers you fed into the targeting solution? Are you watching…carefully…Greggory?"

"I…I am a-watching, *Signore*. Nothing has changed. If it does I will tell you immediately and put the change into the computer. I will then-a tell you what adjustments to make. I promise, *Signore*."

The Professional lowered his eye back into the scope and said, "That is just what ah wanted to hear, Greggory. Just what ah wanted to hear." He inhaled deeply, then let it out in a long, slow cleansing breath. He forced his heart rate to drop another three beats per minute.

"...Your Holiness I deeply appreciate the time you have given me."

"Not at all, Maria," replied the Pope, gracious as always. "May God bless you and all of those watching us." He waited until the red lights on both television cameras went out and the grip staff extinguished the bright lights.

The Pope placed his hands on the arms of his chair—his staff always insisted that every chair had sturdy arms. Since his left hip was replaced a year ago he needed the leverage to lift himself into a standing position without making a painful face. The Pope was definitely not one to request assistance for such a simple task that he had been doing all by himself for over 80 years.

As His Holiness Pope Julian IV rose, so did Bartaromo. "Come, walk with me, Maria. Have you ever stood beside the Pope when he addressed the faithful from this magnificent balcony overlooking St. Peter's Square? I remember the first time Pope John Paul invited me to join him. It was...awesome...as the young ones say." His eyes twinkled at the upcoming opportunity to commune with his flock on this glorious late summer afternoon.

The Professional's eye was now glued to the scope. He watched as the reporter linked her arm though the Pope's and the two seemed to walk right toward him through the French doors that opened onto the balcony. The Professional saw Bartaromo's arm resting inside the Pope's. Probably more to steady the old man than anything else. He ignored a wild cheer from the crowd as they caught their first glimpse of their beloved Pope stepping to the microphone. The Professional's right hand wrapped around the pistol grip integrated into the Barrett's stock. It felt totally familiar, comfortable. Indeed, over the years, the matte black paint on the grip had worn away in the exact spot where he placed his hand time after time after time. He placed his first finger inside the trigger guard and laid the first joint on the center of the trigger. He slowed his heart rate another few beats per minute.

After a career of firing hundreds of thousands of rounds, his trigger finger was in the most comfortable position for him. It allowed the second joint of his finger to remain pointed straight at the target as he pulled back on the trigger. His refined technique made it nearly impossible to push or pull the shot with his trigger finger.

The Professional watched His Holiness Julian IV step to the microphone. His scope was sighted in for exactly this distance. Just behind the Pope's right ear he saw Bartaromo standing. Even at this distance he could clearly hear the man's voice over the loudspeakers. The crosshairs of his scope were glued to the center of the target's forehead. This was the target picture he wanted. The Professional didn't pull the trigger with his finger so much as it was a function of what he saw with his eyes. As soon as the sight picture was exactly what he wanted he began squeezing the trigger. Just his right first finger—not the entire hand as some teach. He would continue squeezing the trigger until either one of the two things happened. First, the sight picture may change and require canceling the shot. Or two, the shot breaks and the weapon fires.

This Pope was an expert at using the media. He stood still at the microphone, looking over the glass lectern that held his notes. His head did not move as he had learned so the television cameras would have no trouble keeping him in focus. It was a warm, late afternoon. A gentle breeze blew in from his left and kept him cool in the heavy vestments he wore. He looked over the white roses covering the top of the balcony and out onto his people. Thousands of people. Maybe hundreds of thousands, he thought as he gazed over the green, grassy amphitheater, passed the monolith and through the two buildings that marked the entry into the Square on *Via della Concillazione*. Way off in the distance, easily discernable even at a mile away, he spotted

Castel Sant'Angelo. Through Rome's summer smog, the sun had turned its circular turret almost blood red.

Every meter of ground in St. Peter's Square was covered with people. Some held up signs. To his left, in the middle of the crowd the Pope read one that said, *Buy GOD stock—Invest in Christ.* The pleasant breeze continued to luff around him, keeping him comfortable. Pope Julian IV was quite enjoying himself. This is what being Pope is all about, he thought. God's humble messenger, taking His word to His people. What an honor. What a privilege.

Finally he raised his right hand. The crowd roared its approval. With his fingers spread wide, he slowly described the sign of the cross, blessing all and blessing this humble address.

The Professional watched the Pontiff's fingers spread. There was obviously a little wind at the target site a mile away. He could see the target's long, voluminous silk sleeves moving definitely left to right as the Pope's right arm raised to give the blessing.

"Greggory? Any change in the settings? Maybe the wind speed? Tell me now, please." The Professional's voice as always at this stage of his firing sequence was soft, calm. He had deliberately slowed his heart rate to where he wanted it.

The assistant checked his instruments. He raised the spotter's glasses to his eyes and focused on the Pope. "I still see the same wind speed as I entered into the computer, *Signore.* Do you have any changes, *prego?*"

The Professional watched the sleeves again. They moved back and forth now, no definite direction. "Na. Wind's swirling a little bit is all. Let's keep it where we set it, shall we?"

The Professional's trigger finger resumed its squeezing, waiting for one of the two things to happen. Cancel the shot or fire. Nothing changed in the site picture. The Professional's heart beat once, then came the definite *Phhhhht* of the Barrett and the deadly bullet was away. His heart resumed beating. Time slowed to almost a standstill. It always did at this distance.

24

The folding butt of the rifle recoiled into his shoulder. He immediately reacquired the target, unconsciously racked the bolt to send another round into the chamber without taking his eye off the target. He waited for the two full seconds it would take the round to reach its target.

With his hands off of the lectern, palms turned upward to heaven, nothing held the Pope's notes in place. The gentle breeze continued to swirl. Suddenly the top two pages lifted off the lectern and flew from left to right onto the balcony. The Pope did not need his notes. Not really. He knew what he would say on this day that the Vatican Bank became a publicly held corporation. Yet it was human nature to turn his head and reach out to grab them. This day, there was more at work than just one extraordinarily beloved man, a television reporter and over one hundred thousand faithful watching.

In that critical instant, the .338 Lapua Magnum projectile tore a hole clean through the Pontiff's left ear. It continued its supersonic downward trajectory unimpeded. It would have hit Maria Bartaromo dead center in the chest had she not quickly stooped to pick up the Pope's two pages the wind had carried to her feet. As it was, the bullet seared a hot, bloody trail through the outer flesh of her shoulder, then buried itself at the base of the stone column behind the lectern.

The Swiss Guards assigned to the Pope's protection detail do not all look like court jesters in the red, purple and yellow striped costumes some of them wear in public. Within one tenth of a second after hearing the unmistakable supersonic snap of the bullet, the guard in his charcoal grey suit was on the Pope. In a single motion the big man's arms wrapped around his charge and launched the two of them through the still open French doors into the office behind the balcony. The three other guards stationed with the Pope were just a hundredth of a second behind. They grabbed the others immediately surrounding the Pope—Bartaromo included—and dived into the office as well, throwing the doors closed behind them. The entire exit took less than two seconds.

The Pope lay there, his ear bleeding a flood of crimson onto the sky-blue carpet. Ear wounds always bleed profusely. The Swiss Guards checked the Pontiff over for any other injuries. The Pope pointed to Maria Bartaromo and ordered his people to treat her first. Her shoulder wound was equally non-life threatening, but bleeding heavily nevertheless. One of the guards already had a field dressing out and was pressing it into her shoulder to stanch the bleeding. For her part, Bartaromo grabbed her cell phone from her pocket and called into CNBC New York headquarters to file her eyewitness account of the assassination attempt on the Pope's life. Maybe this will get me that Pulitzer and fatten up my contract, she thought as her producer picked up.

The Professional had not missed often. This time it was just a freak incident of the target not cooperating. Gotta hand it to them boys, he thought. At this distance you account for the bullet's flight time. You always aim for where your target is *going* to be. Who knew His Holiness would try to catch some papers in the breeze? Never seen a subject get cleared outa the line of fire so fast, he thought again. Yep, gotta hand it to them boys of his. There had been no time—nor a clear shot of any kind—to make another attempt. He knew what came next. He rolled off the sturdy table that had served him well. With the speed and precision touch of the professional he was, his fingers flew over the 98-Bravo and its state of the art sniper's scope. Each part was dismantled to its smallest component and put into the mid-sized case with foam rubber inserts to hold each part. Just might need this again shortly, he thought.

The Professional should have left the weapon and scope and ran. But he couldn't. He had long ago defiled the serial number. Even without the serial number, this was a rare piece of equipment—something few even in the higher reaches of law enforcement had ever seen. Eventually Interpol might trace it back to SEAL Team 1 in Coronado, California, then right to him. He had changed his identity, looks and everything else that was

26

traceable no less than four times since leaving the Navy. He was a ghost, an enigma unidentifiable by any law enforcement agency in the world, though several probably had their suspicions.

The Professional set the Barrett's case on the stone floor and pulled his silenced Sig Sauer 9mm from a small duffel bag containing just his bare essentials. He raised the muzzle of the pistol and fired a bullet into Greggory's forehead that blew out the entire back of his head. No witnesses. Ever.

Then he picked up his luggage and left the sniper's nest, calmly and without running. He made his way down to the secret 13th-century passageways that had probably saved many popes in times of danger. They could just as well serve me, he thought as he put his exfiltration plan into gear. The Professional always had an escape plan. This assignment was not yet completed. The target's protection would now be on high alert. Jest makes the task a wee bit more challenging—and time consuming—is all, he thought as he walked unhurriedly along the ancient stone corridor.

* * *

Chapter 3

His Eminence Cardinal David Caneman swept into his offices
at the Institute for Works of Religion—the Vatican Bank. His
personal suite sat on the top floor of the historic JP Morgan
Building at 23 Wall Street, right next door to the New York
Stock Exchange. The short trip had taken him only five minutes
after the camera's red light faded out. He had quickly shaken
hands with that oaf, Jim Cramer, excused himself and made for
the exit elevators.

The Bank's security guards spotted Caneman as he exited
the private elevator that served just his suite. They quickly
opened the double doors made of heavy, glass-clad
polycarbonate that was capable of resisting penetration from
9mm rounds on up a 12-gauge shotgun blast and everything in
between. A male secretary hustled from behind his desk and
with a practiced expediency helped him out of his red cape.

Without saying a word, Caneman entered his executive
office, pushed the door shut behind him, and grabbed the
television remote from this desktop. He pressed some buttons
and the image of His Holiness arm-in-arm with Maria Bartaromo
walking from the Pope's private study onto the balcony
overlooking Saint Peter's Square emerged. Caneman absently
sat down on the plush sofa in the informal conversation area
where he entertained visiting dignitaries and watched the screen
with unblinking fascination.

His Eminence Cardinal Caneman split his time between his
offices in Vatican City, New York, London and Zurich. He was
a fixture in the world's financial capitals. He ruled the vast
fortune belonging to the Roman Catholic Church. Most of its
investments were held with the Rothschilds in Great Britain and
with JP Morgan in the US. At his insistence, the Bank held
enormous interests in oil—Shell and BP—and weapons—
General Dynamics and BAE. His prized hedge was the famed
Vatican gold bullion. It was worth billions and he kept it in the

Rothschild-controlled Bank of England and the US Federal Reserve Bank.

Caneman watched as the television screen showed the papal flags gently waving in the late afternoon breeze. He saw the Pope step to the microphone and raise his right arm as he always did when addressing the multitudes. Suddenly, the man twisted and lurched slightly to his right to catch some papers that blew off his lectern. "Shit," Caneman's voice exploded in the privacy of his opulent office. In that instant His Eminence Cardinal David Caneman thought that his boss just might actually be the blessed man the Church swore him to be.

The next images were of confusion as the famous balcony immediately emptied. Where the happy crowd was just seconds ago roaring its hearty approval, it was now screaming as one in anguish. Caneman yanked his cell phone out of his vestment inside pocket and pressed a single button. The connection was instantly made. He said, "Your man missed."

"Yes, so it would seem," said the urbane and cultured voice. It carried no concern or worry. As if these things sometimes happened and simply could not be avoided. "I will find out what happened. I am truly sorry. But, as I forewarned you, this business is not an exact science."

"Damn it. I am not interested in exact science," said Caneman. "I require results. The final result is what I have paid $2.5 million US for." He continued watching the screen. Apparently the television people had the camera inside the Pope's office used for the earlier interview now operating and providing the world a live feed. "Your man just managed to clip His Holiness' left ear. That huge elephant's ear. An amateur could have hit it. I paid $2.5 million US for a scratch on his ear? The man's barber accomplishes more when he clips the hair around and inside those enormous ears."

"He will not miss the next time—"

"Next time? You think your man will get another opportunity? You are a fool." Caneman was furious. He stabbed at the red button to disconnect the third party cutout he had used to hire the Professional. The man did not know to whom he was actually speaking. His Eminence was careful with his personal security. Caneman thrust himself back on the cashmere sofa, shaking with anger. "What do we need to do next?", he asked the empty office out loud as he tried to calm himself.

"We do what we set out to do," he answered himself. Cardinal David Caneman believed his own counsel was better than any of the sycophants who worked for him. He had converted to Catholicism just 15 short years ago. He had become a zealot for the Church even though he had been born Jewish. The Jews held no interest for him. They had allowed themselves to be marched off to the gas chambers once already; they would crumble yet again if forced. The Catholics, on the other hand, had a brave history he could understand and truly embrace. He had used his zeal to become a force within the Church in just these few short years. The Roman Catholic Church was his kind of organization—huge, filthy rich and ruthless to anyone who stood in its way.

It took some time, but His Eminence Cardinal David Caneman eventually managed to expunge the fury he felt from his body. He reached over to the sideboard of polished maple for the bottle of Henri IV Dudognon Heritage Cognac. He yanked the crystal cap from the bottle and poured a generous shot of the amber liquid into a bowl-shaped crystal Waterford brandy glass. He hardly tasted the wine as its supremely calming excellence flowed down his throat. Aged for 100 years in barrels that were air dried for five years before use, Caneman was drinking 41 percent pure alcohol. He took another sip and glanced at the bottle. It was certainly the most expensive component. Dipped in 24k gold and sterling platinum, the bottle was adorned with 6,500 brilliant cut diamonds. The cost to the Vatican Bank for Caneman's indulgence was around $2 million US. He barely noticed.

Now he sat there in luxurious silence, cocooned in his private office. He steepled his fingers, as was his habit when deep in thought. He caught a brief glimpse of the NYSE's Big

Board on the television screen. As he predicted, GOD stock was tanking. Even for a failed assassination attempt, it would fall. His phalanx of offshore entities to which he had diverted his personal holdings of original issue GOD stock would make several hundreds of millions from the short positions he had ordered them to take. He had anticipated the stock would drop like a stone on its first day of trading—after the Pope was so suddenly and unexpectedly killed.

Not enough, he realized. Not nearly enough. What to do? He had his mission clearly outlined. But its cost would tax the resources of even the Church's vast holdings. He blew air out in explosive frustration. May as well take advantage of even this limited opportunity, he told himself. Caneman was a disciplined financial engineer. That, he attributed to his Jewish upbringing and his mother's worship of money more than *El Shaddai*, the Almighty One. He had spread his holdings of GOD to brokerage accounts around the world. Always under street name to preserve anonymity and avoid detection of the beneficial owner. He pressed a second single button on his cell phone.

"Close out all the short positions and go long GOD." Then he disconnected the call. He had no doubt that his order would be followed. He had not expected to buy back the stock at the very bottom. Something close, within a few dollars, would be sufficient, he thought. His Eminence Cardinal David Caneman had just turned a profit of several hundred million by shorting GOD into double that, probably much more, depending on where GOD topped out in the next week or so when the Pope emerged back into the public eye with the scratch on that elephant ear of his. "Not nearly enough," Caneman whispered to his empty office once again.

* * *

CHAPTER 4

Summers in the small town of Elkhart, Indiana are balmy.
There is some rain. But a lot of places have rain. Wind
sometimes blows along the flat, open landscape that is normal
for this part of the country—just eight miles per hour on average.
Within city limits, wind speeds are usually less in the summer.
Temperatures were nothing like Dallas or Phoenix, where they
regularly climb into the triple-digits. The Navy's SEALs train in
Arizona to get acclimated to working in blistering environments.
No. Elkhart enjoys moderate temps in July and August in the
high 60's to low 70's. Respectable, but hardly intolerable. The
town has nice summer weather. Jack Schilling likes Elkhart,
Indiana in the summer.

Jack wears his white dress shirt with its collar unbuttoned
and his necktie loosened. His shirtsleeves are rolled down with
the cuffs buttoned as is his custom when in public. He feels the
uncomfortable pull across his back and shoulders. He forced
himself to casually walk out of the Kaito Automotive
Administrative building, across the open campus to the light
truck division's design and engineering lab. The cell phone he
kept in his pocket vibrated urgently again. He ignored it—again.
Schilling deliberately slowed his gait, enjoying the brief walk in
the morning sunshine. This will probably be my last few
minutes of relaxation for a while, he told himself. It seemed
every operation began slowly, seducing you into its web until it
irretrievably entwined you and there was no graceful or
honorable way out. He had turned off the television coverage
just before leaving his office.

Schilling punched in his four-digit access code and the door
lock into Kaito's design engineering lab snapped open. Once
inside, he stamped his shoes to loosen the dirt. Schilling waived
to the security guard behind the bulletproof glass. The guard
buzzed him into the design lab.

"Morning, Brad," said Schilling, stopping at the guard desk to sign in. "Nice day outside. Wish I could get out and take a run. What's the report say for this weekend?"

"Says it's gonna be a peach of a day tomorrow, Mr. Schilling. You and the missus going to the game?"

Schilling knew Brad was a real fan of minor league baseball. In the South Bend Silver Hawks they had one of the finest single-A league teams in the minors. Coveleski Stadium, the Hawks' home field, was just 15 miles east in South Bend. It was built in 1987 and named for Stanley Coveleski, the Hall of Fame pitcher. During the 1920 World Series Coveleski pitched three complete games to lead the Cleveland Indians in their win.

"Naw. Gotta work." Schilling glanced through the glass separating Reception from the engineering facility. Out in the bullpen he saw Helen Kaito intently looking over a drafting table while the engineers apparently explained something to her. Helen was the president of Kaito Automotive's Light Truck division. She was Schilling's boss as well as his wife. They had been married for just 11 months. Schilling felt the vibration of his cell phone erupt urgently again. He knew who it was and what the caller wanted.

"Too bad, Mr. Schilling. The Hawks are having a helluva season so far. I hear it's going to be a real barnburner of a game. The Boston Red Socks minor league team is in town. The Hawks arc starting the new guy, Marc Hankin, on the mound. The parent team just may call him up to the majors after tomorrow. Sure would like to see him pitch here one last time."

Schilling quickly reached into his pants pocket. "Well, Brad, just because I have to work, doesn't mean everyone does." Jack Schilling pulled out four tickets and a parking pass. "Be a shame to waste these, wouldn't it?" The CFO of Katio's light truck division handed over the tickets and the pass. "Enjoy the game, Brad. You and Bobbie have a hot dog for me."

"Just the guy we were talking about," said Helen Kaito as her husband walked into the power train engineering department. She still got a thrill seeing his powerful, athletic grace on the

move. He towered over her at six-feet two inches and 225
pounds of muscle and financial intellect. "These astute engineers
standing here beside me say you'll never go for the added
horsepower my marketing guys say this truck needs to sell. I, on
the other hand, have bet them drinks tonight at McHenry's that
you spend money like a drunken sailor, of which you were
actually one at some long-forgotten point in your life. And that
if more horsepower is what we need, then you'll find a way to
keep the profit margins where they belong."

Jack Schilling again felt the insistent vibration of his cell
phone in his pocket. He smiled in spite of the menacing call.
"Sorry guys. I'd like to join in but I'm afraid I need the
president's attention on another matter. Helen? A moment,
please?"

Helen Kaito knew that voice all too well. Jack's voice was
stiff, tight and invited no nonsense. "Sure, Jack. We'll wrap this
up later," she told the engineers. Helen and Schilling moved
away from the drafting table and walked toward the door, out
into the warm Elkhart summer sunshine. "What's up, sweetie?"
Already she knew that she wasn't going to like what her husband
was going to tell her.

Jack stopped them at the plant's flag park named Hero's
Walk. Kaito Automotive's light truck division flew their flags
proudly. When Jack and Helen returned from their last
adventure, resolving the Deadly Acceleration terrorist plot, they
had drawn up plans for the flag park to honor and respect those
Kaito customers who were killed behind the wheel, victims of a
terrorist group that used Kaito automobiles as the actual weapon.
Though the tragedy that killed almost 3,000 people was found
not to be the fault of Kaito, both Jack and Helen accepted
responsibility. It was the Japanese way. They walked inside the
grassy circle where marble benches and wood picnic tables with
umbrellas were placed so workers could take a break and enjoy
Elkhart's eight months a year of sunshine.

Jack stopped next to one of the stone benches beneath the
flag poles showing the American flag, the Indiana state flag and

34

the red and white ensign of Kaito Automotive Corporation. He glanced as always at the low marble wall that wrapped the interior of the small park. On its inside were inscribed the names of every victim killed during the Deadly Acceleration plot. Schilling would never forget what had happened. He vowed to never let such people seize the advantage like that again. He shook his head. The small park was empty right now. "You haven't seen the news in the last hour have you." It was a statement.

"No," said Helen. "I've been meeting with my engineers. What's happened now?"

"The Pope seems to have survived an assassination attempt. He was hit—NF—sorry, non-fatal wound to the head. A reporter was also hit—a through-and-through to the shoulder. Both will be okay, at least physically."

Helen held a hand to her throat. "My God, Jack. That's awful. Some crazy in the crowd?"

Schilling, felt his cell phone vibrate urgently again in his pocket. He saw her follow his gaze down his pants leg. "It's Smitty—again. He's been calling every few minutes for the last hour—"

"Since the assassination," observed Helen. She was well aware that Smitty—Brian K. Smith, Chief of the SEC's Enforcement Division, Jack's old employer—called every so often since he took over as Chief from Jack. "Better answer him. Maybe there's a connection."

"Oh there's a connection, alright," answered Jack. "The Vatican Bank became a publicly traded company less than two hours ago." He flipped the iPhone around and pressed the speakerphone button. "Smitty, sorry it took me so long to answer. You can't imagine how it is out here in the real world where you actually have to work to earn a living."

The disembodied voice came over the tiny speaker. "Yea, yea, bullshit. Jack. As if I was just another clueless bureaucrat waiting for my two hour lunch time to roll around."

Helen interjected, "Hi Smitty. How are you doing? Dating anyone I need to evaluate for you?"

"Hey, Helen. My favorite computer geek. Naw, Hon. Been too busy trying to keep my feet on the ground here at SEC. God help me, Jack, I don't know how you made it look so easy when you had my job and I worked for you."

"Wasn't so bad, Smitty. I had one very good second in command to shovel all the really hard stuff to. You need to get you one of those. That's why I recruited you right out of the Navy." Jack sat down on the marble bench so he was closer to Helen and they could keep their voices down. His voice deepened and lost all of its earlier playfulness. "So tell me, how's His Holiness and what's going on there in Vatican City?"

Smith's voice became deadly serious as well, "He'll make it, Jack. A single round tore the hell out of his ear, though. Guess the cartoonists won't have that to work with anymore. It would be unseemly making fun of a wound the Holy Father suffered in a failed assassination attempt. That reporter from CNBC, the one doing the interview, standing behind him on the balcony was just as lucky. She took the same round through the shoulder. Stitch her up and she'll be good as new in a few weeks."

"Sounds like both were being watched over today," said Jack. "But that's not the whole story is it, Smitty. Else you wouldn't have been calling me every few minutes since it happened."

There was a brief silence. Jack and Helen waited for Smith's reply. "Guys, whenever there's a violent assault perpetrated against a corporate officer of a company listed on a US stock exchange, the SEC launches an investigation. The Institute for Works of Religion—the Vatican Bank—is now a public company traded on the NYSE. It has a president—"

"That would be Cardinal David Caneman," said Helen. "I've been following their financial drama for the last year."

"Right, Hon. Caneman's the president and CEO. He's supposedly overseen by five cardinals who report to the Vatican's Secretary of State. Only problem is the Vatican's guy died of a stroke last month. In his absence, the Pope stepped in. The Pope is the Vatican Bank's chairman, at least for now."

"The *Camerlengo*," said Helen. "He's the appointed treasurer in succession for the Holy See. In this case, it's the Pope himself in the line of succession. Unusual, but it happened before sometime in the 18th century."

Jack looked at his wife of less than one year. How would she know such a thing, he wondered. Then he asked, "So what do five cardinals and a Pope know about running a financial institution that's now got a market cap of over $200 billion?"

The cell phone crackled a bit. "Yeah, Jack. I figured you'd get yourself briefed up before we talked. You were always one to save time. Thanks. You nailed the question of the day, Jack. As Enforcement Division Chief, it's my responsibility to launch this little investigation. Normally it's no biggie. Put a few of my auditors in the Vatican Bank's New York offices, go over the books, pronounce them clean then issue an unqualified opinion."

"Right," said Jack. "So why are you bothering me? I have month end closing coming up and some power train engineers to convince they need to save money, not spend it."

"Roger that, Jack. Sounds important. Only this investigation's not so normal. First it's the Pope who some guy tried to off. Not your normal run of the mill CEO. Second, it's the Vatican Bank. They have more money than God—or soon will once the billion plus faithful finish buying up their stock, then running up the share price. This deal in the next six months could put Vatican Bank way beyond Goldman, Citi, Chase and Morgan—both Morgans—in terms of financial resources. Any investigation—no matter how perfunctory—needs to be done right. There's only one guy I trust with such an assignment."

Jack had a string of expletives on his tongue, but swallowed them all. He was already way ahead of Smitty in identifying the seriousness of this attack and connecting the dots. He didn't like what he saw. "I'm out of the Navy, Smitty *and* the SEC. A private citizen. Got my hands full right here in Elkhart. I don't want any part of your investigation."

"I figured you'd say that, Jack. Do I need to get the Man himself to give you a call? I will. Sure as I'm sitting here on my butt in DC I will. He told me to say that when he called five minutes after His Holiness went down."

The Man, wondered Jack. He knew who Smith was talking about—the President of the United States. "I thought the President had forgotten about me long ago."

"Jack, nobody—not even a president—forgets the guy who stepped into the line of fire and put two in the chest and forehead of someone who was about to shoot him. Besides, your old man recommended you to him. Apparently he volunteered your services along with Helen's boss."

"My boss?" asked Helen. "You mean *my* father, don't you?"

"Sorry, Hon. They all talk frequently, I understand. Your dad, who just happens to be the chairman of Kaito Automotive, Jack's dad and the President. They're buds. High level, but buddies just the same.

"Smitty, I don't—"

"Come on, Jack. You know you're going to New York for me. Why put us both through this charade? Be in New York at the Vatican Bank's offices by noon tomorrow. Oh, and buddy? Wear a suit. You're representing the SEC. And be polite, for God's sake. You'll be meeting His Eminence the Cardinal David Caneman. I'll have boots on the ground—clerical, admin and support personnel—in the offices waiting for you. But you're running this show, Jack. Out."

The line went dead. Helen stood up from the stone bench as Jack put the phone back in his pocket. "So?" said Helen

"So what?"

"When do we leave?" asked Helen.

"We? Who said anything about we? This is probably just a routine SEC audit. I'm there to cover some bureaucrat's ass is all. Be back in a few days. A week tops—

"Come on, Jack. Someone believes there's a problem. Why else would the President himself have called Smitty and specifically demanded your presence? There's a lot of money on the line here. It's the Vatican, for goodness sake." Helen stopped for a second and thought. "Hmm. I don't think we can get a commercial flight out of here this late in the day to New York. I'd better charter us a jet."

Jack didn't want his wife anywhere near this audit. Big money. High profile people being shot at. Now the President is asking for him—a highly seasoned SEC investigator and former Navy SEAL. Jack knew his way around a balance sheet as well as the business end of an M4A1 assault rifle.

"There is no us, on this one, I'm afraid," Jack said.

"What?"

"Sorry, Helen. It's probably just like Smitty says—routine investigation of a public company launched as an abundance of caution when there's a crime perpetrated against one of its senior officers.

"That's no reason, Jack. You need my help. Where would you have been without me when all those Kaito cars had the deadly acceleration problem? I'll tell you where. Totally out of luck. Up the creek without a paddle. That's where." Helen eyed her husband there in the Elkhart summer sunshine, safe within the granite walls of the memorial park. "I'm coming with you, Jack."

"You're not invited."

"Try this spring roll," said Helen, handing Jack another deep fried delicacy. "I used Hi-Flying Gourmet this time to stock the jet. They're the best." She looked out the executive jet's window as Indiana's flat landscape rolled by 30,000 feet below them while they headed north to New York. "Once we land, where do we begin?"

Jack looked across the narrow isle at his wife. He sat comfortably in the jet's leather seat. He had rolled up his shirtsleeves as soon as they were airborne. He felt like he could breathe again. "Like I said before, sweetie, you're baggage— very pretty baggage—but someone way too important to bring into a dull audit." Besides, Jack thought, Noriko Kaito, would never forgive me if anything were to happen to his daughter. Especially if I knew ahead of time things could turn risky.

Helen uncrossed her long legs, shook off her summer sandals, then tucked one leg under her as she faced Jack. "Okay, Mr. Know-it-all, let's see what you know about the Catholic Church and its relation to Vatican Bank."

Jack paused for a minute. Testing me? She's testing me? He tried to remember his time in Catechism. All that came to mind in the few seconds he knew he had were the Stations of the Cross and the nun's ruler slapping his knuckles.

"That's what I thought," said Helen, eyebrows arching, a look of victory already crossing her face. "Vatican Bank is among the biggest financial powers, wealth accumulators and property owners in the global markets today. Its balance sheet rivals the wealth of most banks, corporations or giant trusts anywhere on earth. And that's before adding in the $200 billion from its recent public offering." She stopped for a second to be sure Jack recognized the importance of her contribution already.

"It's not quite the lily-white institution they would have you believe. The Church ministers to the religious needs of a world where two-thirds of its constituents earn less than $2 a day. About 20 percent of that population is underfed or starving to death. Yet, the Vatican Bank hoards the world's wealth, profits from its stock market accounts and at the same time preaches about its followers giving more so that it can continue its holy work." Helen looked up from the statistics and reports scrolling across her combat laptop. She had commandeered the tough little computer from Jack and Mr. Smith after the Deadly Acceleration adventure. Since then, it was never far from her reach.

"So how did the Vatican accumulate all this wealth over the millennium?" asked Jack.

"Ah, there's the real story, love of my life. They monetized sin—put a price tag on it then sold it to their sinners. The Church's leaders over the centuries knew that people would sin and there wasn't anything they could do about it. So they decided to profit from it. The bishops—and the popes they served—actively marketed guilt, sin and fear for profit by selling indulgences.

"Worshipers were encouraged to pre-pay for sins they hadn't yet committed and earn a pardon ahead of time. Those who didn't pay-up were threatened with eternal damnation. Another method was to get wealthy landowners to cough up their land and fortune to the church on their deathbeds, in exchange for a blessing that would supposedly enable them to go to heaven.

Pope Leo V rebuilt St Peter's Basilica by selling tickets out of hell to get the offenders off the hook. Then later, he sold the same poor souls tickets to heaven so they would be assured of reaching the Promised Land."

Jack selected a tuna sandwich from the tray of goodies on the table between them. "You're painting a picture of the Catholic Church as the biggest mafia on earth. You're saying they ran a protection racket, selling forgiveness from sin. And that's how they accumulated such vast wealth?"

"The practice of teaching people that they can be sinful all their lives and then pay for forgiveness in the end is a basic underpinning of many great religions throughout history. It is one of the chief causes of all the evil and dishonesty in the world. Indeed," said Helen, "if people were not taught about the material benefits of sin by the religious leaders themselves, then the big businesses of religion would die away as unnecessary. When they say that Jesus died for your sin, they want you to feel guilty. But they never, ever say exactly what your sins are that caused the death of someone who lived before you were ever born."

Jack held up his half-eaten tuna sandwich as an indicator that he wanted to speak. "So what's this got to do with the financial state of the Vatican Bank. Which is why I'm going to New York and you talked your way aboard this fancy jet with me?" He looked around its plush opulence of leather and chrome and remembered all those flights on the shabby C-130s, the SEAL's aircraft of choice.

"Apart from teaching you a little something about the entity you're investigating, the Church's wealth—past, present and future—is tied directly to the wealth their protection racket collected from the poor. Through the centuries the popes and the cardinals who worked for them hoarded knowledge. Who do you think kept the masses ignorant and in the dark by denying them a basic education? At times throughout history the Church prohibited anyone from reading or even possessing a Bible, under pain of death.

"Between 1095 and 1291 AD the popes launched no less than seven blood baths—though they called them Christian Crusades, they still amounted to torturing, beheading and mass murdering hundreds of thousands of Muslims in the name of God. The Pope's brutal solders were called Knights Templar or Knights of the Temple of Solomon and evolved into today's secretive brotherhood called the Freemasons."

Jack interrupted, "I know a little something about the Freemasons. Didn't Nick Cage star in that movie about them?"

"A very simplistic story concocted by Hollywood to sell movie tickets. Between 1450 and 1700 AD the Catholic Church followed up their holy terror with the infamous Inquisition. They justified this mass murder by accusing women of witchcraft and branding them as heretics—a crime punishable by death. It was the Freemason's predecessors, the Knights Templar, who carried out this bloody mission—"

"Okay, my expert on Church history and dogma, so you've done some homework on my client. I remember some accusations leveled at the Vatican during the Second World War."

"Right. It's common knowledge to anyone willing to look—as I have—that the Vatican was criticized for supporting Hitler and his Nazi regime during that black time in human history. The Pope is even said to have blessed Adolph Hitler and named him, 'The Envoy of God'.

"This brings us to the present. Over 1,500 priests and bishops have been implicated in the sexual assault of thousands of boys and girls in their trusting congregations and orphanages.

42

With so much money at their disposal to fight these charges and to cover them over when outright fighting didn't work, it's no wonder this abuse has just now surfaced. I'm sure it has been going on for centuries."

Jack sat back in his seat. He felt his ears pop as the jet began its descent into JFK airport in New York. So, this is the client the President of the United States has sent me to investigate, he thought. He sat there wondering what he might discover. "Okay, you know your Church history, I'll give you that. I might even go out on a limb and suggest these massive payoffs are the reason the Vatican Bank needed to go public in the first place. Their capital reserves are low by Church standards. But wasn't there something about a vast store of precious metals and gems belonging to the Church that was accumulated centuries ago and has been hidden ever since?"

Helen fastened her seat belt as the plane lined up on JFK's runway 2-2-Left. "That was only a rumor, Jack. Never amounted to anything. No one has ever proven it even exists. However, I did notice that Cardinal Caneman in his interview earlier with Jim Cramer on CNBC never outright denied that such a treasure existed."

"Of course he wouldn't," observed Jack. "Especially as his stock was going public. He'd want to keep such a ridiculous rumor alive to fuel speculation and thereby boost the share price. I'd call it the treasure premium." Jack wiped his hands on a napkin. "Still, isn't a $200 billion capital structure after going public a big enough war chest for the Vatican Bank? I mean, how much money do they think they need and what are they going to do with it?"

* * *

CHAPTER 5

"How may I assist, Your Eminence?" asked the young man whose desk sat just outside Caneman's private office. He jumped out of his chair even as he spoke the words. The young man was not a priest. He wore an elegant Joseph Abboud business suit and light blue dress shirt. The finely tailored suit did little to hide his physique. The man was a physical specimen. He appeared to be able to give a good accounting of himself in any situation. Even so, there was the unmistakable bulge of a pistol under his left arm that not even the finest tailor could conceal.

"Come with me," said Caneman as he purposefully strode past his first assistant. "Summon the others to the vault." Caneman did not break stride as he hurried out of the Vatican Bank's executive offices. His assistant instantly had his cell phone in hand and texted the emergency code to the four His Eminence had summoned with the location where they were to rendezvous.

The vault of the Vatican Bank is housed on the 40th floor, just two floors below the bank's executive offices located in the tower attached to the JP Morgan Building at 23 Wall Street. The vault area is surprisingly small considering the vast wealth of its owner. Today, the vault houses mostly historical documents, some valuable jewels, a few other antiquities and a minor amount of cash. The Vatican Bank's real assets are electronic entries in stock and bond ledgers as well as mortgage certificates and deeds of trust.

Since Caneman took the CEO's office he placed the vault off limits to everyone but himself and his few invited guests. He now sat at a stark metal table within the vault itself. Its surface was cold to the touch owing to the dehumidified air kept at a constant 64 degrees to preserve the valuable documents housed within.

Caneman shivered slightly despite his heavy vestments. He busied himself watching the television he had installed while

44

waiting for the others to arrive. The television was tuned to CNBC to follow the markets. By now it was late in the trading day. GOD stock had just started its upward climb now that the Pope's survival of the assassination attempt had been announced. Caneman knew it would.

A sudden push of air outward signaled the 5-ton steel door opening. The vault had a slight overpressure to keep out any unconditioned air. The four Caneman had summoned entered the steel room. He observed the vault door close behind the last of them. His well-tailored assistant stopped to turn the combination lock and spin the wheel that threw the dozen, 3-inch diameter bolts into place around the door. They were now locked inside the vault. No one could enter unless they unlocked the door from within.

Caneman knew this was the most private of places on earth. It had its own air supply and telephone connections. It had computer and Internet service protected by the most sophisticated firewalls available. Just as the popes of centuries past had their own private meeting places, so did he. Except, he thought, mine is so much more sophisticated. Befitting the one who will save the Church from itself and those who would stomp on its righteous, fundamental traditions.

He nodded acknowledgement to the four men seated with him at the cold, steel table. Despite the vault's chill, Caneman felt a hot bolt of excitement surge through his body. It is happening, he thought. It is finally happening. Sitting there before him were his most trusted recruits. Each wielded extraordinary power in their own right. One chaired the board of a substantial financial institution. Another was the Chancellor of a respected university. To his left sat the head of a company that manufactured an array of deadly military aircraft and tanks. Finally, there was the managing director of a pharmaceutical company that provided the world with life-saving cancer drugs.

Each shared Caneman's zealous, pathological devotion to a strict fundamentalist view of what the Roman Catholic Church should be—could be once again. All awaited the words that would soon come from His Eminence Cardinal David Caneman.

And there he sat, in his resplendent white Cardinal's vestments with a scarlet *cappo* around his shoulders and matching red *zucchetto*, the silk skullcap. Caneman knew his destiny was to first reclaim, then cleanse the Church of the malignant heresy within and finally to lead it out of the moral dungeon where it now lay.

"Eminence," said the defense contractor, "how will the world view this assault on the Pope? Will they see it is a blasphemy against the Church itself?"

Caneman looked at the four men before him. It was his responsibility to put today's events in proper perspective. "No, gentlemen. The world will view the attempt on the Pope's life as a sign of how far off course he and his predecessors have allowed our beloved Church to stray. The blasphemy is that the attempt failed." Caneman eyed each man for any hint of remorse for what they had almost accomplished. He saw none. This is what they had been working on ever since he took over as head of Vatican Bank. Each man was useful to the cause in his own way.

Caneman began, "Over the last 50 years the Roman Catholic Church has deviated from God's chosen path—the path that over the centuries had once made the institution great. No more. Now the nuns want to be ordained. The priests want to marry." Christ, he thought, a married priest. "What is next? The sacrament of Mass conducted in the local languages rather than the traditional Latin? Birth control? Abortion? Accepting faggot priests?" Though, this he knew was a sore point since a percentage of gay priests showed a disturbing tendency to come out of the closet.

"This free-wheeling movement of change must be stopped. It can be stopped. God has chosen us as His instrument of change," he proclaimed. "We took the first two steps today. One succeeded; the other is still in process. The Vatican Bank is now a publicly traded company, soon with over $200 billion in cash at its disposal."

46

Those seated within the cold metal vault took orders from no man. Except Caneman. Even so, there was pushback. They were used to being listened to when they spoke. The banker among them bent toward the table to speak. His tanned, craggy face was a household image, etched on the world's consciousness from his weekly appearances before the Senate Finance Committee, televised over C-Span, then clipped by every news bureau around the world. He cleared his throat as a respectful way of taking the floor.

"Eminence, there was the rumor of a vast wealth of treasure beyond the Church's current holdings. It was said to be a wealth that the Church has accumulated over the centuries from its outposts the world over."

Caneman knew of the rumor. He hoped it was so much more than just a rumor. He also knew that the $200 billion garnered from today's public stock offering was only the first piece to his puzzle. There was no question that he would need every cent to take over the Church. But this treasure—if it existed—was the second puzzle piece. The public stock offering got me into their pocketbooks. True. But this treasure and the religious artifacts within, guaranteed their hearts will belong to me. Caneman needed both if he was to succeed.

Caneman answered the question, "This so-called treasure does place a premium on GOD's stock price, doesn't it?" He laughed out loud at the greedy speculators to whom the deal managers had allocated huge blocks of overpriced stock. "Of course, who is to say if the premium they have paid will be money well spent?" He let the question hang dramatically in the frosty air over the metal table. Of course, this was the one question they each wanted him to answer. And so he would. Right here. Right now. Just like His Holiness, Pope Alexander VI must have done back in the 16th Century.

His Eminence Cardinal David Caneman slid his metal chair from behind the table, stood and walked over to the rows of safety deposit boxes on one wall. He motioned for his young, well-tailored assistant to come over. Caneman pulled out a ring with six keys on it. The young man produced the single master

47

key that was needed to complete the opening of any single box. Beginning with the first box, Caneman slipped his key into the door and waited for the young man to insert his. The door opened and the assistant carefully pulled the first box from its secure place in the vault. Caneman took the box and placed it unopened on the metal table. They did this three more times until four boxes sat on the table.

"Was the treasure premium so many paid on GOD stock worth it?" asked Caneman. "Gentlemen, you have part of the answer now before you." With the mystery still gathering its aura, he proceeded to open each of the four boxes and remove the heavy jagged piece of stone tablet each contained. His four disciples stood from their chairs to better peer down at each of the tablets.

"May God help me," exclaimed the university Chancellor. It is true, then. These tablets represent the map to the treasure that is said to have been broken apart and distributed to six cardinals. May God have mercy—"

"With all due respect," interceded Caneman, his conversational tone now abandoned, "in this case, God had nothing to do with it. These tablets have been kicking around the Church's worldwide facilities since the time of Pope Alexander VI in the 15th century. They have been lost for over 600 years. I have scoured the earth for them."

"But Your Eminence, how did you know they even existed and weren't just a rumor?" asked the pharmaceutical company's chairman.

"Faith," Caneman said simply. "Faith and much research," Caneman winked at his audience. "Alexander VI was a very smart Pope. He knew the path down which the Church was headed and he desperately wanted to protect it, as do we gathered around this table. Our holy Church is heading in the direction where it actually promotes sins against God. Our clergy are at risk of losing control over those they are charged with leading into Jesus' path." Caneman paused to regain control over his emotions. This was his most profound and gut-wrenching fear for the Church—deviation from the fundamentally righteous path as he saw it.

"So I began my research. It took a full year of study before I guessed where to find the first tablet. Within three months, the second one surfaced. Another year passed before the third one came to me after much study of Church archives. This time, I did not have to guess at its location. My studies directed me right to it."

"But Eminence, after so many centuries, why you?" Only the defense contractor's words were respectful. His tone of voice dripped with sarcasm. "Why did God select you—of all people—to find this wondrous hidden treasure?"

Caneman was ready with his own stiff-arm reply. He chose these men for their tough, prove-it-to-me attitude as well as their complete dedication to the Church and turning it back to a righteous, fundamentalist direction. Caneman redirected the objection toward them. "And you four sitting here with me. Why you? Why would God choose you—of all the people here on earth—to lead the fight to regain His Church? And while we're asking, tell me why now? Why did He select this time in history to make a stand? Certainly there were other times. The Inquisition? The Crusades? Maybe the Salem Witch Trials?" Caneman stopped abruptly. His zealot's gaze seared into the faces of each man before him.

"I will tell you why. There has never been a single time in history when all of the resources needed to succeed in our work stood in the same place and with sufficient resolve. We have a war chest of over $200 billion in cash. We have the world's first and second largest financial institutions. We have the might of the world's greatest manufacturer of weaponry—more to the point, the world-wide *leverage* that company can utilize in our cause. We have the cure for cancer in our midst. It is ours to mete out or withhold as we wish. Finally, we have the prestige and credibility of the greatest university. No gentlemen, if there ever was a time to make our stand, this…is…that…time. If there ever was a small group of men with the very capabilities needed to succeed, we…are…that…group."

Caneman's young assistant placed a red velvet cloth over the table. Caneman walked over and removed each of the four tablet pieces from their safety deposit box and placed them on the cloth. It was a stark contrast, the granite tablet with its jagged edges from the centuries old pounding they took to break them apart sitting on the pristine red velvet backdrop. The words and lines were easily discerned, etched deeply into the granite to guarantee their survival over the centuries.

The university Chancellor exclaimed, "But there are only four tablet pieces. I remember from my study that there were six pieces that Pope Alexander VI distributed in the 15th century—"

Caneman grabbed the floor. "Then you must also remember that each piece was reputed to be indispensible to accurately locating the Church's treasure trove. If just one piece is missing, the map is useless."

"So just where are the last two pieces," asked the raspy voiced defense contractor.

That is the question, thought Caneman. Where are they? "I have researched everything I know of them for two years. Each time, I get a little closer—"

"Close, but no cigar," interrupted the contractor.

"Not yet," replied Caneman calmly. He had argued before with the man. Just stand your ground and challenge him. He wasn't used to such behavior from anyone. Caneman saw its immediate effect.

"Well, what will you do if you can't find it?"

"Oh, I will find it. Count on that. Since the 15th Century when Pope Alexander VI broke apart the ancient map, there have been a total of 34 Popes. My research that uncovered four of the tablets dug into just 21 of them. I still have 13 Popes to go. I will find the fifth and sixth tablets. Of that I am certain. Indeed, I believe that I have located Number Five. I will shortly be traveling to Israel to see if it is what I hope it to be."

"And when you do find the final tablet, Eminence, what then?" asked the pharmaceutical company CEO whose advances had saved so many people from cancer. "What value to our cause will be its location? How will this newfound wealth assist us in restoring the Church to the path of the righteous? We already have $200 billion in cash from the public stock offering. How much more do we need?"

That was the question that Caneman could not wait to answer. "The truth is, gentlemen, I will have to wait until I see what is inside the Church's ancient treasure vault to answer. I believe that I know. But until I see what is actually there, I cannot be sure."

"What do you know, Eminence?" asked the university Chancellor. "What do you think is there that will help our cause? How will you use it?"

* * *

CHAPTER 6

"Hi, everyone," said SMP, as she was known the world over. She spoke with her fresh, bright smile and looked straight into the camera lens, "I'm Sister Mary Pat of the Vatican News Service, coming to you live from our beloved Pope's summer residence here in the beautiful village of Castel Gandolfo." She paused to look down at her notes, then apparently decided to chuck the prepared remarks her producers had given her and just say what was on her mind. It wasn't the first time she had done this nor, she imagined, would it be the last. The performance was vintage Sister Mary Pat. She stuffed the index cards into the pocket of her purple and white habit that were the summer colors of the order of Our Lady of Perpetual Correctness. SMP was famous the world over for her shoot-from-the-hip reporting style and an honesty in her reporting that only came from knowing down deep inside where it counts that she really answered to just one true boss. She kept her age a secret though many other reporters had tried to guess. Sister Mary Pat maintained a trim, fit body type that she insisted the Lord would be proud of. She was a marathon runner when the mood struck her and a long-distance cyclist when it didn't. Truth be told, SMP was single-handedly responsible for generating the Vatican News Service ratings to the point where they now rivaled CNN when it came to secular news of the Roman Catholic Church. Her casual style and friendly reporting of the Vatican's goings-on that the Cardinals all thought was so important gave her street cred among the faithful that few others could match.

"Well folks," Sister Mary Pat began, "the truth is Brian Williams of NBC and little Wolfie Blitzer of CNN got into a bit of a tiff as to which network got the best position here in the village. So my boss at VNS—who pretty much runs the show here when the Pope is in residence—decided to end such pettiness before it really began and have just one pool reporter for this historic meeting. He decided the VNS reporter was it." She paused to give a humble shrug. "So, folks, I guess you're

52

stuck with me for a while." She gave the camera her trademark friendly wink and heart-felt grin.

SMP was the nun every Catholic school kid wished they had for a teacher. What she seldom spoke of was her expertise in grammar usage around the world or that she spoke six languages and had a doctorate degree in Renaissance classical literature from Stanford University out in California. While a student there, SMP established Our Lady of Perpetual Correctness-West. The outlying convent remains operational today even though its founder, SMP, was recalled to Rome.

"Since His Holiness almost had his ear blown off in that assassination attempt, he's been recuperating here at Castel Gandolfo. It's quiet—much more conducive to recovery than Vatican City, I can tell you that." Sister Mary Pat paused for a second, tugged at a gray strand of hair and tucked it under her white hat. "The American President is actually the first official head of state to visit him after that awful business in St. Peter's Square just four days ago. I should say that the President is creating more of a stir than he should for our recovering Pope, if you ask me. Let the poor Pontiff rest, I say."

The beloved reporter looked over her shoulder to see the American President's motorcade of long, black limousines very slowly negotiating the sharply winding cobble stone streets—perfect for the donkey carts in use when the road leading to the main square of the village was built in the 17th Century. "I'm standing on a veranda inside His Holiness' compound looking down on *Piazza Della Liberta*. The small town overlooks Lake Albano—site for the rowing events during the Rome Olympics. It's just 15 miles south-east of Rome, in the Alban Hills. Normally this resort village has a tiny population. But it swells when the Pope is in residence to accommodate all those who think they are indispensible to him." Then, with an honest self-admission, Sister Mary Pat said, "I guess that includes me."

She said without covering her microphone, "John, sweetie, how about swinging that camera around so our viewers can get a glimpse of the President as he arrives." Sister Mary Pat was not one to stand on television formality when it came to serving her viewers. She had a reputation for acting as her own director. Down in the television production trailer, the real director threw up his hands and said with a smile, "That's our Sister Mary Pat, God love her."

"Enough of the motorcade, dearies," said SMP as she saw another chance to educate her viewers. "John, dear, now swing your camera down to the retinue stepping into the Villa's courtyard to receive the guests. The man you see leading the delegation, standing where the limousines will finally stop and wearing the formal black robes, is Monsignor Jose Bettencourt. He is the Holy See's Head of Protocol. In that capacity he's in charge of everything involving the Holy See's relationships with other states. Whenever anyone comes to visit the Vatican higher-ups, he's the man in charge. Today he'll oversee the Americans' visit to our recuperating Pope. I do hope Msgr. Bettencourt shows some restraint in the usual pomp and circumstance associated with such visits. His Holiness needs his rest."

The line of limousines and black SUVs carrying the Secret Service agents wound into the Villa's courtyard. It was large enough to accommodate only two of the modern vehicles. The others in the entourage simply stopped in the middle of the cobblestone street, totally blocking any traffic.

SMP waited for the President's car to stop and for the dignitaries to disembark and be greeted by Bettencourt's retinue. It wasn't until everyone had entered the villa some minutes later that Sister Mary Pat raised her microphone to her lips, "This is a state visit. There's no question about that. However, since we're not in Vatican City, and owing to our Pope's fragile condition, I'm going out on a limb here and assuming it is a private visit rather than formal. There's a big difference, believe me. Even private visits are a minuet of diplomacy and protocol. For example, no parade—out of the question. Nor will His Holiness come out to greet the President. However, I am told gifts will be exchanged in the residence."

54

Figuring that the American President would by now finally be seated inside with the Pope, SMP gathered her ankle-length skirt to avoid dragging it on the stone steps and said, "Follow me everyone. I spoke with His Holiness yesterday and requested a discrete seat near him during this visit. Msgr. Bettencourt didn't like the idea, but His Holiness saw nothing wrong and agreed." She turned to face the camera, winked again and stage whispered, "I must insist that you all maintain a respectful quiet during this meeting. Okay?"

Sister Mary Pat's trust and credibility with the Pontiff literally brought the world in to see the highest level sick-call ever broadcast. The President and the Pope sat comfortably talking pleasantries for some time. SMP sat quietly near the two, whispering stage directions to her cameraman. Then she saw the Pope appeared to tire. The President saw it too and called for his get-well gift.

SMP whispered quietly into her microphone, "This is the ceremonial gift giving that almost always accompanies state visits—even private ones like this." SMP had been a teacher—the very best kind—all of her life. She seldom passed up a chance to turn a normal moment into a learning one. This time was no exception. "Did you know, kiddies," she whispered into her microphone, "that the exchange of gifts among kings and chiefs and presidents and, yes, popes, is a centuries-old tradition. It dates back from the ancient civilizations of Rome and Egypt to the native tribes of North America. Ceremonial gifts have paved the way for peaceful coexistence between peoples of different cultures. They are universal symbols and have become part of diplomacy's lexicon of protocols. Most of the gifts tell something about the country of the giver. But sometimes, they take on a more personal nature if the two people involved know and like one another. Let's see what the American President brought with him," she finished whispering into her microphone.

Sister Mary Pat watched and listened as the President handed over an ornately inscribed and remarkably preserved silver vessel. He said, "Your Holiness, this is a wine vessel that was used by Roman society sometime between 60 B.C. to 600

A.D. in and around Vatican City. The religious symbols inscribed indicate that it was possibly used during religious ceremonies. It was part of the New York Metropolitan Museum's collection. On behalf of the American People, we are returning it to its rightful place."

"Well," whispered Sister Mary Pat, "isn't that nice." Her tone, however, indicated that it was about time. "Wait, kiddies. It appears that the American President has a double-header in mind."

She watched as the President leaned toward the Pope's right ear—the one that wasn't heavily bandaged. She was not close enough to hear what he said. But had she been, she would have heard the American President say, "Your Holiness, I have one other gift for you. It is personal. Something from me to you." He pulled the highly personal gift out of his pocket and handed it to His Holiness.

Why, it's an iPhone," exclaimed SMP, "I'm certain of it. I can see the silver Apple logo. From the small size of the white box it couldn't be anything but. Oh no," SMP sighed as the Pope's face lit up and he opened the little box to remove the device with its curved corners. "Folks, the American President meant well by giving a very personal gift. But the only nice way to say it is that someone evidently did not complete his homework. You see, our Pope is quite the gadgeteer. I happen to know that he has the very latest in all electronics—iPhones included. During an interview he once helped me switch on my Bluetooth. And I have heard that Apple ships our Pope the prototypes of its new devices to try out here in the Vatican.

She continued, "Well, at least the President got the color right—this one is a shiny Cardinal Red in a red velvet case with gold trim. Embroidered on the velvet is the insignia of the Papacy. John, dear, could you please zoom in on the insignia. There, you can see the crossed keys of Simon Peter. One is gold; the other is silver to represent the power of loosing and of binding. Above the keys is the triple-crowned tiara representing the Pope as the supreme pastor, supreme teacher and supreme priest."

The President leaned into the Pope's good ear again as the Pontiff admired the gift, fired it up and launched the music icon to see his personal playlist appear—it was mostly liturgical pieces by Marty Haugen and Sebastian Temple mixed in with some Gregorian Chants. The President had added Neil Young's *Rockin' in the Free* World for fun. Then the Pope pressed the Contacts icon and again the screen faithfully displayed his personal contacts. He looked at the American President with the unasked question in his eyes—*how did you get my personal contacts?*

"Your Holiness, I have an agency—the NSA—that prides itself on being able to get whatever information is needed. They didn't even break a sweat in downloading your personal iPhone items. I had them add two new contacts for you. I'm on there and I hope we will speak frequently. There is one other. It is Jackson Schilling. He is my godson. Should he call or email you it is my hope that you will respond to him without delay. Jack does not waste time—neither his nor anyone else's. If he contacts you, be assured it is important. Perhaps a matter of life and death." The President pulled away.

After a pause while SMP rendered her judgment of the gift, she said, "Perfect. I'd say this is a perfect gift for the Pope. And so does he, actually. He seems quite pleased. Look at that beautiful smile on his face."

SMP continued watching from the corner and whispering excitedly into her microphone. Her cameraman caught what came next on live feed that went out to the world. "Alright kiddies," explained Sister Mary Pat, "the American President has offered his gift, it is now His Holiness' turn. Often gifts from Popes to other heads of state are of a religious nature. But this Pope is known as a bit of a renegade. There's no telling what—"

The Pope reached a hand into his alb, the long, white robe worn under all the rest of his ceremonial garb. He had shunned much of the usual vestment finery owing to his recuperation, the fact that he was not actually in Vatican City and this was a private visit rather than a state visit.

"He's pulling what appears to be a necklace with a pendant on the end of it," said SMP. "The light's a little dim in here. It's difficult to actually see."

With that she caught the Pope's eye, shining with pleasure, and inclined her head, seeking permission to approach. The Pope raised a hand, motioning for she and her cameraman to join him.

"Kiddies, you can see for yourself what is on the end of His Holiness' gold chain. It appears to be a smashed piece of metal—I'll just shut up now and let you listen."

The Pope explained to the President as the world listened, courtesy of the ever astute Sister Mary Pat, "My friend, I would like you to have this," offering him the necklace and pendant. "I certainly have no further use for it. You may notice that it is somewhat heavy. Yes? My security team tells me that the .338 Lapua Magnum is indeed quite heavy. They dug it out of the wall where it lodged after piercing my ear and then Ms. Bartaromo's shoulder."

"Your Holiness," stammered the President as he hefted the smashed piece of lead on a gold chain, "I don't know what to say. This is an historical artifact. I couldn't possibly—"

The Pope waived his hand, dismissing the President's objection. "Take it my son. It was actually Ms. Bartaromo's idea. When our people found it, I offered it to her as a souvenir. It turns out that we both had the same thought—neither one of us wanted to see the thing again. Then she suggested I give it to the first dignitary who comes to visit me. I am afraid that you, Mr. President, are him."

Sister Mary Pat looked on in amazement as she watched her beloved Pope with a twinkle in his eye push the priceless artifact into the President's hand, then close his fingers around it so he wouldn't drop it. The Pope turned to her and gave his trademark wink to his favorite nun.

"Do you think we will make the evening news, Sister?" he then asked.

"Won't be much of a stretch, Your Holiness." Then she saw him raise a hand to his mouth to stifle a yawn.

The American President saw it too and recognized the signal for what it was. "Your Holiness, it is getting late and I am afraid that my visit has tired you beyond what is healthy. I will leave now." The President stood and helped the Pope to his feet. Together they slowly walked down the colonnade, through the many offices that were needed even when the Pope was supposedly on retreat. SMP managed to wedge both she and her cameraman into the front of the line of security people and the others who served the closest needs of their chiefs. She was just behind the two security officers, wearing dark blue suits, but armed to the teeth under their coats. Her microphone was wide open and her television audience worldwide was perfectly situated to hear what came next.

The Pontiff stopped beside an office door, then suddenly opened the latch, spun on the ball of his foot and stepped in as the door swung open. With his other hand—the one the President had linked through his arm to steady the Pope—he pulled him into the vacant office. The line of followers suddenly disrupted. The security team tried to muscle their way into the office.

Sister Mary Pat was being jostled and pushed, but she clearly heard the Pope say as he stuck out his head and put a calming, but firmly unequivocal hand on his security chief's sternum, "I wish to have a private moment with my friend. It will be alright. I do not believe that he is armed. And there is only one bullet between us now—even that one is of little use anymore. We'll just be a few moments." His Holiness shut the office door in the security chief's face.

SMP spoke quickly into her mic, "Oh kiddies don't you know that this is highly irregular. His handlers keep our Pope on a tightly scripted schedule. There is almost never any time for impromptu meetings—even with other heads of state. I wonder what those two are discussing in there."

* * *

CHAPTER 7

Cardinal David Caneman eyeballed the university Chancellor for a moment. The only sound in the Vatican Bank vault was from the air conditioning vent pouring cold air into the steel sarcophagus in which the five men met. Finally, Caneman spoke. "You ask what I know; what I think is in the Church's treasure vault and how it will help our mission to purify? You want to know how I will use it? Whatever 'it' is." Caneman stood from his metal chair at the head of the table. Still dressed in his Cardinal's vestments—white with vivid scarlet—his was a commanding presence. "Very well. I have thought long and hard about these questions. I have prayed to the Holy Father to guide me. This is what I have concluded." He stepped back toward the steel wall behind him.

"First, since Pope Alexander VI broke apart the map to the treasure vault in the 16th Century, that vault has probably not been entered since. What I'm going to find is a lot of dust." The four men laughed as Caneman knew they would at his attempt to break the tension in this steel room. "I hope to find the most extraordinary manuscripts of papyrus that document the life of Christ. I expect to find proof of Church ownership of vast tracts of land in the most populated centers of the world. These contracts, mortgages and title deeds will be traceable to the modern era. But that will take time, enormous amounts of money—which we now have—and hundreds of lawyers. I will set in motion the mechanism to retrieve what property belongs to the Roman Catholic Church, but it is not my highest goal."

Caneman saw each of these most powerful men leaning into the table. He knew he had them enraptured. These men understood vast wealth. But what he envisioned that lay within the Church's treasury was likely something of incomprehensible value known only to him. "What I want to find is an object—a single object that explains everything we stand for in unequivocal terms. This object, whatever it is, will draw the world—believers and those with doubts—into the fold of the Roman Catholic Church. It will be sufficient to turn our Church away from the very dangerous path on which the last ten popes have led her." Caneman stopped and waited for the question he knew would come.

"Eminence, what kind of object possesses such power to knit the faithful and others into one? And to then change the direction of such a huge institution? How valuable is such a thing?" The question came from the University Chancellor—Dr. Neil Palmer. Caneman chose him specifically because he was not a priest. In fact, he had no formal seminary training. He was part archeologist, part a renowned scholar in ancient religions whose credentials were beyond reproach.

"I imagine that my object, by itself, is not particularly valuable. In fact, it is my hope that here in the modern era we still use something like it—as it has evolved over the centuries—in our present everyday life. The better for the world to identify with it and to understand. Dr. Palmer, you asked how valuable is this object? Its intrinsic value is small, inconsequential. Nevertheless, given the right provenance and who in history might have used it, its ability to persuade and to convert masses of people to our theology is priceless."

It was the defense contractor's turn. "Okay, Eminence, I get it. You're after a symbol. Surrounded by a few hundred billion in other more tangible wealth, gold, silver, jewels and trust deeds donated to the Church over the centuries. But still, a symbol. And I agree with you. Such an object and provenance—if it actually exists—is priceless to our cause. So tell me, just how close are you to finding the fifth and sixth map tablets?"

* * *

CHAPTER 8

"Looks clean to me," said Jack Schilling. He tossed the Vatican Bank's balance sheet on the table. His audit team had commandeered the executive conference room. "What am I missing here, people?" He rubbed his tired eyes. Since he and Helen had landed in New York just twenty-four hours ago he had not stopped for more than twenty minutes for a sandwich. It was now 1:30 in the morning. The Bank's offices had long since gone dark except for the areas in which his team now worked.

Jack shrugged his shoulders, trying to get his dress shirt to give him a little more room. He stretched his arms and considered unbuttoning his cuffs and rolling up his sleeves to alleviate the binding. But no, he thought, these accountants are a curious lot. They don't need to know the part of my background etched on my bare arms. He supposed they talked about him— ex-head of the SEC's Enforcement Division, now working for Taiko Motor Corporation as a division CFO. The SEC had managed to keep his military service under wraps.

What he did a year ago in the Oval Office, on the other hand, was public knowledge. Video of Jack had played almost continuously for a week afterward. It showed him in excruciating slow motion stepping from his guest post in the back of the famous room, in one smooth, fluid motion producing a hand gun, then drilling the would-be presidential assassin with a deadly double-tap—one into the center of his chest, the other dead center in the forehead. All before the Secret Service agents who were never beyond arms reach of the President could call out, "Gun!" And even more fortunately, before the assassin could fire a single round.

Back then, as head of the SEC's Enforcement Division, Jack Schilling was authorized and licensed to carry a concealed weapon. That explained how he just happened to have the Sig Sauer P226 in a shoulder rig with him there in the Oval Office for the historic meeting so well documented in the book, *Deadly Acceleration*. It was the right time, right place, right weapon and most importantly the right person firing it. What it didn't explain—the question that it actually begged—was how an SEC accountant came to be so fast and accurate in what had suddenly and unexpectedly devolved into a combat situation.

NBC's Brian Williams wanted to answer that question. He had even shown side-by-side footage of Jack and the Secret Service agents in those fateful seconds. Williams revealed, as only slo-mo video can show, Jack reacting a full quarter second ahead of the fastest man on the Secret Service team present there in the Oval Office. He pointed out that in such situations 0.25 seconds literally meant the difference between life and death.

All it took was a call to NBC's Studio B in New York from the White House. At the President's insistence, his call was routed through the building, into the Evening News production booth and right into Brian Williams' earpiece as he sat there on the set. The President asked if he might have a word with the famous newscaster—right now. The President suggested he might want to go straight to commercial without another word.

Brian Williams is a great American. He did as the President requested. During the three minutes and 40 seconds of ensuing commercial time the President explained that Jack Schilling was quite obviously someone significantly more than just an accountant. And that if Williams insisted on pursuing his supposed revelations, Jack's usefulness to the country would be compromised. "You don't want to limit a national hero's capabilities, now do you, Brian?" the President finished. The famous newscaster replied, "No sir, I do not. I'll just jump to our next story about the Labrador retriever who saved his master's life on a frozen lake in Minnesota."

"Sounds liker a nice story, Brian. I like dog stories. I think I'll just sit right here in the residence and watch you tell it. Pleasure talking with you, Brian." The President put down the receiver without another word.

Jack knew there were questions at the SEC about why would he suddenly be called back into public service for this Vatican Bank audit. There were rumors about him—especially after the

Oval Office episode. Still, no use in confirming them, he thought. Better just keep those sleeves rolled down.

"Sir," said one of the third-year bank auditors. She ran what Jack took to be a nervous hand through her blonde hair. "We've gone through all the cash accounts and the asset accounts for loans receivable from the various philanthropic groups the Bank considers borrowers. I ticked and tied all of the payables. No problems there, I guarantee it—"

"So what're you saying, Audrey? You ready to render an unqualified, clean opinion right now?" She had caught Jack's eye before he left the SEC a year ago. Pretty, *wicked smaht*, with an MBA from UCLA and a CPA out of E&Y. She needs a little seasoning, Jack thought. He was just the one to give it to her.

"No, sir. I am not ready to give any sort of opinion."

That back talk got Jack's attention. He liked sassy accountants. It meant they wouldn't take anything anyone said at face value. Instead they wanted to look at the facts and form their own conclusions. That was why they were all here. They would determine if the attempted assassination of the Pope— who just so happened to be the Vatican Bank's Chairman—was related to a possible adverse financial condition of the institution. "Ooookay, then Audrey. What?"

"It's not what we are seeing here. It's what we're *not* seeing."

Jack suddenly understood where she was going. He decided to give her the street cred among her peers sitting around the table, now listening to their exchange. "Continue."

"Well, every bank has a boatload of off-balance sheet items. They don't appear on the face of the financial statements. Only in obscure financial language in the Notes to Financial Statements at the back—"

Time to test her mettle. Jack sat up straight and looked the promising young woman in the eye, clearly challenging her. "Tell me the extent of the Vatican Bank's financial guarantees. What about its standby letters of credit, it's bank loan commitments and the risk it has undertaken with those derivatives, currency and interest rate swaps. And while you're at it, tell me—no tell all of us—about their over-the-counter options, futures and forward commitments."

And she did. For the next hour Audrey proceeded to dissect the Vatican Bank's unseen underbelly of financial commitments and risks that its stock investors would likely never see. By the time she was finished, Jack saw a pile of analyses, reports and graphs supporting her facts stacked in front of him, courtesy of Ms. Audrey.

"So, what's it mean to you, Audrey? What conclusions can you draw from all this?" Jack finally asked, spreading his arms to encompass the stack of documents before him.

There was a pause. Jack saw the brilliant, young auditor hesitate. Time to let her off the hook, he thought. "Nice job, Audrey. Thorough, complete, clearly presented. Backed up by independently determined facts. Good work. May I offer you my conclusions?"

"Please," she said with relief in her eyes that the boss—especially this one with his reputation for being both tough and smart—wasn't going to chew her ass off.

Jack sat back in his chair and talked to his group as he reasoned through his conclusion out loud. "Vatican Bank was a large institution even before it went public. Now it has over $200 billion in assets—and that doesn't include the treasure that's supposed to exist." Jack paused to let the quiet laughter die. No one really believed a treasure of any sort existed—him included. "The off-balance sheet activity on the surface doesn't appear unusual for a bank of this size. I do find their sophisticated use of swaps, futures and forward contracts—the derivatives Audrey unearthed—odd for any bank. Particularly one with a religious intent such as Vatican Bank. That's sophisticated stuff—"

"It comes from the background of Cardinal David Caneman, the CEO." This interruption came from the door as Helen walked into the conference room. Following her were waiters from Danny Meyers' *Blue Smoke* barbeque restaurant just a short

66

block away. Each waiter carried heavily laden aluminum trays sealed with foil.

"Jack can go forever without eating," Helen said as she moved aside binders and file folders to clear a space on the conference room table for the food trays. "Sometimes he just assumes everyone is like him. So I ordered in. Was I right?" she asked looking around the conference room table at the nodding heads. "That's what I thought. I think you'll like my selections." She yanked the foil cover off one of the trays. A cloud of steam and the rich, smoky smell of what just might possibly be the city's best barbeque ribs wafted into the conference room.

Helen Kaito had been in the public's eye even before meeting Jack Schilling and helping solve the terrorist plot that used Kaito automobiles as its weapon of choice. The world had known her as a spoiled, self-absorbed dilettante who was lucky enough to be the chairman's daughter of the world's largest automotive manufacturer. What the world did not know—was still finding out—was that Helen Kaito had discovered her true self during that awful time when 3,000 people were killed by her company's cars. The satisfaction she had felt during her role in uncovering the *Deadly Acceleration* plot and bringing down the perpetrators was beyond anything the booze and boys could begin to provide. Then, of course, there was Jack Schilling. She had found him to be the most extraordinary and deeply layered individual she had ever known. Since meeting him at Kaito's small truck division in Elkhart, Indiana, then standing beside him during the deadly acceleration plot, they had not been apart.

Afterward, once they both were back working their jobs in Elkhart she suggested that maybe they both might feel better if they got married. Jack's reaction to her suggestion still made her laugh. The brilliant, tough ex-SEAL was speechless for a full minute. Then she saw the smile spread across his chiseled face. He had swept her off the floor and into his arms and said, "I thought you'd never ask." Since then—not quite a year ago— their life together had been immensely happy and satisfying, but relatively uneventful. Until the Pope was shot on the day the Vatican Bank went public.

Once she made sure the SEC auditors had filled their plates and everyone was busily demolishing *Blue Smoke's* best, she took advantage of the quiet. "There's only one Cardinal in the Vatican's inner circle with the background to execute those sophisticated swaps, futures and forward contracts." Helen saw the look of surprise on several faces. "Yeah, I guess that doesn't sound like the New York party girl from my reputation, does it."

Jack spoke up by way of explanation, "Even with all that champagne swilling and bar hopping during her youth, Helen managed to get a Stanford MBA. She also served as corporate treasurer for Kaito's small truck division when her father banished her to the hinterlands after her arrest in New York. What was it for? Something? Ah, public drunkenness." Jack knew his wife was tough enough to take it. "All kidding aside, without her expert help, we probably never would have uncovered the perps using deadly acceleration as a terrorist weapon. Helen knows what she's talking about."

Helen threw Jack a smile. "Right. Well Cardinal David Caneman has an extraordinary background in corporate finance. Before entering the priesthood, he worked for Goldman Sachs in their structured finance group. Eventually, he rose to head the group and was named a partner.

"He is responsible for creating the municipal bond swap transactions all those cities got involved with. He created the transaction, brought in the banks to finance them, then paired them up with the cities who were desperate for cash flow. He was so good at packaging his financial products that the Harvard Endowment *and* Yale along with other ivy-league schools, bought them as well.

"Cardinal David Caneman is one of the most astute financial engineers on the planet. Three years ago when he took over Vatican Bank, it was a prestigious institution, but hardly worthy of investment grade consideration. When His Eminence assumed the helm, he immediately began preparing it for a

68

public offering. He convinced the Holy See that this was the way to get the funding to do the Church's work well into the next century. Caneman is the architect of the modern-day Vatican Bank."

Jack spoke up, "So who is the Vatican Bank's biggest investor? Who stands to make the most if the stock goes up in a big way?"

Helen had done her homework. "Vatican Bank is actually just its slang reference. Actually, the bank's real name is Institute for Works of Religion. With the recent public offering the Bank sold just 45 percent of its ownership. The Roman Catholic Church retained the lion's share of the ownership. So the answer to your question as to who benefits from a stock increase is the Church itself."

Jack said, "Okay. Fine. But doesn't Cardinal David Caneman run the Bank?"

Helen said, "Most people assume that he's the final decision-maker because he is the president and CEO. However, he reports to a seven-member board made up of the highest-ranking Cardinals of the Church. The Pope himself chairs that board right now because the former chairman suddenly died."

Jack arched an eyebrow. "Died? Of what?"

"Heart attack," answered Helen. "These are elderly men, sweetie. They are not really fit for the rigors of international finance that Cardinal David Caneman has placed them into."

Jack casually twirled a pencil in his hand. "Who would succeed the Pope as chairman if he were to suddenly die?"

"You mean like almost happened four days ago?" Helen was right on top of the Vatican Bank's line of succession. "Geez, Jack I see where you're going with this. The answer is that the current President and CEO of the Bank itself would automatically become chairman should the Pope die or become incapacitated until the Holy See could elect a new Pope. They call such a succession, the Camerlengo Chairman. You are not suggesting—"

"I'm not suggesting anything. It's too early and this is a bank audit, not the investigation of an attempted murder. What else do we need to know about the Institue for Works of Religion?"

"Well, the bank funds global projects for the good of humanity. For example, it provides the funds for training people to fight drought and desertification in nine African countries. It provides seed for crops and the funds to teach farming techniques in non-developed countries. That sort of thing. However, the Vatican Bank has a history of scandal too."

"Follow the money," said Jack. "Vast sums of money always bring out the worst in people. What happened most recently?"

"During the 1980s, the Institute was involved in a political and financial scandal. The bank was a lender and financial backer during the $3.5 billion collapse of Banco Ambrosiano. As a result, the head of the Bank then, Archbishop Paul Marcinkus, was almost indicted as an accessory. However, they never filed charges since he was such a high-ranking prelate of the Vatican. He had diplomatic immunity from prosecution."

Audrey set down her plastic knife and fork, wiped the barbeque sauce off of her fingers and said, "I still don't understand what the Bank will do with the $200 billion it just raised from going public. That's a lot of money to spread around the world doing God's work."

"Too damn much money," said Jack. "Especially for a bank whose sole purpose is to act as a conduit for the collection and disbursement of funds to further the Church's philanthropic works. Remember, our job here is to determine if the shot at the Bank's chairman—the Pope—had anything to do with the enterprise and to verify that the books and records of said enterprise fairly present its financial condition."

Jack glanced at the stand-by letter of credit he had pulled from the stack of documents Audrey had given him during her lecture. It was for a small amount by Vatican Bank standards, just $2.5 million. What caught his eye was the beneficiary, the person to whom the Vatican Bank was paying the money—Trident Operations Corporation. Jack looked at his watch—an

70

indestructable stainless steel and black rubber IWC Ingenieur—and said, "It's almost 3:00 a.m. Let's take a break and reconvene at 0900, shall we?"

"Something bothering you?" asked Helen when the exhausted auditors had all left the conference room. She looked at Jack's face. The lines across his forehead had deepened as she learned to notice when he spotted a problem. The creases that ran down his cheeks next to his slightly crooked nose were more pronounced. "What's up?"

Jack picked up the $2.5 million LC written in favor of Trident Operations Corporation. "I skimmed the stack of letters of credit Audrey pulled from the off-balance sheet transaction list. All of them precisely described whatever was being purchased. Some were hard assets like air conditioners for Church installations around the world. Some were for school books being sent to African nations. Some were for medicines shipped in care of Doctors Without Borders. Many were for some pretty big numbers too. This is one big organization. But each had a description of the item so detailed it would make any accountant smile."

He picked up the single document from Trident and let it fall to the table, landing alone outside the stack. "Then there's this one. The description says just, *For services rendered.* Every other one has three authorizing signatures—the Church representative in the field, the Vatican Bank's controller and finally its CEO here in New York. But this one? This one has just one signature—"

"Whose is it?" asked Helen.

"Cardinal David Caneman."

Helen picked up the letter of credit and examined it as a former corporate treasurer would. "Why would the CEO of the Vatican Bank even be involved with such a small disbursement?"

"That's another problem I have. Just who or what is Trident Operations Corporation? What services did it render to the Church that earned it $2.5 million?" Jack picked up a cube of cornbread, smeared some honey on it and took a bite. "Maybe it's my professionally skeptical nature, Helen, but why the name Trident? What operations does this Trident do? Both words together in that particular order mean something to me. They would to any SEAL."

"What does it mean to you?"

"The trident is the Navy SEAL's symbol. He unbuttoned his shirt sleeves and rolled up his cuffs. "See?" There, tatooed on the inside of his left forearm was the SEAL's trident. It began with the old anchor symbolizing the SEAL's roots in the ocean. Attached to the anchor was the three-pronged scepter. It belonged to Poseidon, king of the ocean. The third trident component was the cocked pistol—ready to fire. Finally was the eagle, the symbol of America's freedom, holding everything together. Only this eagle's head was lowered in a sign of humility as the true warrior's strength.

Opposite on the right inside forearm were the words, *The Only Easy Day Was Yesterday.* "Trident Operations could mean a SEAL op—a covert, direct action operation. Authorized and paid for by Cardinal David Caneman."

"So, you think His Eminence might be up to something?"

Jack considered her question for a moment, then shook his head. "Probably not. Most things like this have a simple, plausible explanation. But my skepticism is the CPA in me. I'll run it down myself tomorrow and let you know." He stretched his arms over his head and yawned. "I need to check in with Smitty in DC."

"Jack, it's after 3:00 a.m.," objected Helen.

"Hon, if I don't sleep, Smitty don't sleep. Besides, he made me promise to call him each day. He probably thinks I forgot."

"Wake up, shipmate," said Jack, his voice was jocular with forced enthusiasm.

"What?" answered the groggy voice. "What the fuck?"

"Somewhere it's daylight, buddy and you're burnin' it all to hell."

"Christ, Jack. It's…it's—"

72

"Just after three in the morning," Jack answered for Mr. Smith. He heard a deep, clearing breath come over the phone.

Then a suddenly-wide awake voice saying, "Okay, Jack. I'm with you now. Thought you forgot our daily call."

"I wouldn't do that, buddy. Just a little late is all. I'll give you the essentials first."

"Go."

Jack began in his clear, deliberate briefing voice they had learned over a decade before in the Navy. "Financial statements are clean—that's what my team's unqualified opinion will say. The notes to the financial statements are another thing. I don't like something I saw. It's small, but raises a question."

"What?" asked Smith.

"It's a $2.5 million Stand-by LC for *services rendered.*

"What's *services rendered* mean?" Smith asked.

"That's the thing, shipmate. It could mean anything. But that's only the first thing that caught my attention. Guess who the LC's beneficiary was."

"Come on, Jack. It's three in the morning."

"Sourpuss. The payee was Trident Operations."

There was a long pause on the line as both men considered the possibilities. Then Jack said, "You know, Smitty, this is probably nothing. But given the circumstances of an assassination attempt on the chairman of an NYSE company that just went public, it's a nugget."

"That it is, pal. What's next."

Jack already had his list of assignments for Smith. "I'm going to request an audience with His Eminence Cardinal David Caneman and just ask him. While I'm doing that I want you to get me the details of the assassination attempt."

"What're you thinking, Jack?"

"Just naturally suspicious is all. I want to confirm that this LC has nothing to do with the assassination attempt on the Pope."

"Like what do you want to know about the assassination attempt?"

"Everything about that shot. Distance for starters. What was the round that hit the Pope's ear. Did they find the rifle? What about the spotter, if one was used. Get me everything you can."

"Won't be easy, Jack. We're not just dealing with the Italian *Arma dei Carabinieri*. As if they're not difficult enough. We're actually dealing with the *Gendarmerie* of the Vatican City State. They answer to a higher calling if you get my meaning."

"We're the SEC Enforcement Division. Even so, you just may have to get the Old Man involved," said Jack. "I'll call you again at 0900. By then I should have talked with His Eminence and you should have what we need on that shot."

* * *

Chapter 9

"What is troubling you, my friend?" asked the Pope as he stared into the American President's face inside the vacant office within Castel Gandolfo. Both could hear the small crowd of their retinues outside. "I can see it in your eyes. You are distraught. Friends should have no secrets."

The President looked at the Pope. He guessed this exhibition of clairvoyance was probably the reason the man was chosen to lead so many in their religion. "You're right, Your Holiness. I am troubled about this assassination attempt. Our Securities Exchange Commission is investigating the Vatican Bank to see if there is a link between the assassination attempt and the bank." The President looked into the kindly eyes staring at him, patiently awaiting his explanation. "Even if such an investigation wasn't standard procedure, I would have done something anyway. About 24 percent of the American population is Catholic. I'm Catholic and my family has been for centuries

"And you do not like someone taking a pot shot at your religion's leader?"

"Well, Your Holiness, that is certainly part of it—"

"What is the other part?" asked the Pope

"Common sense requires our involvment. It is no secret that the Church has a fundamentalist faction that is growing in strength. They want to see the Church return to its old dogmas. I cannot help but wonder just how far they might go to achieve their end."

"Yes, Mr. President, I am aware of that. But is dissent not fundamental to every great institution? That does not necessarilly mean the dissenters will try to kill a leader they do not agree with."

The President stood there with the Pontiff, considering how to put what else he wanted to say. "Then there's that damn— sorry, Your Holiness—treasure. What if it really does exit? The power of the Church from such vast wealth would instantly elevate its stature and its capabilities to do good as well as…other things."

The Pope laughed out loud. "Mr. President, I seem to be the only one who maintains that the treasure and the fictitious map of stone that was supposed to lead people to it is pure fantasy. Many things associated with our Church are gross exagerations or outright fiction created for who knows what purposes. I can tell you that there is no Catholic treasure. I can also tell you that the Vatican Bank now has more than enough money to do the work of the Church. Any more would probably not help the cause. I am no economist. But I am told by those who are that there is a law of diminishing returns. I believe the Vatican Bank has now reached that point."

"There is one more small matter, Your Holiness." The President waited a beat to be sure he had the Pontiff's full attention. After all, the man was 83 years old. "I mentioned earlier the man we have from the SEC Enforcement Division auditing the Vatican Bank—"

"Yes, Mr. Schilling, your godson."

"That's right, Father. I heard on the way over that his investigation has turned up a very small anomaly. It is probably nothing. However, Jack will be pursuing it to its end."

"What is this anomaly please?"

"Smitty said it wasn't worth my time to explain Jack's hunch. So I only know that the SEC's audit is not yet being signed off with a clean opinion."

"Well, Mr. President, Cardinal David Caneman has my complete faith and trust. If there is anything to Mr. Schilling's hunch, His Eminence will certainly extend his fullest cooperation to assist in bringing it to light. And if Mr. Schilling is still not satisfied, I believe you said he has my telephone number." The Pope patted the inner pocket of the white *alb* he wore, indicating the new iPhone the President had given him earlier in his visit."

"My experience with Jack is that he is not shy about asking for what he wants. If he feels you can help him, be assured that he will be on your telephone immediately."

The Pope nodded. "I think we are making our people a bit nervous, no? Unless you have something else, perhaps we should open the door."

Mr. Schilling, His Eminence asked me to send his regrets, but he has so many things on his plate what with the attempted assassination on His Holiness' life and the Vatican Bank just going public four days ago—"

"So he is not going to make time to see me," said Jack.

The well-tailored assistant to the Vatican Bank's CEO held Jack in a stony gaze. "I am afraid not."

The two men looked at one another. Jack was no stranger to confrontation, verbal or otherwise. He long ago had learned that it pays to be a winner. This was no exception. He needed to speak directly to the originator and the person who authorized that letter of credit sending $2.5 million to an enterprise with the curious name of Trident Operations. The person who did both was the bank's CEO, Cardinal David Caneman. Finally, the assistant blinked.

"Mr. Schilling, just because His Eminence cannot devote the time you require to solving your audit question does not mean that someone else cannot help you. Just tell me what you need and I will see to it the proper person fits you into his schedule."

Jack waited, considering his response. May as well be crystal clear from the beginning, he thought. "Just becoming a public enterprise is something new to your staff. There are a new set of rules and operating principles that go with holding the public's money in trust. Most things of this nature turn out to be an oversight or easily explained. That is the information I am seeking here—an explanation. Since there was one originator of the payment voucher and the same person authorized cutting the letter of credit, I want that person to tell me himself what it was."

The young assistant looked carefully at the letter of credit sitting on his desk. "Mr. Schilling, $2.5 million is not a significant sum to an institution the size of the Vatican Bank. I doubt that His Eminence even remembers it."

Jack had about enough of this guy. He stood up from his chair. "Maybe $2.5 million is nothing to you or to this bank. But sure as I am standing here that amount of money is enormous to the poor people around the world who so generously gave it to the Church in their collection boxes and offering plates." Jack's voice was rising in his irritation. "It is a huge amount of money to those investors who bought a few shares of Vatican Bank stock just so they could own a piece of their Church." Jack noticed that heads had turned in the office toward their conversation. Just what he wanted. Jack raised his voice yet again and leaned into the face of the young assistant, who was also by now standing. "But what is even more important is the haphazard policy and procedure of money management and funds disbursement that this reveals."

The young assistant's voice now matched Jack's in volume. "And I am telling you there is no way you are going to interrogate—"

Suddenly the door to the office next to the assistant's desk opened. "Peter," said the stern-looking man who quickly emerged, "I'll handle it from here, please." He extended a hand toward Jack. "Marc Greggory. I sit on the non-statutory advisory board of the Vatican Bank. You must be Jack Schilling. I believe that I can help you. Would you please step into my office. We'll let these people get back to their work."

Jack shook Greggory's hand and followed him into his office. It was sparsely furnished, befitting a former army general. Jack knew all about General Marc "Scorpion" Greggory. West Point graduate, career Army. Tours of duty in every conflict that America had faced over the last 40 years. Owing to Jack's closeness to the up-and-coming senator who was now President he had heard Greggory's name trotted out as a possible nominee to the Joint Chiefs of Staff. Then he abruptly left the Army for the Chairmanship of General Ordnance Corp., arguably the world's largest manufacturer of military hardware. His Georgetown Ph.D. in foreign relations along with an MBA from MIT qualified him for that post. He was said to be a strict practicing Catholic. That explains him acting in an advisory role to the Vatican Bank's board of Cardinals, thought Jack.

"So you think you want to speak with Cardinal Caneman," began Greggory. "Son, that young man you just had the shout-fest with is right. It ain't gonna happen."

"Why is that, General?"

Greggory smiled at being referred to by his old rank, took in a deep breath and puffed out his barrel chest. "Because I say so. His Eminence is far too busy to spend time with every bean counter who wants to ask him some clerical question. If we didn't pull the plug at some point, the Cardinal would become less effective and the Bank's commerce would come to a grinding halt." Greggory smiled in what Jack would have termed a *shit-eating grin*. As if he held all the cards and he knew it.

Jack calmly stood and said, "Well then General, I guess you told me, didn't you," and he turned toward the door as if to leave. "Except that," now Jack turned back for what seemed an afterthought, "you are no longer a general and I am no longer in the Navy. Near as I can see, you have no publicly disclosed capacity at the Vatican Bank. You are not listed as one of the senior officers. You are not a member of the statutory board of directors, just the advisory board. You are not shown on the list of shareholders owning more than 10 percent of the common stock."

Greggory said, "I have something far more valuable, son. I have Cardinal Caneman's full faith and trust. I am among his closest advisors."

Jack had encountered difficult executives during his time at the SEC. There is a way to deal with them; Jack knew the way. "Then you'll want to advise him on this. First, tell him that referring to me or any accountant as a bean counter is not the way to earn our everlasting endearment. Caneman will want to remain on our good side. Second, I am not just any accountant. I am the chief bank examiner for the SEC's Enforcement Division. A power curve operates here, General. I am at the top. Finally, I am not satisfied with the explanation of a very large disbursement. Twice I have asked politely to speak with the one man whose signature created and authorized that letter of credit. I have twice been refused access to that individual. What is the conclusion that any reasonable person faced with these circumstances would draw?"

Jack now turned around to face the general full on. "Sir, there is usually a plausible explanation for these things. Rarely do publicly held corporations sidle into the financial gray areas, then try to hide their activities from the auditors. I have asked twice for an interview with Cardinal Caneman. Since you say you are among his closest advisors, pass on this message to him. Tell him that I have stopped the SEC's audit. I will issue a press release through the SEC's New York office explaining that the Vatican Bank was unable to provide sufficient documentary evidence for us to render an opinion on the Bank's financial state of affairs, its operations and the fairness of presentation of its financial statements. And therefore, the SEC will immediately consider steps to delist GOD stock—"

"Now just wait one minute, son."

"Too late, general," said Jack as he maintained his professional, polite tone. "The matter is now out of your hands and those of Cardinal Caneman. My policy is clear. I must seek confirmation from the CEO's supervisor and address the statutory board of directors regarding my findings."

Jack could see the general's face was turning red. "You mean to tell me that you are bringing the Pope into this minor dust-up?"

"Sir, the Vatican Bank's chairman is superior to the CEO in the chain of command. Due to the unfortunate demise of the former chairman, you are correct. The Pope himself has now stepped in as successor and *camerlengo* chairman. It is my hope that His Holiness will satisfactorially illuminate the issues on which I seek guidance."

"And if he won't see you or if his answers prove to be less than enlightening?" asked the general.

80

Jack faced the bureaucrat, "Then I understand delisting a $200 billion bank stock from the New York Stock Exchange can be a very expensive and time-consuming enterprise. There will be investigations by the Enforcement Division's Criminal Activities unit. Any illegal acts perpetrated by the Bank's personnel will be turned over to the Justice Department for prosecution to the fullest extent of the law. And this time there will be no diplomatic immunity."

"That's what the General called it?" asked Smith, "a minor dust-up?"

"That's what he said," Jack confirmed into his cell phone. He was sitting in the audit team's empty conference room. It was 11:17 a.m. The rest of the team was out in the various parts of the bank doing their work. The door was closed. "Something smells here, Smitty. I've been around all sorts of publicly held enterprises. Most are relatively transparent if you know where to look."

"The Vatican Bank isn't transparent?"

"It's murky, shipmate. People seem to behave almost as if they were afraid to speak to my auditors. Anything of substance gets referred up the chain of command. The higher ups in the CEO's office keep a distance from the operations they're responsible for overseeing. Then there's the CEO, Cardinal David Caneman. You'd think he was the Good Lord himself the way they protect and insulate him from everything going on in his own shop." Jack stood and walked to the windows overlooking Wall Street 42 stories below. From here the people on the sidewalk looked like so many ants rushing in and out of their various ant hills.

Investors in GOD stock the world over were his responsibility. The $200 billion they had entrusted to the Vatican Bank was an enormous amount of money. Was it safe? Was Caneman exhibiting the stewardship over such a treasury that investors of a stock traded on an exchange in the United States had a right to expect? Jack shook his head. He did not know. The books and records were clean. The internal controls were documented and followed by those responsible. It was just that $2.5 million letter of credit to Trident Operations that kept surfacing.

"Smitty, I want to see the Pope."

There was a stunned silence on the line between New York and Washington DC. Then, "Wow, Jack. That's a statement you don't hear every day. You had a sudden awakening, buddy? You and over a million other Catholics the world over want to see the Pope."

"No, jerk-off. I mean I *need* to see the Vatican Bank's chairman. Right now, due to the sudden death of the former chairman, that individual just so happens to be the Pope."

Smith said, "I don't know, pal. Getting an audience with the Pope is a pretty tough order. You're gonna have to wait. The guy's schedule is probably jammed."

"He'll see me, Smitty. Count on it." Jack remembered the call he had received in the jet coming out from Elkhart. It was his godfather, the President. After the usual pleasantries and catching up on family, he had given Jack a very special telephone number with instructions to use it if he had to and not to hesitate. "So, what did you find out about our sniper?"

"Jack you gotta understand that working with the Italian police and the Vatican security forces is not easy. It requires extraordinary tact and diplomacy—"

"You asked Helen for help, didn't you."

"She's a student of the art. She did the coaching, but I really did do the talking. Promise."

"Okay. What'd you find out?"

"Yeah. The round fired—and it was just a single round—happened to be a Lapua .338 Magnum Long Range Sierra Match King Hollow Point Boat Tail."

Jack knew the bullet and the various rifles a sniper would most likely pair it with. "What was the range of the shot?"

"Ah, now the field narrows considerably old buddy. Vatican Security lasered the angle of the shot and its ballistics. It came from the *Castel Sant'Angelo*. That's not even in Vatican City, Jack."

"Well, Vatican City isn't a very big place. Helen tells me it's the smallest country in the world."

"She told me the same thing. But Jack, get this. The distance of that shot was almost 1,800 yards—over a mile."

Both men were silent on the line. Over the years they each had learned to read the other's thoughts. Both knew that this had indeed narrowed the field to just a few experts who could make such a shot.

"Did you find the weapon?" asked Jack.

"They did not. But the sniper's nest was not clean. The guy executed his spotter."

Jack said, "That means he's a pro. Certainly an outside contractor. He hired the spotter or he was paired with him and he had no choice in the matter. He left behind no loose ends."

"He also left behind a small windage meter on the roof of a neighboring building. Digital. Very high tech. He used the flags throughout Saint Peter's square and the Vatican flags leading up to the Pope's private balcony to fine-tune his windage right up to the trigger pull."

Jack thought for a moment. Trident Operations ran through his mind. "Smitty, wasn't there a guy in the teams years ago? A sniper. Best shot I ever saw. He won some world competition."

"I remember who you're thinking of, old buddy. I had beers with him after he got back from the world competition in Finland. Something he said stuck in my mind."

"What's that?"

"Jack, he said that the Finns really know their ordnance. In the competition they all used the same ammo. He said it was consistent, high quality and you just never missed with it."

"Lapua .338 magnum load." Jack didn't need to guess.

"You got it, buddy."

Jack thought for a few more moments. "A pro isn't married to his weapon. A pro would just drop it and execute his exfil plan in the situation he found himself. I mean, it's not like he was in Indian territory and might need to shoot his way out. What's that tell you, Smitty?"

"He's not done yet."

"Right. Don't forget. This guy missed once. If he makes his living as a contract shooter, his reputation is now on the line. He'll need to make good on this contract. And if he was one of us, there's that SEAL work ethic."

The words of their instructors at the SEAL Team base in Coronado, California came roaring back to Jack. *First to go and last to leave. No job is done until the job is done, done, done.*

"Talk to me, buddy." Smith's words jerked Jack out of his thoughts.

Jack wanted to be sure he was considering all possibilities. "Could be we're way off base here. Afterall, there are ten, may fifteen guys who could make that shot. Smitty, check with the boys in Coronado and find out where that guy went, whoever he is. Then give whatever you get to our FBI. Make sure they pass it on to Interpol, the Italian authorities and the Vatican Security people. If they think it's too sketchy to share, then let me know and I'll do it in person."

"Sounds like you're going to see the Pope."

"That I am, Smitty. I've got an audit to finish and His Holiness is the man I need to see."

* * *

Chapter 10

The Professional sat quietly. He was just another worker taking a break and sipping a cappuccino in a Rome sidewalk café on a beautiful summer day. He watched the city walk by. His well-used black chauffeur's cap and sunglasses hid most of his face. He had applied a scruffy black beard before setting out for the streets. There was nothing out of the ordinary to attract attention to the man anyone would see as a worker—perhaps the owner of a small business or an enterprising taxi driver. Just one of the mass multitudes gathered in the greater Rome area during the summer.

What no one could see or even guess about the man sitting in the outdoor café was his identity and what he had done. The Professional had perfectly inserted himself into the area's background. He had money, a small, inexpensive place to stay that was out of the way. And he had time—all the time he needed.

He pulled out his cell phone and thumbed through his emails. There were just four—one for each day it had been since the attempted assassination of the Pope. All four came from the same person. Each said pretty much the same thing: What the fuck are you doing? His answer, now that he had decided what he would do, was simple. He typed it into the small keyboard of his cell phone. *A deal is a deal. I will make good on my contract.* He pushed the button that sent the note, then stood and put the cell phone into his pocket. He pulled some Euros from another pocket—enough to pay for his cappuccino and a decent tip but not so large as to be noticed—then exited the café.

The Professional knew the Rome bus schedule and the various lines that went to the destinations he needed by heart. He walked north to the bus station where he bought a ticket and boarded the bus to Lake Albano and Castel Gandolfo.

Once off the bus, he walked around the small village. To anyone watching him—and he was sure no one was—he was just another working man taking a stroll or enjoying a well-earned day off. He peered into the shops that served the village's small population. Slowly he made his way up the hill that overlooked the Castel Gandolfo itself. It was no secret that the Pope was now in residence during his recuperation. A recuperation, the Professional reminded himself, that the man was not really entitled to. To him, the Pope was simply a target that needed to be put down. Nothing more. The Pope had gotten lucky, that was all. It happened. This job was part physics, part ballistics, part engineering. But he had always felt there was something else to it as well. Some called it art; some called it fate. The Professional did not dwell on nomenclature. His target was still standing. His job was to make it fall. He would then move on to the next assignment. This was strictly a business proposition. You did not get involved with any personal aspect of the target.

Because the Pope was in residence there was a crowd into which the Professional melted on the hilltop. Everyone was hoping to catch a glimpse of His Holiness, perhaps strolling the halls of the Castel, regaining his strength or perhaps sitting and taking some sun on a veranda. This was the Professional's hope as well, but for a much different reason.

Today's excursion was purely reconnaissance. He had no weapon with him, didn't need one. He did, however, bring a small pair of binoculars. These were not anything that could be bought at a sporting goods store. They were military grade. He appreciated the precision of the state-of-the-art optics packed into such a small package. To anyone observing him, he appeared to be just one of the large number of faithful hoping to catch a glimpse, no matter how brief. The small binoculars were unusual in nothing but their heft. They weighed twice as much as one would expect of such a small unit.

The Professional raised the precision optics to his eyes—just like so many of his fellow, faithful observers. But the Professional knew exactly what he was looking for. He wanted to see the colonnades and walkways. He committed to memory how they intersected. Where doors were left open to allow the summer breeze to flow inside. He focused the powerful optics inside too. He made careful note of the guards—and there were many—who walked the corridors and stood post inside doorways.

Yes, he thought. They are on high alert as they should be. They know they were lucky once. Saved by a shallow breeze that carried a few scraps of paper. They wonder if another attempt will come. They are taking no chances.

A small flurry of activity on one of the second floor balconies caught his attention. He panned his field of view to the left. There was a deep balcony, almost completely covered by the roof's eves. Yes, there he was. Unmistakable. The Professional watched as his former and future target slowly walked around the corner and onto the balcony. He wore the white alba and clerical collar. But that was not the giveaway. The place was literally crawling with clerics dressed as he was. On his left ear was a heavy bandage, the result of the first attempt.

The other faithful saw him too, though their optics forced them to guess as to who this man was. The Professional knew for sure. There was a commotion on the hilltop. The Pope must have seen and heard it too. They were only 175 yards away. He paused, looked at the crowd, and then walked to the edge of the balcony to greet his well-wishers. He raised his right hand. The world knew the gesture that was about to come exclusively as his very own. He made the sign of the cross, then gave the crowd a thumbs up sign.

The hillside exploded in cheering and clapping for their Pontiff, Pope, religious leader and now a healthy survivor. This Pope was loved the world over. Especially now, that the faithful could breathe a sigh of relief at his recovery. The Professional clearly saw the Pontiff smile broadly to the crowd. His pearly-white teeth gleamed in the bright sunshine. A wisp of white hair blew from beneath his white cap. Two of the Pope's bodyguards quickly appeared and placed themselves between him and the crowd. The Professional saw how they gently, but firmly guided him away from the balcony railing and back inside the villa.

That's fine, thought the Professional as he turned a slow 360, scouting the area surrounding the Castle. There's no chance for a shot, no matter how long, now anyway. He had another idea; a better idea; one that would not fail this time.

* * *

CHAPTER 11

Jack yanked the handle on Helen's roller bag and slung his own duffel over one shoulder as he looked for the exit from Rome's Leonardo da Vinci airport baggage claim area. "There, Helen. Bear left. The sign says ground transportation is this way."

Helen nodded. "I spoke to His Holiness' secretary after you called him on that special cell phone of his. He sent a Vatican car to pick us up. He says we can't miss it."

Jack scanned the line of waiting town cars and limos mixed in with Rome's famous taxis. "The secretary is right. You really can't miss them." He saw a priest dressed in black trousers, a black jacket, black shirt and white clerical collar. He had another priest with him scanning the crowd. Both were standing in front of a black Mercedes SUV with the white and gold Papal flag stenciled on its side in gold. "Looks like we're traveling first class, Helen." Jack made eye contact with the priest and nodded in his direction.

Some old habits die hard. Jack retained several from his years in the teams. One of them was situational awareness. He constantly evaluated his surroundings. Those approaching, whether on foot, car, airplane or any other vehicle received an immediate threat assessment. As Jack and Helen made their way through the crowd to the waiting Mercedes his head was on a constant swivel. Habit. When they approached the waiting priests, both received the same once-over. Nothing out of the ordinary was Jack's two-second conclusion. Maybe a bit bigger and more fit than he would expect of a priest. But these guys worked for the Pope, he decided. They must be the best of the best.

Jack shook hands with both. They insisted on taking the luggage off of his hands. While they loaded them into the Mercedes' back, Jack looked down at his right hand. Something felt odd. He was used to shaking all kinds of hands—men's hands, women's hands, executive hands, worker hands. He cataloged each and made a mental note of what to expect when he shook someone's hand. Habit. Both priests had rough hands—those of a worker. Definitely not those of someone who dealt with the softer side of life.

It took Jack just an instant to process this information and to pair it with the build of both priests. That instant was all he needed. The bustling crowd of travelers was swarming around them, crossing the lane leading to the parking structure, waiting for their own rides. Suddenly Jack felt the muzzle of a pistol jam into his ribs. He looked deep into the priest's eyes. There was conviction there for sure. He saw a zealot; a true believer. He also saw training. The man was not wild-eyed as a novice would be. He was calm, authoritative and apparently believed he had the situation under control.

"Into the car, Mr. Schilling. Now."

Jack felt the barrel thrust deeper into his ribs to emphasize his meaning. He looked over at Helen who was standing too close to the other priest. He saw the man's black-sleeved arm extending inside her coat.

"Is this how His Holiness greats all of his out-of-town guests?" asked Jack. "Seems a bit inhospitable, doesn't it? I mean we fly half-way around the world to come visit. Sure we get picked up in a spiffy Mercedes. But what's with the hardware? Such treatment really isn't necessary. You'll get your tip. Don't you worry."

Jack looked from one priest to the other. Both seemed perplexed at what he was saying. Exactly what I intended, thought Jack. Maybe they're not so professional as they at first seemed. Then time slowed for Jack. What neither knew was that his conversation was meant to give him just enough time to think of what he was going to do to get he and Helen free. In the few seconds the conversation lasted Jack had planned his moves in his mind right down to how he would disarm the two. Time to roll, he thought.

Mistake number one was that Jack's priest left his hands free. Big error. In a flash, Jack's hand shot out and grabbed the barrel of the man's pistol. A quick twist and it was now Jack's. He flipped it around and jammed the barrel into the man's chest, then squeezed the trigger. Elapsed time, just a half second and one was down. Jack's rule was to never give the enemy a second chance to come after you.

Priest number two was watching Jack, rather than Helen. Mistake number two. During the year since their Deadly Acceleration adventure, Jack had given Helen an intensive course on self-preservation—the SEAL way. He had made it fun and somewhat academic to avoid turning her off to it. To his surprise, she took right to it. Jack had watched Helen transform from a former New York party girl, more concerned with swilling champagne and spending her family's billions into one serious woman with a calling in life.

She wasn't quite as fast as he would have liked. Nor was she as smooth as he knew she would eventually become. But she got the job done. Jack watched as his wife thrust her free right hand—her huge purse hung from her left shoulder—in a downward chop. Its knife-edge hit the priest's wrist and instantly deadened it. The gun dropped to the ground. Continuing in the same motion, Helen spun like an Olympic hammer thrower as she pulled that heavy purse from her shoulder, grabbing it by its leather strap and swung it right into the side of the priest's head.

Jack heard the sound of the man's skull splinter as he went down hard onto the pavement. A pool of blood began to form under his head. Jack's eyes met Helen's. He nodded once to her, then bent to the fallen priest as if to render aid. He grabbed the man's head in both hands and gave it a single, short twist.

90

He heard the cervical vertebrae crack. The second priest was also dead.

The whole episode took less than ten seconds. But even now the crowd was beginning to notice. Jack heard one scream, then another. Time to go, he thought. He opened the passenger door for Helen, then ran around to the driver's side. The priest had left the car idling. Jack yanked the gear shift into drive and stomped on the accelerator. He had heard this is how they all drive over here.

Jack figured they might have a five-minute head start before the Rome police would come looking for a black Mercedes G-550 with the Vatican flag stenciled in gold on both doors. How conspicuous can you be, he wondered. He pulled out his cell phone and handed it over to Helen. "Sweetie, how about calling His Holiness and letting him know we got delayed in baggage claim but we're on our way now. Maybe he can get word to the Vatican security agency and let them know that we had a bit of trouble with ground transport and the Rome police shouldn't pick us up. Go ahead, Sweetie. His number is right there on speed dial under Pope."

"Your Holiness, it is my honor to meet you," said Helen as she bowed slightly.

"There is no need to bow, my dear," said the Pontiff, "and please do not try kissing my ring. That ceremony is usually reserved for the clergy. Personally, I think it is a bit over the top what with all the germs going around today. Though some do insist. I make sure I wash it every night and I keep a small bottle of Purell handy when one of them insists."

"A good idea, Your Holiness," said Jack. "Never can tell what little critters people carry on them."

The Pope leaned back in his chair and let loose a laugh that began deep in his belly and made its way up his chest and out his throat. "That is exactly what I was thinking. The President and your father said you have a wry

sense of humor."

"Wait," interrupted Helen. "You know Mr. Schilling?"

The Pope looked at her with a mild curiosity. "Of course, my dear. Young Jack's father has provided financial counsel to the Vatican for over 20 years. He is a good man. I was so saddened when he had that little tiff with the American IRS and had to sit out a few months there in the Lompoc Men's Correctional Institution."

"You are well connected, Your Holiness," said Jack.

The Pontiff bowed his head and chuckled. "Yes, I guess I am at that. I even placed a call to that judge who heard your father's case before sentencing. Can you imagine a Pope asking a judge for clemency and forgiveness? Ah, but at the end of the day even I could not get him off. The best I could do was to lop off three months from his term."

Jack reached across the shiny, bird's eye maple desk there in the Pope's private office, patted the man's arm and said, "That's okay, Your Holiness. Nine months sitting on the bench proved good for him. Made him a better person; more humble—"

"And he learned to cook," said Helen.

The Pope's eyes laughed at that. "So I hear. I spoke with him day before yesterday. He said he would have to cut our conversation a bit short because he was in the middle of making a new lasagna and had to get it into the oven before the pasta noodles he had also made dried out."

"That wouldn't be the chicken and porcini lasagna," asked Jack.

The Pope turned to him and said, "Why yes, I believe that is what he said it was. Why?"

Jack mumbled under his breath, "I've been trying to get him to share that blessed recipe with me for six months now. He won't. Says he hasn't perfected it yet." He watched the Pope rub his still heavily bandaged ear and guessed he was getting uncomfortable. "So, Your Holiness, you know why I asked to see you in person."

"Your description of the problem you discovered in your audit of Vatican Bank was vague. But you made it sound urgent."

"It is," said Jack. "The SEC needs to bless the financial operations, capitalization and a number of other things I won't bore you with that are associated with the Bank. I'm in charge of that. If I cannot say with certainty that the Bank is operating within the guidelines prescribed for a publicly traded company, then GOD's stock will be delisted. That's $200 billion in equity on the line. A good part of that came from small investors who just wanted to own a piece of the Church."

The Pope donned his most understanding look and peered directly at Jack. "But there is more that is troubling you. I can see it in your eyes. You can tell me. I have heard it all, beginning as a parish priest."

Jack was beginning to understand just why this charismatic elderly man had been chosen to lead over a billion of the faithful. "That is true. It is not just the Bank's financial operations. Actually, they're pretty clean. Except for a single transaction of a minor amount—just $2.5 million. My problem is the...the atmosphere of secrecy that lays over the entire organization like a dark cloud."

"Well you know that Vatican Bank has a long history of secrecy. For decades its operations have been kept away from public scrutiny. Taking the Bank public is very new for everyone there." The Pope tugged gently again at the bandage covering his injured ear.

Helen broke in, "The SEC is a regulatory body. It is auditing a public entity. The goal is to *reveal* what it finds to the public. If the Vatican Bank did not wish to invite transparency into its operations, then it should not have gone public."

"That is what I told the board when I was forced to become the *camerlengo* chairman after the unfortunate death of my predecessor. However, Cardinal Caneman had the rest of the Cardinals who made up the board on his side. His judgment is that the Vatican Bank needs to sell its shares to millions of Catholics the world over who want to own a piece of their church. He explained that with such an enormous amount of money the Church could take on even more ambitious projects to help a world that sorely needs its help."

This was the kind of conversation Jack was hoping to have. "And what are those new projects, Your Holiness?"

The Pope shook his head. "So far as I know nothing has changed in the Vatican Bank's mission. It is still there to fund the charitable workings of the Church."

"Why do you think Cardinal Caneman refused to speak with me about that $2.5 million transaction?"

The Pope tugged at his bandage again.

"Your Holiness, if you are tiring and would rather cut this interview short, we can," said Helen.

"Oh no, my dear. You came a very long way to talk with me. I am flattered. I will tell you everything I can." The Pontiff took a sustaining sip from the porcelain teacup sitting before him.

Jack continued. "It was an unusual transaction. Its description lacked the detail usually provided. Indeed, the detail that transactions much smaller than this one always seem to have. The money was paid to an entity that the Bank had never dealt with before. And Caneman approved it himself, circumventing all standard internal controls."

The Pope was curious. He leaned forward and asked, "To what company was this $2.5 million paid?"

Helen said, "It was a business called Trident Operations. Have you ever heard of it, Your Holiness?"

The Pope thought about that for a minute, scratching his chin. "Hmmm. No, no. Nothing comes to mind. The Bank's board reviews all disbursements over $1 million. At least we get a list of them before each board meeting and can raise a question on any one item if we want. I've been the *camerlengo* chairman for just three months now and this Trident Operations does not sound familiar."

Jack had his timing right. He checked the copy of the Trident invoice he had brought with him. "The date on this invoice is just last month. Do you happen to have the list of disbursements the Board's directors receive before each meeting?"

94

"Of course. I keep everything." The Pope opened a desk drawer and leafed through some files. "I must confess that bank finance is not my strong suit. So I keep all the information they send me about the bank. I hope someday I will understand it." The Pope continued leafing through his files. "Ah. Here is the package the Board received prior to last month's meeting." He quickly paged through it until he found the disbursement list. There were just 11 items listed. "I see no Trident on this list." He handed it over to Jack along with the two preceding month's board packages.

Jack leafed through the list, confirmed that Trident was not listed, then performed the same examination on the other two board packages with the same result. He leaned back in his chair and rubbed his chin.

The Pope asked, "What? Is not finding that $2.5 million payment a good thing?"

Helen spoke up. "No Your Holiness. It is a very bad thing—"

Jack broke in, "It seems that someone has sanitized the disbursements shown to your board." He held up the questionable invoice to Trident Operations. "This disbursement is conspicuously missing from your board package. Its absence means some insider with access to the information provided to the board perpetrated a fraud on you directors."

The Pope looked at Jack. There was dismay in his eyes. "Sounds ominous," he said. "Will Vatican Bank have to give back all the money it just raised?"

Jack almost laughed at that. "No, Your Holiness. That would be the very last resort. Most of these things are just oversights. A little digging usually reveals some error or misclassification of an accounting entry. However, now I really do need to get to the bottom of this particular disbursement. We have a set of circumstances building up to what at this point could be construed as a fraud or embezzlement against the bank if it's not explained away. What I need from you is access to all the materials and people I need to conduct my investigation. No more running around and refusing to speak with me. Everything in Cardinal David Caneman's office stops until I am satisfied as to the explanation of this disbursement."

The Pope nodded. "Of course. You shall have everyone's fullest cooperation. Just tell me what you need and whom you wish to speak to. I will personally make sure they cooperate with you fully. As soon as we finish here, I will place a call to Cardinal Caneman and see that he initiates a new level of cooperation."

Just then the door to the Pope's private office opened. The priest who entered had not even taken the time to knock. Jack saw that it was the Pope's assistant whom he had met when they first came into the Castel where the Pontiff was recuperating. The man's face was red and he walked across the carpeted office with what seemed an urgent purpose. Distraught is what Jack thought. The priest leaned close to the Pope's uninjured ear and whispered. Jack knew what was said without even hearing him.

The Pope's hand flew up to his mouth in shock as he turned on Jack. "There were two men dressed as priests killed at the airport shortly after your flight landed. I can connect the dots as well as anyone even if people insist on calling me Your Holiness. You told my assistant that you had what he termed a bit of trouble at baggage claim. Your father has shared with me some of your background. So I must ask if you had anything to do with what happened to those two men?"

Jack was calm, as always when faced with an accusation. He said simply, "They needed killing and I performed the service. You said the deceased men were *dressed* as priests. Do you mean they were not *actually* priests?"

The Pope sat there looking Jack over. He had known his father for years. Never had a reason to think he ever lied, despite his incarceration for tax evasion. The Pope figured his son must be cut from the same cloth. He shook his head. "We are still checking on who they were. Right now we know they did not work in the Vatican or anywhere close to Rome."

"What about the car they were driving?" asked Helen.

"The car did indeed belong to the Vatican motor court." He faced Jack and said, "Apparently you drove it here after taking it from them. However, my assistant tells me that it went missing the day before yesterday."

"Don't they keep records of the whereabouts of the Vatican's official vehicles?" asked Helen.

His Holiness sighed, "I'm afraid our people are not very good at such record keeping. When they cannot find a car or truck, they simply list it as unavailable for service until it shows up again. They usually do." The Pope asked, "Did the death of those two men have anything to do with your visit to see me and this audit of Vatican Bank you are conducting?"

Jack did not respond. Instead, he sat in the relaxed office of the Pontiff's lakeside retreat, thinking. Jack did not like coincidences; didn't believe in them. He thought about the sequence of events in which he was now involved, like it or not. First the Vatican Bank went public and raised $200 billion. Then came the assassination attempt on the Pope. Were the two events connected? He wondered. Jack had received word from Smitty back in DC that the Italian authorities had not yet apprehended the shooter. He'll try again, thought Jack. He was certain of it.

Then the President insisted that he be brought in to do the routine SEC review on the Vatican Bank. Next came that $2.5 million payment to Trident Operations. It was a payment that was out of compliance with the bank's system of internal controls and disbursement safeguards. And that vendor's name—an odd sequence of words that would mean something only to a former SEAL. A third event connected? Then the Vatican Bank's CEO—His Eminence Cardinal David Caneman—refused to speak with him about that strange disbursement. Why? He was used to dealing with reluctant executives. In the end, he always prevailed. Not this time. This time he had to go right to the top of the Roman Catholic Church. And was almost killed—along with Helen—within an hour of landing in Rome.

"Jack?" asked Helen. "Jack, His Holiness asked you a question. Do you think those two men who tried to kill us at the airport have anything to do with our visit to Rome and the audit of Vatican Bank?"

Jack Schilling snapped out of his reverie at the sound of Helen's voice. "Count on it." He turned to the Pope, "Sir, you are in grave danger. I have an idea that I'm going to need your cooperation on something far more urgent than a $2.5 million disbursement."

* * *

CHAPTER 12

The Professional had many disguises. A particularly expert make-up artist in Hollywood trained him after he left the Navy. His arsenal of characters included young, old, male, female, various ethnicities, bald and hairy. He used cotton rods in his cheeks to puff them up when needed. Various sets of false teeth gave him the dental look that matched the persona he was assuming.

He walked slowly along the cobblestones leading up to Castel Gandolfo. Today he was an elderly man serving the Pope's summer residence as a gardener. He was one of dozens of laborers who came and went as needed. This group of employees did not know one another, nor did the guards. There were no regulars. Their work seldom lasted more than a week or two. When His Holiness was in residence, their ranks doubled.

The Professional had forged the identification tag that everyone entering the compound had to present and display at all times. His bore the dirt and grime that one who digs in the villa's flower beds would have. His hands were worn and there was dirt embedded in the lines and creases. A large and well-worn straw hat with a wide brim covered his head and placed his entire face in shade.

The Professional was American, born and raised in Louisiana bayou country. He was Caucasian and despite all his outdoor activities had a fair complexion. Today, however, he was a local Roman and had the ruddy, dark skin of a life spent on the Mediterranean coast. The stain he used on every exposed part of his skin was a perfect match for the region. He was an expert in its application. The deep, coppery color was as if he was born with it. The stain would last for a week at least and was waterproof. He walked in a slouch that took six inches off of his height. He had mastered the speech affectations of a tired old man who had labored hard his entire life. All in fluent Italian, of course.

The Professional was carrying two large flats of white, yellow, pink and red bouvardia. He turned so the guard at the gate could more easily see his ID tag. He was proud of his handiwork. It was perfect. Indeed, he had never made an ID that was questioned or even given a second look. He would stake his life on his work, as he had many times. The guard held up a hand to stop him. He looked at the gardener's worn face, back at the ID tag, back at the gardener. "Where are you planting these today?" the guard asked, his voice congenial. He recognized the gardener. He had been working in the villa and on its grounds for three days now.

The Professional spoke in flawless Italian, "The south beds overlooking the lake, just below the balcony of His Holiness' bedroom. He will see the colors when he awakens in the morning."

The guard brightened and smiled at the mention of their beloved Pope and the thought of pleasing him. "That he will," said the guard, still smiling. He nodded his permission to enter the grounds and held open the heavy iron gate for the Professional.

He worked in the gardens, planting and watering, raking leaves and sweeping. By mid-morning the flowerbeds for which the Professional was responsible this day were truly immaculate—a work of art. The colorful flowers were set just so to make a beautiful and appealing collage for His Holiness' enjoyment. And his back hurt. The Professional was in superior physical condition. The man was a former special warfare operator. Once anyone attained that level of physical and athletic perfection, they rarely allowed themselves to fall very far from the standard. The physical work was not what bothered him. No. The Professional was not used to walking in the slouch that his disguise required. He especially was not used to carrying heavy loads in that same slouch.

"Hey you," said a priest standing around and surveying the villa's grounds. The Professional looked up from his sweeping and made a pointing motion toward himself with his bushy black eyebrows raised. "Yes, you. I need you to cut a large bunch of those flowers from over there," the priest pointed toward a row

100

of brightly colored daisies, snapdragons, birds of paradise and roses. "Then deliver them to Sister Maria on the second floor. She's His Holiness' personal secretary. She'll have a vase ready for you to put in his study.

The Professional hid his elation. He was planning on sneaking onto the second floor to check the layout of the Pope's personal spaces. Instead he had just been given a free pass to wander around up there as he wished. He slowly leaned his broom against the villa's heavy plaster supporting column, careful to hide his enthusiasm for the assignment. He pulled well-used gardening shears from his jeans pocket. His stride toward the flowers the priest had pointed to was slow; that of a worker just doing what he was told to do. But the Professional was not just a worker doing his master's bidding. He had an all too different and deadly agenda. It looks like the opportunity will come faster than anticipated, he thought as he snipped the flowers stalk by stalk.

"You have but to ask, my son," the Pope had said. Jack Schilling saw just what weight those words carried. Within an hour of his request, Jack was dressed in the black slacks, jacket, shirt and white dog collar of the villa's working clergy. He had an authentic identification badge bearing his photo and the various color codes allowing him unlimited access to every nook and cranny of the villa. He looked across the desk at Helen. She wore the purple and white habit of the sisters of Our Lady of Perpetual Correctness. All it took was a call from the Pope's personal secretary. Someone from the most famous order of nuns the world over—since the Vatican News Service's own Sister Mary Pat was a member—had brought it over and instructed Helen on how it was to be worn.

"What'd the Vatican Security detail say?" asked Helen as she looked over the both of them in their new attire.

"They admitted that they stick out like a sore thumb here in their business suits with those curly communications wires coming out of their ears. They gave me a hard time when I asked for a gun and shoulder rig to put under my coat. In the end, a nod from His Holiness got me the gun, rig and a nifty silencer."

"What about me?" Helen asked.

"Don't worry, I got you one too—a Glock-17. It's small enough to fit under the folds of that fancy outfit without anyone being the wiser. Unless you have to use it, that is." Jack had watched Helen progress through the ranks of marksmanship during the past year. By now she had qualified as expert or better on five pistols and several automatic rifles. He ran her through the mock kill house at the Elkhart police academy. Her times had quickly improved along with the errors she made in shooting the innocents that popped up around corners and in doorways as she made her way through the staged course. But she hasn't had anyone firing at her, he thought. That's a whole different experience.

* * *

CHAPTER 13

The cellular connection crackled in Cardinal David Caneman's earpiece. "How much longer?" he demanded.

The Professional looked out of the small window of his tiny apartment buried in the depths of Rome's rundown garment district. From here he could not see the hills in which Castel Gandolfo was located. The best his view could manage was of a narrow, dingy street five floors below with no elevator service. "The job is more complicated now that the authorities are on high alert," he said.

"I do not care how difficult the job is. I paid you $2.5 million for results. You were hired because you are the best there is. You missed with your first attempt—"

Such an accusation inflamed the Professional. "I did not miss. My shot went right where it was aimed. No one could have foreseen the target lunging sideways to grab a piece of paper the wind had blown. No one."

"The stupid old man still lives," fumed Caneman. "He continues driving the Church in a direction never intended by the Twelve Apostles. If I cannot terminate his agenda, he will soon open the priesthood to the nuns. Then God knows what else he'll do."

The Professional cared not a whit about his client's agenda or the reason for which he had ordered the target put down. "I am pursuing an alternate route to achieve our goal."

"What route is that?" asked Caneman.

"I am a subcontractor. I retain the right to conduct my assignment as I see fit, using whatever tools or tactics I deem necessary. Disclosing my methods to anyone—you especially—could place us both in jeopardy."

Caneman was still fuming. Still, as he sat on the hillside overlooking the old city of Bethlehem, he could not fault the logic. He was not one who willingly accepted a subordinate position to someone he deemed his inferior. "When then?"

"When? It will happen when it happens. Even I cannot foretell when the opportunity merges with all the mechanics necessary for execution and then escape. Just know that I am working on this project every day. Your target is my only assignment right now and will be until I have fulfilled our arrangement. That is all."

Caneman heard the unmistakable click of the Professional cutting their connection. He stood among the sandy rocks of the hillside. Even here in the shade it was hot. That's Israel in the summer, he thought. He turned to the goatherd standing next to him along with the man's elderly father and his even older grandfather. All three men were dark-skinned from a lifetime of working in the sun. They were skinny, as all these people seemed to be who lived in the desert. "Where is it?" asked Caneman in near perfect Hebrew.

The grandfather who was brokering the deal spoke up, "Ah, sir, we have what you seek. We were smart enough to leave it in the cave where my grandson found it."

Caneman had spent months doing the research he needed to locate the fifth stone tablet to the map of the Church's treasure vault. Over the centuries, the pieces had scattered to unimaginable corners of the earth. Yet Caneman had managed to locate four of them. His research was second to none. His resources were without equal. Not even the most prestigious universities or museums the world over could match his capability for finding the most valuable artifacts the world would ever know.

He bought three of the tablets from their owners. The cost had been extraordinarily steep for these three. The first went for $75 million. The owner was guessing who this obscenely rich and apparently naïve collector of religious antiquities actually was. Caneman never, ever negotiated as himself on behalf of the Holy See. Never. Every transaction was strictly *off piste*—out of bounds, beyond the normal channels of such purchases.

Caneman saw that the second owner had heard of the collection of tablets that someone was amassing, though he did not know who. The family who owned it were Sicilian immigrants living in New Jersey. They were in the waste management business. Waste management, indeed, thought Caneman. He knew as well as anyone that they were of the Mangano crime family. Caneman proved to be an even tougher negotiator, though. Their tablet sold for $225 million. The amount was trivial to someone with the resources of the Vatican Bank behind him.

The third owner was actually legitimate, though the transaction was not. The Getty Museum in Los Angeles, California had acquired the oddly shaped stone tablet with patches of ancient writing decades ago as a minor part of a much larger acquisition. For all of that time the ungainly and actually quite ugly tablet had sat gathering dust in J. Paul Getty's personal overstock storage vaults. Yes, the head curator knew of its place in the museum's collection archives. However, he had attached no particular significance to it. Would he be willing to part with it? Perhaps. What did the strangely unknown collector have in mind?

Caneman posed as an eccentric collector of religious art. He had in mind a trade. The Church had an extensive collection of masterworks in its own vaults. These rotated around its various displays worldwide. Many pieces—worth hundreds of millions—seemed to have fallen from the Church's inventory lists. Similar to the Church's haphazard recordkeeping that seemed to afflict so many parts of its empire. Would the Getty simply trade a few priceless paintings that no one had seen in decades and that were missing from any collection lists for the tablet?

The professional curator whose Ph.D. and academic pedigree had come from the finest ivy-league schools with internships and department directorships at the world's most prestigious museums knew a rube when he saw one. Perhaps, he had told Caneman. He had *hondled* with the strange collector for a month before selecting his four paintings in exchange for the ugly stone tablet whose value was questionable at best. Caneman knew the four painting's value--$375 million—had the Church put them up for sale. The Church, Caneman knew, did not even have a record of their existence. They were never missed.

Acquisition of the fourth tablet proved unconventional. Caneman spent years locating it. He found it in Slovenia—the family heirloom of a carpenter. It had been handed down from generation to generation for hundreds of years. When Caneman approached the family with an offer to take it off of their hands, they refused. They would not budge. The rock, as they called it, was a precious and interesting piece of their family's history. It was not about money. Caneman saw they were people of simple means to whom money truly meant nothing. In the end, he grew impatient. He contracted out the extermination of the entire family—nine people. There could be no loose ends. He got the rock.

See, sir, look at it," said the goatherd's grandfather. They were standing in a sweltering cave in the hills outside of Bethlehem. The man removed a filthy rag, yellowed with age. Caneman peered downward. There, in the stifling cave, illuminated by the dim, late afternoon light coming into the mouth of the cave sat Tablet Number Five. Despite its age and the conditions in which it had been kept, Caneman saw the unmistakable glow it shared with its four brothers. The old goatherd spat on its surface, then rubbed it with his bare hand. As expected, a shiny sheen appeared on the gray surface as it had on the other four. This was it, he exclaimed to himself. By now, over all these years of research, then tracking and finally acquiring, there was no mistaking it.

Caneman realized that he was alone with these three. They were in the middle of nowhere. He had told no person where he was going and with whom. Merely, that he had a meeting with a local merchant. "How much?" he asked.

The grandfather who served as chief guide, curator and, apparently negotiator, looked at Caneman, then shook his wizened head as if he knew something the disguised man did not. "This is of no value to us," he said hefting the stone tablet. "It buys no new tent for my family. It cannot buy another goat or a camel. You may have it with my best wishes for a long and happy journey to wherever your travels may take you. Whoever you are and whatever you choose to use this for, my hope is that it helps you accomplish your goals." The old man placed the rock in Caneman's hand.

Without another word, the grandfather led his son and grandson out of the cave and to the Toyota pickup parked on the upslope to the cave. The old truck had peeling paint that made it difficult to tell what color was actually intended. Caneman watched the truck sag on long-dead springs as the son climbed in and turned over the tired engine. He heard the engine hiccup from a misfiring cylinder. The son ground the gears into submission. Then the old truck hauled the three of them off into the desert in a listless cloud of searing dust.

Caneman stood at the mouth of the cave and watched as their trail disappeared into the desert. He thought of each of the other four stone tablets and what he had to do to gain control over them. Then he looked down at this most recent Number Five in his hand. By far, this acquisition was the easiest. Perhaps God was rewarding him for his diligence and perseverance. *And* his sacred mission to save His Church from this Pope and those who had gone before him. There was just one way—the Holy way. It was the strict fundamentalist Catholic doctrine that would save the Church and its followers.

Caneman climbed into the Land Rover, hoping that the man he had hired to dispose of the Pope would get it over with quickly. He put the car in gear and backed down the slope, then turned in the direction of Bethlehem with the fifth tablet safely tucked into his leather satchel.

* * *

CHAPTER 14

Jack held his cell phone up to his ear. The Roman Catholic collar chaffed his neck. It was not something he was used to. Nor did he intend to get used to it. This was just a short job; one to assess the Pope's security and look over who they let into the compound, then get back to New York to wrap up the Vatican Bank audit.

"So what'd you find out, Smitty?" Jack asked in a hushed voice. He leaned up against the villa's 16th Century plaster column that overlooked Castel Gandolfo's pristine gardens.

"Okay, pal, you were right, sort of. The boys at SEAL Team 1 out in Coronado confirms the guy I met and had a beer with did indeed win the World Long Rifle Championships back in 2005. He was one of ours, Jack. Spent seven years in the Teams as a sniper. Deployed all over the Middle East, Philippines, South and Central America. Played a role in most of the hot spots. During his time in the Teams he racked up 173 confirmed kills."

Jack was a sponge for information. He stood listening and leaning casually against the pillar. "What did he use?" Jack was well aware that most snipers had a preferred rifle they used for their craft. They usually kept it for their entire career. Though each insisted it was just another rifle—a JAR—everyone knew better. Each sniper made little tweaks and changes to the action, the frame, to the optics they carried that made it uniquely their own.

"I spoke with a Captain William Lama—ex-fighter jock who became an intel officer with the SEALs once his flying days were over. He's the quartermaster who kept the records of the weapons and ordnance issued to the Teams. Lama says this guy—name's John McElwey, by the way—had three rifles that he always took with him on deployment. His favorite was the Barrett M98-Bravo Long Range. That's the one he used to win the World Championships. Lama says that this McElwey never let that gun out of his sight."

108

Jack paused for a moment as one of the villa's gardeners slouching and wearing a wide-brimmed straw hat ambled past him down the colonnade and into the colorful garden. Jack stood there silently watching the man pass. Nothing escaped his observation. "And McElwey's favorite cartridges?"

"You're right in line with me, Jack. Lama looked up his records of ordnance issue. Says the SEAL snipers could get any loads they wanted. Most used a variety depending on the job. But most had a favorite they preferred—especially for what they knew would be long range work. McElwey used exclusively the .338 Lapua Magnum Long Range Sierra Match King Hollow Point Boat Tail projectile. You have any idea the cost of those? About $30 for a box of 20 cartridges. And before you ask, that is the load he used in the World Championships back in '05."

Jack did not have to ask. Though he was not a qualified and designated sniper, he knew his way around the trade. "The 98-Bravo loaded with the .338 Lapua certainly could have made that mile-plus shot at the Pope."

"Yes it could," confirmed Smitty.

"Where's McElwey now?"

"I had Lama check the Navy's records. He mustered out of the Teams in 2006. Didn't go into the reserves as most of the ex-special ops guys do for the pay and the medical benefits. Lama couldn't say for sure, but he doesn't think the guy went over to another government agency. Never attended any of the Teams reunions. He seems to have fallen off the face of the earth, disappeared. But there's one more thing Lama wanted to make sure I knew about our boy. Emphasized it, actually."

"What's that, Smitty?"

"He said this McElwey is one deadly hombre. Was arrested by the San Diego police department three times and brought up on assault charges while his team was back home on stand down. There were other incidents that his commanding officer smoothed over with the local PD. But Lama's point about this guy is that he's crazy aggressive. Once he gets you in his sights we won't stop until you are dead. He uses whatever weapon is available. In Afghanistan there was an incident he told me about. Said McElwey's team was pinned down in an alley and taking fire by two Talib snipers above them in high cover. Sitting ducks. Remember how that feels, boss? Anyway, the story goes that McElwey didn't have a shot. The Talibs were too well-concealed. They had taken out two of our guys already. So he left his hide, crawled across the rooftops to go get them himself. There were two lookouts protecting the Talib snipers. Kids, he told me. One by one McElwey silently crept up to wherever they were hiding—maybe in doorways or under old boxes—and slit their throats then gutted them from pubic bone right up to their sternum. He yanked their internal organs out of them with his bare hands. Left them so they spilled out of the chest cavity onto the dirt. He staged a gruesome scene. Then he moved on to the snipers. Did the same thing to them. When the CO learned what he had done, he wanted to bring him back for court martial. The SEAL commandant put a stop to that. But what this guy did, boss, it was inhuman and unnecessary. Lama said he talked to our guys who had actually seen what he did. It was as if he got off on the brutality of the act of killing. He explained what he had done to the CO of the forward special operations base, saying he wanted to send the message that US soldiers would not tolerate anyone who supported the enemy in trying to kill our troops."

Jack was silent on the phone for a moment, taking in Smitty's report. "Did it work?"

"Apparently so, boss. Local support for the Taliban insurgents went from significant to zero over night. The Talibs were said to be brutal to those who refused to help them, but the US soldiers after what McElwey had done to the kids and the snipers they served was ungodly no matter what god you believe in. Better the devil you know than the one you don't. The last thing Lama said to me was to be very, very careful if we go up against this guy. He's not only a master marksman, he works with blades, garrotes, anything including his bare hands. And he's deadly with all of them. Lama told me he thinks the guy's crazy—insane."

110

"Yeah, well Smitty if it were easy, they would just call in the Marines. Instead they call the SEC."

"Yeah, right boss."

"Okay, can you check on one more thing before you leave DC?"

"Where am I going, boss?" Smith never got over calling Jack Schilling his boss. They had been partners in the Teams through the toughest, most grueling training of any military combat organization in the world. Then later, as Team buddies on some of the most dangerous and blackest of black operations where the lives of both literally were in the other's hands. There was no stronger bond than that forged in combat. Since Schilling was a year older and the more senior of the two, Smith began calling him boss. He never stopped.

"You're coming here. I need someone I can trust and whom I know will do whatever is needed without me having to ask. Take the SEC's jet. Bring two other operators with you—make sure they're guys I know. Don't use a commercial flight. You're going to bring our clandestine load-out of weapons and supplies anyway. If you need the old man's intervention, get it." Jack knew that Smith now would not hesitate contacting the White House for any help he required. When Jack Schilling called, he didn't have to ask a second time. "But before you leave, get the answer to one last question."

"Shoot, boss."

"Since 2006 until now, has the number of assassinations of prominent figures in government, business and elsewhere increased from the previous ten years?"

* * *

CHAPTER 15

The Professional carried the 25-kilo sack of fertilizer on his right shoulder. An old and well-used leather tool belt held the pruning shears, trowels and small hand shovels he used on the flower beds. Even to the highly-trained Swiss Guard standing post at the iron gate to the villa he looked like all the other workers starting their day.

The Professional smiled a friendly grin to the guard and wished him a pleasant day in perfect Italian. The guard briefly held up the gardener's plastic laminated ID card that swung on a lanyard from around his neck. His eyes flitted between the photo on the card and the tanned creases of the gardener's seemingly old and weathered face. He had seen him entering and leaving the villa's grounds each day for the last week. No threat here, he judged. The guard wished the gardener the same pleasant day and admitted him onto the villa's grounds where the Pope remained just 50 meters away on the second floor overlooking Lake Albano while he continued his recuperation from the gardener's first attempted assassination.

The Professional carried his heavy load of fertilizer to the back edge of the villa property where the outside grounds staff maintained their work shed. It was a corrugated metal structure that held the mowers, tools, shovels, wheelbarrows, watering hoses and all the other things required to maintain a property comprising 20 hectares on a pristine hillside overlooking one of the most beautiful lakeside medieval villages in Europe.

Inside the shed, the Professional carefully set down his bag so that it lay flat. He made sure that all the other gardening staff was busy going about their daily maintenance assignments. Then he closed the shed door and jammed a shim under the door in such a way that it could not be opened from the outside. Once certain that he would not be disturbed, he carefully sheared open the fertilizer bag lengthwise as they always did when loading such bulky materials into the wheelbarrows that would carry them to their final resting places. It was true that the bag contained fertilizer. But it contained something else too.

The Professional pulled out four bricks of PE4 plastique explosive. Similar to the more common C4, but the off-white colored PE4 packed a greater punch—27,000 feet per second of explosive force. The Professional was counting on the enormous shock wave to bring down the villa. He needed it to be as large as possible. Each of the PE4 bricks weighed about three kilos—enough to blow not only the villa and everyone in it to kingdom come, but also possibly the entire hillside. He lined the bricks of explosive up against the shed wall. The Professional liked working with plastique. He could shape and mold it to conform to the load-bearing joists he needed to blow. It was stable. No gunshot would initiate its detonation; nor would dropping it on a hard surface. The only way to initiate detonation of plastique was with a combination of extreme heat and a shockwave—such as when the detonator trigger inserted into the shaped charge was fired.

He pulled the four electronic detonator triggers from the fertilizer bag along with some electrical wire and a cellular telephone that would initiate the entire device when he dialed the number. He had completed the basic assembly in his small room in Rome, then made it safe for transport and placed the components inside the fertilizer bag to bring to work today. All that remained now was to complete the assembly by putting the four bricks of PE4 in their inconspicuous places, inserting the detonator triggers into the plastique, wiring them together, connecting the wire to the electronic triggers and then connecting the entire device to the cell phone. This step took him just five minutes more.

The Professional carefully placed the device—now about as large as two shoeboxes—back inside the fertilizer bag and resealed it. He stood back in the dim light of the work shed to inspect his work. He thought that if he lay the bag with the seam side down, no one would be able to tell it had been opened. He placed the bag four rows down in the stack of the other fertilizer bags arranged neatly in the corner. He made sure that he could see the single red marker stripe he had drawn to mark his bag. It would take the gardening staff at least three days to work down the stack of fertilizer bags before his was next up. By then, the villa and the Pope would be in smoldering ruins. The Professional wiped his hands on his work pants, removed the shim from the door jam and left the shed.

By now he knew every inch of the villa. His was a familiar, friendly face to the staff. He had quickly become known as a careful and very deliberate worker. This reputation was hugely assisted by the Pontiff himself who commented on the beautiful flower garden that had just been planted right outside his bedroom. And what a lovely site it was to awaken to the sun shining on those brightly colored daisies and roses with the lake in the background. Word of His Holiness' approval had traveled around the villa. Shortly everyone knew which gardener had so carefully arranged the garden and did the planting to achieve exactly the effect that so pleased their beloved Pope.

Not only did the Professional know where every door and window was located, he had also learned where the major supporting beams were hidden among the ceiling joists and bearing walls. Building a villa on a hillside near a lake was a structural engineering undertaking. Since it had been built in the 16th Century, the achievement was that much more remarkable. The Professional's PE4 would make short work of the huge oaken timbers that supported so much of the villa's tremendous weight on the hillside.

The Professional had in mind particular places to shape his plastique into the villa's structural supports so that it looked like part of the wall. He did not wish to rely on crushing the Pope to death as the villa came crashing down around him. After missing with his first shot in St. Pete's Square, he felt that his reputation could not withstand relying on such luck. He needed His Holiness to meet his maker first as a direct result of the blast itself. Then, if the resulting cataclysm further crushed the body, so much the better. But first, the blast.

114

His Holiness had settled into a predictable routine. He took his meals at the same places, at the same times each day. The only variant was whom he asked to dine with him. He strolled the same paths each day. The Professional knew within a minute or so of just when the Pontiff could be seen passing any particular intersection of pathways around the villa. But even these predictable habits left too much to chance for the Professional. He had a fail-safe, fall back to his plan that would not miss this time.

"You are new here, aren't you, dear?" asked Sister Mary Pat. "I don't believe that I have seen you before."

Helen stopped walking and turned to face the nun who Catholics the world over had come to love and rely on to provide them a direct news feed into Vatican City. "Why yes, Sister, I am. I just arrived yesterday from New York." Helen wondered if nuns shook hands or hugged or what. She decided to hold out her hand and see what happened, "Sister Helen."

SMP took Helen's small hand in both of hers, then pulled her close and kissed both her cheeks. Then leaning away while still holding her hand she conducted a grandmotherly head-to-toe appraisal. She said, "I thought so. His Holiness himself told me of a novitiate nun with a smile so pretty she could make the sun rise at midnight. He asked me to see if you needed any help."

Helen was a seasoned party girl, turned corporate investigator over the last year since she had met Jack Schilling on the Deadly Acceleration job. It took a lot to fool her bullshit meter. But she had to admit such a sincere and warm compliment coming from this purely good person made her glow just a little bit.

Still, Helen could not risk Sister Mary Patrick sniffing out a story—any story—about her, Jack or what they were doing here dressed as a nun and a priest. She knew SMP and the Pope had been friends for three years since she arrived in Vatican City to work for the Vatican News Service. When Jack had questioned His Holiness' decision to bring a reporter into his confidence the answer came fast and clear, "Young man, whatever security clearances you think you might have, I can guarantee Sister Mary Pat's is higher." Then he watched him wink to seal his message. When the Pope left the office Jack had turned to Helen, "What's that supposed to mean? A nun has no security clearance."

"You big oaf," Helen had answered. "He means that Sister Mary Pat answers to a higher authority than either you or I. His Holiness has faith in her because he has decided that her own personal faith is unshakable. There is no higher endorsement than that of a sitting Pope."

The truth was that Helen liked the blousy, calf-length pants of the purple and white habit as it swirled around her legs. She adjusted the minimalized summer headdress. Sister Mary Pat stepped toward her and corrected its positioning. "You'll get the hang of it, dear," she said.

"Thank you, Sister," Helen said and meant it. "I have been watching you on television for a long time. You are famous, a world-class reporter—"

"Please dear, don't go overboard. I'm just a nun trying to serve…and a working reporter on the side. Though, I must admit, I seem to have access to the top dog in the world's largest religion, don't I?"

Helen looked closely at the smiling nun. "Ah Sister, please tell me if I'm wrong, but did His Holiness have a conversation with you about me and Mr. Schilling?"

Sister Mary Pat took Helen's arm in hers and said, "Come dear, let's take a walk." The two proceeded through the villa, past its precisely kept gardens with its army of gardeners to keep it that way and out into the olive grove.

When they were alone, Sister Mary Pat said, "My dear, the Pope did summon me into his office after you both had left. From time to time His Holiness entrusts me with information that is not for public disclosure. He tells me where and when I am to leak it. Our beloved Pope is quite adept at using the media to further the Church's cause.

"He told me that you and your extraordinarily handsome husband are both here on a delicate matter of the highest importance to him personally. He asked me not to divulge your presence or bring into question your true identity. You must understand that such a request coming from His Holiness is the highest level. He is very polite in its statement. But we shall call a spade a spade—his conversation with me was an order. He emphasized his point by saying that revealing you both as something other than the clergy you now appear could place his life in danger. Then he asked me to make contact with you and provide you both with anything you might need. Anything."

Helen said, "He makes a pretty strong case, doesn't he, Sister."

"That he does, my dear. I wouldn't have it any other way. I am privileged to know him as I do. What this Pope says is what he means." SMP stopped and looked Helen in the eye. "He reminded me that I am a friend to the Church and his personal friend as well. Then he asked again that I exercise complete secrecy on this and anything else I may discover involving you two as I offer my services."

"And what do you think you might discover, Sister?" asked Helen.

"No idea, dearie. Oh, of course I'm a bit curious. And I wouldn't shut my ears to anything you might be willing to tell me. But as for asking or ever repeating anything I hear, the devil himself couldn't get it out of me."

Helen made a decision. Their walk had taken them full circle, out of the olive grove in back and returning them onto the villa's grounds. They passed workers and the seemingly endless army of gardeners.

"Excuse me, Sister," said one deeply tanned gardener in a floppy straw hat who bumped into Helen as she and Mary Pat rounded a corner. Helen briefly made eye contact with the gardener before he broke it off and continued on his way. She turned and watched his back as he slowly walked away in the slouched posture of one who has spent a lifetime doing stoop labor and carrying heavy loads. She had a thought that even with

117

that painful posture, he looked to be in pretty good physical shape.

Helen turned back to Sister Mary Pat. "I need to ask you some questions about the workers here and the Pope's schedule."

"Ask away, my dear. What would you like to know?"

"The Professional fought to keep his slouch as he walked away from the two nuns. The older one he recognized. Of course he did. Who didn't? The famous Sister Mary Patrick of the Vatican News Service frequented the villa. During the past week he was here, he had seen her three times. But the other, younger and pretty nun was new. What's she doing, he wondered. During the brief encounter his surveillance training kicked in. He managed to catch her profile. Asian, probably Japanese. Tall, about 5-10. But some Japanese women are quite statuesque. Slender. The habit she wore hid her figure. From the contour of her face and the lines of her neck, he guessed she was in excellent physical shape.

He wondered if she might present any threat to his mission. With all the clothing these people wore around here they could conceal any type of weapon they wished. He decided to keep an eye on the tall, pretty nun. If she exhibited any sort of behavior not in keeping with a member of the clergy he would eliminate her. He would make that decision in the next 24 hours.

"For starters," answered Helen, "that gardener who almost flattened me as we turned the corner. Do you know him?"

"Oh yes," answered SMP, "even though he has been here just a week, he is quite well regarded here in the villa. He seems to have a knack for designing the most beautiful flowerbeds and laying them out exactly where His Holiness is most likely to enjoy them. In fact, His Holiness himself has commented on what an excellent job he is doing."

Helen could care less about the gardener's skill with flowers or what the Pope thought of his work. "But he is new to the villa's staff?"

118

SMP thought for a minute. "Yes. I'm sure of it. I haven't seen him here before this week."

"Is he allowed access to the Pope's spaces?" asked Helen.

"Hmmm. Well, I imagine he is. Yes. Certainly here on the ground floor he has unlimited movement about the gardens and service sheds on the property. I have seen him on the second floor in His Holiness' office carrying bunches of fresh-cut flowers from the beds he planted for Sister Maria. She is His Holiness' personal secretary. Why, dear?"

Helen ignored her question. She thought about the gardener some more. Was the slouch a deliberate affectation? Or was he exactly who he appeared—a hardworking, dedicated employee of villa? She tried to imagine how he would look standing straight up. He'd be about six feet tall. Two inches shorter than Jack. Certainly not a skinny fellow; but not fat either. Solid. Fit was how she would describe such a person. Kind of like how Jack and Smitty look. She had been around Jack's friends in the special operations warfare community enough to know *the look.* Did this guy have it? She made her decision.

"Sister, could you please discretely follow that gardener from a distance so he won't notice you? Then text me where you both are. I'm going to speak with Jack."

"Where is he, Sister?" demanded Jack.

Let's be a little more calm, sweetie," said Helen, "you're scaring her."

"Dearie, I've been scared before. Really scared. Believe me, your Mr. Schilling here does not scare me in the least."

"Where?" demanded Jack.

SMP looked down the villa's colonnade again where she last saw the slouching gardener. The colonnade ran the length of the south side, from the flower gardens, past the olive grove and the hillside that overlooked the villa. "I don't know. I lost him. I followed him through the gardens and waited around a corner while he went into the gardener's service shed where they keep their tools and such. I saw him go in but never saw him come out—"

"Is there a back door to the shed that he might have used?" asked Jack, a knife-edge in his voice.

"I don't know, Mr. Schilling. I have never had the privilege of entering the gardener's service shed. But I imagine it does. They drive their mowers and tractors through there."

Jack made his decision. "Helen, you go get the Pope out of the villa and as far away from here as fast as you can. I'm going to find our gardener." With that he was off at a run, his priest's coat tails flying behind him.

The Professional had removed his villa ID card and lanyard from around his neck. He now looked like any workingman in the tiny, peaceful village of Gandolfo. As he left the north gate—an entry used only by the villa's service staff— he wished the guard a pleasant afternoon. He slowly walked through Gandolfo, along its cobble stone street toward the hill that overlooked the Castle. He climbed the well-worn path to the top plateau where the faithful gathered as they did every afternoon, hoping to catch a glimpse of the Pontiff.

Right on schedule, thought the Professional. He looked at his watch. Another ten minutes and the target will be in position. The Pope worked in his office from one until three every afternoon. At about 3:15 each day, he walked out onto the balcony off of the office, waved to the crowds on the hillside while sipping tea from a china cup. His appearances lasted an average of five minutes and ended with the sign of the cross followed by his now familiar thumbs up signal and the famous Papal smile, then he withdrew back into the villa. The last few days, the Professional had noticed the bandage that had once totally covered his injured left ear was becoming smaller as it healed.

The Professional had built a flower box to place out on the office balcony. Needless to say, after his success with the masterpiece of gardening outside the Pope's bedroom windows, Sister Marie had readily granted this astute and talented gardener permission to enter the office while His Holiness was elsewhere

120

to place the beautiful new flower box. She had actually suggested the colorful plantings the gardener had filled it with. She was thrilled at being involved in the surprise project that would most certainly bring such pleasure to His Holiness.

But the gardener had filled the flower box—measuring a good four meters long by two meters wide—with something additional. Something designed to produce an explosive shock wave that would literally crush the life out of anyone inside the office or within a 40-meter circumference around it. He had chosen the exact placement of the flower box in such a way as to exert maximum damage to the occupants and to the structural integrity of the 16th Century supporting beams that held up this side of the villa. The PE4 plastique explosive was connected to the electronic detonator that was itself connected to the cellular telephone. The cheap cell phone would activate the detonator, fire a small explosive charge into the PE4 which would then detonate into one enormous, explosive fireball.

But that was not all. The Professional had in mind to destroy the entire villa and everyone in it. He had located a service closet on the first floor, below the Pope's offices. The support beams that had held the villa fast to the sloping hillside for all these centuries ran right through the closet. He had begun his work two days ago. He had worked slowly and carefully, molding the pliable PE4 into the joist and connector of this most critical section of the structure. Like the craftsman he was, his work was perfectly smooth and blended in precisely with the surrounding wood. Looking at it in the darkened closet, no one could tell that anything had been added in centuries. The wiring and electronic triggers that activated the explosive rig ran behind one of the giant joists and was all but invisible.

The Professional now stood on the hilltop, cell phone in hand, with all the other Pope watchers hoping to catch a glimpse. His watch was counting down. It now read 3:11 pm. Just four more minutes.

Jack quickly combed through the villa searching for the suspect gardener. He had alerted the security team. Within 90 seconds they had a photo taken of the villa's favorite gardener who had so pleased their beloved Pope with his flower gardens. The gardener's photo had come from the laminated ID card issued to everyone working on the villa grounds. They had texted the photo to all of the security personnel working on the grounds.

Jack glanced down at his cell phone every so often at the gardener's photo. Despite the urgency to find this gardener and make sure he was exactly as he appeared, he worked quickly, but did not hurry. He knew the difference. Quick was efficient and effective. Hurrying was sloppy and prone to errors. He carefully vetted each face he passed, focusing on the puffy cheeks, broad mustache with strands of gray and bushy eyebrows of the man whose photo he held in his left hand.

The Professional stood patiently on the hilltop. His face was now clean-shaven and he had stripped away the theatrical gray bushy eyebrows. His natural brows remained. Gone were the cotton cylinders inside his mouth that made his cheeks puffy. He stood up straight, exposing his full six-foot frame as he held the cell phone in his hand and watched through his special binoculars for the target to appear at his regular place at his regular time. Nothing seemed out of the ordinary below in the villa.

He could not see the determination of the security detail moving through the workers. For a second he caught what seemed a self-important priest briskly striding through the villa on his own urgent business. The Professional didn't give the priest a second thought.

"Your Holiness, you must leave here immediately," Helen almost shouted at the elderly Pontiff still in his office, sitting at his desk. She saw the Pope look up from his reading, a startled look crossing his face. For the briefest of seconds she noticed the colorful flower box on the balcony, just outside the French doors. That's new, she thought. "Now, Your Holiness.

There may be another attempt on your life right here in the villa. I need to get you to safety." Sister Mary Pat and two Swiss security guards followed Helen into the Pope's inner office.

Helen quickly crossed to the desk to help the Pope to his feet. The man was busy gathering the papers he was working on. Then he stopped and shook off her helping hands.

"Helen, I will leave with you. Of course I will. However, my dear, there are some things more important than an old man's life." He turned from her and with surprising agile quickness strode to the coat closet on the opposite side of the office. He bent down and shoved aside two cardboard file boxes. Set into the scuffed and scared oak floor was a metal ring. The Pope grabbed it and lifted up a section of flooring. She heard its aged hinges squeak. Helen peered over his shoulder, watching as he spun the dial of the safe back and forth, hitting the numbers with a practiced ease on the first attempt. Finished entering the numbers, he twisted the T-shaped handle and slowly pulled open the heavy door. His Holiness reached in and removed a metal box about the size that a pair of her Jimmy Choo shoes came in. From the way he hefted it, she could tell it contained something of substance.

"Now, let's not waste any time," said the Pope as he held out a hand indicating Helen should lead the way.

Jack had completed his search of the villa's interior spaces. No gardener. He phoned the chief of security, "Anything?"

"No, Mr. Schilling. Our men have fanned out to all of the gardens and sheds. If your gardener is still on the property, then he must know of a place that our people have not yet discovered."

Jack cut off the chief of the Swiss Guards attached to the villa. *A place that our people have not yet discovered,* he repeated the words to himself. What place? Jack stood still for a moment and slowly turned in a complete circle. He looked at everything as he turned. Within its walls, the villa contained beautiful open spaces, planted with grass, flowers, trees and shrubs. No place to hide there. He continued his circle. Suddenly he was looking over the villa's walls outside into the village of Gandolfo. There. A hillside rose up above the villa. It was less than two hundred yards away. Jack could see the people standing on the hilltop. The Swiss Guards certainly had not gone outside the villa.

Jack was off like a shot. He ran up a path, leading to the village-side entry gate. He stopped barely long enough for the guard to crack an opening to let him out. He was off again, running up the cobblestones as the narrow road—designed for horse carts—wound its way up the hillside. If this gardener is anywhere, he could be on the hillside looking down on the villa with all those others, he thought. Hiding in plain sight. That's exactly where I'd be. But how do you shoot a rifle from a crowd?

The Professional scanned the villa, then checked the time—3:17. The target was late. Off his schedule. For a week the target's appearance on the balcony had not varied more than 60 seconds. This was unusual. The Professional did not like unusual things. They disrupted his routine and his concentration. He raised the high performance binoculars back to his eyes. He saw a priest running—running faster than any real priest could, he observed. That is strike two, he calmly told himself. During the entire time he had been at the villa he had seen no one run. Their business was one of thoughtful contemplation. Slow thought, prayer and deliberation. He caught a last look at the priest as the man deftly slanted his body then thrust it through the iron gate before it was fully open. He would have to presume the priest would turn left and begin his assent up the hillside from where the Professional was watching. That is a 425-yard run up a steep incline on uneven cobblestones. He had measured it twice for just this event.

The Professional shrugged. He would have liked to see exactly where the target was before detonation. However, it didn't really matter. When the entire villa came crashing down the hillside, it and everyone in and around it would be crushed. He reached into his pocket and pulled out the cellular telephone. He pressed the speed dial button to call up the numbers the phone had memorized. There was just one.

The Professional turned and walked away from the villa view. He picked up his pace as his thumb pressed the call button for the single memorized number.

The concussion sent Jack flying across the uneven cobblestones. He felt the slick dust and grit as they slammed into his hands, elbows and knees. His chin skidded onto the ancient cart path, rutted by centuries of wooden wheels going up and down the hillside. He immediately knew what had happened. Even before his body stopped sliding across the cobblestones, he turned and looked down on the once-beautiful villa crumbling in pieces as it cascaded down the hillside.

He had but one thought—Helen. He knew she was somewhere in there. He had sent her to lead the Pope to safety. He didn't see how she would have had time to get clear of the villa before it began its deadly slide down the hill as its walls blew outward and its heavy, red-tiled roof slammed down on top of everything.

Before she heard the roar of the first blast, the concussion knocked Helen to the ground. She did not immediately recognize what had happened. Jack was the one who knew about explosives. Helen had expected a muffled pistol shot, maybe the crack of a rifle. But whatever it was, in the ensuing split second she figured it could not be good. She threw herself over the Pope as the first blast wave crushed them into the hard-packed dirt in the back garden. She saw the ground's perfectly even grooves from the gardener's rakes rushing up at her face.

Blast number two came within a second of the first. Helen felt a heavy weight slam onto her back, followed by two more in quick succession. The first blow crushed her lungs. The second and third, knocked the air right out of her. She fought for breath. Gasping, she tried to relax and pull a first small breath into her deflated lungs. I can only guess His Holiness is having a much harder time than I, she thought. The second breath was a little easier and a little deeper. The third and fourth came faster.

Helen wiggled herself free from the pile of bodies and took another gulp of air. As her vision returned from the blackness that the lack of air had caused, she pulled the Pope out from under the three bodies. She helped him sit upright and saw the old priest-turned-CEO of the Roman Catholic Church and Chairman of its Vatican Bank was breathing in ragged breaths, but nevertheless he was breathing. He still clutched that metal container, the size of a shoebox.

Helen dared to look at the three. Two of them—Sister Mary Patrick and one of the Swiss Guards she recognized as accompanying them—were moving, breathing shallowly and checking themselves over. The other Swiss guard, however was not moving. He was the one on top of all of them. She saw a length of iron rebar sticking through his back and coming out of his chest, where his heart was. The man had been impaled by debris shot like a cannon from the concussion wave. Helen quickly looked away from the gruesome horror.

"So sorry to have almost crushed the life out of you, dearie," exclaimed Sister Mary Pat as she shook off the dust and fragments still clinging to her. SMP went to the Pope and put her arm around him. Once she was sure he would survive the two blasts, she looked at Helen and then at the impaled guard. "Oh my heavens," she said. "I did not know him, yet I know many like him. Guarding His Holiness is a privilege to them." She reached out a hand to touch the other surviving guard. "Each would lay down their own life to save that of His Holiness. That is exactly what this extraordinary young man did." The other guard returned SMP's clasp and held it for a single, silent moment.

"Let's get out of here," said Helen. She glanced back from where they had come and saw what was left of the villa as it continued collapsing down the hillside into a large crater. The once-beautiful colonnade they had run through just minutes

126

before was now a mass of crushed plaster and concrete. The blast had rendered the huge 16th-century supporting beams into sawdust.

Helen helped the Pope to his feet. She put one arm around him while Sister Mary Pat took up the other side for support. The remaining Swiss Guard took up point as the wobbly foursome prepared to move away from the collapsing structure. "Here," offered Helen to the Pope, "let me take that for you." She made an effort to remove the metal container from his grasp.

The Pope immediately jerked the box from her grasp. "I may be an old priest, but I am still quite capable of carrying the Church's artifacts entrusted to my care."

"Whew, that was close," said Jack. He had run down the hillside to the remains of the villa. His search through the rubble covered him in dust and debris. He looked like a gray ghost to Helen as he climbed out of the ruins to the back gardens, away from the hillside.

"How did you know we got out?" asked Helen.

Jack urged them to move, placing a four-foot high red-brick fence between them and the hillside overlooking the crater. All the while he looked up, scanning the hillside for a large former SEAL. "Lucky guess. I figured you were either dead or you pulled His Holiness out just in time and had the good sense to go in the only direction that would save you." Jack knew what caused this catastrophe. The unmistakable cloying smell of PE4 explosive still hung in the air.

Sister Mary Pat exclaimed, "His Holiness seems to have nine lives. First the assassin and now this explosion. The world will not believe its good fortune."

"Sorry, Sister," said Jack. "The world is going to have to wait a while longer to celebrate the Pope's survival."

"Why is that, my son?" asked the Pope.

Jack looked at the remaining Swiss guard. He was alert and had his Sig-Sauer machine pistol out. He continued scanning the area for threats. Then Jack looked back at the Pope. "Let's allow the one who did this to think that he succeeded in killing his target. As long as you are alive and he knows it, his job is not finished. Letting the world think you're dead eliminates the threat against you." Jack whispered something in the Swiss guard's ear. The guard quickly nodded his head and knelt beside his fallen comrade. He began stripping off the dead man's black suit jacket, then his tie, his shirt and next his pants. It took them just minutes to disrobe the dead guard.

Jack brushed off the guard's clothes as best he could. "Here, Your Holiness, please put these on. It's the best disguise we have at the moment."

The Pope looked at the clothes Jack held out to him. Then he looked back at the Swiss guard who had given his life to protect him. "May God bless you, my son," said the Pope and he made the sign of the cross, then took the clothes. He quickly stripped out of his dusty white *alb*, put the suit pants on, the shirt and then the jacket while Jack and the guard dressed the deceased in the Pope's clothes.

"Let's move," said Jack. He looked at all the people flooding into the villa's compound to help with the rescue. They were all running in the opposite direction, toward the crater. Still it was only a matter of time before their small band was noticed.

The Pope did not move. He stood there in the bloody, dusty suit of the dead Swiss Guard as if pondering something.

"Are we forgetting something, Your Holiness?" asked Sister Mary Pat, gently placing an arm around the 83-year-old Pontiff.

The Pope held up his hand. The gesture asked for another second to think. Then the Pope removed his *zucchetto*, the white skullcap he wore. Next he took off his red velvet loafers. "If we are attempting to deceive my people, then we may as well do it right," he said. Finally, with reluctance he looked down at the *piscatoris*. It was the large gold Ring of the Fisherman that was every bit as much a part of the official regalia as was the *mitre* head gear.

All of them knew the ring as the symbol of the Papacy. Like the *zucchetto* and red slippers, the Pope's dead stand-in would have to wear everything just as the Pope had. Jack saw the look

128

of astonishment on Sister Mary Pat's face. "What? It's just a ring," he said. "Let's properly dress this heroic young man and get out of here."

Helen chimed in, "It is not just a ring."

Jack was impatiently tapping his foot on the gravel as he looked around them and saw more and more people racing to the aid of those unfortunates trapped in the fallen villa.

The Pope looked down at the third finger of his right hand. "I have not had this ring off since the Dean of the College of Cardinals put it there at my inauguration. Only the most extreme circumstances could get me to remove it."

Helen quickly glared at Jack, silencing him. "Well, Your Holiness, having someone try to kill you twice is about as extreme as I want you to get." Helen looked at Jack and the surviving Swiss Guard as they arranged the Pope's clothes on the body, put the skullcap in place and slid the red velvet loafers onto his feet. Now Jack carefully removed the Pope's remaining white bandages covering his still-healing ear and affixed then to the left ear of the dead Swiss Guard.

From a distance, the corpse could indeed pass for the Pontiff, impaled by a length of rebar.

Helen simply held out her hand and asked, "Please, Your Holiness."

The Pope slipped the *piscatoris* off of his right ring finger and placed it in Helen's outstretched hand. "I hope you find this assassin soon, my dear. I need to resume my official duties."

"We have a good idea who the man is we're looking for," said Jack.

Helen placed the ring on the finger of the dead Swiss Guard.

But it was the surviving Swiss Guard who asked the obvious question. "You know who did this? You know who the assassin is?"

Jack looked at the Swiss Guard again. He didn't trust anyone right now. "We have a pretty good idea," Jack repeated.

"Who is the son of a bitch?" demanded Helen. "Sorry, Your Holiness."

"No worries, my dear," said the Pope. "I have heard it before. I too would like to know the answer to that question. Since I am the subject of his interest."

Jack looked back, then up to the hillside as the group continued to move, keeping the low brick fence between them and the hillside's line of sight. The smoke cloud and debris that still hung in the air like a heavy fog, further shielded them from prying eyes. Jack knew what his target looked like. Smitty had sent a photo to his cell phone. "He was a SEAL sniper. Famous, actually. The way we put two and two together was his win at the world long rifle championships and his preference for a specific type of cartridge. There aren't many men in the world who could have made the shot that almost killed His Holiness. And even fewer still who use that particular cartridge."

"But he missed," said Sister Mary Pat.

Jack shook his head as they cleared the villa compound and approached the public streets of Gandolfo. "He didn't miss, Sister. Smitty studied the video. His round went exactly where it was supposed to go. Had it not been for the Pope suddenly lunging for that paper blown away, the guy would have accomplished his mission."

Jack noticed the Swiss Guard had been on and off his cell phone since he had arrived. Then a nondescript Laforza—the Italian version of a Chevy Suburban—rolled up to their ragged, filthy group.

"Right here, Your Holiness," said the Swiss Guard, now closing his cell phone as he stepped to the truck and opened the back door."

Jack looked the Laforza over. It had driven through the dust cloud and was covered with the stuff. Definitely not the type of transportation the head of the largest church in the world would use, he thought. Even better that the windows were so caked with dust and grime, seeing the occupants inside was impossible. That and the dark suit the Pope now wore made his true identity indistinguishable. "This will do," said Jack. He took the Pope's arm and helped him into the car. He made sure Helen and Sister

Mary Pat were safely in as well. Then he climbed in after them and shut the door.

The Swiss Guard gave one final look around, then entered. Jack heard him say, "The Vatican Intelligence Agency will take care of your security from here, Your Holiness. They will keep you hidden until we catch this criminal."

* * *

CHAPTER 16

His Eminence Cardinal David Caneman virtually floated toward the Customs desk at New York's JFK International Airport. The fine leather of his Italian loafers clicked softly on the airport's linoleum floor. For the flight from Tel Aviv he chose to pack his clerical regalia, opting instead for a grey chalk stripe summer-weight Brioni two-button suit. The aluminum briefcase he carried by his side contained the fifth tablet he went to Israel to retrieve. He did not feel its weight so much as he did the possibilities it represented. His hand gripped the metal carry handle as if the case held the answer to all of mankind's sins. Part of the answer, he reminded himself. There was yet a sixth and final tablet out there somewhere. Still, the artifact held inside the aluminum briefcase was priceless, he thought.

The truth was, he had no idea what the Roman Catholic Church's treasure hoard held beyond the expected objects of precious metal and priceless gems. To a religious zealot like Caneman, these mere trinkets were of far lesser importance than the singular object—whatever it turned out to be—whose provenance would unite the Catholic world like no other event in Church history. It existed, he told himself. Its presence somewhere was his white-hot, absolute belief. He had based his life, his entry into the Church's clergy and his ascension to the head of its most powerful bank on its existence.

Think of it, he almost exclaimed out loud as he waited impatiently for his turn at the Customs desk. This object— whatever it is—will prove beyond any doubt that the fundamental doctrine of the Church which has served it so well for so many centuries before now is the one and only true way. With the weight of this overwhelming evidence, those who ignore the one truth will forever live in morbid fear of the consequences. They will learn to hide their repressed doubts and counter theories. They will fear the new fundamentalist Church will pass judgment on them as it has against so many in centuries

132

past. Did not the doubters suffer dearly for their intransigence? That was then and so it forever shall be the way. Amen.

Caneman watched as one after another, the passengers answered the Customs agents' questions, had their picture taken, retrieved their passports, and then shuffled out with their luggage in tow. The power that such mere government functionaries wield over its people is nothing close to the force this Church will have over them when they see the truth, mused Caneman. For it is a power they give willingly—a power over something so much dearer—their souls rather than just their pocketbooks. Disobey God's fundamental commandments and suffer the consequences, thought Caneman. Distrust of the un-Godly, like the homosexuals for instance, will turn the tide against the idiocy that currently passes for being politically correct. The Church will judge what is politically correct and what is not. And over a billion followers will take its doctrine into their lives as Christ commanded they do over 2,000 years ago. Fail to obey and they will—.

"Next," called the bored voice of the Customs agent. Caneman jerked from his reverie as he saw the man cup his hand and motion for him to approach the elevated desk. His porter shoved a cart carrying his two suitcases after him. Caneman handed him his passport.

With a practiced flip of the Vatican State passport, the agent quickly scanned the name and photo of its owner. Suddenly the man stepped back and carefully set the passport back down on the table as if it were of extraordinary value. "Welcome home, Your Eminence," the man said with a new reverence in his voice. "I saw you on the television two weeks ago when your Vatican Bank was all over the financial news. Then the Pope was shot. And now this…"

Caneman heard the man's voice trail off in sorrow. Have you heard any news? Do you know if the Holy Father survived?"

What, thought Caneman. Survived? "Sir," he said, I have been in an airplane for the last 12 hours. What has happened? Tell me now." Then Caneman heard his own impatient,

133

demanding voice. "Please, sir, I just want to know what you are talking about. Is it His Holiness? Is he alright?"

Caneman watched as the Customs agent's face dissolved into deep sorrow and sympathy. "Your Eminence, I am going to process you right through here," he said as his fingers flew over the keyboard and he flipped through the passport and stamped it in the appropriate places with an urgent smack of finality. "Then I want you to get out of here and call the Vatican. Here." The agent handed Caneman his documents and passport without even a glace at the aluminum briefcase. In fact, it held perhaps the most priceless artifact illegally smuggled from the Holy Land since the Dead Sea Scrolls were discovered by goat herds in a cave on the banks of the Dead Sea in 1947. There was no doubt that this tablet would help reveal something far more important.

Caneman's mind was racing at the possibility. Could it be true, he wondered. Had the Professional finally succeeded? He felt the cell phone vibrate in his pocket. He reached in and turned its screen toward him. It was *him*. "Thank you, sir. Go with God," Caneman told the customs agent and hurriedly left the crowded Customs area. He quickly walked to a deserted corner of the hall with the phone to his ear.

"Speak," commanded Caneman.

"Is that how you talk to the one who may have just killed your Pope?" answered the Professional, his voice a blistering sneer.

"*May* have killed the Pope. Are you not sure?" Caneman felt the pang of anxiety crawl up his spine.

"This is what I am sure of: the villa in which he was staying along with his retinue suffered two massive explosions approximately 15 minutes ago. The concussion probably killed anyone in the Pope's office or in any of the adjoining rooms. The second explosion followed within two seconds and ripped apart the ancient oak beams that supported the entire villa and held the structure fast to the hillside. The villa and all of its rooms collapsed down into one giant, smoking cauldron."

"But the Pope was killed?" said Caneman. He heard the expectant sound of his own voice. "He must have been."

The Professional screwed his wireless earpiece into his ear so he could speak hands free. He peered through his hi-tech binoculars. He was crouched in a hidden perch well away from the crowded hilltop overlooking the villa where all the spectators were watching. The Professional was trained at using his environment to camouflage his presence. His green uniform of the villa's gardening crew blended perfectly with the leaves and branches surrounding him. Through the binoculars he clearly saw the crumpled remains of the man dressed in what was unmistakably the informal, working clothes of the Pope. The once pristine white *alba* was now smeared with blood across the back. A length of rebar entered the back, then exited through the chest. He glassed the binoculars over the scene. The man's left ear still bore the unmistakable bandages as it healed from the bullet wound sustained two weeks ago. He scanned down to his feet and saw the Pope's signature red velvet slippers that he wore. Then he was surrounded by rescue workers doing everything they could to help get him out of the still crumbling crater.

The Professional knew it was hopeless. No one could survive the concussive force of the PE4 high explosive he had planted in the flower box on the balcony outside the Pope's office. He estimated there would have been five tons of concussive force concentrated in a sudden blast that lasted less than a second and focused its energy directly into the office. The rebar had pierced his back and thrust out his chest like an ancient jousting lance. Then came the catastrophic mayhem as supporting beams, walls and the red tiled roof came crashing down on top of him. And finally, the whole mass cascaded down the hill, burying him under tons of wood, rock and plaster debris.

"But the Pope was killed," repeated Caneman.

Probably." The Professional said slowly, paused then continued. "If he somehow survived the concussion of the blast, he was likely crushed as the building collapsed. In my business, a confirmed kill requires me to observe unequivocal proof of death—preferably a body with no vital signs of life. As you might surmise, the entire area is clogged with police, paramedic and rescue crews searching the ruins for survivors. Since I am quickly but carefully making my exit from the target area, you will likely hear confirmation of the Pope's death before I do."

Caneman could not help himself, "But you think he was killed?"

The Professional waited a full, agonizing ten seconds. The target was finally dead. Of that the Professional was now dead certain. The only other thing he could have done was place two fingers on the target's jugular to feel for a pulse. He wasn't about to do that. No need. The Professional lowered the binoculars from his eyes a final time, capped their lenses and returned them to his worn leather work bag, slung across his shoulder like a satchel. "Yes. Unless I hear otherwise, my contract has been executed as agreed." He carefully made his way out of his hiding blind and began his egress from the target site. Mission accomplished.

Caneman heard the Professional click off, closing the line. He lowered the cell phone from his ear and let the news sink in. The aluminum briefcase holding the fifth tablet weighed about fifteen pounds. Yet it felt weightless in his hand. He had forgotten about it completely while he had spoken to the Professional. Now, with His Holiness gone, he held the next key to restoring the Church to its rightful, fundamental place. He turned, impatiently gestured for the porter to follow him and quickly walked to the ground transport area where his driver with the limousine would surely be waiting for him.

* * *

CHAPTER 17

CNBC business commentator, Jim Cramer, sat in the broadcast booth above the floor of the New York Stock Exchange. Beside him sat his co-anchor, Maria Bartaromo. Her left arm was still in a sling as her shoulder continued to heal from the bullet wound. Both watched their television monitor showing CNN's live feed from the blast site in Gandolfo, Italy.

Cramer began his commentary in a somber voice—completely different from the high-pitched urgency he usually had for this segment of the show. "Folks, like everyone else, we are watching events as they unfold in Italy—"

Bartaromo interrupted, "It is not our intent to divert attention from the tragedy that has suddenly befallen the Catholic Church and the 1.2 billion of its followers worldwide, of which I am one. So please, forgive my colleague and I if we focus on the financial perspective to this awful event. We are just doing our jobs."

"Of course, Maria, just doing our jobs," repeated Cramer. "The Exchange has suspended trading in GOD stock, pending restoration of an orderly market."

"What's that mean, Jim?" asked Bartaromo for benefit of her viewers. She knew perfectly well what it meant.

"It means that GOD is tanking. That's what it means." Cramer's voice began to creep up in pitch as it always did when he became excited. "And if the Exchange didn't step in to seize control over the supply/demand ratio, a lot of investors would be unnecessarily hurt financially. Right now, GOD is at the mercy of events unrelated to the Vatican Bank's balance sheet or its prospects for future profitability. Investors are reacting on pure emotion—quite understandably—at the Pope's apparent death in the Gandolfo villa. So the Exchange is doing them a favor and stopping GOD from trading—"

"Wait, I see something," Bartaromo jumped in. She unconsciously rubbed her left shoulder where the bullet meant for the Pope had entered then exited without hitting anything vital. "They are bringing up someone on a stretcher. Oh my

God. He is all wrapped up in white. He's caked in the dust and grime from the blast hole, but I can see it was once white. The Pope traditionally wears white—it's called an *alba*—when he is working in private. White is the color reserved for the Pope. Whoever this is, and I am not saying it is the Pope, but whoever it is must be important because all excavation work has now stopped in the blast crater and workers are flooding in from all over the site to help. I can see the victim is still wearing a white skullcap—the *zucchetti*—that the Pope attached to his white hair with a bobby pin. Everyone is concentrating on getting this single victim up the hillside that has caved in around him. Those who cannot help have removed their hats and placed them over their hearts."

Jim Cramer spoke slowly, carefully to his audience. "Folks, let me say again that it is not my intent to insensitively dwell on the financial side of what has apparently just occurred in Gandolfo, Italy. I'm just a guy doing his job despite the tragedy unfolding." Cramer peered into the camera lens for a full five seconds—a lifetime by his rapid-fire standards.

With his point made, Cramer looked down to the floor of the New York Stock Exchange to the Big Board that showed all stocks being traded. "GOD stock has stopped trading on its low of the day. That's what happens when the Exchange steps in for a stock that is in free-fall."

Bartaromo tore her eyes away from the monitor showing the rescue workers still climbing up the loose, crumbling walls of the crater. "Explain how this helps investors." Her voice was flat, without the inflection of her usual curiosity.

"Sure, sure Maria. The Exchange's action staves off panic selling. Now, GOD stock may well continue its free-fall once these events have played out and it resumes regular trading. But at least investors will have had time to digest the impact of these occurrences and make their own decision to pull the ripcord or ride out the cataclysm."

138

"I know, Jim, that you are not shy about giving your opinion or advice on what investors should do. So what do you think?"

Cramer paused for a moment, looking at the live feed from CNN appearing on his own monitor. He shook his head. "Stand pat. Do not follow the herd of sellers on this one folks. About now the institutions with their programmed trading algorithms have already determined that this is a black swan event—an occurrence that no one could have predicted and that adversely affects the stock—and have already sent out their sell orders. If you look at a graph of GOD stock from the time this tragedy was announced and hit the airwaves until the NYSE suspended trading, you'll see a straight downward line. And I suspect the sell orders are piling up at all the brokerage firms making a market in GOD stock." Cramer stopped for a moment to cement his point. Then he looked down the throat of the camera lens.

"If you're an individual investor—one of the millions who own GOD—maybe you have a hundred, a thousand or even ten thousand shares, stand pat and keep your powder dry. Any sell order you place will go to the back of the line. The market makers are there to serve their big institutional customers first. These whales pay their year-end bonuses. The little guys will get screwed six ways to Sunday."

Maria Bartaromo's eyes flew wide open at this remark. "How so, Jim?"

"I'll tell ya how," responded Cramer, his voice rising another octave as his ire rose at the inherent unfairness of the stock market. "Say you place a sell order now. GOD stopped trading at 53. You figure that you're out at 53 and compute your loss using that number. No way, Jose. When GOD resumes trading it'll be a fast market, I guarantee. The floor specialists will be inundated with a tsunami of sell orders. It'll be like trying to catch a falling knife. The whales—the broker's biggest customers—get out first. The stock price will continue to drop even further. So your sell order at 53, may not be executed until GOD hits the mid-40's or lower. What a shock you'd be in for and what an unanticipated loss."

Bartaromo took control. "So that's why you tell the individual investors to just sit tight."

"Absolutely, Maria. If you sell now, you're selling at the bottom—and we don't even know yet what that bottom will be. So just wait. There'll be a Papal conclave to appoint a new Pope. The Catholic Church will survive. It has for centuries. So will the Vatican Bank. It may take some time for GOD stock to rise from the ashes, but rise it will."

His Eminence Cardinal David Caneman stood facing the television in his Vatican Bank office. He still held the aluminum briefcase containing the precious fifth stone tablet. He had rushed from the airport straight to Wall Street when he heard more news of the Pope.

It was the middle of the trading day here in New York. The Vatican Bank's executive offices were fully functioning— including the securities trading room. It was staffed around the clock. Somewhere in the world a market was always open and trading. Caneman's policy was that the Vatican Bank would be an enthusiastic market participant at all times.

Caneman's brain functioned as the high-level financial engineer he was. There were few men in the securities business with the authority or the fortitude to make the decision he was about to. Jim Cramer's words flowing from the television intruded on his thoughts. Cramer urged his idiot viewers to keep your powder dry—don't sell into this catastrophic slide in GOD's price, he had said.

His Eminence Cardinal David Caneman knew better. Cramer was a hack—a creation of the media whose sole purpose was to sell advertising minutes. Caneman set the briefcase on the floor inside the credenza behind his desk, closed and locked its door. He desperately wanted to hold the stone tablet again. He wanted to observe the beautiful lines of the partial map it contained and the Latin words that were probably directions. That would have to wait a bit, he told himself. It would give him something to look forward to as he set off to do financial battle on the world's bourses.

Caneman punched the keyboard of his desktop computer. Up popped the pages of his GOD stock portfolio. There, in columns of numbers were the shares, the purchase prices and where they were domiciled. He took a deep breath and went over the trading strategy he had cobbled together during the trip from the airport. After the first assassination attempt on His Holiness GOD stock had dropped like the stone in the credenza behind him. He had known in advance of the attempt and the effect it would have on GOD's price. He had shorted the stock, betting that it would drop. He looked at his profit and loss sheet. Those transactions had netted him $234 million. The holdings were spread around the world on a network of anonymous accounts owned by a maze of corporations, partnerships and offshore entities. None of it would trace back to him.

When it had become clear His Holiness would survive, Caneman reversed his short positions and went long on GOD stock. That was a week before he left for Israel. His trades were not nearly so profitable since everyone on Wall Street did the same thing—everyone, that is, with even an ounce of fortitude and the decision-making power to back it up. It was actually a fairly small and elite group. But they controlled billions of investible funds.

When he returned from getting the stone tablet and was back in Tel Aviv, he checked his securities positions. Reversing his shorts and betting that GOD would again rise in price had netted him $53 million. Not bad. Even better that the SEC's insider alert system would ignore what he was doing since so many others had done the same thing and it was a rather obvious and very public tactic. All totaled, his profits on paper were $287 million and change. On paper, he reminded himself, meant little. It was the profit after closing out the positions that really counted. That was his problem now.

He realized that he had committed the sin of greed while in Tel Aviv. He should have closed out more of those long positions that favored a rising GOD price. Instead, he only took

$50 million off the table. The rest—$237 million—he had left in play. The NYSE had suspended trading in GOD stock while he was still at JFK airport. Right now its value was half what it had been before the villa crashed around His Holiness and killed him. There was no way of telling where the stock price would settle, but he knew that it would be even lower, much lower. What to do? He was now in the same position as the naïve faithful who had bought GOD just to have a piece of the Church.

Caneman sat there in his opulent office with its red and gold Persian rugs, the antique side tables and cushy couches. His view took in Wall Street and the surrounding neighborhoods in the distance. He knew the answer. He did not deserve to suffer such a loss. He had taken the Vatican Bank from financial obscurity to the worldwide player in the financial markets it now was. Rome owed him. Besides, they would never miss it. Not after he obtained the missing sixth stone tablet that made the map to the Church's treasury complete. The vastness of riches surely contained in the treasury would completely eclipse such a paltry sum.

His Eminence Cardinal David Caneman made his decision. He grabbed his GOD stock inventory sheets from his chrome and glass desktop and strode out of his office to the elevators and down one floor. The guard stationed at the entry doors to the Vatican Bank securities trading floor instantly snapped to attention on seeing Caneman striding toward him. The guard quickly swiped his card key across the sensor and held the door open for Cardinal Caneman.

Caneman marched through without breaking stride or even glancing at the guard. Young men with shirtsleeves rolled up and telephones stuck in their ears or headsets affixed to the top of their heads turned to see where The Cardinal was headed but did not stop their talking.

His Eminence was known on the trading floor. He made regular appearances down here. Vatican Bank's securities trading operations were his personal creation. Through his design, the Church managed to take in its significant

142

contributions and hugely expand them by trading aggressively on the world markets. Most of the profits—that numbered in the mid-hundreds of millions annually—went back to the Church. Though there was a significant carve-out for the young traders here in this room. The average income was over $5 million. There were several particularly aggressive traders whose bonus reached into the eight figures. Caneman believed that the spoils belonged to the victors.

The head of the Vatican Bank's trading operations put his telephone back in its cradle without signing off his conversation and stood up from his desk as Caneman entered his glass-walled office. "Yes, Your Eminence. What can we do for you on this tragic day?"

As calmly as he could, Caneman placed the GOD stock inventory sheets on the head trader's desk. "Mathew, this is a list of long positions in Vatican Bank stock I still have on the books."

The young man—just 36 years old, making $15 million annually with a net worth exceeding $100 million—leaned over the desk and leafed through the pages. He let out a slow whistle when he came to the end and saw the total footings. "Eminence, that portfolio had a book value of over $237 million before His Holiness was lost." The trader shook his head and did the math in his head. "Now it has a value of just $166 million, a loss of over $70 million on the day. And trading is suspended. I can't even get you out."

Caneman already knew this. "Actually, you can not only get these positions sold, but in so doing, Mathew, you will be showing the world our bank's true faith in the Church's ability to survive this tragedy and move on with a new-found resolve." Caneman could feel the strength of his conviction as he spoke.

"You mean, Vatican Bank will buy all this stock? At what price? I cannot even calculate the risk since no one knows where it will open or even *when* it will reopen."

Caneman continued as if he did not even hear the head trader's objections. "I will issue a press release describing this purchase and the Bank's continued faith and support of the Church in this time of need."

The young millionaire heard his marching orders loud and clear. "You're talking about a private sale, then. Go around the stock exchange. Just a buy and sell between two private parties. Clear the transactions through Goldman Sachs in New York—"

Caneman interrupted, "Yes. But it is best to spread it around. Use BNP Paribas in France and Union Bank of Switzerland as well."

The trader knew this transaction was absurd. His Eminence cannot be serious, he thought. "And where will I set the purchase price?"

Caneman thought for a moment. He had already committed the sin of greed when he failed to close out his long positions before the Professional had fully executed his contract. It had cost him $161 million. He would not make that mistake again. He decided to take a 10 percent haircut on the transaction. The $24 million I will give up shall serve as penance and remind me to follow the scripture, he told himself. "Make an average price of $77 per share. I know it is well above the closing price before the NYSE suspended trading. Making an above-market offer to accumulate such a large block of stock quickly is not unheard of though. Besides, Vatican Bank just issued $200 billion in stock. We can afford it. Do it."

The trader knew he must put a stop to this before His Eminence went any further. "There is another problem. The SEC Enforcement Division's audit. While you were returning from your business trip, they threatened to issue a qualified opinion on Vatican Bank. We received the first notification just an hour ago."

His Eminence Cardinal David Caneman stood there dumbfounded. Caneman knew that a qualified opinion on a publicly held company was tantamount to a death sentence. It said that the balance sheet issued to the public for investment purposes was wrong. His first reaction was that maybe he had misjudged that bean-counting auditor, Jackson Schilling. Should

I have spoken to him when he asked, he wondered. Too late now, he thought.

"Eminence, they are talking about delisting GOD stock from the New York Stock Exchange and unwinding the public offering. We would have to return the $200 billion in stock proceeds."

Talking about delisting a stock? Caneman had seen stocks removed from the New York Stock Exchange. When the SEC began talking about such a draconian punishment it almost always happened. Yes, he thought GOD will most surely be delisted and then the public offering will be unwound. There goes the $200 billion our crusade desperately needs.

"Eminence? What should I do about your private stock transaction?" asked the trader.

But Caneman was already making for the office door. Over his shoulder he said, "Get it done before they speak any more of delisting the stock. By God, get it done." He strode down the plush carpeted hall to the elevators. His mind raced. With the $200 billion potentially evaporated, finding the sixth stone tablet, then locating the Church's treasure vault was an immediate and critical necessity. His mind was in overdrive. His research into just where the sixth tablet might be had recently revealed some interesting information. His brain snapped back to the Pope's death. What about His Holiness? How did this most recent of events affect the scenario? The elevator doors whooshed open on the executive floor. Caneman almost jumped out as he raced for his office. Ah, he thought, one door closes and a window opens. Caneman saw a new aspect to his plan emerge as he entered his office. No one could see the smile that crossed his face in the emptiness that was his inner sanctum.

* * *

CHAPTER 18

His Eminence Cardinal David Caneman stood before the assembly there in the Vatican's Sistine Chapel. His gaze scanned out over the College of Cardinals. It was a sea of brilliant red capes and the red *zucchetti* they all wore on their heads. Caneman thought the skullcaps did little to hide what was either white or gray hair or no hair at all. The chamber—an auditorium, actually with stadium seating installed a day ago just for this event—was full of the Cardinals who were gathered at this sad papal conclave to elect a new Pope. These were old men chosen to perform an historic ritual that had gone on for centuries. As the youngest Cardinal, Caneman knew deep in his heart that the Church's future rested on the shoulders of the younger generation—his generation. Only he and his disciples could restore the Church to the fundamentalist ideal that would return it to the glory his church once enjoyed.

As *camerlengo*, Caneman was the Chamberlain of the Holy See in the Pope's absence. *And the Pope was permanently absent.* He had assumed the role of *camerlengo* shortly after turning around the Vatican Bank. For decades its dealings and wealth had been the most closely guarded secret of the Church. Caneman had opened the windows, blew away the acrid dust of past corruption and let the sunshine of transparency flood inside. For the first time the world saw the extraordinary wealth Vatican Bank's accounts held. Caneman described to the media and to the world the humanitarian uses the Church put forth in the billions it disbursed annually to those many charities. He showed how the money was handled; how it was accounted for using the same modern accounting principles that Wall Street understood. From the beginning, his plan included taking Vatican Bank public and raising the serious money his grand scheme needed to succeed. There was no dispute that Caneman controlled the Church's money. His power within the corps of Cardinals soared. His Holiness himself sought out Caneman's counsel. The post of *camerlengo*—the one to act in the Pope's absence—was assured long ago.

His Eminence Cardinal David Caneman had waited the prescribed time following the tragic death of His Holiness when Castel Gandolfo exploded. On that awful day, the Swiss guards had acted quickly to preserve the Holy Father's dignity. Even before the body had been raised from the site of the explosion they wrapped it in white linen. When asked about the shroud covering the Pope, the Swiss guards to a man had shaken their heads and said His Holiness was all but unrecognizable due to the extent of his injuries from the explosion. Still, the press managed to get a long-range photo of the length of rebar that pierced the body's back, straight through, then out the chest. To the world, there was no doubt the Pope had been tragically killed.

As *camerlengo,* Cardinal Caneman was responsible for bringing to order the chaos that ensued in the Church after the Pope's death. Standing before this assembly of those who led 1.2 billion Catholic followers worldwide, he could attest that this was no easy task. Made even harder, he told himself, by needing a preordained outcome. Like herding cats, he thought.

Just as he had done at Vatican Bank, Cardinal Caneman decided to break with tradition. At least part of this conclave for the very first time in history would be open for the world to see. Caneman had invited the Vatican News Service inside the Sistine Chapel and granted them a live video feed. He had requested the proceedings be covered by their most famous reporter, Sister Mary Patrick, the deceased Pope's good friend. Only the Sister was missing since Castel Gandolfo exploded. She was presumed dead, buried under the tons of rubble that crews with cadaver dogs continued to pick through with new fragments of remains being discovered daily.

Caneman was no fool. Even if his fellow Cardinals fumed at the thought of a public Papal conclave, he understood its dynamics all too well. The press would look upon him as their savior who finally opened the conclave. Yes, the 146 Cardinals assembled here might be pissed off, he thought, but there are 1.2

billion followers who are grateful to me for showing the world just how a Pope is elected. So grateful, in fact, that they will give me their support as the young breath of fresh air this Church so desperately needs.

His Eminence Cardinal David Caneman stepped behind the rostrum and faced the assembled church leaders, representing every country where the Catholic Church has a presence. He thumbed on the transmitter switch of his lapel microphone. Showtime. For the benefit of the television audience, he began by explaining what would happen over the next few days.

"Your Eminences and to everyone around the world watching, I am Cardinal David Caneman, chamberlain of this Holy conclave. It has been this way for centuries. The papal conclave is simply a meeting of the College of Cardinals— mortal men all, nothing more. The papal conclave always follows the sad passing of the Pope. Its purpose is to elect a successor pope. In this case, it is particularly sad since His Holiness was tragically killed in the explosion of the Pope's summer retreat where he was recovering from a gunshot wound, the result of an assassination attempt." Here Caneman paused to take a sip from the crystal tumbler filled with spring water. He saw that all eyes in the chapel along with the uncounted millions were on him and him alone watching this historic broadcast worldwide. He relished the attention.

"Our purpose on this sad occasion is to elect a new Bishop of Rome, more commonly called the Pope. No need to remind those assembled in this holy shrine of their catechism. But for all those around the world watching, we Roman Catholics consider the Pope to be the apostolic successor to Saint Peter. As such, he is the earthly head of the Roman Catholic Church. It is a belief held by many—me included—that the Pope should answer only to God. The Roman Catholic Church has used conclave since it was decreed by Pope Gregory X in 1274 during the Second Council of Lyons. It is the oldest ongoing method for choosing the leader of any institution here on earth." Caneman gazed around the sea of cardinal red and saw them fidgeting in their seats, growing impatient. He looked directly into the primary camera he had ordered positioned facing straight into the rostrum.

"But enough of the history lesson. Let us proceed with the first tradition." Caneman nodded his head, indicating one of the acolytes should approach the rostrum. He carried a red velvet pillow with the gold embroidery of the Vatican flag. On it was the *annulus piscatoris*. Caneman unfastened the pin holding the large gold ring in place and held it up in both hands. The cameras zoomed in as he knew they would. A close-up of the large gold ring, so seldom seen by commoners, traveled around the world at the speed of light. People saw the embossed image of a priest sitting in a wood fishing skiff pulling his nets from the ocean.

"We have here our beloved Pope's ring of the fisherman. He wore it every day. Indeed, he had it on the third finger of his left hand on the day of his tragic death." Caneman stopped short, seeming to gather himself in the face of this great loss. Then he looked out over the assembled cardinals and into the television camera facing him. He seemed the picture of sincerity and humility.

"Such a ring is made for every pope at the time of their Papal coronation. The Piscatory Ring was used in ancient times to officially seal the Pope's most private communications that went out to the Catholic world."

Caneman paused for dramatic effect. Now that they had seen the beautiful gold ring, he had the world's rapt attention. "Now I am duty-bound to commit what may at first seem a blasphemy on such an historic object." He nodded again to the acolytes offstage. This time two approached, wearing white robes. One held a large silver hammer; the other a slab of granite. They placed both on the floor, then quickly exited.

Caneman came around the rostrum with the large and beautiful Piscatory Ring. He wrapped it in a simple piece of white silk with gold embroidery and placed it on the granite slab. Next he picked up the silver papal hammer. He raised it above his head and sent it crashing down on the ring. He raised the hammer a second time and hit the ring again. Cardinal Caneman took the silk back to his rostrum and unwrapped the ring. He held it up for all to see the total destruction of the deceased pope's ring.

"It is my duty as *camerlengo* during this sad time of *sede vacante*—the interim period—to destroy the seal of the Papal Piscatory Ring. This ceremony dates back to Pope Clement IV in 1265. On the death of the Pope the ring used for sealing the Pope's private correspondence is destroyed. This was done to prevent anyone from using the ring to officially seal backdated or forged documents." Caneman handed the destroyed ring to an acolyte who would then hand it to the Vatican's official historian and archivist for safekeeping. Once again he faced the camera, appearing every bit the Holy Church's interim leader. "In this day of Internet and email correspondence, destroying an historic artifact so that it cannot be used to seal official correspondence may seem silly." He smiled to show the world he shared the thought with them and agreed. "However, as we work our way through this conclave and elect a new Pope, you will see firsthand that our Church rests on a solid bedrock of tradition. It is these very traditions that make us who we are."

Caneman said, "Let us pray for wisdom as we begin discussion and balloting for the next Bishop of Rome."

Jack lowered his cell phone. He had been in constant contact with the New York office of the SEC's Enforcement Division since they left the ruins of Castel Gandolfo.

"What'd they say?" asked Helen, handing him a cup of coffee from the machine on the kitchen counter.

"Thanks, hHon. I just spoke with that cute, smart auditor you met at Vatican Bank—"

"Audrey?"

"Yeah. She's on top of it. I knew she was the right choice. We're going to continue the suspension of GOD stock trading indefinitely. The SEC's audit is still pending so far as the public is concerned. No official qualified opinion. Just rumors of one generated by a threatening letter I sent the Vatican Bank's CEO."

"That couldn't be good for its financial reputation," said Helen.

"It's not. I got the SEC's chairman to speak with His Eminence Cardinal David Caneman himself. We're telling him to voluntarily unwind their public offering or we'll do it for them."

"Geeze, Jack. That's $200 billion the Vatican Bank has to give back to investors—"

"Ain't it a hoot? Embarrassing as hell for Caneman. But it'll save the US taxpayers a bundle in the lawsuits and administrative time if we had to do it." Jack stood at the safe house's kitchen window and moved the curtain slightly to the side so he could see out. The Italian countryside rolled out before him. He picked out the Swiss guards concealed around the property to the point of being invisible in their *gilly suits*. He saw them only because he knew exactly where to look and could see the grass and straw embedded in their clothing that was their camouflage slowly rising and falling as they breathed. "How's our houseguest?"

"Oh he's antsy," replied Helen. "Wouldn't you be? Getting your ear shot off of by some sniper then, even before you recovered from that, almost being blown up in your own home."

Jack nodded as he let the curtain slip back into place. "And now watching the one you put so much trust in turn out to be nothing but an opportunist bent on taking your position." Jack walked out of the kitchen toward the safe house's living room.

"Ah Jack. Come in, come in my son. Take a load off, as they say."

The Pope turned away from the television set—a nice 60-incher. High definition Jack noticed. The 83-year-old Pontiff wore blue jeans and a white collared cotton shirt with New Balance running shoes from the small inventory of clothes the Swiss guards kept here in the safe house. The Pope looked like a regular guy catching a ball game in front of the TV on a lazy Saturday afternoon. Except this was no ball game he was watching nor was this any casual Saturday afternoon. D-day was approaching for 1.2 billion Catholics around the world. And this man sitting on the couch was their spiritual leader in exile.

Jack sat in the armchair to the Pope's side. "Who's winning?" he asked.

Sister Mary Pat sat on the couch beside the Pope. She had traded her nun's habit for slacks, a t-shirt and trail boots. "Oh, Mr. Schilling, Cardinal Caneman seems to be wooing them all. He is making all the right moves, he is. The biggest one, however, was his insistence that this conclave be televised for the first time. He is a hero to Roman Catholics the world over. Indeed, one of my favorite television personalities is interviewing him right now. Right there in Rome…Vatican City to be exact. Just an hour's drive north of here. Oh how I wish I could catch a live glimpse of him."

Jack looked more closely at the screen. "Dr. Sanjay Gupta? Isn't he a neurosurgeon?"

"He is indeed," said SMP. "Still performs brain surgery several days a week in spite of his TV and book commitments. He is so nice, so insightful," she exclaimed. "I must admit that I am a real fan," she exclaimed nodding her head enthusiastically.

Jack sat down to hear the famous Gupta, brain surgeon turned television personality.

Helen entered the room carrying a tray with a large plate of spaghetti carbonara, crusty Italian bread and a bottle of Chianti. "Do you wish it was you covering the conclave inside the Sistine Chapel?" she asked Sister Mary Pat as she set the plates down.

SMP looked at Helen with an expression of incredulity. "My dear, you cannot be serious. The world is watching this conclave live. There is no scoop there. The most any reporter can do is repeat back to the masses what they have already seen on live TV. Oh no. The real story is right here in this very room and he's sitting here beside me." She patted the Pope on his hand. "How many people in their lives ever get to spend hours, let alone days with a sitting Pope? Get to talk with him as a real person. Get to hear of his worries and innermost thoughts.

152

None. Though I must confess, I do not understand why the need for all these Swiss guards and your three associates, Mr. Schilling."

The Sister was referring to Smitty and the two additional SEALs Jack had asked him to bring into the mission. They were specifically trained for this to a level far beyond that of the Swiss guards. All were professionals. The Swiss had immediately accepted the "suggestions" that Jack, Smitty and the other two had made. Now the safe house was a fortress with electronic sensors, motion detectors, infrared cameras and determined, careful men carrying the most deadly firearms and each knew exactly how to use them. They had almost been defeated twice by this assassin. They were not about to let it happen again.

"And those nasty-looking guns everyone is carrying around here," finished Sister Mary Pat. "The world saw His Holiness die at Castel Gandolfo. At least the poor man whom they *think* was the Pope. Where is the risk, I ask you?"

Jack had spent seven years in special operations before leaving the Navy and joining the SEC's Enforcement Division. He had become a strategic weapon in America's war on terror. To any enemy he was an unknown, unseen tactical nightmare— the kind and ilk of which they could never imagine until it was too late. Jack, Smitty—who had taken his place at the SEC when he retired—and the other two SEALs were a lethal, aggressive unit that projected a deadly force many times beyond their small number. The Swiss guards outside along with their technology, weapons systems and training could hold off even the most determined force—at least for a while.

"Sister and Your Holiness, let me tell you the risk we face here." Jack paused while Helen handed him a bowl of carbonara. It smelled just like he taught her to make back in Elkhart. He took a forkful, tasted it and threw her a wink. Helen bowed her head slightly with a smile. "We may have fooled some people with the white shroud on that dead body carried by the guards out of the smoking hole that used to be your villa. The funeral and the burial following was nothing short of showmanship. It appears that we may have even fooled His

Eminence Cardinal David Caneman. But I doubt we fooled the one person who really counts in this calculus."

"Who is that, Mr. Schilling?" asked the Pope.

"The unholy devil who shot off your ear and blew up your villa," answered Helen. She set down her bowl of pasta. It was almost gone. She liked her own cooking even more than Jack did.

Jack wiped his mouth on a napkin and stepped back into the conversation. "See, completing the mission is the most important thing we do. Finishing is ingrained into each SEAL from their first day in BUDs training. Basic Underwater Demolition school is all about the integrity of completion. Fail to complete and you are not the man you thought you were. It's the code we live by."

The Pope still had half of his pasta left. He turned to Helen and said, "How's the Chianti, my dear? Does it go well with your excellent carbonara? Not too tart?"

"Why no, Your Holiness, it's perfect actually."

"You sure, my dear? It didn't become too warm sitting here in this room?"

"Would you like to try it—"

The Pope reached over to Helen's glass of wine and took it, raised it to his lips and sipped. "Mmmmm," he said and rolled his eyes toward heaven. "You're right, my dear. Not too tart or sweet. It pairs perfectly with the sweet tomatoes in your excellent sauce." He took another sip and sat back contentedly, still holding Helen's wine glass and with no apparent intention of returning it. "Temperature is just right too."

The Pope set his now-empty bowl down next Helen's and bit off a corner of garlic bread. He spoke around the bread, punctuating his speech with the as yet uneaten end as would any family member around the dinner table. "And this assassin was one of your SEALs?"

Jack had watched the proceedings with the wine, pasta and bread. Just another guy sitting around the table having dinner.

154

Except this one is the spiritual leader of over a billion people. "Not much escapes you, Your Holiness."

"I could not help overhearing you talking on that cell phone of yours. It is a small house," said the Pope.

Jack nodded, accepting the fact. "Yes. We are almost sure of it. From the sniper rounds fired in St. Pete's Square, the impossibly long distance of the shot, to the PE4 explosive used on the Gandolfo villa. It's him."

The Pope took another sip of wine after Helen had refilled his glass. He sat there thinking and watching the television as Cardinal Caneman led the procession of cardinals in the pre-game ceremonies leading up to the first ballot to elect the new Pope. His Holiness' face was a calm, serene mask. The Pope was gathering information in an arena with which he had little familiarity. Yet, he was still the chess master who was contemplating his next move against a younger and possibly slightly naïve adversary. Then he turned his head to Jack. "But he must have seen the television coverage of the body and the rebar protruding through the man's back and chest. There was no question of the death. The Piscatory Ring and the red shoes, not to mention the white *zucchetto* on his head. Who could that have been if not the Pope?"

Jack looked at the Pope. He had known admirals, generals, CEOs of the world's most powerful industrial companies. Owing to his father's closeness with the first family, he had rubbed shoulders with America's highest-ranking politicians on both sides of the aisle. Each seemed to have an agenda. Most sought power for the prestige it brought them. A very few simply wanted to serve. For these, it was their talents that had brought them to the most exalted corridors of power. They did not need confirmation of their worth or ego satisfaction. They worked for the simple necessity of getting the job done. The current occupant of the White House Jack counted among these rare individuals. And the Pope seemed to be cut from the same cloth. "Yes, Your Holiness. That is the illusion we created. It is what the world wanted to see. So that is what we gave them. Except the ring, the shoes and the skullcap were just ornaments.

To one trained to confirm his kill beyond the shadow of a doubt, it leaves one unanswered question."

"And that question is?" asked SMP

"Who's the guy with all these ornaments wrapped inside that shroud so no one could see his face? What about the standard DNA testing done in every coroner's office? Especially on high profile heads of state. Of which the Pope surely is one. What about confirmation from those with an intimate knowledge of what the Pope looked like in real life and who actually had eyes on the deceased? The medical examiner and the mortician, for example? What about them? Why has there been no statement from them? These are the questions the assassin must be asking. I would if I were him."

The Pope turned from the television showing the inner workings of a papal conclave for the very first time to a world all too eager to soak up its majesty and historical traditions. "Who do you think is the real enemy here?" he asked.

"The assassin who tried to kill you," emphatically declared Sister Mary Pat, speaking to the Pope. "Who else could it possibly be?"

"Yes," followed Helen, "but Jack doesn't think he's convinced that his mission is complete."

The Pope looked at Jack. Their eyes locked on each other in complete understanding. "No," said Jack. "The real enemy here is not the assassin. He is just an instrument. A means to an end. The real enemy—whomever he or they are—wants to take over the Roman Catholic Church."

The Pope raised his glass in salute to Jack's sudden comprehension. Then he leaned toward Sister Mary Pat sitting on the couch next to him and whispered into her ear. She immediately got up to go do his errand.

"So do you know who this group is, and who leads them?" asked Helen.

The Pope looked back at the television and His Eminence Cardinal David Caneman continuing his oration. "Oh my dear, I have a very good idea who that person is and what he wants."

156

"Is this what you wanted me to get, Your Holiness?" asked Sister Mary Pat, now holding the metal strong box. It was scratched; its gray paint faded and missing in spots, several dents marred its surface. A similarly rusted and battered padlock secured its lid to the body.

Jack saw the Pope's eyes light up at the sight of the ancient metal box.

"Ah, yes, Sister, that is exactly what I wanted. Thank you. The Pope reached inside his shirt and pulled out a single key he wore on a chain around his neck. The key was rusted; its surface was pitted and it looked very old.

The Pope paused for another sip of the Chianti he had sweet-talked out of Helen's grasp. "Come close, everyone. Behold one of the best-kept secrets of the Papacy in the last six centuries. This box is what I took those precious minutes to retrieve when you were trying to get me out of Castel Gandolfo just before it exploded." He struggled to insert the ancient key into the lock. Try as he might, the teeth were just too old to allow the key entry.

Jack sat there watching the Pope struggle. He left the couch and knelt before the heavy duffel bag containing his personal supplies he had asked Smitty to bring from the States. He pulled out a can of WD-40. The Pope was still struggling with the lock and key. "Your Holiness?" said Jack. "May I have a try?" He held the lock up to get a good angle on the keyhole and inserted the red plastic tube that came out of the can's nozzle. After a good spraying, he wiped off the excess with a napkin and sprayed a coat of the all-purpose lubricant on the key for good measure.

"There," he said. "That should improve things. Why don't you try now, Your Holiness?" Jack handed the Pope the box and key. He noticed how heavy it was. Whatever it held was hugely dense.

The Pope jiggled the key into the keyhole, this time with only minor difficulty. Before he turned the key to open the lock he said, "This is what they are after. It is what they believe is worth executing an old man for." He turned the key. The lock fell open. The old metal hinges gave a protesting squeak as he opened the box.

His Eminence Cardinal David Caneman walked the marble halls outside the Sistine Chapel. It had been three hours since he had recessed conclave after his opening oration. He was but one of more than 150 cardinals preparing to reenter the chapel for the next session. This time they would celebrate a Mass that was intended to put them in a serene state of mind for this, Day 2 of Papal Conclave—an election, in reality. Caneman spotted Cardinal Michael Fararro, dean of the College of Cardinals. He would be last in the procession of red-capped cardinals when they all finally entered the Chapel proper. Fararro would carry a golden staff and swing a silver thurible— the ceremonial incense burner that trailed the procession with a sweet, smoky aroma. Caneman was more than familiar with the smell Cardinal Fararro's thurible gave off. It was a throwback to the old days when the cardinals did not bathe regularly and they needed the masking effects of the incense. He thought the centuries-old tradition of the procession and Mass was more theater than anything else. Caneman stood apart from the other cardinals—just one of the crowd, but then again, not ordinary in any sense of the word. Everyone noticed His Eminence Cardinal David Caneman. He knew that he was the Church's fair-haired boy.

He was special. He felt it. He saw how the other cardinals stopped their conversation when he approached and quickly stepped aside to let him through the narrow passages in and around the Vatican. He had righted the cumbersome, ancient ship that was the Vatican Bank with its sordid history of questionable practices and intrigue. He had restored once again the account balances that allowed the Church to function. It was only a short time before he was appointed *camerlengo*, the chamberlain of Vatican City. It was largely a ceremonial post, but one that was recognizable. The *camerlengo* served as the Vatican head during the brief period between the time one pope vacated his position and the new pope was elected. As *camerlengo* he was right in the center of the proceedings. Exactly where he needed to be.

Caneman stood erect. Alone. Apparently ready to serve his God. His plan would bring the Church to heel and right the terrible deviations from its fundamentalist doctrine. He knew he wouldn't be standing alone for long. Over the last few days here in the Vatican preparing for conclave, he seldom had more than a few moments of downtime. Just as he intended.

"Excuse me, Your Eminence." Caneman slowly looked down from appearing to serenely admire the frescos of the chapel. His gaze eventually stopped on Cardinal Angelo Chicarelli facing him, resplendent in his scarlet *zucchetti* and scarlet cape, his eyes narrowed and chin frowned into a serious expression.

"Yes, Your Eminence," Caneman answered. "You look troubled, my friend. How may I help?" His voice positively dripped concern.

Chicarelli slowly nodded as if the weight of the entire Roman Catholic empire were on his shoulders and his alone. Perhaps he felt it was. "Your Eminence, ours is a solemn responsibility. The next pope will guide the Church into an age of technology, political agendas, financial imperatives and things most of our aging brothers cannot imagine."

Chicarelli was opening a dialog of papal lobbying. He knew it and Caneman knew it. The lobbying was masked as merely conversation, the cardinals all getting reacquainted or meeting others from the far reaches of the Church's empire for the first time. But it was an elegant form of lobbying just the same. Caneman nodded gravely. He had endured seven such conversations of intense consensus building over the last two days leading up to the selection voting that was to begin in the next few days. Except Chicarelli was different. He represented a *faction* of cardinals. Some said that Chicarelli's group comprised about a third of the potential votes. Caneman knew what he said in the next few moments would be distributed, communicated, dissected and interpreted by as many as 50 cardinals who would be voting for the next pope in a solid, uniform block.

"Come, Michael. We have known one another since I was ordained. There are no secrets between us," said Caneman.

Cardinal Michael Fararro smiled at the honor of such gracious familiarity coming from the man known as God's Banker. "Thank you, Your Eminence. Yes, we do go back a long way. Do you know what they call you around the Vatican now that you have engineered this public stock offering that brought $200 billion into the Church?"

Caneman put an arm around the older man's shoulder and gently guided him farther away from earshot of the gathering crowd of cardinals. "What is that, my friend?"

"Mother Teresa with an MBA," answered Fararro.

Caneman let out a dismissing sniff at the term as he knew modesty required. Inwardly, though he would rather have been aligned with St. Michael—a leader in triumph over the powers of hell. I have earned it. My fundamentalist movement has earned it, he reminded himself. When I bring the ancient papal treasure to light, there will be no stopping us.

"They mean nothing but respect, Your Eminence," said Fararro, seeing the scowl on Caneman's face. "It is no secret that you are on the short list for the first round of voting for the next pope. You are well-known and respected throughout the Church's kingdom. Even by those who have never met you, they know of your accomplishments within the Vatican Bank. And I need not remind you that in these times, money speaks very loudly. It is the fuel by which the Church is able to continue doing its work."

Caneman knew exactly what the elderly but still immensely powerful Cardinal Michael Fararro was talking about. It was rumored that the financially secretive Roman Catholic Church had spent almost $150 billion in all of its activities last year. Caneman knew the figure was actually $171.6 billion. After all, it was he who wrote the checks. Over half went to health care networks and to pay for its million-person payroll along with the others the Church helped.

Let those without a clue as to the real numbers worry about settling those child abuse lawsuits brought by the victims against those idiot, faggot priests. He fumed whenever he thought about the tremendous damage to the Church's public image they had done and probably continued doing. Not to mention the millions he had paid to the Church's public relations and lobbying firms just to keep public opinion even. In truth he knew the $3.3 billion paid out in legal settlements was but a gnat on the elephant's ass. Further, that the diocese in Europe and America had actually made the payments out of their own funds, not his Vatican Bank. The financially naïve priests who ran the diocese in the hinterlands had stupidly panicked at the figure the lawyers presented them. They immediately did the worst thing they could do—sell off the Church's most valuable assets, its real estate—to restore their cash balances. Never mind that real estate was an asset class on the upswing around the world. They sold the Church's properties at the market's bottom for pennies on the dollar. Then they came to his Vatican Bank for assistance.

From there sprang His Eminence Cardinal David Caneman's base of power within the Church. He was gracious to the naïve bishops who filed into his New York offices, hat in hand. He was understanding. *'Of course Vatican Bank can help you out, Bishop. A loan? Naturally. After all, Father, this was not your fault. We are all brothers in His service are we not? How much do you need?'* Then, on occasions where the Bishops begging to borrow were in positions of influence: *'Father are you sure that will be enough? Let me add another $10 million. Better safe than sorry.'* Caneman knew Europe and America—North and South respectively—were in his pocket. But what about the others?

And now that bean counter from the SEC had threatened the possibility of delisting GOD stock and the public offering being unwound with the $200 billion going back to the investors. Caneman knew Wall Street. Such a suggestion all too easily could become a self-fulfilling prophecy. Of course the bean

161

counter knew that too. I must be careful how I handle this Jackson Schilling, Caneman told himself.

Caneman admitted he had an urgent problem. If the $200 billion repayment was made, the Church's coffers would suddenly deflate like a punctured balloon. The Church's account balances would be brought so low that within six months it would be unable to meet its enormous payroll. And with those depleted account balances went his power base. Not on my watch, he vowed.

I need that sixth and final stone tablet, the voice inside his head shouted. I need it right now, by God. Not only for the vast riches that must surely be buried in the Church's ancient treasury, but for the object I can turn into the icon that will bind the Church and lead it back to the doctrine of righteousness. The five stone tablets Caneman now had that comprised the treasure map were useless without the sixth. I must get my hands on that sixth tablet, he silently fumed. But where? Then a thought occurred to him. That stupid, overly cautious 16th Century Pope Alexander VI created the map, then broke it into six pieces. Could it be that the secret of the tablet's locations had stayed with the popes after all? Did they pass it from pope to pope over the centuries like a common household knickknack? Was it indeed hiding in plain site?

"Your Eminence?" asked Cardinal Fararro. "What would you like me to tell the other Cardinals when they ask of your strategy to restore the Church to the path of righteous fundamentalist doctrine? Please, David, give me something I can take to them in which they can believe."

Caneman thought for a few seconds. He was unhurried in his reply. Seemingly almost casual. So much rode on what he said next. He saw the others turn their way, hoping to catch a word here or a phrase there. "Tell them, Michael, that the one who supported them in their darkest hours when they needed help the most; that the one who refilled the Church's checkbook with the funds so essential to fulfilling His wishes is *working the problem.*"

162

Cardinal Michael Fararro stood there before the ornately carved entrance to the Sistine Chapel looking up into Caneman's eyes. Then a broad smile of understanding broke over his dark, Mediterranean face. He nodded in sudden comprehension at the total political astuteness and authority of that simple statement. Let the voting cardinals themselves figure out the meaning of Cardinal Caneman's reply. After all, that is what our Savior did first in the 10 Commandments and then in the Holy Bible. That Cardinal Caneman has succeeded so magnificently in the past is credible witness of the comfort we can all take when he promises he is *working the problem.*

"Excellent, David. Brilliant. I shall tell them exactly that. Thank you, David. Thank you. Thank you."

Jack heard the creak of old metal hinges as the Pope pried open the lid to his strongbox. "What's that, Your Holiness? Looks like a rock," said Sister Mary Pat as she peered in along with Helen. "Oh my word," she said, clapping her hands to her mouth in amazement. "This is it? *This is really, it,* Your Holiness?" She unashamedly threw her arms around the Pope's neck.

The Pope, exiled and dressed casually as a common laborer reached into the box and with both hands cradling the 15-pound stone tablet and lifted it out. "Yes, SMP, this is really it. For centuries, this stone with its inscriptions and map legends has been handed down from pope to pope." Then he seemed to lose his grip and fumbled the stone, apparently about to drop it.

"Oh my God," said Helen and Sister Mary Pat simultaneously.

The Pope magically regained control and faced them with the smile and humor that over a billion Catholics the world over had come to love. "Here take it, my dear," he said offering the ancient stone tablet to Helen. "It won't bite. Promise. It is the men who wish to possess it that I worry about."

"What is it?" asked Helen as she took the rock in both hands. "I mean, I hate to sound ignorant, but to me it looks like a rock with some ornate carving."

The Pope replied, "Quite alright, my dear. I would not expect even the most learned theologian to recognize the meaning of what you hold in your hands this very moment. Sister Mary Pat's understanding of this piece of history speaks for her deep research into the faith and the folklore that belongs uniquely to the Church." He nodded his head to her with the deepest affection and respect. Helen set the heavy tablet down on the coffee table beside the plate of the few uneaten bruschetta.

"Let me explain a little Catholic history," said the Pope. "Not what they teach in catechism. The real stuff. The things known only to the popes as they communicated with one another over the centuries from one incumbent to his successor and then to the one who followed him.

Jack reached over and grabbed the bottle of Chianti to refresh His Holiness' wine glass. We're talking two-thousand years of history here. He figured this might take a while.

"Thank you, Jack. It does have a medicinal effect, doesn't it?"

"Absolutely, Your Holiness."

The Pope took a sip and smiled. "Pope Alexander VI in the 16th Century was very wise. He knew that the vast amounts of wealth the Catholic Church had accumulated by then had the power to corrupt even the most devout clergy. He decided not to let any single individual get his hands on the Church's treasure."

Jack asked, "But wasn't the Church's wealth scattered throughout its kingdom—around the world?"

"One would think," answered the Pope. "But no. Even back then the Church was centrally controlled from Rome just as it is today. The popes wanted the Church's missions and lesser outposts to look to them for leadership in religious doctrine. The best way to do that was to make them all beholden to the central leadership for their very existence. Since money was their sustenance—just as it is today—the Church stockpiled its vast wealth in a central location. It was doled out to the orders and sects who deserved it—"

164

"Deserved it?" interrupted Sister Mary Pat. "Not likely. It was given to those who did the Pope's favors or who held some power that the popes could use."

"I see that I have hit a sore point," said the Pope. "You are correct, Sister. But let us not stray from the point. That being the Church's wealth was concentrated in a very small place. Over the centuries, the Popes found they needed more power to control the vastness of the Church's expanding empire. So they did what anyone would do—"

Helen said, "They moved the treasure into a single vault and granted access to just a very few of their most loyal lieutenants."

"Correct," responded His Holiness. "But soon even this was not sufficient security. So Pope Alexander VI decided to move the treasure to a secret location known only to him and a handful of his most faithful and most trusted. He made a map of the location in case something happened to him." His Holiness paused to look at his audience. "Back then, I'm afraid the Popes didn't live very long."

He took another sip of Chianti and continued, "Alexander VI broke the map into six pieces. He distributed five of the pieces among his most loyal cardinals and kept the sixth one for himself. The story says that each of the pieces of tablet contained specific parts of the map. However, by themselves not even five of the pieces if assembled together would have led someone to the exact location of the treasure vault."

Jack asked, "You say vault. You don't mean like a bank vault, do you?"

"No. Certainly not, Jack. I imagine the treasure that was accumulated over so many hundreds of years from around the world could never fit into a man-made vault. No. I imagine the vault of the pope's folklore is actually a natural cavern someplace. If it exists at all and if it has not been looted empty by now."

Helen said, "You mean, you don't know where this secret vault is located?"

The Pope looked at Helen, then at the single stone tablet on the table before them. "No, of course not. This is the single piece of tablet that Pope Alexander VI kept for himself. It has secretly been handed down from Pope to Pope for hundreds of years. This is a tradition that only a very few know about. Over the years it has lost its credibility and is now just folklore. I received this tablet in a ceremony that was more of a private, insider's joke than anything else."

"So what makes you think there really is a treasure vault filled with vast riches accumulated over centuries?" Jack asked.

The Pope sat for a moment as he considered Jack's question. "Well, why not? We know the Church's history and reputation as a cash machine and a...a...oh what is that insect trap they advertise on television?"

"You mean the roach motel?" asked Helen.

"Yes. That's it exactly. Roaches check in but they don't check out. The Church—especially the Vatican Bank under Cardinal Caneman—operates that way. Money comes in but it doesn't seem to go out. At least not without his say-so."

"But what makes you think a treasure vault really exists?" asked Jack again.

"Why, Cardinal Caneman himself. He needs there to be a vast amount of wealth to make up for the $200 billion in proceeds from the Vatican Bank's stock that you are going to make him repay. When I was younger I was quite the mountaineer. When climbing, you occasionally come upon a situation where a handhold just has to be there or you are going to fall. You put your faith in finding that life-saving hold before gravity does its work. That is the situation in which Cardinal Caneman now finds himself. The treasure vault absolutely must be there for him to be elected the next pope."

Jack looked up, now with complete comprehension. "And he had better find it fast or he is unlikely to sway the papal conclave in his favor."

His Holiness nodded, "He has about three days I would guess. That is about how long it will likely take for the conclave to vote in a new pope."

Jack said, "Maybe I'll speed that along and ramp up the pressure he's under. I'll have the SEC issue a press release after the markets close today announcing the Enforcement Division's qualified opinion on the Vatican Bank's financial statements and our final recommendation that the Bank unwind its public offering and return the investors their money. So far this was just a private threat from the SEC to Vatican Bank. But a press release imparts a whole new sense of urgency. That should light a fire under His Eminence Cardinal Caneman."

"Careful with him, my son. He is a man to be dealt with very carefully. He is brilliant and totally focused on what he wants. He controls the Church's purse strings. That gives him extraordinary power."

Jack nodded. He was no stranger to dealing with the powerful and unprincipled. "Your Holiness, if Cardinal Caneman does have some of these stone tablets, where do you think he keeps them?"

The Pope looked back at Jack. "If I were him, with my base of power in the New York offices of the Vatican Bank, I would keep them in my own private vault right there in the bank. It is safe and no one would ever find out about them until I was ready."

"What makes you think he may not actually be dead?" Cardinal David Caneman had to work to keep the terseness from his voice. The truth was, he had wondered the same thing himself. As soon as he spoke the words, he knew he should not have asked the question.

The Professional held his cell phone to his ear. "I was unable to confirm the kill as I normally would have. The site was too hot. I had to leave too soon. I thought that I would get confirmation from secondary sources—"

"Secondary sources?" demanded Caneman. "What secondary sources?" He was back in his suite at the fancy La Maison Royale right there in the center of Rome between St. Peter's Square and Castel Sant'Angelo. Caneman always had his

167

secretary book him at La Maison. Some of the city's finest
restaurants surrounded the property.

He had removed his vestments and his Roman collar. He
had been checking his emails and conducting Vatican Bank's
business when his private cell phone had rang.

The Professional ignored Caneman's interruption. "The
news media is usually a good secondary source. Also those who
are close to the target frequently provide confirmation. But that
hasn't happened in this case, has it?"

Caneman thought for a long moment. He had put this
possibility out of his mind when it became clear that he was the
frontrunner in this conclave. Events had begun to run on their
own. Faster and faster the attention came until he knew without
a doubt that his election was much more than a possibility.

But how could the Pope *not* be dead? He sat there in the
chic interior of his rooms within La Maison, pondering. He
breathed in the luxurious smell of new silk wall coverings and
freshly cleaned wool carpets. No one could have survived being
run through with that piece of rebar and then being buried under
the Villa Gandolfo when it exploded and slid down the hillside.
He answered the question, "As you said, no information from
secondary sources has come forward in this case. That is out of
respect for His Holiness. And also the fact that the injuries were
so disfiguring no one would want to see the body."

The Professional nodded in his empty, one-room apartment.
He was secluded right there in the seediest part of Rome. It was
a very far cry from timeless, classical beauty of La Maison.
Hiding in plain sight was always his preference when the
airports, shipping ports, bus stations and every mode of
transportation leaving the area were being watched like never
before. "You see? No one in a position to positively identify the
target and confirm death has come forward."

Caneman said a little too quickly, "But the photos of the
rebar and the body—"

"There were many bodies lying about Gandolfo that day,
Your Eminence." The Professional spoke his client's title with a

168

slight hint of mockery. "It would have been an easy task to take one of them and wrap it so no one could see who it actually was. Better still if the body had a catastrophic injury such as being run through with a length of rebar. Such an image tends to stifle inquiry."

Caneman's mind was racing. "No. It was His Holiness the Pope. The hospital personnel and morticians removed personal belongings from his body that were his and his alone. His shoes; his *zuccetti;* the piscatore ring. All of them belonged to the Pope and none other. He never went anywhere without them. I held the piscatore ring in my own hands before I hammered it into unrecognizable oblivion this very afternoon. It was his ring. I have seen it a thousand times."

"Of course it was his ring." The Professional wanted to follow with, *you idiot*. But he did not. "What if they merely undressed the real pope, removed these readily recognizable personal items and redressed the corpse with the rebar running through from back to front? Then they wrapped the body in that blanket and made a show of bringing it up from the ruins of Gandolfo. What if they did that?"

Caneman took another sip of his Macallan whisky. Ballsey, he thought. It was a term he had often used when he was on the trading desk at Goldman Sachs in the years before becoming a priest. It took brass ones to commit the tens of millions to the wildly fluctuating securities markets that he had. That was for sure. The press coverage of the Gandolfo explosion was immense. "The Pope's personal Swiss guards carried the body themselves," he said. "They never leave the Pope's side. Never."

"See? Just another credibility chip. And we still don't know for sure if the body inside that shroud and that the world saw buried in full Roman Catholic tradition that was televised for all to see—we still don't know if it was *him*."

Caneman could not argue the point. If this was a ruse, it was one he could not tolerate. "But why fake the Pope's death?"

"I might have the answer," said the Professional. "I have the necessary contacts within the Swiss Guards and the *Polizia di*

Stato to find out. If I am right, then I will take what steps are necessary."

* * *

CHAPTER 19

Night was falling in the rolling hills and meadows surrounding the old farmhouse. Helen finished checking the Pope's left ear. "Looks like it's healing just fine, Your Holiness. A few more days and we can take out the stitches. Several are already starting to come out on their own." She set down the cotton swab containing Neosporin she had used to cover the stitches.

"That would be nice," said the Pope as they all sat around the dinner table. Sister Mary Pat had already cleared the dinner dishes. "The stitches do tend to itch a bit."

Helen nodded. "Okay, then. Let's see how it looks in the morning. I have alcohol and some very sharp scissors with me—"

Jack turned to Helen and said, "Ever removed stitches before, Hon?" He saw the head shake he was looking for.

"But I'll bet you haven't either," she said.

Jack was an extremely well-trained and experienced operator. Extensive first aid and even some kinds of emergency battlefield surgery was part of that training.

Before Jack could answer, Mr. Smith walked in. "You'd lose that bet, Helen. I've personally watched Jack stitch up some nasty wounds and then a couple of weeks later remove the stitches."

"He worked on you?" Helen asked.

"Me? Hell no. Sorry Father. I wouldn't let him touch me. But I have seen him operate on *himself*. Does an adequate job. Won't win any beauty contests. But adequate."

Jack turned to the Pope, "Don't listen to these two, Your Holiness. I am really quite an excellent surgeon. I've been watching your ear. I'll remove your stitches myself day after tomorrow. By the way, I've always wanted to ask this question."

"Ask away, my son," said the Pope. "There are no secrets in this house. At least, not with me."

Jack leaned forward in his chair opposite this most approachable Pontiff. He was beginning to understand what so many people saw in him. There was a peace within him that came out when he spoke to you. Almost as if just by talking with the man, he transferred to you a personal tranquility and conviction that a better day was coming. "What does a Pope actually do? I mean, what's an average day like?"

The Pope set his wine glass down on the table and shook his head. "You will be disappointed, I'm sure, Jack. It's a job. Of course, being Pope has its ups and downs, like any other job. But in the end, it's really quite ordinary."

Ordinary, Jack wondered. What's ordinary about leading over a billion people? He persisted, "But what do you *do*?"

The Pope pulled out his iPhone and removed it from the red velvet-covered case the American President had given him. "Let's see," he said thumbing through its calendar. "I downloaded my contacts, calendar and music from the iCloud. My schedulers usually have me going every minute of every day. Probably like you. My schedule is usually set weeks, even months in advance."

He glanced down at the screen. "This seems a bit odd. A man whom the world presumes dead, looking up his schedule for today and talking about it as if he were still alive. But I am still very much alive. Am I not?" The Pope glanced around the safe house living room to make sure they got his joke then returned to the digital calendar. "Hmmm. Had I been in Vatican City today, my schedule would have begun at 6:00 a.m. I get up, open the windows to my private apartment that looks out over St. Peter's Square and get dressed in my workout clothes. I had a small gym installed two years ago just off the bathroom. I turn on CNN then do ten minutes of stretching, some weight work, then jump on the Versa-Climber for 20 minutes. The whole routine takes about 45 minutes. Then I shower and go downstairs for breakfast in the kitchen. I like talking with the cooks and the housekeepers over breakfast. We eat family style in my house. Whatever everyone is eating, that's what I eat also."

Helen asked, "What do you usually have, Your Holiness?"

"For breakfast? Despite what you may have heard, we Popes eat the same things you do. Lately, Chef has been making a marvelous granola. I have that with a single packet of Splenda and a cup of vanilla flavored soy milk. Chef heats the whole concoction in the microwave for exactly 80 seconds. While he's doing that, I have a piece of fruit. Right now the ruby grapefruits in Rome are excellent. Is that detailed enough?"

"Perfect. Then what?"

The Pope consulted the digital calendar in his iPhone again. "Hmmm. Let's see. Today at 7:30 a.m. I was going by car to the Basilica of the Virgin Mary to pray with a congregation from Ghana before the icon of the Madonna. Oh, I see here that I made a note that the car we use should come from the regular Vatican motor pool, not that fancy Rolls Royce they like putting me into."

The Pope looked up from his calendar at Jack. Seeing he still had everyone's attention he continued. "Oookayyy. Then at 9:45 a.m. I was to leave—again by car—to the Sistine Chapel where I would have conducted a mid-morning Mass. I see that I made another note here telling the Swiss Guards to invite some of the visitors on the tour into the Mass if they cared to join us as my personal guest."

"Wow," said Helen, "I bet that would have made their day."

"Exactly, my dear. One of the perks of being Pope is to make an ordinary day something to remember. Mass would have lasted about an hour and fifteen minutes. I see that I had fifteen minutes free afterwards. My security detail knows me quite well. They would have seen the free time in the published schedule they receive and selected a few people from those guests attending the Mass. They would have invited them back to the Vestibule so that I might have the opportunity to meet them and exchange a few words. Can you imagine what a story those people would have for the folks back home? First being invited by the Pope himself to join him for Mass and then having a few private minutes speaking to the Pope afterwards."

"What else?" asked Jack.

"You all are really curious, aren't you? By now it is 12:15 p.m. on my schedule. Time for lunch. Today this would have been a working lunch with five financial experts—including

David Caneman, by the way. It would have been held in the Pope's private dining room in the Vatican. The purpose was to prep me for the upcoming Vatican Bank board meeting. Not being a financial professional like Cardinal Caneman, I always like to have some private tutoring by the experts before the meeting. We had scheduled this luncheon to last for two hours. And so you don't have to ask, Chef serves a light pasta with a grilled fish and small salad on Thursdays. Everyone eats the same thing for lunch, again served family style. I find that I cannot really tolerate much red meat anymore. Definitely no pork products of any kind. My cardiologist approves of that. So Chef makes me a lot of healthy whole-wheat pasta, veggies, fruits, fish and occasionally an ostrich steak to splurge."

"When does your workday end?" asked Jack.

The Pope laughed at this. "When does *your* workday end, Jack?"

"It doesn't. Mine is a 24/7 job," said Jack.

"So is the Pope's. This afternoon I was scheduled to work in the office until six. I make and return telephone calls, do paperwork, draft soliloquies for Mass and generally do what any other CEO does." His finger flicked the phone's screen to page down his schedule. "At 6 p.m. there was a reception and Vatican State dinner to be held in the residence's main dining hall for Cardinals and Bishops visiting from South America. My secretary made a note reminding me to change into the Pope's full regalia for this event." The Pope looked up from his calendar. "Do you know the weight of that red velvet cape and all that goes with it? I loaded it all on my bathroom scale once— 28 pounds. Not to mention that it's summertime here in Rome. Oh well, we all have our crosses to bear, don't we? They all expect the Pope to look like the Pope. I wouldn't want to disappoint them. I like the South Americans. They're committed and doing a wonderful job for the Church. The State dinner would have wrapped up around 9:00 p.m. I would have presided over Evensong services until 10:10 p.m. Then back to my private residence. Every day I get exactly 100 emails the staff

174

thinks are important enough to filter to me. I finally had to ask them to limit it to just the top 100 emails—my staff handles the rest. I answer all 100 every day. I don't go to bed until I've caught up. By midnight or so I take a few minutes for my personal reading. I like history. Sometimes historical novels. Then I go to bed." He looked up from his cell phone. "Anything else you want to know?"

The safe house living room was silent for a moment. Jack knew that there were just a handful of people in the entire world who knew what he had just heard. Both Helen and Sister Mary Pat began quizzing the Pope for even more details. Jack saw Smith raise an eyebrow. It was their signal. He got up off the couch and walked out the back door onto the veranda overlooking the fields in back. Jack felt the warm summer evening wrap around him. He smelled the fertile fields and the rich grasses that covered the acres surrounding the farmhouse. "What's up, Smitty?"

"Just got off the phone with the old man. He wants to talk to both of us soon as we get a chance."

"What's he want?"

"He's pissed, Jack. The President's Chief of Staff called me to ask why I couldn't control my people."

"What's he pissed about? We saved the Pope and brought him to a safe house. What's wrong with that?"

Smith scratched his chin. "Well, for starters you had your people leak to the press that the SEC was threatening to issue a qualified opinion on the Vatican Bank's financial statements. The old man thinks that's something for Cardinal Caneman at Vatican Bank to announce. Then apparently you had one of your new kids—pretty girl by the name of Audrey, I think—leak to the press that the SEC is recommending the Vatican Bank unwind its public offering and return the investors their money."

"Yeah? So? Caneman isn't playing nice. I needed to get his attention."

"Jack, holding the guy's feet to the fire like you did is not the way to go about it. He went straight to the head of the SEC. It didn't take long for the President to get wind of it."

Jack felt the vibration of the cell phone in his pocket. He held up a single finger, indicating for Smith to wait. He looked down at the screen and saw who the caller was. "Hey, dad, what's up?"

"Quite a bit, I hear," said the distant voice. "This is not a secure line I take it."

"No. Are you calling about all the hot water Smitty just told me I'm in?"

"Put me on speaker, will you?" Jack pressed the button and held the phone between them.

"Hey, Mr. Schilling," said Smith. "What's going on there in DC?" After his role in the Deadly Acceleration case last year, Mr. Schilling had asked to be appointed to the IRS as head of its Offshore Asset Recovery division. No one was better qualified than the elder Mr. Schilling. He was an expert at hiding assets from the taxation authorities—it had been his business for over 30 years. He had always said that it takes one to know one and he knew 'em all. He had business dealings and was friends with heads of state, CEOs and some of the world's most famous and infamous. He had known the current American president since he was a junior congressman. Their relationship ran so deep that he made him part of the family by appointing him Jack's godfather.

"You ask what's going on here in DC? Quite a lot, no thanks to you two," the voice said over the line. "I just got a call from Jack's godfather."

Jack and Smith both looked at one another. Smith mouthed the words, "I told you he was pissed."

"It wouldn't look right for the President to circumvent the chain of command and get on the horn to you directly. So he asked me to."

Smith said, "Look Mr. Schilling, if anyone's to blame, it's me. I kept tabs on Jack's audit and knew what he was going to do—"

"Going to do?" said Mr. Schilling. "Going to do? You mean that leak to the press about the qualified opinion and then

176

another leak to the press about unwinding the Vatican's public offering? Is that all we're talking about here? And I thought there was a really big fuckup." He ended this sentence screaming into the phone.

Jack spoke up, "Well, it seems that the head of the SEC as well as the President both seem to think my methods lacked a certain amount of judgment."

Mr. Schilling wasn't about to let his son off the hook so easily. "Oh, I don't know, Jack. We're only talking about the Roman Catholic Church with over a billion followers, a portion of whom have invested some of what little they have in GOD stock." The little cell phone was silent for a moment. Then, "Let me guess. Caneman refused to give you the time of day. There were questions about certain disbursements. You couldn't get any answers going up the chain of command. When Caneman slammed his door in your face, you wanted to get his attention. That about sum things up?"

Jack and Smith looked at one another. Neither had to ask how he knew exactly what happened.

"Thought so," said Mr. Schilling. "Listen guys, I know Caneman. Matter of fact, he was a client of my firm while he was with Goldman Sachs and for a short period after he entered seminary. We've maintained our relationship over the years. He's an arrogant bastard. But, Jack, you already know that. He's a real religious zealot, though. You gotta give him that. A few years ago he became obsessed with collecting religious artifacts. Never could understand it. Focused on a granite tablet. Said it was Catholic folklore. The tablet was actually part of a map from the 16th Century. It supposedly showed where the Church's wealth was stored."

Jack jumped in, "How many pieces does he have?"

"Well, back then he had three. I saw them. They're impressive. Gray pieces of granite with the tops polished to a shine. Lines of Latin running across and partial carvings of the map, I suppose, done in beautiful relief. Keeps them in the Vatican Bank's vault there in New York. But that was two years ago. This guy Caneman doesn't allow anyone or anything to stand in his way. That's how he got to the lofty place he now finds himself. And rumor says he's a potential candidate for Pope at this conclave. A shame what happened to His Holiness. I knew him too."

"You did?" asked Smith.

"Of course I did. With all that money sloshing around, you don't think I'd let the opportunity to manage some of it slip away, do you? He's a great man. But he's also tough. Most people don't know that. Box him into a situation that compromises his Church or his personal integrity and watch out. You'll have your hands full."

Jack and Smith looked at one another. Caneman's three pieces of the map along with the one the Pope has in his possession right now makes the puzzle map two-thirds complete. Jack said, "Good to know."

There was silence on the line. Jack heard his dad slowly say, "I see." It was all Mr. Schilling needed to say. Jack knew his message had been received.

"How's my favorite daughter-in-law? You being good to her? Respecting her?"

Smith broke in, "He better be, sir. If he doesn't he'll have to deal with me."

"And me as well," said Mr. Schilling. "I love that girl as if she were my own daughter. How's her carbonara coming along? As I recall it was one of our mutual acquaintances' favorite pasta dishes."

Jack smiled. The old guy was getting it. "Pretty good. Actually we just had it for dinner. But this batch she made without the sausage. One of our guests doesn't eat pork of any kind."

"Really? Without the sausage it'll need a great Chianti as a supporting actor."

Jack said, "She served that too. Turns out the same guest who doesn't eat pork really loved the Chianti."

There was another brief pause. Then Mr. Schilling said, "Thought so, son. Well, I've a flight to catch. But before that, I think I'll have a talk with your godfather. See you two soon."

The Professional peered through the Barrett's ATN day/night scope. He perched on a small hill over a mile away from the old farmhouse outside of Rome. There was open space around the house for at least 50 meters in all directions. He saw the lights burned brightly inside the house. It had taken him just one day to learn what he needed to know from his contacts in Rome's law enforcement community. While in the Navy, his SEAL team worked on three drug interdiction cases against European narco traffickers moving product into the U.S. Across Europe his team was greeted with huge respect and admiration. Nowhere was that more evident than in Italy with the *Carabinieri*, a special military branch that takes on the role as the country's military and territorial police force. His position as one of the team's three snipers and word of his rapacious confirmed kills had raised him that much farther up the totem of respect. Indeed, his reputation as winner of the World Long Rifle championships had preceded his arrival.

The Vatican Security Service was a whole new animal. Guarding the Holy City and the Pope was largely a boring job. The Professional would never have wanted it. Personal protection was not in his nature. Just the opposite, he had learned early on in BUD/s training. The Swiss guards manning Vatican Security had quickly become his buddies. While in country, when the team stood down, awaiting its next assignment, they had invited him out to their training range to share some of his expertise. The Professional was gracious in sharing his skill. You just never know when such friendly contacts will come in handy, he had told himself back then. When he left the Service and went to work on his own for whomever was willing to pay his exorbitant fee he not only maintained his contacts all over Europe but he managed to expand them. His current requirement for information had proven the value of this effort.

It was these contacts that he had called on now. Yet, he was not surprised to learn that no one knew anything. That was the point. It only confirmed what he had suspected as soon as he had seen the "Pope's" sheet-wrapped corpse being hauled up out of the crater that was once Castel Gandolfo.

He was careful not to raise suspicion. In the end any inexperienced lack of subtlety would have only gotten him blank stares. He could not afford for them to become the questioners. No, he was after inconsistencies and dead ends rather than hard answers to direct questions. His conversations with those in a position to know were oblique. From several meetings for coffee, tea and eventually for drinks he pieced together his own conclusions. In the end, these led him to this farmhouse out here in the middle of nowhere in the dead of night.

He shifted his position, lying flat prone on the ground. Stalks of long, fragrant Italian fescue grass were all around him. The sounds of the night were numerous and individually identifiable if you knew what to listen for. He heard the skittering of rodents scurrying into their burrows, out of sight of the owls that hunted them at night. Off in the distance, coyotes howled. And the breeze blew the grass that concealed his hide.

Throughout his day of surreptitious questioning he wondered, *where was the Target's body taken? Did the Vatican medical examiner make a definitive conclusion as to cause of death?* The answers were less important than the person occupying this farmhouse tonight. The Professional saw right through the subterfuge. The Target was alive. He had somehow survived the explosion at Castel Gandolfo. He must have. But there was more. His Eminence Cardinal David Caneman wanted the top job. That was obvious to the Professional. But a man like him, used to vast amounts of money, needed something more. What did the un-dead Target possess that would be more valuable to Caneman than the man's life?

Now that he knew his location, the Professional knew it was a matter of waiting for exactly the right moment to strike. He peered through the ATN scope, scanning the distance

180

between his hide and the farmhouse. He knew what to look for. There. An elongated mound of straw in the hay field that rose just about 18 inches off the ground. Not unusual. There were many such mounds of hay in this hay field. But this one moved. Slowly. Rhythmically. It was a trained operator in a gilly suit whose steady, shallow breathing was all the tell an equally trained operator needed for confirmation of his location.

Now that he knew what to look for, the Professional swung the Barrett around the entire area surrounding the farmhouse. He counted eight guards posted at varying intervals around the property. Together, they combined to cover every entry point to the property.

The Professional knew that there could be only one reason why so many highly trained guards had been placed around a defendable, nondescript location in the middle of nowhere, but still close enough to Rome to be of use for its occupant. The Target himself was somewhere behind those thick walls. Yes, the Pope was far from dead. Of that the Professional was now certain.

The Professional lay there quite comfortable in the fescue grass on this warm summer night. He had time and the element of surprise on his side. He next needed to identify the surveillance equipment he knew must be deployed around the property. Surely, they would use infrared cameras, motion detectors, trip wires, pressure pads and the like. Child's play for an experienced operator like him. He looked down on the yellow light spilling from the windows and thought it not beyond the possibility that they might even use a drone surveillance aircraft flying high over the property to look down on whomever might come their way.

* * *

CHAPTER 20

Jack held a hand to his mouth, stifling a yawn. "It's late, guys. Why don't we all get some sleep?" He could hear the quiet of the Italian farmland all around them. There were no busy roads, no airports with their roaring jet engines nearby. There was nothing but the bleating of some sheep up on the hillsides and rustle of the tall grass outside as the breeze blew.

Smith agreed. "We can't stay here forever. But it would take someone with extraordinary contacts in just the right places weeks or even months to piece together this subterfuge. Then they'd have to figure out where on earth the Pope is hiding. We're safe." Smith got up off the couch.

Jack rose from the chair he had been sitting in. "I'm going to make one more tour around the property and check in with the guys. See you in a while, Helen." Jack walked out the front door, down the three wood stairs that sagged in the center from years of heavy work boots coming and going. He landed on the gravel that surrounded the house. There was no moon this dark night so he was careful where he stepped as he headed toward the equipment shed where the surveillance systems were housed. He also had some thinking to do about his father's claim of actually seeing three of the mysterious stone tablets in the Vatican Bank's New York vault. He was wondering just how to get into the vault to see for himself how they fit with the single tablet the Pope had shown him this evening.

The Professional raised the Barrett's scope. Immediately he saw the big guy—all 6-2, 225 pounds of him—a target that would be hard to miss at any range, even without the high-powered riflescope he had mounted on the Barrett. "Jackson Schilling," the Professional said softly into the night. "I would recognize that arrogant walk anywhere." He pressed the small button on the side of the ATN scope. It launched a micro-second laser burst from the system's range finder. "Hmmm," he read the distance through the scope's reticle. "Just 1542 yards." His

Louisiana drawl was ever so soft—no more than a whisper—as the breeze whisked his words away. "No sweat."

Jack's body stood out like a green giant in the night scope's optics on this dark night. The Professional watched as he quickly opened the door to an old maintenance shed and disappeared inside.

"What's up, guys?" asked Jack. He looked over the array of screens and monitors set up on the dusty old workbenches that lined the shed's perimeter.

"Got a problem with the MQ," said one of the young men who sat behind a monitor and held a joystick between his right thumb and forefinger. He never took his eyes off of the screen in front of him. It showed an aerial picture of the entire property and surrounding landscape as shown from the MQ-1 Predator's nose-mounted camera. "The infrared system crapped out."

"What? Now you can't see the sheep and goats roaming around out there," Jack teased. He thought all this high-tech gear was no substitute for human eyes on target.

"Oh I can see 'em all right. Just much easier to work off their heat signature than having to actually set eyeballs on 'em. I still have the mini-predator in reserve. It doesn't have an infrared system so it doesn't give us the advantage that this does."

"Hellfire missile system still operational?" asked Jack. He didn't trust the Italian maintenance crew. The drone belonged to the *Carabinieri* who had official responsibility for this mission. Their lone drone pilot was currently off on vacation. That left the operation and maintenance of the Predator up to Jack's small group.

"Oh yeah. Missile's are still up. Got a sheep you want offed? I'll show you." Jack wasn't disturbed about what seemed a minor system failure. After all, they still had aerial surveillance up and running. And he knew if the Italian drone failed completely he still had the CIA's latest mini-drone combat system inside the farmhouse sitting in an aluminum container no larger than a big suitcase. Still, he knew that even an experienced operator having to rely on his interpretation of the visual image appearing on his screen wasn't nearly as reliable as an infrared heat-signature. Fuck it, he thought. No one knows we're here. And they never will. The Pope will be out of here in a few days.

Jack walked down the line of young men seated at the workbenches. He stopped at each of the closed circuit TV stations, the motion detection station and the trip wire station. Everything seemed working just fine—nominal was the term he had used in his former life. Just the drone was having a minor glitch.

The Professional moved his eye away from the scope. He wasn't going to shoot anyone tonight. Tonight was for recon. He had only just got here and taken up station in the rocks on the hillside. The rocks were still warm from the day's sun. His heat signature blended in perfectly with the warmth surrounding him. The tall fescue grass hid his image. He was visually, thermographically and electronically invisible. Just how I like it, he drawled to himself.

The Professional slowly and with a minimum of movement unwrapped a peanut butter sandwich. He slowly bit into the Italian sourdough bread and chewed. This was the perfect sniper's food—silent in its consumption, good calories, rich in carbs and not fatty. Perfect. He just as slowly and with the same minimum of movement raised the tube on his camelback water bladder to his lips and sucked down the cool liquid—25 percent energy replacement with glucose powder and 75 percent mineral water.

As he ate and drank, the Professional watched the farmhouse through the high-powered spotter's scope he had carried into his hide. This too had an integrated starlight night vision system. To most anyone—even the Green Berets with whom his SEAL team had once trained—the entire area seemed deserted. But the Professional knew better.

He knew he was looking down on a precisely choreographed slow motion dance. He appreciated the care and stealth of the skilled craftsmen who moved below him on the flat farmland. By

184

now he had spotted the three snipers dressed in gilly suits so they blended perfectly into the landscape. The only thing that gave them away was the small movement of their breathing. At that, the Professional had to respect their craft. He had missed them several times. It wasn't until he placed their image in the spotter's scope so that the mound he thought might be one of them was in front of a stationary backdrop—a rock or the roofline of the farmhouse. Then he watched for the line from their image slowly moving up and down the line of the stationary backdrop—sometimes as little as an inch or two. But that was all it took. The Professional was now familiar with the particular stalks of grass and twigs that each had used to make up their gilly suit. Visually, they were each as unique to the Professional as would be a brother and a sister.

He took another slow bite of his sandwich. The creamy peanut butter (never chunky because the nuts might make a crunching noise) lay deliciously on his pallet. The snipers were in rotation again below him. One would ever so slowly creep up to the one he was relieving. When the replacement was in place, the primary would creep away to replace this brother farther down the line. This leapfrogging kept everyone from getting stale, allowed them some movement and retained a fresh field of view over time. When their six-hour shift was over, others would don their own gilly suits and creep out from the farmhouse.

The Professional slowly ate, drank and watched. When the time came when he was satisfied that he knew everything he needed to know about personnel, weaponry, intrusion alarms and where the target was—he would silently pick off each of the snipers. The Barrett was silenced. At this distance no one at the farmhouse would hear a thing. By the time he completed his recon, he would know where the trip wires, pressure pads, heat sensors and motion detectors were located. Already he had spotted five of them. There were surely others. He had all night and all day tomorrow to find them. He was confident he would.

Jack sat on the edge of the bed, stripped down to his running shorts and a grey T-shirt with SEC stenciled in yellow military logotype across the chest. Helen lay beside him reading more about the history of the Vatican Bank and the scandals that had enveloped it over the decades.

"Who are you calling at this hour?" she asked, noticing that Jack had picked up his cell phone.

"It's just six p.m. in New York. She'll still be working," answered Jack.

"Audrey? You're calling Audrey, aren't you?"

Jack leaned over and kissed Helen's thigh, naked on this warm summer night. "You have nothing to worry about, Hon. She's at least six years your junior—"

"She's adorable. Blonde, statuesque, knockout figure. I saw the way all you guys fawned over her. She had you eating out of her pretty little hand."

Jack nodded as he keyed the number into his cell phone. "That's exactly why I'm calling her and not one of my more senior auditors. Besides, none of the others have anything on Audrey when it comes to brains and the tenacity to use that intellect."

"What's she going to do?" asked Helen.

Jack held up a single finger as his call connected.

"Hi, Mr. Schilling," Audrey said, "you're still somewhere out of the country, aren't you?"

"That I am, Audrey. You're on speaker now. Helen is right here with me."

"Hello, Mrs. Schilling, how are you?"

"Please, just call me Helen. And I am just peachy. Did you and your team eat dinner?"

"Ah, no Ma'am. Not yet. We were thinking about ordering in Chinese. We're drafting our final audit report tonight."

"That's what I thought. Okay, by the time Jack is finished with you, I will have ordered for your group from Number One Little House Chinese Restaurant. Chef Lee's General Tso chicken and shrimp with broccoli is spectacular. It's right there in the financial district on William Street between Beaver and Mill Lane. Do you know where I'm talking about?"

"Oh sure, Helen. I've walked by there with my boyfriend, but never ate there."

Jack interjected, "You have a boyfriend, Audrey?" Then he saw the scowl Helen shot him. "Yeah, of course you do. Anyway, I need you to do something for me." He took the phone off speaker as Helen picked up her own cell phone to place the dinner order all the way from Italy. "This is important, Audrey. It is also none of anyone else's business. So keep it between us."

"Yes, sir. Okay. I'm up for it, whatever it is. Count on me, Mr. Schilling. What is it you want me to do?

"There are some physical assets in the vault on the 40th floor that I am pretty certain were not part of this audit's inventory. I need you to somehow get into that vault and use your cell phone to photograph them and send them to me."

"Mr. Schilling, the vault on 40 is off limits. It is Cardinal Caneman's private vault. They told us there was no bank property there and refused us entrance to complete our asset observation."

"Yeah, Audrey. I figured that. Just the same, I need you to get in there, find the safe deposit boxes these assets are in and photograph them. If it were easy I would have asked one of the senior guys to do it."

Audrey laughed at that. "Well, I've met the Cardinal's personal assistant, Enzo. Seems like a nice enough guy. Wears really nice clothes. I caught him staring my way."

"What's that mean?" asked Jack.

"I guess it means that he noticed me and that he likes what he saw. I believe that he has access to the vault as the Cardinal's personal assistant. When the Cardinal's advisory board has meetings in there he goes in first and sets it up. You know, with water, coffee and usually something to eat. I saw him nine days ago carrying a tray of pastries into the elevator. I'm certain of the timing because that was the day the Pope was shot. He was going down to 40."

"Perfect. You just might have a future with the CIA, Audrey." She had no idea that Jack knew what he was talking about and actually had the connections to fulfill that claim.

Audrey laughed at that. "I'm just a hardworking accountant, Mr. Schilling. What is it that you want me to photograph?"

"There are at least three granite tablets, maybe one or two more. Each has carved images and inscriptions on them. They're probably kept in separate safe deposit boxes. Each one weighs about 15 pounds and is the size of a small shoebox. I have seen one tablet. The carving appears on just one side. I need a clear photo of each. Maybe point the camera straight down at the tablet. That's all. Take the photos of each tablet and email them to me." Jack paused. "Think you can do that?"

"Taking the photos, sure. We'll see about the rest. This is a challenge. First I have to get Enzo, the Cardinal's assistant, to give me a tour of the vault. Then concoct a plausible story that gets him to open the safe deposit boxes and show me these shoebox-sized stone tablets you think they contain. Finally, I'll need to get him to allow me to photograph them. I presume these are private and quite valuable?"

Smart girl. "They are. Also, we don't want the Cardinal to know you were even in his vault let alone photographed his precious tablets."

"That's not a problem. His assistant isn't supposed to let anyone in there. Since he and I will be the only ones who know I was there, he won't tell that he breached security. I won't. So His Eminence shouldn't be any the wiser."

Jack asked, "When are you going to do it?"

"Ummm. Actually, I saw him just a few moments ago. I think I'll start the ball rolling right after I run a brush through my hair and fix my makeup. I'll ask one of the seniors to go get our dinner. And please thank Helen for looking after us."

"Done. Call me when you've executed and your mission is secure."

"What?"

"Just give me a call to let me know that the photos are on the way."

"Sure thing, Mr. Schilling."

"Working late this evening, Enzo?" asked Audrey as she sauntered up to his desk. She stood off to the side so the desk provided no barrier. Hand on one hip, with ankles crossed and the toe of one high heel resting comfortably on the carpet, she presented a dazzling image. Good thing I decided to wear a short dress today, she thought.

The well-dressed personal assistant to His Eminence Cardinal David Caneman hadn't seen her coming. He had been arranging the Cardinal's media interview schedule while he was in Rome during the papal conclave. Enzo was startled. He was totally unprepared for the vision of loveliness standing beside his desk. He stood so that he wouldn't have to look up at her so much. Audrey was a good four inches taller than the Italian in her heels.

In perfect English, peppered with an Italian accent he said, "So sorry, Audrey. I did not see you coming. I was just sending His Eminence tomorrow's schedule." He looked down at his keyboard, moved the mouse to his email Send button and clicked it. "There. All finished. How may I be of service to you?"

Audrey was a novice at getting men to do something for her that they shouldn't just because of the way she looked. But she was a fast learner. She looked down, deep into his eyes and said, "There is something I've been dying to see in the Bank. I was wondering if there's a chance—"

"Something to see? Here in Vatican Bank? But you auditors have access to everywhere." Enzo's hands came up with open palms—the Italian gesture of confusion. He watched as the woman shifted, then rested one lovely hip on his desk. His gaze traveled across her bare, tanned thigh, across her knee, then down her well-muscled calf to a slender ankle. He noticed her high heel had slipped off of her foot that was hanging in the air. The shoe dangled from a single, well-manicured toe.

"Not everywhere, Enzo. You have been gracious to all of us and especially to me. I do appreciate your hospitality. But I would just love for you to show me the Vatican Bank's private vault." She wiggled her dangling foot with the shoe precariously still attached. "In my three years as an auditor, would you believe I have never seen such a thing? I hear it is beautiful, all that polished steel." She was guessing. Of course Audrey had been inside her share of vaults. Most were cold, dull metal affairs.

"Yes, I suppose to some the interior of the Cardinal's private vault would be beautiful. To those of us few who are entrusted with its safekeeping, it is just another place to work. No one is allowed in there without the Cardinal's permission or unless they are on official bank business."

Audrey allowed the shoe to slip off of her toe. She gently rubbed her bare foot against the man's shin. "Oh come now, Enzo. You are just too modest. You have access to the vault. Just a quick look is all I want. Promise." Her foot wondered a little further up the warm, soft cashmere of his suit. She abruptly removed her foot from his leg and slid her shoe back on.

"Okay, Enzo. I was just teasing. You know that, right? I do need to see the vault. And my reason does have to do with the audit. So, my request is indeed official bank business." She looked him in the eye.

Enzo took a step back from her. His lips relaxed from the thin line that had turned them white. His eyebrows fell from their worried, crinkled position. The poor man was relieved. "Whew, *Senora*. You really had me worried there. But what is with the theatrics?"

"Look, Enzo, I like you. I was just flirting a little bit. I need you to do me this favor. I know it is an imposition. I know that I am asking you to do something that maybe you shouldn't. But it will be my ass if I don't conduct a physical observation of two categories of assets that must be in that vault. They are listed on the asset sub ledger and we cannot find them anywhere." Audrey was totally winging it now.

190

"And what are these two categories of assets please?"

May as well jump right in, she told herself. "The first is real estate related. I need to observe and prove the existence of the land deed documents for the tower and the Apostolic Palace, where the Bank's headquarters are housed in Rome and also the lease for the Bank's New York offices—"

"And the second category?"

She smiled and shook her head as if it was silly. "You're not going to believe this. I am skeptical myself. My senior manager thinks he saw some stones or rocks in the asset inventory. He figures they must be squirreled away in the Cardinal's vault. He has asked me to observe them, count them and photograph them. We will take the photos to an expert for valuation. Everything in the strictest confidence, of course." She held her breath. Now was the moment of truth.

Enzo looked at her there on the 42nd floor of Vatican Bank's now deserted New York offices. Then a broad smile split his face horizontally. His Italian accent just became thicker, "*Senora*, this is no problem. Since you are on official bank business, of course. I can let you into the vault and take the land deeds and leases from their files for you to inspect. Those pages for the Apostolic Palace are quite old. You will have to wear white cotton gloves when handling them and be very careful. The New York office lease is less rare. They do not require cotton gloves. As for the rocks—yes, there are some stone tablets. Actually, His Eminence just recently added a new one. Now there are five. The Cardinal has asked me to open their safe deposit boxes and set them on the work table twice before during meetings with his advisory board. They are heavy. I was always excused before they opened the boxes so I have never actually seen them myself. But His Eminence refers to them as *the stones*. I too would like to see them. By now the 40th floor is deserted except of the cleaning crew. We go now."

Audrey shivered in the cold of the vault. The clingy silk dress she wore provided nothing in the way of warmth. She removed the white cotton gloves and handed back the thick real estate file folders to Enzo. They were just part of her ploy anyway. She did not want him thinking that she was there solely for the stones. He might have become suspicious and not granted her request. Though she was fascinated at the Apostolic Palace documents she had glanced over. Ancient and interesting how they did business so long ago.

"One part of my mission completed, Enzo. One to go."

"Si, *Senora*. Now for the stones." He pulled two sets of keys from a leather satchel that he had brought into the vault with them.

The vault door was closed and locked. No one knew they were in here. Nor could anyone from the outside enter. The time lock would not engage for exactly sixteen minutes more. The shiny steel cavern was theirs until then.

They worked as a team. Enzo simultaneously turned the two required keys to open each safe deposit drawer. Audrey then pulled the heavy boxes out of their resting place and set them on the brushed aluminum table while Enzo inserted both keys into the next box.

When all five were sitting in a neat row on the table with their lids open, Audrey and Enzo both walked their length, admiring the polished, smooth surface of the granite tablets. The ornate carvings were beautiful. But they made no sense whatsoever. They reminded Audrey of a jigsaw puzzle. She thought perhaps if they had more time they might be able to move the heavy stone pieces around so they made sense. She looked at her watch and knew she had to get her photographs and get out before the time lock sealed them in until morning.

"That's perfect, Enzo." Audrey pulled her cell phone from her auditor's bag. "Now I'll just get my photos and we can leave." She decided to photograph each stone tablet first as it sat in its own safe deposit box. All the boxes were facing the same way. Maybe Caneman had placed the tablets in their boxes so they were positioned correctly. She clicked away, taking each photo from directly above the tablet and making sure it was in

192

focus and held steady, just as Schilling had ordered. To be on the safe side, she snapped two photos of each tablet.

Then as an afterthought she said, "Say Enzo what do you think of a side view of each stone out of their box?" Without waiting for his answer she began removing the first tablet from its metal container.

Enzo nervously looked at this watch. "*Senora*, we have just seven minutes until the time lock seals us inside for the night." To be found inside the vault that was forbidden to everyone but His Eminence Cardinal David Caneman and his specially invited guests would have meant certain dismissal from Vatican Bank and probably jail time.

Only Caneman had the code to break the time lock and open the vault after hours. Since he traveled so often and was in and out of the Vatican Bank offices at odd hours, he often required access to the vault after it was sealed for the night. Occasionally, when he was out of the country he called in to his night staff, gave them the special code to unlock the sealed vault to get him some papers. Then he reset the code via remote computer access.

Audrey quickly photographed the stone tablet from both sides. "No problem. You put this one back while I get the next one." She took the next tablet out of its box while Enzo hurriedly grabbed the first and returned it to its original position inside the box. "Hurry *Senora*—"

"I know Enzo. Five minutes left." She finished with the number two stone tablet and grabbed the third from its box. Her photography was going faster now. There was a rhythm to her work. Three minutes. She heard Enzo muttering in rapid Italian under his breath. Number four was completed. She grabbed the last tablet. Out of the corner of her eye she saw Enzo putting the rock back in its box and slamming the lid shut. He had already placed the other three boxes containing their tablets back into the metal cabinet and locked them in.

"There. Done," said Audrey. Just 45 seconds remained before the time lock sealed them inside. "Hurry, Enzo." He grabbed the rock and set it in its box. He slammed the lid shut and ran with it the entire length of the vault to the cabinet. Then he thrust it back in place and banged its door closed. He yanked the key from the lock.

Audrey hit the large red button that opened the vault door. She looked up at the digital clock mounted on the huge metal door to the vault counting down the seconds until it would automatically swing shut for the night. She stood on the polished steel threshold of the vault door and grabbed Enzo's outstretched hand as he ran toward her even as the massive steel door began its inexorable swing shut. She pulled him through to the outside. Both breathed hard. There was a finely oiled metallic sound as sixteen three-inch circular steel studs all simultaneously moved into place around the vault door, sealing it shut for the night.

Audrey slipped her cell phone containing all of her pictures inside her jacket pocket. It was payback time, she knew. "Enzo you are so nice to do this for me. I cannot thank you enough."

"Well, *Senora*, I can think of something."

Oh boy, thought Audrey. "Yes, Enzo? What can I do for you?"

The same smile split his face in half again. "Relax, Miss Audrey. You have nothing to worry about from me. My boyfriend always says I am completely harmless until you get to know me. I was simply wondering if you might have time for dinner with Adolpho and I. It is a beautiful summer evening here in New York. We could dine *al fresco*."

Audrey's laugh was one of deep and colossal relief. They were out of the vault now and walking to the elevators. "Yes, I would love to join you and Adolpho this evening. Let me quickly send an email to my boss who is waiting and I'll meet you in the lobby in ten minutes."

* * *

194

Chapter 21

"Wake up, Your Holiness," said Jack. He shook the Pontiff's shoulder again. "Come on, duty calls, sir."

"What? What?" asked the still-groggy Pontiff. The warm summer breeze blew in through the open window. "Jack? It is still dark outside—"

"Yeah, yeah. It's 2:30 in the morning. So? Come on. I have something that cannot wait. I need you right now."

The Pope was wide awake, fearing that Jack would shake his shoulder again as if it were one of those barbells he probably lifted just for fun. "Okay Jack. I am up. What is so important? Is Helen ill?" Already he was slipping into his robe and slippers.

"Naw, Your Holiness. Helen is fine. She's still in bed sleeping." Jack held out his cell phone showing Audrey's photos of the five stone tablets lined up in a row. "This is what's so important. I thought you would want to see it immediately."

The Pope reached toward his bedside table, almost knocking over his glass of water, and grabbed his glasses. "What do you have there, my son?" Without another word he took Jack's cell phone in his hands and proceeded to examine the images of the stone tablets. First as a whole with all five tablets in a row. Then he scrolled through the camera roll and looked at each individually. There were photos of each rock beginning from overhead to see the inscriptions, then from each side, showing the crags, protrusions and crevices from when it was broken apart so many centuries ago. "Such perfection in the photographic detail," he said. "I can see that each one is different. God bless Steve Jobs and his idea to upgrade the iPhone's camera system. Where did you get these?"

Jack ignored the question. Even with the Pope he kept some things close until absolutely necessary to reveal. "The proof is right here in your hand—"

"That the stone tablets actually exist," finished the Pope. "That there just might actually be a shred of truth to the story of the Church's vast treasure."

Jack said, "So we have the complete map now, don't we?"

The Pope smiled slyly. "We have six carved rocks. Only the Vatican's folklore says there are exactly six. Over the centuries that number might have become understated. There could be more. And these pictures of tablets," he lifted Jack's phone that he still held, "these tablets might not even be the real thing. Even if they are, what they represent—if anything—remains a question." He squinted down again at the photographs on Jack's tiny screen. Then he tilted his glasses in order to increase their magnification. "Still, you have made quite a find, haven't you? I am so happy that you have allowed me to share your discovery— even in the middle of the night. Is there any way to print these photos so we can begin putting this puzzle together?"

The Professional put down his peanut butter sandwich. He aimed the spotting scope through the open window as soon as he saw the bedroom light switch on like a beacon in the night in the otherwise darkened farmhouse. He watched as Jackson Schilling conversed with the target. Both men's backs were to the open window. The target had left the curtains open—to enjoy the warm evening's breeze, he supposed. The angle at which the target held the cell phone provided a perfect view of its screen. At this distance, the Professional's spotting scope provided a crisp, clear image of exactly what the target was looking at. "Hmmm," the Professional drawled softly into the still-warm rocks surrounding his hide, "a row of five metal boxes—safe deposit boxes if *Ahm* not mistaken—with rocks in them. Rocks?"

He shifted slightly to get more comfortable for his telephone call. He softly drawled the client's name into the earpiece whose microphone extended an inch and a half down his jawline. The cellular telephone resting in a pack not two feet away from him instantly made the connection.

"*Ah* have some information that you might be interested in, *Yer Eminence.*" He spoke the man's title with his usual slight mocking disdain.

196

"It is the middle of the night," complained a groggy Cardinal Caneman—"

"Not hardly, *Yer Eminence*. Just early mornin'." From the news reports the Professional monitored, he knew, along with the rest of the world, that His Eminence Cardinal David Caneman was in Rome presiding over the papal conclave. "If you would rather wait until you have had your breakfast and morning walk around the Vatican, *Ah* am certainly willin' to accommodate."

Caneman hated the man's soft, Louisiana drawl. It sounded menacing. He always spoke in such hushed tones it seemed he was afraid that his conversation would be overheard. "No. Go ahead. You would not have intruded on me at this hour if it were not important. Tell me."

"Well, *awright* then. First, the target is very much alive." He waited while Caneman sucked in his breath. "That is correct. Remember that *Ah* expressed my misgivings at bein' unable to confirm the kill? Then again when they wrapped the target's body in that shroud so no one could identify who it actually was?" the Professional listened to Caneman breathing. "You there? *Yer Eminence?*"

"I am here. I…I just was not expecting this news. I suppose His Holiness has his reasons for staying in hiding."

"Oh he does. He surely does. He knows that my contract was not honored. My guess is also that by now—thanks to Jackson Schilling—they know that *Ah* am a man who always makes good on his promises. But that is not the news *Ah* wanted you to know. *Ah* will put down the target. His luck will run out. Ever-one's does eventually. No. What *Ah* wanted you to know about was a series of images the target and Schilling were a-lookin' at on his cell phone."

"Images?" asked Caneman. "What images?"

"Strange images, *Yer Eminence*. There were a bunch of 'em. Five metal safe deposit boxes sittin' on a shiny metal table with their lids open—"

Caneman suddenly jerked upright as he sat on the edge of his bed. "What was in the five boxes? Tell me now."

The Professional was one not to be rushed. "*Ah* will tell you. Then we will negotiate a new price. Sittin' in each of the boxes was a rock. Each looked about the same size. Granite, *Ah* would guess. The tops were sawed flat and all polished. There was some carving on each of the rocks."

Caneman felt his mouth go dry. His brain seemed to freeze on the image of the metal boxes sitting in *his* private vault, lids open with the ancient stone tablets exposed for some interloper to see. His only comfort was that even with detailed close-ups of his five tablets they would do no one any good without the sixth. He needed to find the sixth.

"Now don't go off and shoot the messenger here, *Yer Eminence.* There was somethin' else *Ah* saw."

"What?" demanded Caneman.

"Well, the target laid the cell phone with the images of the rocks aside. Then he reached under the bed and pulled out a really old lookin' strongbox. He lifted it onto the bed. Seemed a little heavy, the way he held it and the way it sank into the mattress. Then he pulled a key from a lan'rd 'round his neck and used it to open the lock on the box."

Caneman felt things going from bad to worse. "Did you see what was in the box?"

"Oh *Ah* saw it *alraht.* There was a rock in the target's box. Looked to be identical to those in the images on the cell phone." The Professional paused to let his information sink in.

Caneman was silent, thinking. The papal key. Worn around the neck? Of course. There was a rumor of such a ceremony where little artifacts were handed down from pope to pope. Sentimental trinkets everyone supposed. No real value. Nothing of any significance. But the sixth stone tablet? Could His Holiness actually have possession of the sixth stone tablet?

The Professional said, "Now *Ah* believe that *Ah* can obtain the target's strong box and its contents shortly after *Ah* complete my original assignment. Is that somethin' that you might be interested in, *Yer Eminence*?" The Professional first wanted to establish demand and gauge its strength before he began negotiating price.

Caneman abandoned his usual cool demeanor. "Yes. Yes. That stone tablet is something I am interested in obtaining. Yes. For the love of God." He knew that his credibility with the cardinals voting in conclave for the next pope would soar when he revealed first the complete map to the Church's treasure vault. Even better if he could actually show them the vault. He had three days tops to accomplish that.

"That is what *Ah* was hopin' to hear, *Yer Eminence*. Let us just treat this rock as a separate transaction apart from puttin' down the target. *Ah* will complete that contract within the next 24 hours. Count on it. That will be a long-distance shot. *Ah* really am not at very much risk. The rock, however, is somethin' else altogether. *Ah* will have to enter the lion's den. There are snipers—trained just like me—along with all sorts of sophisticated intrusion detection devices. *Ah* will be at enormous risk if *Ah* am not careful. *Ah* think $20 million is fair, don't you?"

$20 million, thought Caneman. The truth was he had paid over 10 times that for one of the earlier tablets—and nothing for another. "Yes. Given that you are placing yourself in so much danger to retrieve the tablet I think $20 million is fair. Steep, but fair."

"That's good, *Yer Eminence*. That's *real* good. When *Ah* have completed the first contract and have the rock in *mah* possession *Ah* will call you with delivery instructions for my money and will tell you how you can get the rock." the Professional pressed *End* to cut the connection. He had not revealed just where the target and the rock were located. That was valuable information that he had gone to considerable trouble to obtain. Intellectual property, he called it. No way was he going to reveal it to a mere client. During the entire telephone call he had continued watching Schilling leave the room and come back a short time later with life-size hardcopy photographic prints of the five rocks. He and the target sat side-by-side on the bed twisting and turning the photos, trying to match them to the real one.

He laid the spotting scope aside and thought that if this transaction worked out the way he knew it would, this might be his last assignment. No sense in pressin' one's luck, he whispered into the summer night that enveloped him like a warm cloak. Ever-one's luck runs out some time, don't it?

* * *

Chapter 22

"What are you two doing up at this hour?" asked a sleepy Helen as she stumbled into the Pope's bedroom and leaned against Jack. She hadn't changed out of the XL-sized navy blue shirt with *Carabinieri* emblazoned in gold across the front that she used as a sleeping shirt. It was part of the inventory of clothes the safe house owner kept on hand for its guests.

"Ah, sorry to awaken you, my dear," said the Pope. I had the same reaction when Jack shook me awake a while ago. But it was worth it, believe me—"

"Is that so?" asked Sister Mary Pat as she came in already dressed in her jeans and t-shirt. "And what does young Jack think he is doing pestering an elderly man who is still recuperating from a gunshot wound in the middle of the night?"

The warm summer breeze blew in through the open window, ruffling the curtains. Outside, the horses whinnied and a dog barked at some unseen and inconsequential disturbance. Jack peered out the window briefly, then returned his attention to the room and its new visitors. That was a mistake.

The Pope defended their late night meeting. "It is actually just going on 3:00 in the morning. We were discussing something that cannot wait."

SMP was skeptical. She took nursing His Holiness back to health seriously. "Uh-huh. And just what is so important it cannot wait until morning, after a good night's sleep and a healthy, nourishing breakfast? Hmmm?"

The Pope grabbed Jack's phone off of the bed and fired up the images. "This." He turned the phone around so they could both see what was on its screen.

Both Sister Mary Pat and Helen leaned in to look at the small screen. "Oh my word," said Mary Pat as she looked at the granite tablets with their ornate carvings sitting in their safe deposit boxes. "They have cloned themselves?"

"No, my humorous friend," exclaimed the Pope. He was relishing the excitement after the days of boredom. "Each one is different. These five are the mates to the one we have right here in my strongbox. They are located in...um Jack where did you say they are?"

"I didn't say," answered Jack.

Helen gently took the cell phone from the Pope and looked more closely at it. "That is the inside of a bank vault. Hmmm. If I'm not mistaken it must be in New York. And the only bank vault in New York with any connection to holy artifacts would be—"

"The Vatican Bank vault," answered the Pope and SMP at the same time.

Jack finally gave up his secrecy. "One of my auditors talked her way into Cardinal Caneman's private vault and obtained these photographs about ten minutes ago—I'm not sure how she did it."

"That was Audrey?" asked Helen.

Jack just winked at her in answer.

"Turn it again...no *that* one," said the Pope. They had moved into the dining room where the large table provided a flat surface for them to set the five pages of the tablet photographs from New York alongside the real rock from his strong box.

Helen ran a hand through her hair. "We've been at this an hour. It's not getting us anywhere. No matter which way we turn them or what order we place them, nothing lines up. It's like a puzzle with no solution."

"We need the real things," said Jack. "The jagged edges from when the tablet was split six ways would then line up in a snap."

"The problem, my son, is that we are here and the five tablets are in New York."

Sister Mary Pat said, "What we need is a 3-D graphic printer to make life-size facsimile copies of each tablet. Your auditor took the right photographs. We just need to make the connection."

Helen stopped studying the paper images sitting on the table. "That's it exactly, Mary Pat. If Audrey has a 3-D printer there in Vatican Bank, we can photograph our tablet from all sides and send it to her. Then she can print all six tablets—"

"Oh, oh, I see," exclaimed the Pope, now in total excited comprehension. "Then she can just fit the cut sides together so they align perfectly and *voila*, she has the completed, correct map right there in front of her. Ingenious, Sister Mary Pat."

But Helen was already on the phone, calling Audrey. Sister Mary Pat had taken the new red phone the American President had given to the Pope to begin photographing the real tablet sitting on the table in front of her. "This phone must have the most modern and highest resolution camera yet," she said.

"Okay, Helen," said Audrey. She ended the call, set down her cell phone and waited. She wondered just where she might find the 3D graphic printer Helen talked about. And if she did, how she would figure out how to use it. Audrey knew better than to ask too many questions of either Jack or his wife. She was proud of her ability to figure out how to get things done without being told every step. It was something—one of many things—she respected and admired about her boss. Once he trusted you, he just told you the result he expected, then left you alone to execute and implement whatever it took to achieve them.

He has one helluva reputation, she thought while her laptop lay there, inert. Top-notch accountant, that's for sure. But definitely not just a nerdy bean counter. He knew how to lead. He respected and protected his people. All of us—me included, she admitted—would follow him to the gates of hell and beyond. And that square set of his jaw when he wanted something. Jack Schilling was certainly not one to wait patiently for anything. Like everyone else, she had seen the video last year of Jack drawing down on the assassin in the Oval Office.

He was smooth. The slow motion clips had shown that before the network news organizations yanked them off the air. Even so, she had watched as her boss made his decision in a split second and pulled his pistol from a shoulder holster. With everyone else at the SEC Enforcement Division, she had watched the boss bring the barrel of his gun up, level with first the chest, then the forehead of the President's would-be assailant. The boss's aim was true. The man was dead before he hit the floor. Then Jack had calmly kept the gun leveled at the rest of the Chinese delegation sitting near the President until the Secret Service could regain control of the Oval Office. Jackson Schilling was someone she truly admired. She had seen the tattoos on the insides of his forearms: *The only easy day was yesterday* and that emblem of the Navy SEALS.

It took no more than 90 seconds before Helen's email hit Audrey's laptop computer. She saw the photographs of the sixth tablet attached. She put all the image files of the now six ornately carved rocks on a memory stick and yanked it from the side of her laptop. Audrey looked around the deserted conference room on the 39th floor of the Vatican Bank building. By now it was way past normal working hours and everyone had left. She asked herself where a 3-D graphic printer would be? May as well start in the office services suite, she told herself. That's where they keep all the copier equipment.

Audrey knew what a 3D printer was but had never used one. Their popularity was steadily increasing. She supposed she'd learn how they worked eventually. She just didn't realize it would have to be tonight. She understood they were capable of translating all sorts of media into life sized, 3D replicas of whatever was fed into their readers—engineering drawings, blue prints and photographic images like what Helen had sent her and she had loaded onto the memory stick in her hand. They produced their output in many different mediums—plastic, steel for tools, someday perhaps even human tissue. Still, she didn't know why a bank would need one.

Audrey turned on the lights in the office services suite and began looking around. Everything she saw—every piece of equipment, telephones, computers, large computer screens for detailed graphic display—were new and of the latest generation.

Hmmm, she thought. Okay guys, where do you keep the graphic artists for the documents you release to the public? Ah, she spotted a sign hanging from the ceiling designating the Graphic Arts Department.

Jack Schilling was a combat analyst. His senses operated both on a conscious plane and subconsciously. Earlier he had heard the horses whinnie and the dogs bark at some unseen and inconsequential disturbance. He had consciously heard it. He even peered out the window of the Pope's bedroom briefly to see if any threat existed. Nothing. Probably just a breeze blowing the tall grass; maybe a rodent being taken by a fox in the night. Nothing. As they were all working at the dining room table, trying to fit the paper images of the six pieces of stone tablet into the right alignment and the right order, his subconscious continued working.

Suddenly, the silence of what was *not* present moved from his subconscious and surfaced into his consciousness. Jack had insisted on wearing an ear bud so he could monitor what his four SEALS and the other *Carabinieri* guards were constantly talking about on the communications net at all times. Now the chatter had stopped. His earpiece went eerily silent.

The Professional cycled the bolt of the 98-Bravo. Another .338 Lapua Magnum Long Range Sierra Match King Hollow Point Boat Tail cartridge slid smoothly, then seated into the chamber. Target acquired. Through the Day/Night scope the target looked like a green log with a head, two arms and two legs lying concealed in the tall grass and facing about 45 degrees to his left. The target had all manner of grass and twigs coming out of his clothing so he blended in with his surroundings. But the Professional knew what to look for. The target could not conceal his breathing. No matter how shallow he made it, his silhouette still rose and fell in predictable, regular intervals. That was the dead giveaway. The Professional's finger increased pressure on the trigger. Phhhhfffft. The supersonic round escaped the 27-inch barrel, extended another 12 inches by the silencer. Elapsed time

205

from when he cycled the bolt until the target lay inert forevermore: 3.2 seconds.

"Three down. Three to go," his Louisiana drawl whispered to the rocks surrounding him. "Time for some fireworks."

"Get down," said Jack. His order wasn't shouted, nor was it panicked. Instead, it was a command with such an urgent intensity that Helen, Sister Mary Pat and the Pope could not ignore it. They instantly looked up from their work on the images of the stone tablets. Each paused for just a second to understand Jack's command. Then all three dived for the floor beneath the table.

Jack's palm slapped the large red push-button on the dining room wall plate. The entire house instantly went black. The *Carabinieri* had installed master kill switches for the lighting in every room throughout their safe house. At least they got that right, thought Jack. He grabbed his M4A1 assault rifle from its place leaning against the table's leg just 12 inches away. He swiftly crawled toward the window overlooking the front yard. Jack felt Smitty's presence now right beside him.

"Heard—rather didn't hear—the same thing you did, boss," said Smitty. "Comm net is operating. I heard you call, *get down* and came a-runnin'. Both men peered into the blackness outside.

The Professional looked at the luminous buttons on his radio frequency control console. Several days ago he had set up his arsenal of diversions around the rock outcropping surrounding the farmhouse. His finger hovered over the pushbutton on the top row, left. He looked up, noticing the farmhouse suddenly plunge into darkness. Every light went dark at the same instant. "Well, that's no s'prise," he calmly whispered. Ol' Jackson Schilling was prob'ly listening for his sentries and didn't hear anythin' so he hit the panic button. Won't help him. Nothin'l help him now. The Professional felt

206

no remorse, no regret. This was a job. Nothing more. Finish it, then move on to the next.

The Professional looked down once again at the glow of buttons on his control console. His finger selected one then firmly pressed it. From the southern-most end of his rocky hillside—about 300 meters away a *whoosh* sounded in the night as the launch tube fired the first of the RPGs. The Professional held his binoculars on the target at which he had aimed the remote launcher. The rocket propelled grenade left a gray exhaust trail, just visible against the night sky, as it streaked toward its target. The wood stairway leading up the porch to the front door of the farmhouse suddenly exploded into slivers of wood and pieces of the supporting stones.

The Professional was on the move. Things would happen rapidly now. He pressed three more of the buttons on his control console as he moved among the rocks of his hide. Now the farmhouse and the front and back yards were exploding as the Professional's carefully aimed ordnance hit their targets. He paused after ten more steps, leaned against a boulder for support, rested the 98-Bravo's barrel on a sand bag sitting on the rocks in front of him. He had prepositioned the firing post during his planning of the assault. He had located his next target over an hour ago. He squeezed the trigger. Phhhhfffft. The target's shallow breathing ceased forever.

The Professional moved twice more; twice firing with the same deadly results. Then, with the sentries down, he left the safety of his hide and quickly made his way toward the farmhouse. He had three more buttons on his console left to fire. He pressed one when he reached a point 100 yards from the farmhouse. Suddenly the shed in back where he had seen the technicians working and controlling their drone aircraft exploded in a hail of splinters. It was instantly ablaze. The Professional didn't waste any time in advancing on the farmhouse.

Jack raised his head. He peeked over the windowsill. He was just in time to see the gray exhaust trail of the next RPG arcing across the still-black sky and heading toward the bedroom wing of the farmhouse. He moved to duck behind the couch and covered Helen with his body, waiting for the explosion to come. Suddenly the entire house rocked with the RPG's concussive force. A cloud of dust from the century-old structure blew through the living and dining rooms where they were huddled together, covering everything with gray dust.

"What," said Sister Mary Pat managing to maintain the calm in her voice, "did they bring an army to attack us?"

Jack and Smitty's eyes met. Both said at the same time, "Force projection."

"What is that," SMP asked, "a new kind of weapon?"

"No," answered Helen as she wriggled out from beneath her husband and took a deep breath, then coughed out a lung full of the choking dust. "It's a technique to make your small force seem much larger than it is."

Just then the staccato sound of automatic rifle fire sounded from right inside the front yard. It was close. No more than 50 yards away. The walls around them exploded as if they were matchsticks. The *Carabinieri's* safe house was not armored. It was never intended to be impenetrable. The old structure could not withstand attack from modern weapons. It protected its occupants from the simple fact that no one knew where it—or they—were located. Except today.

Jack crawled back to the front window as bullets whizzed overhead. They sounded like a herd of angry hornets before smacking into the walls with a violent thud. He raised his M4 rifle and loosed a deadly stream of lead from one end of the front yard to the other. But he stayed exposed a fraction of a second too long. A bullet smashed through the windowsill and buried itself in the muscle inside his left shoulder, right next to the axillary artery—the large blood vessel that carries oxygenated blood into the arm and chest. Jack felt the round hit, knew the armor hadn't stopped it. There wasn't much pain, just a dull ache on his side. He kept firing—no time to take inventory of the hit. He saw his vision growing narrow as if looking through a tube that was getting smaller and smaller. Everything was getting cold. Very cold. Then the blackness of the night enveloped him and he collapsed. The M4 fell silent, still in his hands.

"Jack," screamed Helen when she heard his rifle stop firing and saw him crumple beneath the window. She crab-walked to him, ignoring the bullets still flying overhead. This was the man she thought was made of steel rather than flesh and bone. It never occurred to her that he could be taken down. Her only thought was to get who did this to Jack. She snatched up his M4 and fired into the front yard until its magazine was exhausted. Then, without thinking, Jack's year of training her kicked in. She reached down to his motionless leg and grabbed the fresh magazine he always kept in the left front pocket of his cargo pants and smacked it into the M4's receiver. Savagely, she grabbed the bolt and cycled it, chambering the next round. Her finger curved around the trigger and she started pulling in controlled, short two-burst volleys.

The Professional entered from the back of the house. He was clad entirely in black and wore body armor over his chest and legs. No helmet. He didn't want anything obstructing his peripheral vision. He figured the target would likely be in the front room where he had watched them all working earlier. He swiftly and silently rounded the corner doorway leading into the large room. With controlled, bursts from his rifle, the Professional placed shots in the most likely places anyone could hide. He was rewarded when the old man stood up from behind the couch and actually advanced on him. He knew exactly who this was. The Pope had no weapon. Of course he wouldn't, the Professional thought, he is a man of God. Instead, he held out his steel crucifix as if it were armor plating. The Professional heard him say in Italian, "Stop in the name of the Pope and the Roman Catholic Church."

It didn't take more than a half second. The Professional raised his assault rifle and shot the target twice in the chest. He crumpled to the floor. What he failed to see during the short time he was fixated on the target were the other two on either side of the doorway and now two feet behind him as he advanced further into the room.

Sister Mary Pat loved her Pope. First as leader of her Church. But even more so as her friend. She paused only for a split second, seeing him crumble to the floor, suddenly inert. The basest of instincts took over. Her beloved friend was dead. Killed by this monster. He would die too. She grabbed up the wrought iron shovel from the fireplace set, hefted it to her shoulder and swung it at him with all of her 115-pound strength. She should have taken the heavy poker. The shovel lost some of its velocity due to the wind resistance its flat surface created. Even so, when it hit his shoulder, the blow was strong enough to spin him around. But the fireplace shovel bounced off the body armor protecting his shoulder.

From the other side of the door jam, Helen saw Mary Pat pull back the shovel for another attempt. She raised Jack's M4. Over the last year in Elkhart, he had taught her how to use many tactical weapons. Now this compact, automatic rifle felt as familiar in her hands as her own toothbrush. Time slowed as Jack had promised it did for all warriors during combat. She watched as if detached from the scene as the barrel of the assault rifle came up to the center of the target's chest. She squeezed the trigger as Jack had taught her, allowing the kick of the rounds to raise the barrel up, stitching the armored chest with lead right into his head. The intruder's brain sprayed over the once white walls with bone, gray matter and blood spatter. He collapsed to the floor. His rifle fell from his hands. No threat to anyone, anymore.

Helen didn't waste any time watching. She whirled around with the rifle's muzzle pointed outward, scanning her target area for any new threats to come her way. Now the house and its surroundings were eerily silent. Nothing moved. Then she heard the heavy shovel hit the floor with a solitary clatter as Mary Pat dropped it. The grief-stricken nun went to her friend, the Pope. Helen went to Jack.

210

Back in New York in the offices of the Vatican Bank, Audrey slid the memory stick into the desktop computer that had a thick black cable snaking into the 3D graphics printer. She stared in amazement as the computer read the content of her memory stick and brought up the printing menu for the 3D printer.

"Okay," she whispered softly in the empty room, "what now?" But the printer software walked her through each of the five steps she needed to begin printing the first stone tablet. She waited while the amazing printer thought about printing her tablet. The print routine was automated. How about that, she thought.

Then slowly, up from the plotting board rose a neon green, 3-dimensional replica of the first stone tablet in ABS plastic. Having seen the real thing in Cardinal David Caneman's vault earlier she figured it to be about half scale. She watched as it grew out of the printer's plotting bed. "This is even greater detail than I had imagined," said aloud as she eyed the thick, ragged sides of the stone and saw how they were fractured and split from when Pope Alexander VI broke it apart centuries ago. "So this is how Helen thinks I'm going to fit the six stones together and solve her puzzle for her."

Audrey didn't waste any time. She didn't want to be caught in here. When the first tablet was done printing, she carefully removed it to allow it to cool and immediately set the printer to rendering the next tablet. She took a red felt tipped pen from the caddy on the graphic designer's desk and wrote the file number on the top of the first tablet. She ran her hand over the top, her fingers slid over the rough sides of its ornate carving and lettering.

By the time she got to the fourth of six tablets, Audrey felt she might have overstayed her welcome. Her watch said it was past one in the morning. If a night guard saw the lights and heard her working in these spaces she would have a hard time explaining herself. As fast as the little printer was, it seemed to move with agonizing slowness. "Like any computer, she said softly. The more urgent your project, the slower they seem to go."

Suddenly, she heard the door to the Office Services suite rattle. Audrey had pulled the door shut after her when she entered. It locked electronically after her. All the auditors had master card keys allowing them entry into all but the most sensitive areas of the bank. She could see the beam from a flashlight moving up and down through the cracks in the doorframe outside. The printer was still running. Even though it sounded like a small vacuum cleaner, the noise right now, at this hour, seemed deafening. Then the night guard left as quickly and silently as he had come.

Audrey let out a long, relieved breath as the fifth replica of the stone tablet slowly sprouted up from the plotting bed. She picked it up, marked it and set it alongside the other four. The sixth and final one had already begun its print run.

Fifteen minutes later she had the last one. "What now?" she thought as she eyed the line of neon green stone tablet replicas. But even then she could see how the sixth stone that Helen had sent could actually be the key to the puzzle. It was the only one with ragged edges on all four sides. The others had at least one smooth side, designating it as an outside edge. "Just like a jigsaw puzzle," she whispered to herself.

She set Helen's stone tablet in the middle and began trying to fit the others around it. Each side was enormously detailed in its niches and grooves. Like a piece of broken ceramic, there was a perfect fit for each one. Other ways might be close. But in the end there was only one perfect fit.

There. She found the first match. The tablet edges just slid in place like they belonged to one another, which they did. But they hadn't been together in centuries. Audrey looked at the perfect seam. She grabbed both replicas and tried to slide them apart. Their nooks and crannies grabbed one another and prevented any movement.

"Perfect," she said. "Next." Audrey picked up another tablet. From here, it was only a little easier. She had one tablet, true, and now just six sides to try fitting it into. After five minutes of trying every combination of side matching, she looked down on the inscriptions. The one she had in her hand seemed to be a continuation of the second stone. Though she couldn't read the writing, it seemed that a little swirl on one continued right into the next. She tried it.

The stone replicas slid into their correct places. Audrey blew out a ragged breath. Three down and three to go, she thought. She had been at the matching for 90 minutes now. The last three took just 30 minutes to match.

She sat back against the chair and looked at her handiwork. There before her on the graphic artist's desk sat the Vatican's map to a legendary vault of untold riches—all in neon green ABS plastic. She lifted her cell phone and took photos of the completed puzzle from all angles including several from overhead, looking down on the map.

Just then the electronic card reader controlling the door to the Graphics Department cycled. The door slammed open. Audrey heard the sound of heavy boots entering the outer rooms. Lights suddenly glared all over. The door to the Graphic Arts suite smashed inward and three men rushed her.

She had no warning. She was caught sitting at the desk, the six stone replicas before her arranged in their perfect order. She slid her phone into the desk drawer and shut it. The three men were across the room and on her in the next second. The lead man grabbed the neon green replicas. The second man backhanded her across the jaw with such force that it knocked her off the chair and slammed her head into the corner of the desk. She was only vaguely aware of the kicks and punches that followed before she passed out.

Smitty knelt beside Jack and looked down at his face. It was the color of pale parchment. A gray blanket of dust covered everything in the old Italian farmhouse. Even the air was so thick they chewed, rather than breathed it.

"Okay, boss, here's what we've got," said Smitty in his precise military voice. "You took one to the side of your upper chest. From the loss of blood I see, looks like it may have nicked the axillary artery."

Jack made his eyes look up at his SEAL partner and best friend, then at Helen who kneeled beside him, holding his hand. He couldn't move so he blinked twice.

"Good, buddy. You understand. You're conscious and coherent. That's all I need to know. I'm not much of a surgeon but I'm the best you got right here, right now. We're gonna save you, buddy."

Jack moved his eyes to the left toward the Pope.

Helen understood what his eye movement actually meant. "His Holiness was shot at. Two bullets to his chest. But somehow they didn't penetrate. Lots of blood, but it looks worse than it is."

Two more blinks.

"He's breathing, sweetie. Mary Pat just said she has an erratic pulse—A-fib it sounds like. The man's over 80 years old and frail."

Two blinks.

"Work on him first? I knew you'd say that. We did. He's as stable as we can get him. Smitty had the *Carabinieri* order up a chopper. It's 15 minutes out. That's supersonic for Italy, even for the Pope. They don't know the identity of their patient. They'll transport him to the Level 1 trauma center at Niguarda Ca'Granda Hospital in Milan. There's nothing with the capabilities he needs any closer. Sister Mary Pat used her influence to get a hospital jet fueled and waiting on the runway at Leonardo Da Vince airport. They'll have a fully staffed trauma facility on board for the 46 minute flight."

"No more talk," ordered Smitty.

Two blinks.

"Nonsense, buddy. I'm your best hope. The way I look at it," Smitty gently plunged the hypodermic needle filled with a measured dose of morphine into Jack's right arm, "you got no downside here." He watched Jack's already hooded eyes close.

Smitty had already washed his hands in the kitchen sink and then poured iodine over them from the extensive first aid kit he found in the safe house basement. He pulled on the latex gloves from the first aid kit and rinsed them in iodine too. He carefully pulled away Jack's shirt and the Kevlar vest he had still been wearing since his last patrol outside an hour ago. The bullet had entered the unprotected side of his chest where the two sections of Kevlar didn't quite meet.

"Bad luck," was all Smitty said as he pulled the plain white gauze that Helen had put over the bullet hole while they had attended to the Pope earlier. The wound began to seep blood once the gauze pack was removed. Smitty grabbed a forceps from the kit, spread the sides of the hole apart and carefully probed the area.

"Hmmm. Maybe we got lucky here," he said shining his hi-intensity light into the wound as the forceps and his fingers parted the flesh. He poked a second hemostat into the wound, opening a deep path all the way inside until he could see the axillary artery. "It's intact, Helen. The artery wasn't nicked. With all the blood, I feared the worst, but it's the secondary vessels surrounding the major axillary artery that are bleeding. Bad. But not *that* bad. Our boy isn't out of the woods by any means. But…well, let's just see what we can do until the helo gets here to transport our two patients.

Smitty continued poking with the forceps until he hit something solid. "There you are, you SOB," he said. He clamped the forceps around the object, careful to avoid any contact with the axillary artery. He carefully pulled out the forceps. In its pincers was the 9-millimeter bullet that had caused his friend such grief. It was deformed, probably from having ricocheted off of a rib, bouncing around inside and finally lodging just beside the axillary artery. The wound began bleeding profusely from all the pushing and pulling Smitty was doing.

He dropped the bullet in his hand and quickly rolled it on his pants leg to get off most of the blood, then put it in his pocket. Jack will want this later, he told himself. Yes you will, buddy.

215

And I'll be there to give it to you. Then, to Helen, "Reach into the kit and pull out three green packets of QuickClot combat gauze." Just like Jack, Smitty's voice was controlled, commanding and not in any way panicked. Just deliberate and very focused.

Helen saw them immediately. The packages were an unmistakable olive drab green. They were clearly marked as QuickClot and had six niches for easy tearing with bloody fingers all around the package. She tore the top from the first pack and pulled the end of the gauze out.

"That's perfect, Hon. Just that much exposed to this dirty atmosphere at a time." Smitty took the pack in his bloody, gloved hands and began feeding the QuickClot combat gauze from its sterile package into the bullet hole.

"This stuff will stop the bleeding within two or three minutes," he said. "It's got a coagulating medication impregnated into the fabric. Begins working on contact with blood."

He was careful not to further tear any of the surrounding blood vessels as he packed the wound tightly. And he was especially careful when he reached the depth of the major axillary artery. He kept gently feeding the gauze into the entrance wound, pushing it into the bullet hole and surrounding tissue with his index finger. When one packet was completely fed into the wound, he looked up. Helen had already torn open the second gauze pack and handed it to him, exposed end first. The bullet hole took just over half of the second pack before it was complete and tightly filled.

When he was satisfied he couldn't get any more into the wound, Smitty squared up the remaining gauze with surgical scissors from the first aid kit to make a neat bandage and laid it over the wound. Then he opened the next gauze pack and began wrapping the wound tightly, making a combat field pressure bandage. When he was done, he had a neat, sterile bandage that showed no sign of further bleeding.

216

Next, he inserted one empty green pack of QuickClot under one of the bandage seams so the physician who saw Jack would know that a hemostatic agent was used on the wound. Finally, he completed the patient card that came with the QuickClot pack and gave them as much information about Jack and the wound as he could. He inserted that beneath the bandage as well. Lastly, he injected Jack with a syringe of antibiotics from the kit into his arm and patted him on the shoulder.

Audrey awoke to the dark room. Her head throbbed where it had smashed into the corner of the desk. She tentatively put her hand to the worst of the pain and felt the thick wetness of her own blood, sticky in her matted hair. She slowly sat up there on the dark floor of the graphic design space and immediately felt a wave of nausea roll over her. The side of her face was a mass of pain where the second thug had hit her. After a few more breaths she could feel where they had punched and kicked her. It hurt her chest to breathe. Probably broke a rib, she thought.

After a moment, she tried slowly swiveling her head. She scanned the room. No one here but me, she told herself when she was satisfied that she was alone. The computer was still powered up; so was the 3D graphics printer. Just as she left them. Then she noticed that the 6 half-size neon green plastic replicas of the stone tablets she had printed were gone. That must be what they wanted, she reasoned. She looked on the side of the computer where she had inserted the memory stick containing the files she had printed. Empty. Then she remembered that it also contained the SEC's workpapers, notes and a draft of the audit team's report.

That made her mad. Those workpapers and notes are SEC property. They are confidential and not to be shared with any third parties. She felt awful. It was her job as the audit senior on the job to ensure proper custodianship of all confidential documents associated with the project. What's Jack going to think of me now? His good opinion of her was something she valued above almost anyone else's in her life. Of course she would call him immediately and confess her error. She would explain. Not embellish. Nor would she offer any excuse. Just state the facts, then throw herself on his mercy. He was a fair man, she knew. Still, from experience, she also knew that he did not tolerate such breaches and prepared herself for whatever might come.

Audrey slowly and gingerly curled her feet up under her and grabbed on to the side of the desk. Using her arms and legs she slowly pushed and pulled herself into a standing position. Her head hurt like hell. So did her chest and ribs where they kicked her. But she was up. She leaned over and flipped the light switch on the wall next to the desk.

She heard a ringing sound. At first she thought it was from inside her head. Then she recognized her own cell phone's antique bell ringer tone. It was muffled. Out of the fog of her struggling memory she recalled putting the smartphone inside the graphic designer's desk drawer when the intruders rushed into the room. The ringing persisted a fourth time. They must not have seen me put it there, she thought. Audrey reached inside, snatched up the phone and answered the call. Caller ID on the screen said it was Helen from somewhere in Italy.

"Hello? Helen?"

"Audrey, yes, yes it's me. You don't sound so good. Are you okay, sweetie?"

Even though the boss's wife wasn't even 10 years older than most of the auditors, she had assumed the role of den mother when Jack was assigned this one last case. She made sure they ate, had plenty to drink and insisted that Jack send them all home when she saw the schedule was wearing everyone out. In some cases, Helen had a faster line of communication with the audit staff than did the boss.

"No, Helen. No I'm not okay. I was just attacked by three thugs right here in Vatican Bank. They stole the replicas of the stone tablets I had printed for you. I'm so sorry—"

"Screw that, Audrey. Your wellbeing is far more important than those plastic replicas. That's why I was calling. My idea of using that to solve the puzzle probably wouldn't have worked anyway."

Audrey was feeling better just speaking with Helen. "You were calling to see how I was feeling? Why?"

Suddenly Helen's voice took on a faraway tone. "Because, sweetie, we were also attacked. By a professional. By a guy who knew what he was doing. I wanted to be sure they didn't connect us with you."

"And the boss? Jack wasn't hurt, was he?"

It took Helen a heartbeat to find her voice. "Jack was hurt, yes. Very badly. He's lost a lot of blood. Right now I'm on an air ambulance flying from Rome to the trauma center hospital in Milan. I didn't have a moment to call you until now." Helen looked from her seat across the aisle of the converted Boeing 737 hospital jet. There were two trauma teams aboard. One was dedicated to the Pope, the other to Jack. They were the only two patients on a jet equipped to handle four times that.

Audrey blurted, "Jack was hurt?" She had always thought of him as a rock that nothing could even scratch. It wasn't just his physically imposing stature and hard-muscled physique. It was his intellect—sharp as a skinning knife. She heard stories of how Jack Schilling would verbally put down any CEO who dared attempt to intimidate one of his auditors. He dealt with them swiftly and finally. Then, in private, he would calmly speak with the auditor to find out what happened. If the auditor was at fault, they would be knocked down, but then picked up, dusted off and made sure that they had learned from the experience so it would never be repeated. But the boss would do it in private. Never with anyone else present to cause undue embarrassment to the person.

Audrey had once heard Jack raise his voice to the chairman of a publicly held rail company. They were in the chairman's office behind closed doors, so he must have been shouting at the man. He began saying that the auditor in question had his complete faith and trust. And that he personally knew him to be one of the finest, most honest and careful young men God had ever placed here on this earth. Before Jack excused himself

Audrey had heard him end by saying, *Sir, you would do well to strive for half the integrity of the young man about whom you are complaining.*

"But he's going to be okay, isn't he?" asked Audrey.

"I don't know, sweetie. They're doing everything they can. The next 24 hours will tell."

Audrey couldn't think of anything to say. So she apologized for not protecting the replicas of the tablets.

"That's okay, honey. It's minor compared to what else has happened—"

"But I took pictures." Audrey's brain had reengaged. "Before they attacked me, I was able to assemble the puzzle perfectly. I presumed that's why you wanted me to make the graphic replicas. You were right. They eventually fit together. I took photos from all sides and then from above the completed puzzle."

There was silence on the other end as Helen digested this bit of new information. "Did you now, Audrey. You solved the puzzle and took pictures of the completed map? Using your cell phone, I presume?"

"Uh huh."

"Well, sweetie, do you think you might be able to email me those photos?"

Audrey took her phone from her ear, placed it on speaker and accessed her email. "The best ones are on their way, Helen."

Helen said, "Thank you, sweetie. Now you go and make sure all the doors to your area are locked tight. Then just sit right down and get comfy. I'm calling the police and paramedics for you as soon as I get off the phone. I've Googled the exact longitude and latitude coordinates for your location. Don't move. Engine Company 28 is just one block away from you. They have a paramedic ambulance right there. I've passed them dozens of times. I will give them all the information and my contact info so I can check up on how you're doing. As of right now, you're on the bench. Understood?"

"Yes, Ma'am," answered Audrey. "You sound like the boss."

"A kinder, gentler boss, I hope. But when it comes to you—all of you—regarding your wellbeing I have the same steel spine. Stay put. I just received your email with the photos. Gotta go. Jack is waking up." With one eye on Jack and the other on her cell phone, Helen called the New York City Fire Department, Engine Company 28 and then the NYPD to get them over to Audrey's location.

Jack was indeed waking up. He was agitated, arms and legs moving in uncontrolled spasms. The doctor and two nurses surrounded his bed that was bolted to the plane's bulkhead. Suddenly the slow, steady rhythm of his heart rate monitor was interrupted. It went into intermittent pulses and finally began speeding way up beyond normal.

Hypovolemic shock," said the doctor. His voice was urgent, but not panicked. Jack had lost a lot of blood. So much that there wasn't enough flowing
through his body's organs. His skin was cold and pale. His blood pressure plummeted.

The doctor said to the nurse "Hypertonic saline. Push it to accelerated flow." Immediately one of Jack's nurses hung a new bag from the overhead hooks surrounding his bed. She quickly plugged the new bag into the IV line already attached and adjusted the drip monitor machine.

Within just a few minutes Helen could hear Jack's heart rate monitor beeping out what sounded to her like a more normal rhythm. "What's happening to him, Doctor?" she asked.

The Italian ER physician checked Jack's vitals on the monitors attached to the bulkhead surrounding him, then turned to her. "Mr. Schilling has lost almost 35 percent of his total blood volume. The heart beat monitor you heard sounding rapidly erratic was his body trying to make up for the loss in blood volume. I pushed into him a large dose of hypertonic solution—actually 7.5 percent sodium chloride, super salt water. It acts like magnets, drawing fluid from tissues into the bloodstream. That's how I was able to increase his blood volume so quickly. I've already ordered a transfusion when we get to the hospital—"

"Just tell me the prognosis," said Helen, cutting him off.

The doctor looked at her for a moment. "The good news is that your husband is in phenomenally good shape physically. If there was ever a patient with a likelihood of coming out of such trauma without lingering aftereffects, it is he. He got exactly the right first aid before we arrived. Whoever removed the bullet saved us the time of doing it and greatly reduced the risk of it shifting during transport, possibly nicking the axillary artery. They did a good job. The hospital in Milan is a Level 1 trauma center. If I were your husband with this injury, it is where I would want to be taken. For the next 20 minutes of this flight, there is nothing you can do. Please, just try to relax. We'll watch Mr. Schilling. Look. Already his skin color is improving and his heartbeat is moving into a more stable rhythm."

Helen looked across the aisle at Jack. The doctor was right. He was still asleep, but his color had returned a bit. She put her arm around Smitty who was standing beside Jack's bed, one hand on his shoulder. The man hadn't left Jack's side the entire flight. "You did good, Smitty. The doctor said so." Helen was trying to take his mind off of Jack for at least a few minutes.

"The Navy taught us all basic first aid. Then in the teams we all seemed to get way too much practical field experience in stitching up one another. It was a procedure I've done before, though usually with more than one shooter continuing to fire at me and my patient." Smitty shook his head. "Jack's one tough cowboy. He'll make it through this."

"And you kept the bullet you dug out of him," said Helen, "I saw you drop it into your pocket."

Smitty nodded his great head, "You don't miss much, Hon. It's tradition. We all keep the metal shot into us by the bad guys—"

"Jack too?"

"You mean he's never shown you his collection?" Smitty grinned. "It's really something. Quite diverse."

222

Helen wasn't surprised. Even after a year of marriage, the depth of her husband seemed bottomless. She had seen the scars over various parts of his body. Of course she had. When she asked about them, he just smiled and said that it was the price of freedom. He had never shown her the bullet collection Smitty spoke of. "So what do we do after everyone is okay?"

"We go take care of who ever hired this guy. He was one of us, you know."

Helen nodded. "Jack told me. One of the best snipers who ever came out of the teams—"

Just then alarms from the monitors connected to the Pope went off. Helen heard at least two, maybe more, she couldn't be sure over the roar of the jet engines in the cabin. She watched as the medical team watching over His Holiness quickly went into action. They had no idea who the man really was. Helen first saw them shove Sister Mary Pat out of the way. Like Smitty, she hadn't left her friend's side since they left the farmhouse, boarded the chopper, then were loaded onto this jet ambulance.

Helen saw what seemed a well-choreographed dance of hands and instruments. All led by the physician in charge of the Pope. Helen cast a questioning look toward Jack's physician who was also turned toward the emergency now taking place in the aft part of the jet.

"Myocardial infarction," he said. "Heart attack." He stood by, making no move toward the team unless and until he was asked. "They're giving him Plavix, a drug that acts like a super aspirin to prevent any more new clots from forming. In a minute, they'll call ahead to the hospital's cardiac catheter lab to prepare for an emergency angioplasty. They need to open his blocked coronary arteries to allow the blood to flow more freely to his heart."

"Doc, what do his gunshot wounds have to do with a heart attack?" asked Smitty.

"Right. I examined him before we took off. He *was* shot twice. You are correct. But your friend is one of the luckiest people on God's green earth. Neither bullet did much harm compared to what they could have done. The blood everyone saw was actually collateral damage. Purely superficial. One bullet hit a big steel cross he was wearing. It apparently ricocheted harmlessly away. The cross had sharp edges though. It sliced across his chest on impact, cutting a shallow six-inch gash. That is what caused all the blood you saw. Messy, but nothing serious. He'll have a bruise in the shape of his cross for a while. The other shot hit a small bible he kept in his breast pocket. It penetrated the bible right up to the book of Revelations—"

"The last book in the bible," said Helen. "Almost the very end."

"That's right, Mrs. Schilling. The very end. The bullet pierced the skin and bruised a rib. Again, it made a bloody mess, but did no real damage. In all they took 52 stitches to patch him up. Is this man a priest?" asked the doctor.

Helen said, "He's just a very, very good man."

"So what knocked him out?" asked Smitty.

"He is an elderly man who apparently leads a rather sedentary life," answered the physician. "Certainly there was a huge concussion from the bullets hitting him. Probably knocked the wind out of him. Brain function seems fine. That trauma and maybe the shock from having a gun fired at him just knocked him unconscious. The heart attack is probably unrelated to the gunshot. Just a coincidence of timing. Imagine how you would feel if the same thing happened to you."

"It has, Doc. More than once," said Smitty. He nodded toward Jack, "It has to your patient over there too."

The air ambulance was cleared for immediate landing at Milan's Linate airport. It was smaller than Malpensa airport that served most of the intercontinental flights. Linate was also closer to Niguarda Ca'Granda Hospital. Helen felt the 737 jet hit the runway, heard the roar of the engines as the pilot used his thrust reversers to immediately slow the plane. The deceleration threw her against her seat belt. Then back again when the plane lurched to a full stop. It was the fastest stop on a jet she had ever experienced. Through the windows she saw the red and cobalt flashing lights of four Italian *Carabinieri* cars standing guard and a helicopter with its rotor blades already spinning.

She stood out of the way as the doctors already had their two critical patients readied for transport. In what seemed seconds they were all off the jet and seated in the chopper. She heard the roar of its engine as the pilot spooled up the rotor and they lifted off in a high-speed sweeping turn over the terminal, making a fast, low-level dash for Ca'Granda Hospital.

"How are you fairing, Honey," came the soft voice from the back of the helicopter. Helen turned around to see Mr. Schilling, Jack's father.

"How did you get here so fast?" She couldn't stand in the crowded medevac helicopter what with two patients, two doctors, two nurses, Smitty, Sister Mary Pat, her and now Mr. Schilling. Instead she reached her hand back and across the isle to grasp her father-in-law's outstretched hand. They clasped for a full minute. Contact with the man she had become so close to even before she fell in love with his son during the *Deadly Acceleration* episode last year felt reassuring. She didn't want to let go of his warm grasp.

"I was already in the air when Smitty called my cell and told me what happened and where you were headed. I simply had my pilot divert the G650 to Milan instead of Rome. Made a few calls to some contacts to find out where you were and to get me on this bird. Here I am. Easy." His eyes took on a more serious glare. "How are both of our boys?"

Helen told her father-in-law what the doctors explained about Jack's condition and the low blood volume. Mr. Schilling nodded gravely. She knew he had heard such medical news about his son before. Then she explained about the Pope's relatively minor collateral injuries and the heart attack that followed. That was the serious injury. "Both guys are in critical condition. His Holiness is elderly, so between the two, he's in worse shape. Jack, of course, is Jack. Nothing can stop him."

"You better believe it, Hon. I've never known Jackson to walk away from a fight. He's tough and has that Schilling will to live. He'll make it," Mr. Schilling finished as he pulled his cell phone out and punched a button on speed dial. Helen heard him say, "Hi Gracie, Jack Schilling here. Is the President available?" Apparently he was available to him because Schilling began talking after a pause of only seconds.

* * *

Chapter 23

The President sat up in his chair. He ground his cell phone into his ear and nodded gravely. He muttered a few, "Uh huh's," then thanked Jack Schilling, his head of the IRS Offshore Asset Collection Division. "Keep me informed as to his progress—"

His secretary in the anteroom outside the Oval Office buzzed him on the Critical Line. She never did that unless it was important. They had a standing agreement: when she buzzed him on that particular line, he dropped everything and picked up. No exceptions.

"Wait just a second, Jack. Gracie's buzzing me. Stand by." The President picked up the Critical Line. "Yes?"

"Mr. President, the Navy SEALs are here to see you, sir."

"The SEALs?" The President was a Marine. He still thought of himself as a Marine. All Marines—no matter their age or time out of uniform—thought of themselves as Marines and would until the day they died. He guessed it was the same for the SEALs. "Tom Nickl?" Commander Thomas Nickl ran the SEAL teams currently in operation on the east coast. He was as gravel-voiced and hard-bitten as they come. He was also armed with a Ph.D. from Georgetown in International Relations.

"No sir. In point of fact, the Marine standing post at the Northwest Appointments Gate says it is the Naval Special Warfare Group-II. *America's Squadron*, sir." General Charles Krulack, the 31st Commandant of the Marine Corps. and a diehard Dallas Cowboys fan had given Group-II the moniker, *America's Squadron* in a manner similar to his beloved Cowboys who were called, *America's Team*. It stuck.

The President knew the G-II well. He had been a gun-totting leatherneck during the first Gulf War. The G-II had been there right beside him. They had a proud and storied history reaching back to the Viet Nam era. More of this unit's men were killed or wounded in combat than any other expeditionary force in America's military. They were indeed, *America's Squadron* as they quietly said, because boasting was not the SEAL's way.

"What's his name, Gracie?"

"Sir…it's not just one man—"

The President noticed a silence sweeping through the West Wing. He noticed because this was one of the noisiest offices in which he had ever worked. Phones rang all the time. The clatter of computer keyboards was incessant and people were talking—sometimes loudly, passionately arguing—in the hallways. Now all that had suddenly stopped. Dead silence echoed around him.

"Well how many SEALs could there be who want to see me today, Gracie?"

"Sir, the Gate says there are 243 members of the Naval Special Warfare Group-II who have come to see you."

The President turned around to look through the thick, ballistic glass windows that lined the wall behind his desk. Sure enough, he spotted two neat lines of men, women and children standing at attention and politely waiting permission to step through the Northwest Gate and into the White House compound. Still the White House was eerily quiet. Never had the President heard such silence around him in his six years in office.

"Ah, okay, Gracie. Whatever it is they want, I'm definitely going to listen. Tell the Gate to admit them." That's a lot of people for the Oval Office, he thought. "Gracie, please ask them to file onto the South Lawn. It's a nice summer day. They'll be comfortable there." The President looked at his watch. "And Gracie?"

"Yes, sir?"

"Apologize for the short notice, but call down to the mess and ask them to rustle up drinks and lunch for 243 of our finest Americans."

"Already done, sir. They're rolling out the barbeques and basting up ribs, dogs and burgers."

"Perfect, thanks. And Gracie, I think we still have the Navy band in the Rose Garden after the First Lady's address. Please ask them to relocate to the South Lawn and prepare to play the

SEAL's song." The President set down the telephone receiver. Whatever it is they want, ribs, burgers and their song should be appropriate under any circumstances. He picked up his cell phone on the desk, the line still open. The eerie silence almost echoed in the most important office on earth. He looked out the windows again.

He saw young men still wearing the uniform. Older men wearing only the green blouse that they still had. Some wore green campaign hats. There were women in street clothes carrying small flags. There were children too. Some of the men were on crutches, at least 20 were in wheel chairs, pushed by Marines currently serving and wearing their Dress Blues.

He picked up his cell phone. "Jack, you still there?"

"Yes, Mr. President. And I heard everything. Damn, it's quiet there for once. So you have some visitors?"

"Any idea what they want?"

Jackson Schilling said, "I think I do, sir. This will be a tearjerker if I'm right. Sir, this is why you sought the Presidency. These men have taken bullets for you. Many have died for you. So have their sons, brothers, husbands, fathers and grandfathers. Treat them with reverence and respect. Don't blow it, Sir. And Sir, the SEALs don't have a song. They're not like the Marines with their Hymn or the Navy with that *Anchors Away.* Maybe just have the Navy band play *God Bless America.*"

The President put his cell phone back in his pocket. Then he heard it. Applause. It began as a single person clapping out at the Northwest Gate. Then two, then four. *America's Squadron* marched into the compound in two neat, orderly rows. Gardeners dressed in green set down their rakes; caretakers in their white jumpsuits dropped their brooms; men and women dressed in business suits urgently rushing in and out of the White House suddenly stopped out of respect. As the first SEALs marched silently past each of the onlookers, briefcases fell to the ground and their owners began clapping too. At any one time there are several hundred people in and around the White House and its grounds. Today each stopped what they were doing and clapped. They didn't stop clapping as they all followed

America's Squadron onto the South Lawn. Not until the last member of Naval Special Warfare Group-II—all 243 of them today—was safely inside the compound did the clapping stop. Mr. Schilling was right. This was going to be a real tearjerker.

The President also dropped what he was doing.

"Sir you can't just leave," the President's Chief of Staff called after him. "You're meeting with the Australian Prime Minister in five minutes, for God's sake. Then there's the Daughters of the American Revolution. Sir..."

The President stopped and turned around. "Give them my apologies, or something." The President glanced out a hallway window. Still the G-II quietly marched toward the South Lawn.

"But sir...the Australians came from...Australia to see you. We've been planning this for months."

The President turned and began jogging out of the West Wing. But he called back over his shoulder, "Then invite them all to join us outside."

The President's Secret Service detail raced to keep up with their boss. They were serious men wearing dark suits and talking quickly into their wrist-mikes as they ran after their president. By the time he arrived on the South Lawn, the SEALs were already standing in ten neat lines that stretched back over 20 deep. At the head of the group in the middle stood a lone lieutenant on crutches with his left leg in a cast that ran from hip to ankle. Someone had painted it camo green, gray and brown to blend with the rest of the desert dust battle dress utilities he wore.

The President watched the young man brace his plastered leg and struggle to pass one crutch into his left hand. The President took half a step forward to offer assistance. Then he saw the look of defiance in the young lieutenant's eyes. It said as loudly as if he had spoken the words, *I will not succumb to this injury.* The President knew the look; shared the same defiant attitude when he was recovering from a 7.62x39mm round he took in the shoulder from a Talib AK-47 one dark night in Ramadi while on patrol. He stepped back.

The young SEAL slowly raised his right hand in salute. All 243 of *America's Squadron* saluted their President at the same time.

"Oorah, son," said the President.

The young lieutenant hadn't expected that from America's chief executive. "Oorah, Mr. President," he said back in a loud and proud voice that did justice to any man or woman who ever wore the uniform.

"Oorah," thundered 243 voices behind him.

The President stood in the summer sunshine of Washington DC. At this moment, he realized there was no place on this earth that he would rather be than right here. The finest examples of courage and bravery in the American people he had the privilege of serving stretched before him. These people had taken time out of their busy lives to come here to the White House to see him. About what the President still couldn't say. But he could smell the ribs already beginning to smoke next to the hastily erected canopies that shaded picnic tables off to the side near where they land Marine 1, the presidential helicopter.

A White House staffer had already brought a microphone and plugged it into the permanently installed outlet. They often used this spot for events when the weather was nice. The President stepped up and said, "America's Squadron, I salute you and the American people salute you. I am..." he bowed his head for a moment as it slowly began to dawn on him why they might be here. "...I am humbled that you have taken the time to come here to what is truly *your* house. You have fought for it and have bled for it. Your families have paid dearly for it. I am just its temporary caretaker. But make no mistake, it is yours and by God always will be yours."

The President turned the mike around for the young lieutenant to use if he wanted. The Navy SEAL crutched up to it and leaned forward on his metal crutches. "Mr. President, each of us brings to you a part of us today. It's a little known fact that many of us serving in harm's way have a private collection. It is testimony and a reminder of the pain we have suffered. But it is much more than that. It also says that we were not beaten. Some may call it gruesome. But they don't understand the meaning because they have never been shot or taken shrapnel in combat."

Now the President knew the full purpose of their visit. His shoulder ached from the 7.62 cal. round from so many years ago. He had to admit he had never stopped thinking about it.

The young man continued. "Sir, each of us has been wounded in combat protecting our country. We don't want thanks. We don't need any special help or attention. Sir, we just want to win—to beat hell out of those attempting to bring harm to our people and friends. That is who we are—America's first string and first line of defense. We are America's Squadron." When he finished the words, a shout of *Oorah* from those 243 standing behind him thundered even louder this time.

"When I saw the Pope on TV give you the bullet that almost tore his head off just a week ago I had an idea. If I kept the bullet that shattered my leg, there must be others who kept theirs too."

It took less than an instant for the President to think of the bullet they had dug out of him. It was in plastic zip-lock bag in the upper right drawer of the Resolute desk in the Oval Office. He kept it there to remind himself what being a Marine sometimes felt like.

"So I began asking around. Turns out, Mr. President, that when offered the bullet or shrapnel from the medics, most of us keep it. But until now we didn't know what to do with it. Now we do."

This time the young SEAL now offered the President his crutch to hold while he fished into his BDU blouse pocket and pulled out a clear plastic box. He handed it to the President.

"Sir, I give you this to keep as a reminder of our country's strength. When you send us into harm's way know that we go willingly. No one twisted any arms to get us to serve. We all share a common trust in you that you know what you're doing. We are proud to serve. *Oorah!*" Then he saluted, held out his hand to take his crutch back that the President was still holding and crutched away.

Next a man in a wheel chair rolled up to the President. A Master Gunnery Sargeant in Dress Blues pushed the chair. The man was over 80 years old. "Took one in the spine, son," he said and offered a similar plastic box with the bullet. Written on the box was his name—Sam Barr, Colonel, *UDT*. The President saw it said, *Binh Gia, Viet Nam, February 7, 1965*. He offered a snappy salute. The President watched as he rolled away. When he turned his head back he saw a line had formed of all those waiting to give him their contribution. A blonde-haired girl, about 10 years old stood looking straight up into his eyes. She gave him a larger plastic box. Its date was just a year ago. She said, "My dad was killed by an IED. He loved his country and he loved his SEALs. I miss him. But I understand what he did was important." She turned and left the President feeling so humble.

The next in line walked ramrod straight to the podium on two titanium legs. He held a Belgian Malinois on a brown leather leash by his side. The President noticed the dog limped. He also saw the dog's eyes never left his partner.

The SEAL said in a clear, definite voice, "Tuck, at ease." The dog's butt hit the deck in an instant. His tail kept wagging, though.

The SEAL held out two boxes. The location marked on both was Combat Outpost Zerok, Paktika Province, Afghanistan. The date was 18 months ago. The President noticed tags hanging from the dog's collar. One said Tucker, War Service Dog. The President knew that this was as highly trained a fighting team as the military had ever produced. In briefings, the President had seen video of these war dogs. He could imagine this magnificent animal now sitting before him charging through rivers, leaping over walls and fearlessly entering buildings wearing canine body armor and night vision goggles with a remote camera strapped to his back while his buddies watched from a safe distance. He remembered the footage of just such a dog running flat out like a bullet after an aggressor. He hit him at full speed, knocking him to the ground like a line backer, then grabbing his arm, sinking his teeth into the thick padded bite guard, and whipping his head from side to side as if trying to tear the arm off.

"Is Tucker parachute certified?" the President asked.

"Sir, my boy and I made 23 combat jumps into Indian Country before… We jumped in tandem. I had him strapped to my chest. Tuck wore goggles specially fitted to his face so the wind didn't damage his eyes. He also wore an oxygen rig around this nose and mouth just like I did for high altitude jumps."

The President understood that Tucker was every bit a Navy SEAL as was his partner and as anyone among these 243.

"Insurgent rocket got us both, Sir," the young man with the titanium legs said. "Tuck stood watch over me until they choppered us both out of there. He took two rounds, but never left me. Proud to serve, Sir." The President saluted this brave soldier and Tucker. Then he saw Tucker raise his right paw to shake. The President kneeled before him and took his paw. Tucker stared straight into the President's eyes without waiver. "Tucker, atten-hut." The dog withdrew his paw and stood up. "Let's go." The President watched as they both proudly walked away toward the chow tents and picnic tables.

That was how the President spent his lunch break and much of that afternoon. The Australian delegation and the Daughters of the American Revolution had already joined them for a barbeque lunch on the South Lawn. Still, the President stood there, receiving the plastic boxes containing lead fragments. Most you couldn't tell what they were. Some were fairly recent; some, quite old. He knew the bigger chunks of metal were probably shrapnel or whatever the Talibs could scrounge up to put in IEDs. He shook hands with many, hugged the mothers, daughters and sisters. Said a few words to each. Took as much time as each wanted. During all this the Navy band softly played the *Marine's Hymn* and *God Bless America*. The President guessed Mr. Schilling was right, that the SEALs probably didn't have a song they called their own. Have to fix that, he thought.

When staffers saw how many plastic boxes were accumulating they set up several tables with blue and gold US

234

Naval Special Warfare blankets covering the tops. They reverently set each box on the tables in what had now become a place of national honor. Not until the last box was laid to rest did the President walk toward the lunch tent with the young, pretty wife who had given it to him.

She said, "Mr. President, you sure do have a lot of metal on those tables. What are you gonna do with 'em?"

He knew her name because she had introduced herself with tears in her eyes as she handed over her own plastic box minutes before. "Sara, I know one thing for sure. There is no one who will take these out of the White House. Not while I'm here and never if I have anything to say about it."

"They're artifacts, Mr. President. Just like that bullet the Pope gave you. Reminders of the American people's strength and resolve. My husband, Bobby, told me before his last deployment to Afghanistan what he thinks makes SEALs so tough. You were a Marine, so maybe you won't understand." She bent her lovely head down and a slight smile crossed her lips. She was a SEAL's wife, after all. "But for my husband it really meant something. Wanna hear?"

They were walking, still 50 yards from the crowded tents. "Absolutely, Sara. Speak real slow and maybe I'll get it."

"Right." The slight smile flashed across her full lips again at the private joke she had just shared with the President of the United States. "Well, my husband said that he was sometimes scared out there on the operations they conducted. Especially at night. Who wouldn't be, right?" She gave a nervous laugh as if the thought still frightened her. "But he knew his purpose and he had faith and trust in his training. Even more so, he had faith and love in his fellow SEALs. They were family. He knew that no matter what happened they would take care of each other. And if the worst happened, they would take care of me. And they have. There was one more thing. He said that you could shoot a SEAL. You could throw a grenade at a SEAL. If you knock a SEAL down, chances are he'll get right back up and come after ya. But if he can't get up that last time, there'll be 10 SEALs, 50 SEALs,

100 SEALs who will take his place. He ended by sayin', *Don't mess with Naval Special Warfare.*"

They walked a little further in silence. Sara leaned into the President. More for human contact, he guessed. He put his arm around her as he had his daughters when he knew they needed his comfort. Then she stopped and took a step back so they both faced each other.

"You go get 'em, Mr. President. Get whoever it is killed the Pope. He was an ally of ours wasn't he? A friend? Git 'em, Mr. President. Use the SEALs if you have to. That's what we're here for." She wiped a tear from her cheek.

The President had listened carefully to Jackson Schilling, Senior before he left for Italy. He knew that Jackson's son was in a safe house outside of Rome and that the Pope was in fact alive, not blown up as the world believed. Jack had been shot and badly injured. The Pope had suffered a heart attack after being shot twice. Jack was a *former* SEAL and the *former* head of the SEC's Enforcement Division. Now he was in private industry. He also knew that Smitty—also a former SEAL—was with Jack and that he probably brought at least two other operators with him. The President thought, four special ops guys without any support from me against how many? The President's people had created plausible deniability in case things went south. America's hands were clean. His State Department didn't want to have a diplomatic scandal with Italy on its hands. He also knew that the Italian *Carabinieri* was largely ineffective and had done almost nothing to find the Pope's assassin. In Sara's eyes it was so simple. Put a SEAL team on a jet to Rome. Let them shoot up the place until they found who they were looking for. Then rendition them back here—if they survived capture, that is. He knew that in the real world it just didn't work that way, much as he would like it to work exactly that way.

"It's not just me telling you, Mr. President. Bobby would have told you to go get 'em if he were here. I'm speakin' for him." Sara smiled a beautiful, now relaxed smile. She had done what she knew she had to do; said what she knew she had to say.

Christ, he thought. He would like nothing better than to do what Sara was asking—deploy a covert SEAL team with all the support they needed to Italy to hunt down the Pope's assassins. But it was impossible. Congress would hang him by his balls if they found out. So would the Italian government as well as the United Nations. He would be impeached, convicted, then tried at the International Court of Justice in the Hague. Even that didn't bother him as much as the loss of face that America would suffer in the eyes of the world. Much as he would have liked to do exactly as Sara asked, the President thought that he was doing the next best thing.

She brushed a strand of blonde hair from her face and smiled again, "Then Bobby would have said, *Let's go get some ribs and have us a beer.*"

The President said, "I think I would have liked your Bobby. Let's go do just that, shall we?" He was grateful for the break in tension he felt rising inside of him.

* * *

Chapter 24

His Eminence Cardinal David Caneman knelt at the small altar in the tiny chapel just off the main hall of the immensely ornate Sistine Chapel. It lacked the colorful frescos that adorned the ceiling of the main gallery where the Holy Conclave was about to begin. Caneman could hear the Cardinals in the main hall filing in, taking their seats and talking among themselves as they waited for his appearance. Legend had it that Michelangelo used this very room for storage of his paints and scaffolding during creation of his masterpiece that was the Sistine Chapel.

Caneman looked around this small, intimate room, known only to those closest to the current pope and absolutely closed to the public. It was off-limits to the Vatican Museum curators as well. As a consequence, the room was not even listed in the Sistine inventory, nor were any of its sparse furnishings. Caneman had been here only twice with His Holiness. For centuries popes had used the room—called the Chapel of St. Christopher among the few who knew of its existence—as a place to catch their breath and spend a moment in quiet meditation before entering the main gallery of the Sistine where they once again would command the hundreds of millions of Catholic faithful worldwide.

Caneman lifted his head to the simple five-foot high wooden cross, hung on the wall above the small altar. Had they ever been given a chance to examine it—which they had not—curators of the Vatican Museum would have gladly explained it was hewn from a solid piece of rare Brazilian moon wood and was probably more than 500 years old. Caneman didn't care about priceless antique crosses. Instead, he felt the weight from centuries of responsibility his predecessors must have felt in this inner sanctum within an inner sanctum before entering the gallery where every eye would be on him.

Nor did Caneman pray for divine guidance as had so many kneeling in this exact spot done in the past. He had his own thoughts and they were not on prayer. He would lead this conclave to its inevitable conclusion. Within a week, maybe a little more, he would be elected the next Pope. It was his destiny. Of that he was certain. What he was less certain of, however, was the exact location of the Church's treasury vault. His men at the Vatican Bank in New York had sent him the green replicas of the six stone tablets. It would have been easier if the Professional had succeeded in getting him the final sixth stone tablet from that farmhouse in the countryside. He could only assume that he had succeeded in fulfilling his contract and that the Pope was now deceased. What other explanation could there be for his not communicating back to him that the job was done? The Professional was a man of few words. He would not have reported success, only the need to take another shot at the target. So he must have killed the Pope. What happened to the sixth stone tablet the man spoke of was unknown. He may have encountered some problem in getting it to him. Caneman could not take the time to wait for it. He had to move forward with conclave.

As he thought about it, in this digital age having the real tablet didn't matter that much anyway. Now that he had the exact replicas of all six tablets in his possession.

When he opened the FedEx box three days ago and saw what his people in New York had sent him, he was stunned. Somehow, all six tablets that formed the Church's treasure map were finally in the same place after so many centuries. Even if they weren't the real thing, they were close enough. All he had to do was assemble them the way the original tablet had been before being broken apart and scattered to the Catholic empire's four winds.

He worked for two hours straight on the plastic replicas. He missed several meetings that he should have attended before conclave convened for real. He thought of it as an investment of his time. Then the stones finally clicked together with a final and definite solution. Like a holy Rubik's Cube. Their edges aligned perfectly. He tried to move them from side-to-side just to be sure. They didn't budge. He had the treasure map. Finally. He took a breath and had himself a small tumbler of Macallan's whiskey in quiet, solo celebration and he gave thanks. Then he set to work trying to interpret what the ancient map told. It took him another 48 hours before he thought he had the location nailed down.

"Attention on deck!" came the command from the first SEAL who saw the President walk under the shade canopy on the South Lawn. All immediately put down their knives and forks and stood to attention. Even after six years in the White House the President still hadn't gotten used to such treatment. His eyes scanned the picnic tables and fell on Tucker, the war service dog. He noticed that Tucker had immediately dropped the huge beef rib bone he was gnawing on and stood with the rest of his SEALs—eyes level and staring straight ahead, not moving a muscle.

"As you were," said the President, his gaze still on Tucker. The brave canine laid back down and grabbed the beef rib bone again. He also noticed that his partner's hand dropped to the scruff of his furry neck and ruffled it in appreciation.

"I thought I might join you," the President said, "if I'm not intruding," he felt he had to add. "What's good here?"

Everyone under the canopy put down their knives and forks for the second time in less than a minute. Damn, wondered the President, am I going to have to watch what I say around these boys?

From the last table in the back a young man stood. He was average height, maybe a little above average in build. That was all that anyone could call average about this man. Meeting him on the street, you would never guess his extraordinary capabilities from a single, casual glance.

He said in a deeply resonant voice, not overly loud, but that definitely commanded your attention. "Sir, America is good. Though according to some of our elected officials, they feel the need to apologize for us to the rest of the world."

Another young man stood. "Mr. President, my SEAL team is good. Really, really good. So are my swim buddy, his great wife and their two spectacular children."

He sat down and another rose. "Sir, our country elected you to lead. That's good. You have our trust, sir. I'd say that's pretty good since most of us are skeptical, hard-to-please sons of bitches."

Next, Tucker's partner stood on his new titanium legs. The President noticed that Tucker also stood on his hind legs with his front paws resting on the tabletop. "Sir, we all think the Pope was good. Though only about a quarter of us are Catholic. He got a raw deal, sir. Shot once, then blown up. It would be good if you got the people who did this. Really good, sir."

A menacing growl erupted from Tucker's throat as he continued to rest his front paws on the table.

"What's that, boy?" asked his partner in a theatrically loud voice. "You want a piece of the Pope's attackers too?" Tucker barked twice in a loud, full-throated and frightening voice.

The President felt that galvanizing bark spread over all those under the canopy. Tucker's partner still had everyone's attention. "Mr. President, use us. The Italians don't seem to be doing one damn thing to get the Pope's assassins. Let America's Squadron go get the bastards. Just like with me and Tucker, Sir, sometimes you just gotta drop the leash and trust your partner. Do it, Sir."

The President slowly stood and faced the Naval Special Warfare Group-II. He remained stock still, his face a mask—at least he hoped it was. He said nothing. He didn't have to.

The President's eyes locked on the 80-year-old in his wheel chair. They stared at one another across generations of warriors protecting the country they loved and its allies. Then Col. Samuel Barr, USMC, UDT, Ret. nodded his approval and pumped his frail, thin fist in the air one last time. He got it.

One by one and in groups, the 243 members of *America's Squadron* stood. A few elbows jabbed their partners as they realized what the President's silence was saying. Sara, standing beside her new friend, said in a soft voice, "Oorah, Mr. President." From the front of the canopy it began, "Oorah,

Oorah." It spread like rolling thunder. Across the South Lawn and out onto the public streets.

Message received. Loud and clear.

His Eminence Cardinal David Caneman lifted his head toward the Brazilian moon wood cross on the wall of Saint Christopher's Chapel. His right hand made the sign of the cross over his chest. To anyone watching it appeared this *Camerlengo* was asking for divine guidance. Caneman knew that he really didn't need it. Not with this conclave. Then he rocked back on his heels and pushed himself up from the kneeling rail. Hearing movement in the private holy room that was off-limits even to them, His Eminence Cardinal David Caneman's personal attendant and the two acolytes stood outside the closed door waiting for him.

Caneman had learned that someone of his high position in the Church did not rush—for anything or anyone. Let them wait. It only cemented his position of exaltation and authority. As *Camerlengo* he held the ultimate position anyway. He made a shuffling noise with his shoes on the small chapel's centuries-old rough concrete floor. The preceding popes who used the room had never upgraded the floor. Caneman thought that this would be something he would do—a small gift to his successors as they prepared to receive an audience in the famed Sistine Chapel.

Hearing movement on the other side of the wood door, the *Camerlengo's* chief of staff nodded to the acolytes. Simultaneously, they opened the double doors. His Eminence Cardinal David Caneman emerged into a private vestibule behind the Sistine's main altar.

He walked up the three steps to the altar with head bowed and hands clasped in front of him as if in meditation from having just spoken personally with the Almighty himself. Smoke from the incense wafted over him. From the corner of his eye he saw the sea of cardinal red flooding the ornate room set out before him. Michelangelo himself could not have imagined a more

242

fitting occasion for the display of his frescoes. He made a left turn onto the altar proper that led to the elaborately carved wooden lectern where he would make his address. The sound of his heels tap-tapped on the marble floor before he gained the red and gold carpet that covered most of the altar. The intense smell of the incense was even stronger up here. Of course it would be, he quickly thought. Smoke rises and I am now a good three feet above them. Strange what inconsequential things we think of at the most important of moments, he thought.

His Eminence Cardinal David Caneman, *Camerlengo* of Vatican City, stepped to the lectern with command and authority. His first words were, *"Extra omnes!"* It was tradition that his first order as *Camerlengo* of this conclave was to order everyone but the Cardinals who would be electing the next pope to leave the Chapel immediately. It signaled the beginning of conclave.

He gave a slight nod of his head to the two acolytes standing way in the back—about 120 feet away. The Sistine Chapel has the same dimensions as the Temple of Solomon on Jerusalem's Temple Mount described in the Old Testament. When Pope Sixtus IV had it built in 1477 he made sure that the dimensions were exact. It is no accident that the famous Chapel bears its builder's name.

The two acolytes standing in the back were watching for His Eminence' signal. They immediately stepped to the side and grasped both handles of the immense double oak doors that protected the chamber. They walked the doors closed so as to be outside when they shut. Two bishops stepped into their places outside. Their job was to seal the doors shut with locks and chains. This holy conclave was now in session.

His Eminence Cardinal David Caneman raised both hands, palms facing upward to Heaven and commanded his congregation of cardinals to rise. There was a rustling of their red silk vestments as the 147 chosen cardinals stood before him in respect and reverence for the position he held in the Church. The Sistine Chapel was actually quite chilly inside. The floors were stone. The ceiling soared 65 feet overhead, pulling any remaining warm air with it. Though not an enormous room,

Caneman would not call it warmly intimate either. He was glad that he had the foresight to wear his ski underwear beneath his vestments.

"Let us pray," commanded Caneman. The assembled cardinals sat back down. They would have knelt had there been kneeling rails. Still, Caneman noted that about a third of them did kneel in prayer without benefit of the padded kneeling rails.

With the opening prayer out of the way, Caneman quickly dispatched the housekeeping chores that were his responsibility as *Camerlengo*. He led the traditional oath of strictest secrecy every conclave opened with. What went on in this august chamber must be known only to God and to these men seated before him. Next he read the list of cardinals he had selected to assist with the *interregnum* governance of the Church. As he read the short list he looked up and noticed each to a man gave his head a serious nod as if expecting the assignment. But the huge smiles on their faces made them no different than the schoolboys learning of their selection to the soccer team. In truth these men would have little, if anything, of substance to do. Caneman had made sure in the months leading up to the Pope's scheduled death that everything within Vatican Bank as well as Vatican City in Rome functioned as it should. Any necessary decisions during *sede vacante*—empty seat—before election of the next pope, Caneman had delegated to those loyal to him and his cause. Of course, before making any decision they would inform him. Caneman quickly proceeded to his other business according to the Apostolic Constitution—the definitive authority on procedures for holding a papal election.

Finally the time has arrived, thought Caneman. He was beginning the wrap-up of the last Gospel text from John 21. He quickly spoke of Jesus telling his disciples to cast their nets into the sea. Indeed, Caneman reflected on the symbolism. The Pope's fisherman's ring—that would soon adorn his own finger—actually depicts Peter casting out his net to be a fisher of men. He ran through the part where Jesus told Peter, "Feed my

244

sheep." He glanced down at the *pallium* that wound around the back of his neck, then forward, over both shoulders, to join in a cross that flowed down the front of his robe. The vestment was certainly evocative of a shepherd's wool band worn when carrying his stray sheep back to the flock.

He finished this last prayer and waited as the cardinals all sat back, settling into their chairs for what they expected to be the first of several long days of deliberation. His Eminence Cardinal David Caneman made them wait a moment longer while he took a sip of the spring water in a crystal tumbler left there on the podium by one of the faithful acolytes. He set the tumbler down and raised his head to address the cardinals.

"Your Eminences, my Brothers in His service, we are gathered here for the most holy and important of our duties: To select the next Bishop Of Rome—the successor Pope following the tragic death of—"

Here Caneman's voice cracked and he fell silent for a single theatrical beat, seemingly for the purpose of composing himself. No one in the Chapel failed to notice the apparent grief on the young *Camerlengo's* face. He must truly be God's Banker.

"However, I must delay the start of this conclave for three days—"

Hearing this unexpected announcement, the cardinals stirred. The Chapel filled with murmurs. Caneman raised his hands slightly in a gesture that commanded immediate silence without expending any of his authoritative capital.

"I am sorry, Brothers. But it is canon law that all of the appointed electors must be present at conclave. Unfortunately, due to the suddenness of this *sede vacante* and the urgent need to convene this conclave there are three of us who have not managed to get to Rome yet. They are, His Eminence Antonios Naguib from Egypt. As you know Antonios' country is caught up in civil war. He is being held by Taliban rebels. My people are desperately trying to gain his safe release and arrange his travel to Rome.

"Next is His Eminence Alexandre José Maria dos Santos of Mozambique. Father Alex is 88 years old and in poor health. I have personally spoken to his cardiologist about travel. Alex is gaining strength daily. They expect he will be out of danger and able to travel within two days. Finally there is His Eminence Laurent Monsengwo Pasinya from the Democratic Republic of Congo. We have been unsuccessful in getting word to Father Pasinya so far of our urgent need for his presence. He is running a ministry in the farthest, most inaccessible reaches of his parish. There is no communication whatsoever. We have sent a team on foot through the jungle to locate and return him to Rome." Caneman looked out over his audience in rapt attention. "Again, I am advised that this effort will take at least a day out and a day back, then a day to travel here to Rome. So that is why I have postponed the start of this conclave for the absolute minimum of three days."

Caneman paused. He expected that each of the cardinals to a man would accept his every word without question. There was truth to the situations of His Eminence Alexandre José Maria dos Santos of Mozambique and His Eminence Laurent Monsengwo Pasinya of Congo. And His Eminence Antonios Naguib from Egypt was indeed being held by Taliban rebels. However, they were in the employ and being handsomely paid to hold the Cardinal by a small company funded through a variety of offshore entities and special purpose corporations that ultimately led to the Vatican Bank, should anyone chose to look, which no one ever would. Cardinal Naguib would be released when Caneman decided it was time to reconvene conclave and he was ready for the first vote.

His Eminence Cardinal David Caneman said, "So, Brothers, we have no further business to conduct here today. By the powers vested in me as *Camerlengo*, I declare this Papal Conclave closed." He turned away from the podium that was ornately dressed in the cardinal and gold of the Papacy and walked back the way he came, through the private side entrance and into the Chapel's secure dressing room. As the oak doors closed behind him he heard the volume of whispers turn first to murmurs and then to urgent chattering among the cardinals at this most sudden and unusual turn of events.

"I won't lie to you, Jack," said Helen. "He's still in grave danger. But, he's the Pope. And he did somehow manage to survive two gunshots to the chest at close range. Those bullets hitting his steel cross—"

"Are unexplainable by anything but divine intervention," interrupted Sister Mary Pat as she quietly walked into Jack's hospital room. "It seems that our Pope has a date with destiny. No man armed merely with a gun is going to deny him of it."

Jack sat up in his hospital bed at Niguarda Ca'Granda Hospital. His face contorted with the effort.

Helen said, "Here wait a second. I'll raise the back of your bed for you. No need to strain those stitches."

"Have you seen His Holiness lately?" asked Jack.

"I just came from his room," answered Sister Mary Pat. "He's sleeping. That heart attack—his second, though few people know that little fact—did some damage. He's weak. The doctors say the emergency angioplasty cleared the worst of his blockage. But they quickly add that he is 83 years old and not in the best of physical shape owing to his sedentary life." Sister Mary Pat lifted her head to face both Helen and Jack. "But they don't know him. He is the strongest-willed, most stubborn man I have met. You can shoot His Holiness. You can knock him down. He'll get up again and again. Then he'll forgive you."

Jack said, "I know a whole group of men like that—except for the forgiving part. The guys I know would come after you with extreme prejudice. So will he make it?"

Jack's question was simple, direct. Just like the man who asked it. Sister Mary Pat said, "His doctors are not optimistic. They have done all that they can. They tell me to pray for him. If he survives the next few days, then he has a better chance. But now, his life is in another's hands."

"While we've been sequestered here," said Helen, "and are under armed guard, SMP and I have been working out the map that Audrey sent from New York."

247

Jack immediately perked up. One of his people was down. She was his responsibility. "How's she doing?"

Helen said, "I spoke with the ER physician after she finished working on Audrey. She's going to be fine. Right now she has a concussion from where she slammed her head onto the desk after one of them smashed her in the jaw."

"Where is she?" asked Jack.

"I called her mom. The family has a nice home on Martha's Vineyard. They brought her out there to recover and take some time off. She's going to be just fine, Jack. Don't worry about her. She's worried sick about you, though."

"No need. I'm fine too. Or I will be soon as I get out of this place. You said something about the map you and SMP were working on?"

Helen saw some of the typical Jack Schilling slowly emerging as he immediately shifted the subject away from himself and on to a challenge that he found more interesting. "Right. Audrey assembled and photographed the completed map to the Church's treasure vault before they found her. While she waited for the paramedics, she emailed the final image to me." Helen reached inside her backpack—a nice, hand-tooled leather piece designed by Tignanelo—and pulled out the printed map. She handed it over for Jack to take a close look at.

He held the image up to the fluorescent lights of his hospital room. "Whew, this makes no sense. There's no orientation to north."

Sister Mary Pat spoke up. "Well, there is if you know what to look for—"

Helen interrupted. "It turns out that our SMP is a student of ancient Church texts. She picked right up on the map's likely direction."

Sister Mary Pat humbly said, "The popes of the 10th through 16th centuries didn't bother themselves with the worldly issues of which way was north. I figured I may as well put that doctorate of mine in Renaissance classical literature to work. I am well-versed in reading and interpreting old manuscripts. This one did not prove that much of a challenge. At least I know what continent it is talking about."

"You do?" asked Helen. "You didn't tell me that."

"Dear, you seemed to be having such fun turning the images this way and that, trying to figure it all out. I didn't want to spoil it for you. But yes, given a number of *ifs* I can put us within 10 kilometers or so of the spot where the map says this supposed treasure vault is located."

Jack stared hard at the nun he had become so fond of. He understood why her popularity had transitioned out of just covering news of the Catholic Church for the Vatican News Service and was now a featured contributor to NBC, CBS and CNN. And she didn't say a word about her discovery, he thought. The lady keeps her own counsel. He liked that. "What kind of *ifs?*" he asked while painfully reaching for the plastic cup of water with the straw. Helen moved to get if for him. She stopped after seeing the look of determination on his face.

"Hon, if I'm going on a treasure hunting expedition, I had better be able to reach for my own water. What *ifs?*" he repeated his question.

"For starters, the scale of the map." Sister Mary Pat reached over and turned the photographic image of the map Jack was holding on its end. "There. Viewing maps right side up usually helps. As for scales, there really aren't any. So I have to rely on the distance some of the references they use are apart from one another. Then I create my own scale. Another *if* is the body of water here," she pointed to a large wavy carving on the stone image near what could be a ragged coastline. "This ocean or sea is not marked in any way."

"But you know what it is?" asked Helen.

"Yes, I believe I do. The earth's coastal shape is one thing that doesn't change much over a geologically insignificant amount of time as a few thousand years. It's the Mediterranean Ocean. And I would say that from Milan we are within a day's journey to the location." Sister Mary Pat looked at them both with a skeptical frown. "That is, if this treasure vault exists at all. That is something I am most skeptical about. The Catholic

Church is rife with rumors and fiction created over the centuries to retain the faithful's interest."

Jack shook his head as if to clear it from the anesthetic his body was trying to shake off. "So where is the vault, Sister?"

She gently took the photographic image of the ancient map from his hands and looked at it again. "Well, it appears to be about halfway between Rome and Naples. The nearest town to where a natural stone vault of any kind could be is in Formia, Italy. It makes sense, since the town is right on the coast and just about 20 miles from the larger, better known city of Cassino, located at the foot of Monte Cairo."

She paused, seeing Jack's puzzled look. "Think of the boot shape of Italy. Well, the area we're talking about is on the shin portion of the boot about where the top of a nicely styled woman's boot would end."

Helen asked, "Why this particular area? What's so special about it that the Church would put its vault?"

SMP looked at them. Then she thought of her dear friend, His Holiness, lying unconscious in the next room over. Would he live? His doctors had done what they could. They had told her that his life was now in God's hands. To Sister Mary Pat that was good enough. He had survived an assassination attempt that did nothing more than nick his big ear, a bomb blast that leveled Castel Gandolfo, then two gunshots to the chest that were blocked by that large steel cross he insisted on wearing. What was a little blockage in an artery to such an extraordinary man? She put the thought aside for the moment.

"What is so special about Formia? My dear I did a little research while your Jackson was out cold from his surgery. Formia, or its immediate area along the coast, is a perfect place for a natural vault. First, it is an ancient port city. They would have had to float all the loot into the area by boat. There were no airports, planes or trains during the time most of the things they hid were being laid away. It had to be by boat. Formia is the site of the ancient Roman port of Gianola. Also, the city of Formia sits right on the Roman Apian Way. It was smack on one of the busiest thoroughfares of ancient Roman times. After the fall of the Western Roman Empire, Formia and its neighbor, Cassino, for centuries continued their relative prominence for trade both over land and by sea. The Church would naturally have chosen a place well-traveled with sufficient roads and access.

"Today Formia still has some of the Roman port ruins. The Tomb of Cicero—near where he was assassinated on the Apian Way in 43 BC—is still there. Also, the Church of *San Giovanni Battista e Lorenzo*, one of the Roman Catholic Church's first posts outside of Rome is there. The area is littered with churches. There is also The Church of *San Lucia* that opened in the 15th century and the Church of *Sant 'Erasmo*—"

Jack jumped in when SMP stopped to take a breath. "I get the churches. But Sister, we're looking for a natural vault, not a church."

"Right you are, Jackson," SMP exclaimed. "I was just coming to that. I did some more research. Now the Church wasn't overly concerned with the preservation of their loot for archeological purposes—you know, absence of light, constant temperature of 55 degrees Fahrenheit and humidity of 10%. No. They wanted safety and security. They were going to sell these one day. So what do people do with their treasure?"

Helen piped up, "They bury it."

SMP pointed her long, graceful forefinger at Helen. "Give that child a new rosary," she exclaimed as if she were teaching catechism and was rewarding a particularly bright student. "My research led me to the geological composition of this particular coastal area. Naturally, since it is on the coast, we're dealing with a lot of sandstone. However, there are some natural caverns and caves in the area. Uncharted and unexplored, so say the maps. I am thinking that if we could find a system of such caverns leading down to the port or within a short distance from it, we just may be in the right area."

Jack lay there in his hospital bed. His side ached as the painkillers wore off. He had asked his doctor to begin tapering them off as quickly as possible. He nodded his head. "Okay. So it seems you have located the possible spot for this supposed treasure—"

Helen said, "Now all we have to do is go get it."

"Maybe not so easy as that," said Jack. "This could be dangerous. When you both thought I was sleeping, I was actually thinking. I put a few things together. We may not be the only ones who think they've found where the vault is located. Don't forget…"

Helen finished for him, "Don't forget poor Audrey spent a night in the hospital recovering from an attack—maybe by our competition. Now they have the parts of the map. They may not have put it together yet, though. And even if they have, they probably don't have Sister Mary Pat's geographic and historic perspective. At least we don't have to worry about the assassin any more."

"Don't be so sure of that," said Jack. "Whatever they gave me to reduce that pain clarified a few things. First, you always have a backup. If one is good, then two is better. That's the reason they teach combat shooters to double-tap their targets. The guy who tried to kill the Pope may not be alone—probably isn't. His master may well have a backup. That's why I decided to let the world think the Pope was dead and we kept him out of sight."

"So who is behind all of this?" asked Sister Mary Pat.

Jack looked at her. "The man who has most to gain from the Pope's death. The man who I have made almost desperate for money and credibility by closing down his Vatican Bank." Jack understood strategy. He learned it from a practical, combat perspective during his seven years in the teams as a special warfare operator. Then, in business school he learned the refinements of financial combat. Wall Street was just a cleaner, less straightforward form of combat. At least when someone pointed a gun at you, their intention was clear. Not so in business. Your real enemies usually posed as your friends and vice versa. And their roles changed from deal to deal. One month the firm and the CEO who led it might be on your side. The next month, with a new deal, they might be trying to cut out your heart. Jack knew that his suggestion to unwind Vatican Bank's public offering and return the $200 billion raised to the investors had infuriated Caneman. Jack knew that he was at least partly responsible for the attempts on the Pope's life. He intended to right that wrong.

"So you think that Cardinal David Caneman, *Camerlengo* of Vatican City, is responsible for these assassination attempts?" Sister Mary Pat's voice trailed off in incredulity.

"Here's what I think," said Jack. "Caneman is on the short list for this papal enclave to elect him Pope. But there *is* a list. His credibility is suffering now that the SEC is suggesting that Vatican Bank unwind its public securities auction and return the money to investors. He needs two things: Money, for sure. He must replenish Vatican Bank's cash reserves to keep the Church flush. If not, then he may as well quit now because the financial mess he created happened on his watch and everyone knows it. Second, he needs something that elevates his status way above that of any other candidate. He needs to find the Church's ancient vault of priceless religious artifacts. If he has these two things—money and glory—then he'll be elected the next Pope. Guaranteed."

Jack sat back, suddenly exhausted. The trauma of the bullet wound, coupled with the loss of blood would make anyone weak. He was regaining his blood volume and along with it, his appetite. Both were helping him regain his strength. Still, ramping his stamina back up to 100 percent would take some time.

Helen and Sister Mary Pat looked at one another. Helen said, "Jack, while you were out, Cardinal Caneman put the papal conclave into recess. He said it was because not all the voting cardinals could be located. It will be three days at least before he reconvenes the conclave. Caneman has not been seen or heard from since."

Sister Mary Pat said, "Oh he is a smart one, that David Caneman. I think he may have already put together the map fragments and figured out where the vault is located. He is probably on his way to Formia right now."

* * *

Chapter 25

"Your Eminence, suspending conclave? Really, David? A suspension? Without telling your cardinals what you are up to?" The rapid-fire questions came from Dr. Neil Palmer who was speaking from the fine, butter-soft leather seat of the Cessna Citation executive jet as it crossed the Atlantic. When Caneman's call came, summoning him to Rome, he knew the time had come. He and his team immediately left the comfortable confines of his Chancellor's office at NYU to join Caneman in this historic adventure.

Since Caneman had recruited him into his clandestine advisory board, they had spoken at frequent intervals. Dr. Palmer filled in those arcane parts of the Church's history and Vatican lore that he himself had not taken the time to research. And Palmer possessed one other critical asset. The man was one of the world's great authorities on the centuries-old rumor of an ancient treasure vault the Church had used to hide its plunder of foreign lands.

When Caneman acquired the first stone tablet, he opened his conversations with Palmer. Back then he was not even a cardinal. But he was the Vatican Bank's executive vice president in charge of worldwide investment operations. His phenomenal success with growing the Bank's investment portfolio became a factor guiding the ever-expanding influence of the Church's religious works. People noticed. Over the course of just ten years, the young priest from Wall Street's Goldman Sachs had gained a following among the Pope's inner circle of advisors. The hundreds of millions in investment income generated under his control had vaulted him to priestly stardom. Soon there were rumors of being elevated to a Cardinal. Just one year later it became fact. Caneman vaulted from a stellar priesthood, past the bishops, archbishops, metropolitans and primates right into a cardinal's post. Only the major archbishops and patriarchs separated him from the papacy. And these two positions were largely administrative anyway. None were in contention for the top spot. Yes, being a cardinal was where Caneman wanted to be.

When the Vatican Bank's then-CEO was forced out under a cloud of innuendo and suspicion—one of a long line who had been similarly ousted—they naturally looked to Caneman to clean up the scandal of financial improprieties they had left behind.

That Caneman did. He cleaned house the likes of which the Vatican Bank had never seen. The old priests who ran the accounting and finance departments were suddenly reassigned to parishes far removed from Wall Street. In their place Caneman inserted the finest financial professionals that money could buy—none of whom were clergy. They were the young Wall Street sharks he was used to working with. They were the freshly minted MBAs—both men and women—from Harvard, Wharton, Michigan, Stanford and Yale. Each had lives that revolved solely around profit and loss. Actually, more profit than loss. Each was hungry, not so humble and very, very focused. It didn't matter to any of them where they worked. Just so they had the authority and the capital to make money—for their institutions and, more importantly, for themselves.

At the same time, however, now Cardinal Caneman had positioned himself to fulfill the agenda he had set for himself and his Church—to restore it to its fundamentalist glory. Originally just his theological advisor, Dr. Neil Palmer became one of just five confidantes for organizing this palace coup.

He posed the question to Palmer late one evening in the Vatican Bank offices while inspecting that first stone tablet. "What if there really is such a treasure vault, Doctor? What would it look like? What might it contain that would help our cause?"

Dr. Neil Palmer was no priest. He was, however, one of the most learned and self-confident men that Caneman had ever come across. His Ph.D. came from the famed University of Michigan in archeology—specifically biblical archeology.

256

His dissertation not only argued for the existence of the Kingdom of David in the desert around Jerusalem, but he actually went out there to the desert and found it right where he said it would be. His was the fastest defense of any doctoral dissertation ever at Michigan. He brought back high definition video footage of his excavation and the site. Using Hollywood's most advanced animation techniques he showed the dissertation review committee what the ancient city of David that had been lost for so many centuries must have been like. His film cut from the conjecture of animation to the reality of the colonnades, amphitheaters, offices, homes and baths buried in the ruins that he and his team had unearthed. The video featured none other than the great biblical scholar and archaeologist W. F. Albright confirming the discovery the young Neil Palmer had made.

Then he shut off the video presentation and pulled a gold medallion from his dusty, canvas backpack. It featured a menorah, *shofar* (ram's horn) and a Torah scroll. All three symbols are sacred and iconic Jewish emblems. He reached into his backpack a second time and pulled a handful of gold coins— 36 in number—and casually tossed the priceless artifacts onto the doctoral evaluation committee's table.

Caneman heard the same account from two of the five dissertation fellows who sat on Palmer's review committee. *The young archeologist walked into the thesis defense committee, played his video, then presented his golden artifacts. Afterward, he just stood there, letting his discovery speak for itself. After maybe a minute, he said, "Any questions, gentlemen?" We had his dissertation right there in front of us. All dissertations are theory. We got up to inspect the medallion and the coins. These were fact. We were speechless. Theory, backed up by hard evidence. Then he said, " 'Nuff said," and he walked out of the committee room. The vote in favor of a successful dissertation defense and granting him his doctorate was immediate and unanimous.*

That account spoke volumes to Caneman. Here was a man with whom he could identify. One who shared his own self-confidence. One who had complete faith in his own abilities.

When he said something was so, he backed it up with hard evidence and accomplishment—just like Caneman himself.

That evening almost ten years ago. Now in the Vatican Bank offices, after everyone had left, Caneman repeated his question to Palmer, "What might such a treasure vault contain?"

NYU's youngest tenured professor ever had sat back in the plush couch there in Caneman's office. He was not a man to rush his judgment for anyone. That is what Caneman respected about him. He had attained the highest academic office at one of the world's finest educational institutions because he trusted himself above all comers. When he said something, you could count on it being so.

"Well, David," they had agreed after their first meeting to drop the titles of Doctor and Your Eminence, at least when they were in private. Such trappings of office just got in the way of real, honest communication. "If such a vault exists, it is very, very old and low tech. You will not likely find much in the way of security—"

"Its security lies in its secrecy," Caneman interrupted.

Palmer slowly nodded his head as if reluctantly conceding the point. "Yes, in part. But understand also that it would be very difficult to find. This stone you have acquired may be truly the first of the reputed six stone tablets that Pope Alexander VI cut up in the 16th Century. Then again, it may just be part of the Catholic Church's folklore—part of yet another fabrication to keep the masses within the fold. Or there may be just five stone tablets or more than six. We don't know. No one knows for sure."

With the acquisition of each successive stone tablet, they had similar private conversations. As the number of tablets in Caneman's collection grew so did the seriousness of their conversations. The two powerful men began making plans for how to use the riches from the vault—if it existed and if any human could find it. Caneman was supremely confident that if it could be found, Dr. Neil Palmer was the man who would do it.

Now the Skype phone conversation between Caneman and Palmer as the small jet raced to Rome had reached a new level of seriousness. "David, I have the images of the six stone tablets that you have put together. Congratulations, my friend. It seems that you have indeed solved the riddle of the Church's treasure vault."

Caneman sat back, sinking comfortably into the couch in his suite at Rome's most exclusive small hotel. "So now will you answer my question? What does this vault look like on the inside?"

"Since you showed me the fifth tablet, I have been pondering this question. I anticipated there would be a sixth and that you would find it. First, the place will be very dusty. Remember that if we are lucky it has not been opened for centuries. Think of one of the Egyptian Pharaoh's tombs. There will be vermin of all types inside. The timbers holding the ceilings will have rotted away centuries ago in parts and the ceiling will probably have collapsed in places. Priceless artifacts either will be buried forever or damaged beyond recognition. My research indicates that the priests back then were an orderly lot. They likely would have segregated the plunder by type of article or by location from which it was taken."

"Neil, you make the Catholic Church sound like thieves and looters of their own followers."

"They were, David. These were men who believed that God put them here in His service to build His Church. Anything they did to further that cause was justified in His name. They needed money to accomplish that mission. The only way they could get it was by first baptizing followers to join the church, then convincing them to give the Church their most valuable worldly possessions. Their success with this scheme lay in their total commitment to the ideal that they were God's own earthly servants. That was their justification for their crimes. They reasoned they were entitled to this plunder precisely because they were doing it for a higher purpose. That is why they so often targeted the wealthiest people, then accused them of all sorts of crimes against the Church. Believe me, David, it is no different than what the Chinese and former Russian communist parties along with the dictatorships emerging then toppling worldwide have done for decades. Make it a crime punishable by death or worse to criticize the regime. This tactic maintains the power base and keeps the multitudes in line."

"But what should we expect to find in there?" asked Caneman. He knew Church history as well as anyone; didn't need a lecture on the dirty underbelly of the Church. His cause was different, his methods clean and sophisticated, his motives pure. No one would die during his takeover. He repeated his question, "What should we expect to find?"

Palmer knew when to accept the Cardinal's change of subject. "Well, David, I suppose it will be a museum curator's dream come true. There will be rows upon rows of the most incredible documents and manuscripts chronicling the Church's thrust into new territories. There will be deeds of trust allowing the Church to claim some of the earth's most valuable real estate. Expect also to find transcripts of some of the most famous trials for crimes against the Church. We already have the actual court documents from the trial of the Knights Templar and the very papers from Galileo's heresy trial. So too we have the written request for an annulment of Henry VIII's marriage. Expect those kinds of documents with high-level historical import. Perhaps even parts of the Bible that have heretofore gone undiscovered. Expect to see some original Bible sections that were deliberately hidden away by ancient popes never to be seen because they did not match their impression of what should be the true word of God. The very materials that these manuscripts were written on chronicle the advancement of the written word. The oldest will be written on animal skin. Then parchment of one type or another. Papyrus will figure prominently in the later materials used. Eventually there will be the early types of paper. These will be the most delicate."

"But what about the treasure?" probed Caneman.

"That *is* the treasure. It is priceless, David."

260

"Priceless to the historians and to the Church. Not to be vulgar or to insult your historical sensitivities, *Doctor*, what I am asking about is the gold, silver and other valuables with a marketable price tag."

"Oh there will be that in spades, be assured, David. The Catholic Church has never been shy about taking earthly possessions from its parishioners so willing to give. And some not so willing. As testimony of the heretics who were stoned or burned to death, then their wealth confiscated by the Church."

"You know what I mean, Neil."

"Yes, Your Eminence. I know. You are after a talisman—a symbol on which the Church can regain its theological edge and superiority. With this sudden, undeniable proof that He walked this earth among us, you will restore the Church to its ecclesiastical and fundamentalist purity in the eyes of the common man."

"That is it in a nutshell."

The learned professor of biblical archeology turned university administrator ran a hand through his stylishly cut hair as he raced across the Atlantic at a speed close to Mach 1 at an altitude of 45,000 feet. The pause over the Skype connection endured without Caneman impatiently breaking it. Then, "Telling you the genre of the types of things to expect in this vault—if it even exists—was the easy part. You are now asking me to say if it contains a particular item of religious significance. And you haven't even told me what that item is."

"I don't know what it is, Neil. All I know is that when I see it, then I will know."

"I understand my friend. Here is my answer. The priests putting their plunder into a vault would likely stick to items of intrinsic value. Items that had a certain liquidity of the time— that they could use to pay for building the Church. Ideally, these would be precious metals and gems. Items of jewelry would also fall into this category."

Caneman interrupted, "They would stockpile items that did not likely lose their value over time. These priests had something in common with today's investment bankers. They took positions

261

in commodities and enterprises that had an upside potential for future appreciation in their value."

Neil Palmer nodded his head. "Something like that." This was as much of an agreement to Caneman's rush to the treasure vault that may or may not exist as he was willing to concede. "The point I mean to make is a cautionary one, David. Value and liquidity would have been the main criterion by which the ancients would consign property to the vault. If we find everyday items of no particular intrinsic value—"

"Then we have what I seek," insisted Caneman. "Because a normal item of no value would have some sort of historical significance to justify its place in the vault."

Over the Atlantic speeding toward Rome the professor said, "That is the point I was making, yes. Let us hope that if we find the vault and if we discover some of these apparently valueless artifacts, the priests who put them there did so for a very good reason. And they documented that reason with some sort of irrefutable provenance proving its place in history."

His Eminence Cardinal David Caneman felt the hair on his arms stand up with excitement. We are moving ever closer; inexorably nearer to the objective, he promised himself. When I have it, there will be no doubt that I have crossed the chasm from a mere financial engineer to one who rightfully takes his place among the giants of the one true faith. One who saves his Church from itself and who turns it in the proper direction.

Caneman's shoulders tensed as he realized his dream of installing a global Catholic authority with himself as its Supreme Leader was taking its final shape. He would rule from the Vatican in Rome. But his control would span areas far greater than just the religious aspect of the Church's kingdom. He would control the financial and the political doctrine of vast areas on every continent. He would enforce his strict fundamentalist Catholic ideals with financial means. In the small regions—like Washington DC—where financial and political means might prove ineffective there was always the General's military force he could rely on.

262

That was the reason why Caneman had brought General Marc "Scorpion" Greggory into his inner circle. As Chairman of General Ordnance Corp.—the world's largest manufacturer and seller of advanced military hardware—Caneman had all the tools he needed at his disposal.

Caneman willed his voice to stay calm and not rise in excited pitch. "So Neil, you have had a few hours to study the map. Where do we begin looking?"

Palmer glanced back into the cabin of the executive jet. It was configured to hold twenty-four. His archeological team was crammed back there studying the ancient map he had given them once they were airborne. Their excavation tools, instruments as well as a host of explosives and assorted weaponry overflowed the aircraft's storage holds. Each man and the three women on the team were all experts—in archeology, some in theology. Some were also experts in armed combat. Caneman had insisted that a security force accompany him in case they met resistance.

Palmer had known them all for years. Some had been graduate students he personally recruited to the cause. Others had come from the military by way of Scorpion Greggory. They shared his faith along with Caneman's views of the need to turn the Church in a new direction. Each brought something extraordinary to what he was sure would be a monumental undertaking. It was part scholarly endeavor; part gutsy risk-taking based on prior successful expeditions. Palmer knew they didn't have much time to pinpoint the likely spots of the treasure vault and then find a way into it. No more than two unsuccessful attempts, then by the third, they would have likely exhausted their time before Caneman would have to reconvene conclave. Palmer knew the clock was ticking. He understood that Caneman felt the pressure even more.

All that they had worked for these many years was now on the line. First there was the tremendous time and the expense of first finding, then acquiring the six stone tablets. Then putting the puzzle together. If they failed to find the vault or even if they did locate it but could not identify the one artifact that Caneman sought would turn him from hero of the Vatican to its enemy overnight. The Cause could not withstand such a defeat.

The learned academic returned to his telephone call. "David, the final tablet really was the key to this puzzle. No one could have deciphered the map without that sixth tablet. It is not an easy solution. Actually, I haven't yet discovered the exact location—"

Dr. Neil Palmer had worked in the field of archeology his entire professional life. He had handled priceless manuscripts, uncovered ancient artifacts that others skipped over without a clue as to their historic significance. He had laid bare entire cities of empires long extinct and buried beneath the sands of time. Now this priest asked after just a few hours with the map— and a photo of the map at that—where he should begin digging? Well, he actually knew the answer.

"But you do know *approximately* where the vault is located?" Caneman blurted out, impatient and feeling the precious seconds slipping through his fingers. Already the time he had bought by adjourning the conclave was fast dissolving.

"I can put you within a few kilometers of the site, yes. After just two hours studying the map, that is all you can expect. Give me the rest of our flight time to decipher Pope Alexander IV's coded message to us future generations."

The professor is insufferable, thought Caneman. The Church's empire is at stake and he speaks as if to a lecture hall filled with dim-witted undergraduates. He struggled to keep his voice calm, "Where should we begin staging our search, Neil?"

"Let us begin in Formia, Italy, then. The town is rather small and has quite a history within the Catholic Church. It actually is the perfect place to bury the Church's treasure trove. I will land in Rome and then my team and I will motor to Formia immediately."

"Excellent, Neil. I will make arrangements for your transport immediately."

* * *

CHAPTER 26

"Excuse me, Your Holi—*Sir*," exclaimed Sister Mary Pat as she caught herself before blurting out just whom she was addressing. Her voice was stern and commanding, as if addressing one of her elementary school students from so many years ago. "You are *not* leaving this hospital. Is that clear?"

The Pope looked out from beneath the covers of his hospital bed. He wore none of the regalia of his high office. Not even the papal white *zuchetti* on his head. The weakened Pontiff mustered all of his fragile strength. "Now see here, Mary Pat. I do not answer to you. You know to whom I answer—"

"And if He were here do you know what He would say?" SMP did not wait for her friend to answer. "I'll tell you what He'd say. He would say that you are being foolish. He would tell you that the last thing He needs right now is someone who just dropped dead from his own stubborn inclinations. That is what He would say."

Jack and Helen walked into the hospital room to see the both of them staring each other down. "What's going on in here?" Jack asked. His voice once again carried its knife edge of authority. Jack didn't want some meaningless argument between these two to screw up all the work they had done in getting the Pope into this hospital anonymously.

Helen said, "We could hear your voices rising way out in the hallway, even with your door closed. Keep this up and the whole city will know the handsome gentleman in this room is not the retired corporate executive his chart says he is."

Jack walked over to the bedside and grabbed the Pope's hand in his. He held it for almost a minute, looking into his eyes while Sister Mary Pat prattled on about the lunacy of the Pontiff leaving the hospital.

Even while she scolded him, she continued fluffing up the Pope's pillows. When he sat up objecting to all the attention, she placed a firm hand on his shoulder, pressing him back into the mattress then sat back down on the edge of the hospital bed.

266

"Perhaps you two will be able to talk some sense into *His Stubbornness*. He thinks he's going with us to Formia. Can you imagine?"

The Pope spoke up on his own behalf. "Finding the treasure vault, stopping David Caneman and his thugs from taking over the Church is its leader's responsibility. That is me. Should Caneman discover the vault with all of its treasure, his base of power will solidify instantly. When he returns to Rome and restarts the conclave, there will be no stopping his election to the papacy. That will be the end of the progress the Church has made over the last 100 years. It will thrust the billion faithful followers back into the dark ages of fundamentalist doctrine."

Jack still held onto the Pope's hand. He felt the thin, parchment-like skin stretched over the old bones. He was surprised at the strength the Pope showed when he squeezed back on Jack's grip. Almost as if daring him into an arm wrestling match right there. Jack let go of the Pope's fragile hand. He said, "You are worried about religious doctrine here. No one gets killed arguing doctrine."

The Pope and Sister Mary Pat both turned to Jack and stared at him.

"Well, they don't, do they?" Jack insisted.

"Oh dear boy," answered SMP, "they do indeed get killed. Over the ages that is exactly how the Church's fundamentalist factions enforced and coerced the people into submission."

The Pope added, "The Church evolved past such methods long ago. However, returning to Caneman's strict doctrine will reinstate the fear that dark period brought on." The Pope reached a hand out toward his water glass. Helen grabbed for it and handed it over.

The Pope sipped through the straw and continued, "What is at stake here is not just the Catholic Church. After all, there are many other religious institutions in the world. What is at stake is the growth of a disease that will damage the social fabric of society worldwide for years to come if allowed to go unchecked. Do not underestimate our followers. There are over 1.2 billion of us."

Jack shook his head, "Sorry, Your Holiness, but I don't see how—"

"You know the fear, brutality and inhumane acts that Al Qaeda has served up on those populations that have bowed to its fundamentalist Muslim doctrine in the name of Allah. In the towns where their rule of Sharia law dominates the population there is nothing but suffering. Sharia, like Caneman's fundamentalist Catholicism, is the strictest interpretation of the infallible law of God. Versus the gentler human interpretation of God's laws. Tell them, Mary Pat. You're better qualified than I am."

Sister Mary Pat took up the lecture. "The Taliban rose to power by promising peace in a region that had already suffered ten years of war with the Soviet Union. Not to mention the follow-on fighting between various Islamic factions after the Russians withdrew with their tail between their legs. The Taliban, which actually means *students*, surfaced in 1994. It was a product of the many followers who had attended conservative Muslim schools in Pakistan."

Jack watched Sister Mary Pat pause and reach for the Pope's water cup. She sipped from the same straw.

"Then in 1996, the Taliban took Kabul, the capital of Afghanistan. They have remained the dominant controlling force there to this day."

The Pope took up the reins. "If Caneman gains leadership of over a billion faithful Church followers, we will see an upheaval of organized violence the likes of which the Taliban theocracy can only wish for."

Jack said, "With all due respect, these are men running around in robes without any organized infrastructure and lacking the weaponry needed to conquer anything."

"Ah, my son, that is where you are wrong. History is replete with religious crusades that were extraordinarily organized and had weapons that were the most modern of their time. The crusaders invaded their targeted lands and brutally oppressed, enslaved and murdered those who disagreed with them. We have

268

seen what today's jihadists can do. They are not nearly so well organized as would be modern day Catholic crusaders. Nor do they have access to much more than AK-47s and rudimentary roadside bombs. Look how they have tied up the mighty US of A in over a decade of war costing a trillion dollars and so many American lives.

"No. A Catholic crusade led by someone as savvy as His Eminence Cardinal David Caneman would be more fearsome than Al Qaeda by a factor of 10. He is smart and organized. He is a charismatic leader. He understands the strategic use of money and has already demonstrated he has access to a hundred times the resources of Osama bin Laden. Even if you force him to return the $200 billion in investment money from the Vatican Bank's public stock offering he will not give up."

The Pope paused to take a breath and a sip from the water cup that he was now sharing with Sister Mary Pat.

Jack looked at the Pontiff with renewed respect. Here was a man who had his ear shot off, was blown up, shot again twice in the chest and suffered a heart attack. And what he wanted most was to get out of this hospital and jump back in the fight. Jack knew the feeling. He had seen it in his SEALs. But they were trained for it. What kind of training did His Holiness have? "You're a crusader," he told the Pope.

His Holiness' face crinkled into that charismatic smile and then his distinctive laugh the world had come to love during his short reign. He said, "And here I thought I was just a guy with big ears trying to do his job."

Sister Mary Pat was not convinced. "May God have mercy on us all if Caneman discovers the treasury of the Catholic Church. Its treasure will certainly be worth much more than the $200 billion from the Vatican's stock. But there is likely a more strategic treasure buried within. If so and if he finds it he will use it to his extraordinary advantage."

"What extraordinary advantage is that?" asked Helen.

The Pope shook his head from side to side. Jack saw the lines in his famous face set into a chiseled resolve. This guy is a rock, he thought to himself. Who am I to keep him laying in bed if what he really wants is to fight for his cause? I'd do the exact the same thing.

"You don't know what Caneman is looking for?" asked Helen.

"No," said the Pope, "I do not know what he's looking for in the vault. I suspect neither does Caneman. I have been thinking about it as I lay here in this bed. It will be an artifact. A symbol. Something that will gather the masses to him. It will make him immediately credible with all Catholics worldwide. With it, his election to the papacy will be a foregone conclusion. As will be the masses' demand for his leadership."

"Okay, Your Holiness," said Jack, "I might buy the theory of Caneman's fundamentalist leanings generating a new and maybe stricter faction. But a violent, menacing movement the likes of which you're describing would take decades to mount—"

"Not so, my son. A world free from bombs, weapons of mass destruction and those who would use them without a second thought is what's at stake here. You must understand that the risks could not be any higher. We saw how quickly Al Qaeda came to power in the Middle East—just 16 years beginning with financing in the 1990's from Osama Bin Laden's personal wealth and the 1996 bombing of the US embassies in the East African cities of Dar es Salaam and Nairobi. It didn't take long before Al Qaeda was a lethal force on the world stage."

Jack watched as the Pontiff shook his head and scowled. He continued, "I suppose the modern communications brought by the Internet and email had a great deal to do with that along with social media like Twitter and YouTube."

Jack knew the Pope was skilled in all things computer and most especially in the social media. I guess someone in his position has to be, he thought. Jack related to the Pope's lesson. He had spent time in Afghanistan. He had looked down the barrels of Al Qaeda's AK-47's; had carried broken and bloodied US troops from the wreckage of Hum-Vees that were unlucky enough to encounter roadside bombs. There was no question Al

270

Qaeda's low-tech, rag-tag followers were highly effective at intimidating and coercing its followers. Caneman was something else. If he was an enemy, Jack did not know what he could expect him to do. He took another close look at the Pope. He made his decision.

Jack said to the Pope, "Well if you're going with us, you'd better get dressed in something sturdier than that flimsy blue gown and shower slippers they had us both wearing. It won't last two minutes scrambling up and down hills and crawling through caves."

A light went on in the Pope's eyes. He pushed aside Sister Mary Pat's hand again offering the water cup and sat up straight.

"Jack." Helen's sharp voice brought both Jack and the Pope up short. "Mary Pat does have a point when she urges caution." She turned fully toward the Pope now. "I spoke with your cardiologist before I picked up my silly husband—and had to help him get dressed, by the way. You two are quite a pair. One was shot, the other escaped, what, four near misses? The doctor said that you are not nearly out of the woods yet. Your vital signs are improving but they need constant monitoring and professional attention should things go south in a hurry."

The Pope spoke up in his own defense, "There is no going south. There is only going out the door into the sunshine to join in your adventure."

"Oh?" demanded Sister Mary Pat, "and you know this how? Are you one of those seers I've heard about? You have inside information as to when your time with us is terminated?"

"Well, you know Sister," said the Pope, "with this office is said to come a direct line of communication with the Boss upstairs."

"So you have Him on speed dial with that fancy iPhone the American President gave you?" Sister Mary Pat nodded her head toward the red iPhone sitting on the bedside table. She noted that it had never been beyond arm's reach since the Pope received it in Gandolfo.

Jack looked at his watch, "Here's what we've got, Your Holiness. I'm leading this expedition for some very good reasons. Smitty is my second and he's bringing with us four new Spec Ops guys along with their supplies. Sister Mary Pat is chief navigator because she knows the terrain and the maps. Helen is coming…why is Helen coming again?"

"Helen is coming," interjected Helen, "because someone needs to play den mother to you two geniuses. And Helen is coming because she's your wife. If you want to stay married, you had better find a place for her."

Jack understood. "Right. So Helen is on the team." Facing the Pope now and leaning over the edge of his hospital bed so he could look him in the eye, Jack said, "You are our most valuable asset in this operation. It will be you who walks into that conclave and retakes your command whether or not this treasure exists. I find it difficult risking you on a mission that may well turn out to be a boondoggle. Tell me why you need to go."

The Pope held Jack's gaze as steadily as if he were a combatant. "I bring a perspective to this expedition none of you has thought of yet. It is true that Sister Mary Pat knows the maps and the history of the treasure vault. That Ph.D. of hers may yet turn out to be good for something. Nevertheless, I am not without portfolio as well. When you find the vault, what then? What will you do? How will you identify the thing—the one single artifact out of thousands—that Caneman seeks? How will you know what it represents should you somehow stumble upon it?" The Pope paused, allowing his question to float in the air between them.

"The answer is, that you cannot. The stakes are far too high for false modesty. So I must be frank. It will take a scholar with the sensitivity to the masses that no one other than the Pope himself possesses. Jack, when you go up against an enemy with far greater firepower than you, do you leave your biggest gun behind? Young man, I am your biggest gun."

No one in the room laughed at the outrageous comment spoken by the 83-year-old leader of over a billion faithful.

The Pope knew that if their expedition was to be successful they would have to work as a team. He had Jack on his side. Jack commanded the team. But his endorsement would not be enough. He turned to face Sister Mary Pat as she began her argument.

"Your Holiness, you would definitely add a unique perspective on the twists and turns this map is going to take us." She shook the map pages already in her hand. "You want to go. I can see that. And you deserve to go. But it would be irresponsible to the 1.2 billion of your followers to place you in harm's way."

Helen chimed in next. "See, Your Holiness, a team can only move as fast as its slowest member. In all honestly, that would be you. A team is only as strong as its weakest member. It's not a value judgment. Jack has introduced me to some tough guys in the last year. But you are way up there at the top of my list. You are 83 years old, in good shape for being 83, but still. You just suffered three attempts on your life, each connecting in a significant way—an ear was blown off, you survived a horrific explosion and you were shot twice, but somehow managed to ward off both bullets. Don't ask me how. Then with all the excitement, your heart gave out. Whose wouldn't?"

Helen leaned into the Pope's face and grabbed his frail hand. She could feel the fragile skin and bones inside her own strong hand. The bones moved in the old hand that had literally blessed millions as she gently squeezed, "Your Holiness, don't you think that maybe you've given enough?"

The Pope rose from his pillow and sat up straight. "You said yourself that I earned a place on your expedition."

"And so you have," this time Jack answered, putting an end to the discussion. "But you must understand who is in command—"

"You are," replied the Pope immediately.

"When I say the area is too hot risk-wise and you are to seek cover in place, will I get an argument?"

"No, there will be no argument."

"Ever?"

"Never. No argument. You're the boss," then the Pope couldn't resist, "my son."

273

* * *

CHAPTER 27

"Pretty slick," said Helen as the group exited from three Italian-made Iveco Massifs—SUVs that were every bit as ubiquitous here in Italy as the Chevy Suburban is in America. The rugged off-road trucks were manufactured by the thousands by Fiat's truck division. Each was powered by a versatile 3.0-liter turbo diesel. The design came from the famous Giorgetto Giugiaro, named Car Designer of the Century in 1999 and inducted into the Automotive Hall of Fame in 2002. Giugiaro didn't limit his designs to just cars. Oh no. He was responsible for Nikon's camera bodies as well as the prototype designs for some of Apple's early computers. He even developed a new pasta shape called *marille*.

The three trucks were parked on the hospital's underground delivery ramp. "I think His Holiness was finally mollified," Jack said to Smitty as they stood next to one of the Ivecos. Jack grabbed a heavy duffel bag from the back and winced as its weight pulled his left shoulder, stretching his stitches. "The Pope is a smart guy. He gets it." He set the bag down and caught Helen's severe stare as she stopped before putting her own duffel in the back. Jack winked at her. He spoke softly, "Say Smitty, could I have a little help here with *your* supplies?"

"Sure thing," said Smitty, "I thought we agreed that you were using your brain in this op rather than your brawn."

Jack turned back to Helen as the rest of the group loaded their gear into the three SUVs and made ready to depart.

Jack helped the Pope into his seat—it was the third row. He would share it with Sister Mary Pat. Jack whispered to Helen, "His Holiness is focused on the mission, same as we are. For a different reason, but the result will be the same. And you've gotta admit, it's one hell of an adventure, tracking down and uncovering the world's greatest treasure stash."

"Or maybe just another of the world's myths surrounding the Catholic Church," said Sister Mary Pat, as she twisted and turned herself into the third row seat beside the Pope. SMP carried a nylon backpack stuffed with maps and journals that she hoped would help her guide them to what she was sure could only be an underground cavern on the coast. She was certain she knew where to look. It was the only subterranean structure on the geological maps of the area that was elevated enough to keep the sea water out and protect the loot the Church had accumulated and hidden away. They would be in Formia in twelve to eighteen hours depending on the weather.

Neil Palmer stabbed his finger at the map. "We are just a few minutes outside of Formia, David." The rain that had pounded the caravan of spanking new Mercedes vehicles since they left Rome had finally quit. The countryside was drying out. Behind them, Palmer could only guess the deluge that persisted in the mountains over which they had come.

He drew a circle around the small town on the Mediterranean coast with his index finger, then looked across the back seat of the black Mercedes G550 at Caneman. His Eminence would not have traveled in anything of a lesser status—even when he was supposed to be conducting a clandestine operation. Some habits never die. "As you can see, it is not a very big place. We are in luck."

Caneman glanced first at the map Palmer held up to him, then out the Mercedes window. It was late afternoon. The sun was beginning to set. Formia's coast was dotted with small inlets and coves surrounding the harbor. Lights were beginning to flicker on in the stores and restaurants surrounding the quay and on the boats bobbing in their slips and at anchor out in the harbor.

"Where are we going first?" Caneman demanded. They were in a caravan that included six of the imposing Mercedes G550s— the G-Wagons as they were known. Each carried six of Palmer's archeologists. A large Mercedes van followed with their tools, explosives, lighting equipment and some weapons. A second van was empty. Caneman had brought it along to carry their plunder back to Rome. He was betting the future of the entire worldwide

Catholic Church that what they would find could fill the van many times over.

"Well David, an expedition to find a specific vault from a particular period takes time. If I were mounting such a mission for a museum or a university I would spend three months alone in preparing the archaeological predictive model."

"What is that?" asked Caneman.

Palmer nodded, "It is a tool that indicates the probability that an archaeological site will occur in a certain area. We use it to determine where to look for sites based on known factors we have determined through research—"

"And you haven't had the time to do the research, have you," complained Caneman.

"Ah, my friend, that is where you are wrong. When you acquired the fourth stone tablet three years ago, I assigned the research project to my graduate students. At that time it was an exercise. More to teach them the techniques of archeological research rather than anything concrete. Still they came up with some very interesting theories as to where the old popes from centuries past would have squirreled away their plunder from the faithful. They ruled out the new world for obvious reasons. They centered on the coast of Italy. Still it is a very large search area—thousands of square miles."

Caneman saw that their convoy had now traveled through the harbor and were on the road leading down to the southern coastal edge of Formia as they began leaving the harbor area. He listened to Palmer drone on.

"Then when you obtained the fifth tablet, the research quickly turned more serious. I figured that it was only a matter of time before you found the sixth and final tablet. I funneled some grant money to the project—about $4 million and actually hired two professional, real-life archeologists to assist. They are with us now. One is an expert in finding tombs—has discovered Hazor, the largest biblical-era site in Israel, concentrating on the Israelite and Canaanite periods. He also unearthed Shipwreck 43 in Aboukir Bay, Egypt. 43 is just one of 64 ancient wrecks in the area. Naturally, our guy's wreck has proven the most valuable not only from an archeological standpoint, but from a financial one as well. He can pinpoint the opening of a cave, a tomb, or a vault just by looking over the natural contours of the surrounding landscape. But he doesn't leave it to such chance. He has some of the most sophisticated equipment for the job there is. It's in the van behind us. All totaled, we have about $1 million worth of the most modern archeological detection equipment at our disposal."

Palmer continued, now fully warmed to his subject. "I included something else, David. Something that only experience in the field would identify the need for."

"What is that?" asked Caneman.

"Security. I have every intention of succeeding in this expedition. When I succeed, I will have discovered the greatest archeological find of this or possibly any other century. Priceless objects of art, statues, paintings, manuscripts and precious metals and gems will be exposed for the first time in centuries. They must be safeguarded from the instant we have identified the site. Even before the first shovelful of earth is pitched aside. Therefore, I have selected each of my crew here in the field not only for their academic credentials and their experience on other archeological digs, but they also know how to defend a site. We have handguns and automatic rifles."

Caneman nodded. "I'm a step ahead of you, Neil. I brought with us a former Army general and several of his hand-picked troops. They're not in this convoy. They prefer traveling alone, unnoticed until we arrive at the site."

Palmer stared for a few seconds. Then he nodded his approval. He continued, "In addition to the first professional archeologist, my other man has an even more impressive resume of accomplishments and archeological firsts. He has a subspecialty in religious artifacts. If he can't recognize whatever it is you're looking for once we uncover the vault, there is no human alive who can."

Caneman said, "I am impressed, Neil. You have assembled a world-class team and their equipment in record time."

278

Palmer bowed his head only slightly to acknowledge the rare compliment. "I have at that, David. However, it was not in record time. I have been expecting we would be doing this for the last year. So I began assembling my team back then as well. That is when our predictive model changed focus for the better. Suddenly it pointed to this area like a laser pointer on a wall map. My two professionals used factors my grad students never thought of—distance from the sea, ground steepness, soil type, and the other things that will likely define the treasury site. For some reason—we believe that it was politically influenced within the Church over the centuries—there was never any archaeological expedition mounted in this region. Odd, don't you think? Over these hundreds of years not one recorded expedition into the Formia area searching for the greatest treasure trove in history. A treasury that would exceed the ancient Egyptians by a factor of at least 10. Why do you think that is, David?"

Caneman considered the question. He knew the answer. He knew that he understood Vatican politics better than any man on the planet. Caneman didn't think the popes of centuries ago were much different than those of today. They still conducted the same ancient ceremonies; read the same two-thousand year-old sacraments. They had dealt with similar challenges to their authority as he was currently experiencing. Sure, the old popes commanded armies and had the authority to mount military strikes against the Church's enemies. He continued watching the Italian coastline speed past as the day transformed from pink to a deeper red as the sun slipped below the ocean's horizon out at sea. Then it receded into purple, growing ever deeper and sliding into blackness as night fell around the ancient city of Formia.

Caneman believed that when he became Pope he too would have the obligation and the resources to mount assaults on the Church's enemies. He expected that in the beginning such show of force would be necessary to deal with the old guard in the countries that refused to accept the new role of the Catholic Church in their social fabric. The difference would be that his assaults would be financial in nature and target the politicians who controlled the Church's enemies.

279

David Caneman was a brilliant financial engineer. He had
used his Harvard MBA to create the new Vatican Bank. Today it
was stronger, more powerful and among the world's most
respected financial institutions. What happened with the recent
stock offering was but a minor bump in the road.

David Caneman grew up in a family who lacked both
financial resources and a basic understanding of simple
economics. By the time he was a freshman in college he had
mastered the real life mechanics of both. Caneman had financed
his own college education—both undergraduate and Harvard's
business school—by trading the stock of mid-cap companies. He
researched each position he took into his portfolio. He scoured
the publications first for disruptive, break-out technologies.
When he had that, he drilled down into the enterprises competing
in that space. He searched for the lesser-known participants.
Those which had patented technologies that appeared able to
take out the competition. He accumulated their stock—usually it
sold in the single digits when he first began buying.

Caneman's unique trading strategy left no room for error. If
a company failed to live up to the targets he set for it within the
time he had allotted, he sold his positions and moved on to the
next. Those stocks that performed, climbed the charts. Caneman
bought only through the first 25 percent of the stock's climb.
These he let ride. His war chest quickly grew. Within three years
he had accumulated $8 million in profits—after living and
college expenses.

During graduate school his fortune became more substantial.
Armed with a new MBA he marched into the offices of Goldman
Sachs and talked his way into its trading operations. His trading
account profits and his methodology actually did the talking for
him. Anyone so young who could accomplish what he apparently
had was someone Goldman wanted on one of their desks. Doing
what, they weren't sure. But they hired Caneman anyway.

Still, making money was just a means to an end for
Caneman. He knew what he wanted—power and control. He
took his time in selecting the venue that his considerable

financial skills would allow him to rise the fastest. He settled on the Catholic Church. Even though he was born Jewish, conversion was easy for such a man. Caneman was not wed to any religious persuasion. Such a chameleon could easily assume the mantle of whatever faith best suited his needs. While still at Goldman, he brought in one of the largest private accounts the institution had seen—the Vatican Bank. He made himself known to the bank's executives. Word got around about the young financial *wunderkind*. When he asked the Vatican Bank's managing director about attending seminary and becoming ordained, the gates opened wide.

His mentor—none other than Vatican Bank's CFO, Senior Cardinal Scott Brooks—personally selected St. Joseph's Seminary and College, nicknamed Dunwoodie, after the Yonkers, New York neighborhood in which it is located. Dunwoodie is considered the West Point of seminaries. Its curriculum is comprehensive and its discipline is strict. It is one of the more prestigious and theologically orthodox Roman Catholic seminaries in the United States.

Caneman soared through Dunwoodie, amassing an impressive list of academic firsts. He maintained contact with His Eminence Cardinal Brooks, knowing full well that his progress was being tracked at the Church's highest levels. Exactly what he planned. He also continued his association with Goldman Sachs, though on an abbreviated basis. He still managed to earn a combined salary and piece of the profits he created in the mid six figures.

After graduation and ordination, Caneman was, of course, sent to the Vatican Bank as his first assignment. This was a young man whose considerable talents were far too valuable to spend in some outlying parish ministering to a know-nothing, go-nowhere congregation. He rose up the ranks of executives at the Bank. Within three years—thanks to his department's trading profits—he was running the largest division of the Bank. Effectively, he was second in command of the most storied financial institution in the world.

Soon he implemented his plan to clean house, revamp operations and take over. His new system of internal accounting controls appeared innocuous at first. Soon it began revealing—as Caneman knew it would—the corruption and deceit at the Bank's highest levels. Among the first to go was his mentor, Cardinal Brooks. The man's demise came as no surprise. He was an embezzler of the first order. Over the years, Cardinal Brooks had amassed personal assets amounting to $50 million. He had squirreled it away in anonymous accounts around the world. Caneman naturally knew exactly where the Cardinal's plunder was stashed. He made short work of raiding Brooks' accounts and repatriating it back to Vatican Bank.

The Pope fired Brooks personally while Caneman stood by watching. As for the rest, Caneman really had to do very little other than watch his corrupt colleagues hang themselves. One did literally—early one foggy morning he was found hanged by the neck from a lamppost in London.

Caneman was soon called to Rome again, raised to the level of Cardinal and made CEO of Vatican Bank. He was given the assignment to clean it up. This he did. Within one year, its accounting books and records seemed so clean, they were the envy of any multinational US corporation. Most men at this stage would call it a career. The chief executive of one of the world's most prestigious banks; rich beyond imagination, despite the vow of poverty which didn't apply to cardinals anyway. And he had the ear of the Pope himself. What else was there?

Much more, thought Caneman. Much more. All this was preordained. Planned. Simple, really, when you mapped out the steps it took to get him here. What would not be so simple was the next step. That was to stop the dangerous modernization of the Church. Priests were misbehaving, committing crimes. A movement of priests wanted to marry. The nuns wanted to be ordained. The nuns, for God's sake, Caneman exclaimed to himself. The Church was losing its power and influence more and more each day. Where would it stop? He knew and he found it unacceptable.

Caneman had the means to stop the Church's insidious slide to ruination. He had the small but powerful advisors who commanded vast resources—financial, medical, military and spiritual. Along with the huge fortune his Bank had amassed by going public, he was on the verge of discovering the Church's centuries old treasure trove. If the public stock offering was overturned, the treasure was essential to his plan. Without the treasure, he knew he would fail. David Caneman was not someone who had ever failed at anything. He wasn't about to start now.

Caneman knew how he would do it. With the treasure and especially with the single artifact he knew must exist within the ancient vault he would begin his global conquest. How do you take over a country though? Caneman had studied the masters: North Korea's Kim Jong Il, Uganda's Idi Amin Dada, Russia's Vladimir Lenin and Japan's Emperor Hirohito. Compared to them, Iraq's Saddam Hussein and Al Qaeda's Osama bin Laden were rank amateurs. Caneman knew how to take over a country. He considered it rather easy, actually.

The first step was to swoop in as if you and your followers were a kindly uncle concerned for the citizens' welfare. Give them what their current regime had failed to provide: food, cooking oil and gasoline to start. Then running water and a sewage treatment system. After all, he was the Church,. All it took was money. He had that in abundance. And there was not a government on earth who would dare fault the Catholic Church's motives for simply trying to make life better in these backwater countries. With their immediate needs taken care of, now offer them safety and protection. Keep them ever mindful that what you just gave them could be taken away in an instant by outside forces unfriendly to Caneman's cause.

Certainly the takeover process required the elimination of the politicians and control over their political system. All that took was a few well-aimed, clandestine bullets and some money discretely spread around the proper levels.

Next Caneman knew he must offer proper guidance to the masses. Again, not so difficult. The media was more than accommodating to give free airtime if they believed it could fill up their advertising schedule. His plan for global domination by his Church called for control over the broadcast media, social networking, Internet and the news agencies.

With the media brought to heel, Caneman's list next called for control over the country's police and law enforcement agencies. With the political regime taken care of, this became no more than a matter of signing the right laws into effect and properly managing the budgets of the enforcement agencies. With the police in his pocket, he would finally turn to the judicial systems. He would replace those judges currently sitting on the bench with those more attuned to God's one true law.

Eventually, as time went on, Caneman planned to repurpose the social and cultural icons—the churches, theaters and sports stadiums—into facilities that enhanced the fundamentalist doctrines of the Roman Catholic Church under Pope Caneman. If you had the resources and the methodology, Caneman thought, it all really wasn't that difficult.

Indeed, he thought as he sat there in the G-Wagon's back seat while his motorcade swooped down the coastline, *my weapons are so much more potent.* When you command a bank with the vast resources of the Vatican your weapons are many and formidable. Money talks louder than any gun. Forget the multitudes of foot soldiers. First compromise those who command them. Even more, he thought, those who commanded the commanders. Eventually he would have the supreme commanders in his pocket. He would not stop even then. He wanted the politicos who commanded the supreme commanders. Get them on the payroll. Make them beholden. The hearts and minds of the entire country would soon follow. *Just watch me,* he thought.

"Why do you think that is, David?" asked Palmer.

"Hmmm?" Caneman growled as he reluctantly left his reverie.

284

"Not one recorded expedition into Formia during these hundreds of years. Good God man, it is likely the greatest treasure trove in history. But not one expedition to find it."

Caneman turned in his leather seat to face the famous archeologist turned college president. In the fading light he looked him in the eye. "Because the Church and its agents like the Knights Templar have contacts everywhere. Had there ever been a team that appeared to be getting close to the real location of the Church's treasury, they would have been…discouraged from continuing their efforts."

"That is my conclusion as well. So, someone within the Church was entrusted with this information and charged with keeping the secret of its location safe from intruders. Over the centuries this responsibility was passed from person to person. So I directed an archeological survey of the area from Formia all the way on down to Pozzuoli. Still, it was a ridiculously large area. But I believed we were at least in the right ballpark. Now I am certain we can identify the site with a precision no expedition has ever been able to accomplish."

Caneman knew something about archeology himself. After all, he *was* able to obtain all six of the ancient stone tablets that comprised the map that got them here in the first place. "Dr. Palmer," he said, "we have just three days to not only find the site but to excavate and obtain the one treasure that I am looking for. Even if you are within 100 meters of the vault, you might still burn all that time just finding the entrance."

"Ah, David, that is where you are mistaken—"

"This is a large area to search for a single centuries-old door," interrupted Caneman.

Palmer laughed mirthlessly in the now darkened cabin of the lead Mercedes. The five other G550s and their two equipment vans followed. "As I said, we have two real-life professional archeologists with us, David. They have the equipment we will need for a very fast assessment, penetration and excavation."

"What kind of equipment?" asked Caneman. "So far as I knew the most valuable tool any archeologist had in his knapsack was a hand trowel."

Palmer looked at the new pope-to-be through the darkness. "Perhaps in another era the trowel actually was the archeologist's best friend." Palmer sighed deeply as if explaining yet again to a dull student. "Now however, we live in the age of ground-penetrating radar. Such devices—about the size and look of a good lawn mover—can make short work of identifying what lies beneath and behind suspected entrances to ancient tombs and vaults."

"I've never heard of that used in archeology," said Caneman.

"It greatly speeds up the search, David. Ground-penetrating radar uses radar pulses to image the subsurface of whatever structure you're investigating. It detects the reflected signals from subsurface objects and spaces. Nowadays, we use GPR on all sorts of structures: rock, soil, ice, fresh water, pavements and structures. It can detect objects, changes in material, voids and cracks—"

"But can it find the entrance to the vault?"

"Of course," replied Palmer as if this were mere child's play. "And unlike excavation, GPR locates artifacts and maps features without risk of damage. I have used GPR to locate Roman coins at depths of 20 meters through porous sand."

"I am not concerned with the damage to the vault we might do," shouted a suddenly agitated David Caneman. The startled driver turned in his seat to look at the Cardinal and his outburst. Caneman was irritated that the learned Dr. Palmer still failed to grasp the urgency and import of what their expedition needed to find and why.

* * *

CHAPTER 28

Jack was used to riding in military vehicles of all kinds—
HMMWV's, M1 Abrams battle tanks, inflatable boats,
helicopters—but the three Italian-made Iveco Massifs that Smitty
had somehow obtained for their tiny crew of eight was
something else. It was large, reeked of diesel and had seen much
better days in the distant past. It was all Smitty could get on such
short notice. The rain that had begun as dark clouds started
dropping their torrent over the countryside. Quickly the road
turned to a sloppy amalgam of old, cracked asphalt, mud and
other debris. The Iveco in this slop reminded Jack of a lumbering
rhino. It bumped along the sodden and muddy Italian roadway
like a small boat over choppy water. The ride irritated the hell
out of his bullet wound. He tried as best he could to protect it
from the jarring motion of the truck.

Jack, Ellen, His Holiness, Mr. Schilling and Sister Mary Pat
rode in the first Massif. The other four special operators and their
meager supplies were stuffed into the other two. Their convoy
was not nearly so well equipped nor luxurious by expedition
standards as Caneman's. And he was way ahead of them with
more than three times the number of people and millions more in
equipment.

Jack asked Smitty, "Where do you think the competition is
right now?" Smitty became the logistics master of their operation
while Jack was laid up.

"They're about a day ahead," Smitty said. "I contacted the
Rome office of the *Carabinieri*. Asked if a caravan had left there
recently. Sure enough one blew out of the city a day ago. My
guess is that it is Cardinal David Caneman's caravan on their
way to search for the vault."

"But where would they look first?" asked Sister Mary Pat.
She had her maps spread out over her lap and Helen's who sat
next to her. She trained her flashlight over first one map, then
another. "I mean, locating the general area wasn't so hard. I think
I did a pretty good job of it if I do say so myself. But that work is
a galaxy away from knowing just where to stick your pick and

shovel into the sand and expect to uncover a centuries-old doorway."

Mr. Schilling turned around from the front seat and spoke. His was the voice of experience—if not from experience as an archeologist, then from many missions to uncover hidden treasure on behalf of the IRS. Since the Deadly Acceleration escapade two years ago, he had served as the IRS head of off-shore asset recovery. "If I may, Sister and Smitty, do you have any idea what they are driving?"

Smitty echoed, "Driving? Mr. S you want to know about their cars?"

"I certainly do, son. The type of car will tell us what resources Caneman has at his beck and call. It will also tell us how concerned he is about security and discovery. So do you know?"

Smitty was resourceful and comprehensive. It came from his military training. "I asked the *Carabinieri* in Rome that same question. Didn't think much of it when I asked, just wanted to know. Turns out they have six new Mercedes G550s and two large Mercedes Step-Vans."

Mr. Schilling rubbed his chin for a moment, thinking about Smitty's answer. The rest waited as the Massif bumped along the road at too leisurely a pace for anyone's liking. "The G-wagon is an expensive piece of equipment," Schilling began. "Just what someone with an unlimited budget and no thought of maintaining a low profile would use. Each one costs about $114K in US dollars. And Caneman's got six of them. And two Mercedes vans. That tells me he's sparing no expense and has money to burn on this. He's a serious player who won't go home empty handed."

Mr. Schilling looked at Sister Mary Pat. "What type of equipment would you want if money were no object and there was no problem in getting your wish list out here?"

SMP answered immediately. "I would get one of those ground penetrating radar devices. Two of them actually. One I would have rigged for running along the ground so I could see the vault opening below me. The other would be the newest vertical mounted version. The vault opening might be in a rock wall or even perhaps overhead."

Jack asked, "Well, Sister why didn't you say something? We could have at least tried to get what you needed."

"I am sorry, Jackson. I didn't even consider it. They cost about $50,000 US each."

Jack's voice had a steely edge, "Sister don't ever do that again."

SMP looked at Jack's dark, angry eyes and the firm set of his jaw. She could tell he was infuriated. His penetrating look caused her to shrink into the Iveco's seat back. So this is what a pissed off SEAL looks like, she thought. "But I didn't do anything," she exclaimed, trying to defend against whatever made Jack so angry with her. "It's not like I went out and spent your money without asking—"

Mr. Schilling gently cut her off. "What he means, Sister, is that our little group is not without our own resources. Nothing like the hundreds of billions that Vatican Bank and Cardinal David Caneman have available. But still, a cash outlay of $100,000 for the devices you would need to find a vault containing treasure worth in excess of several billions is a small sum. Truly." His voice was gentle, soothing to SMP's bruised feelings. "Had you simply let me know what you needed, I have my AMEX black card right here in my pocket. It could have paid for…for…"

"The ground penetrating radar," prompted Jack. Then he fell darkly silent again.

"Right, the ground penetrating radar in an instant," said Mr. Schilling. "See Sister, among other things Jack and Smitty are logistical experts. They could have obtained it for you even if it required hiring a private jet to fly it in from wherever it was."

Helen poked Jack in his sore side. He spoke up, "Sorry Sister if I jumped down your throat. I'm just used to getting whatever the job requires and having it staged for deployment when we need it. That's how I learned and how I had the SEC

Enforcement Division working before I left for private enterprise."

Helen tried to lighten the moment, "I can vouch for the fact that is how my husband also runs his part of Kaito's small truck division as well as the kitchen in our home."

Sister Mary Pat finally understood the extent of the Schilling's resources. A cash payment in excess of $100,000 apparently didn't bother them in the least. What bothered them was not having the equipment their resources could have brought to this expedition. Knowing that now, she agreed, she should have said something. "So what do we do now?" she asked.

Mr. Schilling said, "It's too late to get that kind of equipment. We're out in the middle of nowhere. It's raining bullets. Let me ask, what do you think your chances really are of actually finding the vault?"

All eyes in the Italian SUV focused on Sister Mary Pat sitting with the Pope on the third row bench seat. Outside the storm continued pounding their 3-car caravan and the sloppy road on which they persisted. She thought about her answer. She was well educated. But biblical archaeology had been only a minor of hers—a passing interest really—on her way to a Ph.D. in medieval European Catholic history. I am not a professional archeologist, she thought. That's really what we need here. Two would be ideal. Along with all the equipment and a few dozen research assistants to handle the digging and excavation.

SMP said, "Let me be honest to all here—Your Holiness especially—this task is so far above my level it is incomprehensible. True, I have studied the maps and applied a good deal of what little I know to get us to the general vicinity of where I believe the Catholic Church buried its treasure vault. But—and let me be perfectly frank here—that feat was elementary to a real professional. They would have determined that the area around Formia was the most likely place in a matter of hours with the map of the six tablets put together. It took we three—Helen, His Holiness any myself—many times that."

Sister Mary Pat looked at them in the waning light as the storm intensified before them. Lightning flashed ahead of them in bright white bolts thundering down from the sky. Behind them the dark clouds had gathered, forming a solid wall of storm. On either side of the roadway, sheets of rain—solid as granite slabs—pelted the asphalt, obliterating any road markings.

The Iveco SUVs relentlessly slogged through it. Sister Mary Pat continued, "I am afraid that I have probably maxed out my knowledge base just in getting us to the general area. What a true professional would do next is dial in the exact location to within perhaps 100 meters using surface surveys of possible sites, then digging shallow test pits followed by deployment of the ground penetrating radar. A really well-funded expedition would also bring along a wire logging sonar rig to be used in the most promising sites. I was on a dig near Tel Aviv in my senior year where just such a Directional Sonar Caliper System managed to create full 3D-images of the subsurface caverns we discovered. Wire logging uses angular-resolved sonic distance measurements. The scanning accuracy inside of the caverns is amazing—even if they're filled with salt water." She stopped and raised her eyebrows at the obvious application of such equipment searching for an ancient vault right down on the seashore near Formia, Italy.

Sister Mary Pat said, "In a real expedition—maybe one sponsored by the British Museum—all this work would go rather quickly. Probably a week or two tops. They would have enough highly skilled people," she continued, "that they could begin digging in at least three of the most promising locations very quickly. That is how they would spread their risk of hitting a dry hole as it is called in professional archeological circles. Then once they finally find the vault, the real work begins. They would carefully penetrate the vault so they did not disturb any of the priceless antiquities. And don't forget, they would also have several structural engineers—perhaps mining engineers—to prop up the ceiling with joists that will keep the vault from falling in on itself while they worked.

"Then, assuming they found what they were looking for, they would have others outside staging and categorizing what they found. No expense would be spared on such a project. This is the most valuable archeological dig the world has seen outside of the Middle East."

Jack had stopped listening to Sister Mary Pat. His gaze moved on to Smitty who sat in the front seat with a cell phone pressed into his ear to better hear over the pounding rain. Jack thought Smitty looked overly agitated at his telephone call. Then the former SEAL, now having taken Jack's place at the SEC Enforcement Division when Jack took the CFO job at Taiko Automotive, abruptly removed the cell phone, smashed the end call button and blew out an exasperated breath.

"One of your missed dates decided she had enough of your cancelled dinners?" Jack asked Smitty.

Jack's protégé turned around from the front seat. "Screw you, boss. When Smitty comes a-knockin' they never go a-packin'."

"What then?"

The conversation turned serious as Jack knew it would after their meaningless banter. It was their way of lightening some of the frightening moments they had found themselves facing over the years both in the Navy and at the CIA before they went to work for the SEC.

Smitty said, "My contacts at the *Carabinieri* have all just clammed up, boss. I called people I know in offices from Rome all the way down the coast past Formia. There is no information whatsoever about the caravan I was told left Rome yesterday."

Jack nodded. Son of a bitch, he thought. "What's that mean?" But he already knew.

"It means that someone got to the *Carabinieri*. If they got to my guys, then they got to those above and probably below them as well. We won't be getting any more help from the *Carabinieri* or any of its sources on this outing, Boss."

292

Jack thought for a moment. Then, "But it does tell us so much more."

All eyes in the Iveco Massif turned Jack's way. "What does it tell us?" asked the Pope. He was slouched as comfortably as possible in the corner braced against the door and the back seat while the Italian-made SUV navigated the ruts and potholes of the saturated roadbed.

Jack thought for a few more seconds. "It tells us that Sister Mary Pat is exactly correct. The vault we're after is in Formia— or at least somewhere in the immediate vicinity. Why else would the good Cardinal use his power and the Vatican's iron-fisted influence to gain the silence of an organization so large as the *Carabinieri* from Rome all the way out on a straight line toward Formia?"

The Pope spoke up. "Jack is correct. The Holy See routinely uses its influence to bend the attention of entire public agencies either toward or away from things and issues in which it is interested. Myself, I have been guilty of mentioning my special interest in something, then, poof it somehow happens. I don't ask how. Thus is the incredible power of the Holy See."

The others began talking excitedly. Jack just sat there, silent. Helen noticed that Jack was not participating—totally unlike him. He was a commanding presence in any forum. His wife of just one year knew her husband as someone whose mere presence exuded a certain authority because of his reputation, what he had done—both actual and the rumors about him—and the various jobs he had held. She fell silent and just watched Jack sit there in the dark now that the sun had fully set. One by one the others stopped talking and looked Jack's way for his guidance.

When he was ready Jack said, "Cardinal David Caneman has placed a security net around the area. Probably from Rome where Smitty discovered they left from all the way down the coast way past Formia, if Sister Mary Pat is right. It is a blackout of any information having to do with his activities in the area. He wouldn't do that unless he was dead sure he was onto the vault's location."

Jack thought for another minute. "Smitty's right too. We won't be getting any help from the *Carabinieri*. But I think there's every likelihood that we could be getting some interference from them." Then he asked Sister Mary Pat, "What types of security concerns do archeologist have?" His inflection seemed rhetorical, innocent and of no real consequence. Just a question in which he might have had a passing interest.

"Security? Why in the past few years it has become of immense interest. Most well-funded expeditions in the Middle East have a paid security staff. They are there to not only protect any antiquities that might be discovered but also to keep safe the expedition staff from marauders. These digs are often located in dangerous parts and off the beaten path. Additionally, it is no secret that the really heavy lifting in these expeditions is done by locals they hire on a daily basis for pennies. The locals can, and do, leak information to others outside the dig about what was recently found. Then these people turn into thieves. There have been incidents where too-well-informed groups of thieves swoop down into a camp and know where to go to find exactly the artifacts they're looking for. Several teams have lost people and many more have been injured. The security force keeps the locals employed by the expedition in line and makes sure they do not carry any weapons that could bring harm to the expedition. They also provide a form of protection. Security is becoming a huge concern. Why do you ask?"

Jack was silent for a moment as he thought. Then, "Formia is a civilized place. Certainly not like Syria or Iraq where some of the expeditions you mentioned may have run into trouble. So, I'm thinking, if Caneman's expedition—large as Smitty says it is—has invested an inordinate amount in extra manpower, vehicles and equipment, that might be a dead giveaway."

"Giveaway to what?" asked Helen.

The Pope spoke up. He was tracking Jack's thought process precisely. "A giveaway as to just where they are concentrating their efforts. The more security and people in general they have on a site, the more likely that is where they have discovered the vault."

"So we're beaten," said Mary Pat. "They have more people, much more equipment and more security staff to protect them than we do. They have at least a day's head start. They will find the vault long before we could ever hope to."

Jack nodded. "Exactly, Sister. That's what I'm counting on." Jack leaned toward the third back seat where she was sitting. "Not to throw discredit at your archeological skills in any way, Sister Mary Pat," Jack reassured her. "But you are correct. We are much too small a team to compete with them in locating and excavating the vault. So why try? Why not let them do our work for us. Then, once they've discovered the vault and blown their way in to begin the excavation, we walk in and relieve them of the loot and take over. Sort of take a page from the marauders of the Middle East digs."

Mary Pat asked, "Even if your plan to raid the camp could be done, where would we look for them? Archeologists don't exactly advertise where their digs are located. They're just like fishermen who never divulge the location of their favorite fishing holes. If the *Carabinieri* are no longer providing you with information, how will we find them?"

Jack looked at Smitty. Both nodded in the silent communication they had established so many years ago. Then they both turned to the back seat where the Pope sat. Helen was watching this mental telepathy. She found it fascinating how Jack and Smitty did it. Apparently the Pope was getting some of it too because after a few seconds of staring one another down he smiled his understanding and nodded his head. Then he pulled that new red iPhone the American President had given him from its red velvet case with the gold papal insignia on it and dialed a number. Helen saw that Jack and Smitty were apparently satisfied because they both turned back and stared out into the storm, waiting.

Helen sat beside the Pope so even over the pounding rain and the lurching of the Iveco as it ran over rocks and dived into potholes she could overhear one side of his conversation. She listened:

"Yes, Mr. President it is really me…no I am not dead. Jack, Helen, Mary Pat and Smitty are taking good care of me…My body? That poor soul was one of the Swiss guards assigned to my protection service. He did what he volunteered to do and paid for it with his life. The best way to honor his sacrifice is to prevail against David Caneman's attempt to highjack the Church…Well, my friend, as it turns out there is something that you can do. We need to find out just where a certain archeological expedition is going on the coast of western Italy near Formia…yes, that's right, Formia. It will be a large expedition. Your godson told me they have six Mercedes G550 SUVs and two large step vans—Mercedes also."

Helen was getting a good understanding of how the Pope was cajoling the President to do his bidding. She continued listening.

"This is not rocket science, my friend…you can figure out what I am asking. But just to save you the mental effort, let me spell it out," said the Pope. "I believe the United States still has the funds to keep its surveillance satellites aloft. Perhaps not the trillions of dollars to provide medical care for its people as that silly healthcare plan your idiot predecessor tried foisting on your people. But money for military offensives and weaponry, yes, absolutely. So why don't you just task one of those satellites flying over Italy to make a slight modification to its track and let me know where this expedition is going. Oh, and one other thing. I'd like your surveillance people to photograph His Eminence' digs—Sister Mary Pat tells me there will likely be two or three—with particular attention to the surrounding countryside so I can orient myself as to where they are. Can you do that for me, Mr. President?"

Helen saw His Holiness nod at the cell phone and push the button to end his conversation. Then he said to Jack and Smitty, "He says he'll make it happen. Though I must say he was not at all pleased at being ordered about by a mere cleric." The Pope chuckled at this reference to the highest office in the world's largest institution. "He told me that he should have some satellite imagery for us in an hour or so. He will have the NSA send it right to my iPhone. I do hope they have the good sense to include the still photos in jpg files and maybe a video of the fly-over in an mp4 file."

Helen looked at both Jack and Smitty. She was impressed, and more than a little surprised at His Holiness' depth of computer knowledge. Sister Mary Pat leaned over to her and said, "Don't be surprised, dear. I was listening too. His Holiness is quite the gadgeteer. Computers and personal data devices are among his favorites. Indeed, in his spare time he can often be found down in the Vatican's IT department commiserating with the real experts in this stuff. Though I must say, he did once set up my new MacBook Air for me with Wi-Fi and email. It took him less than five minutes where I had been working at it for several hours."

* * *

CHAPTER 29

Cardinal David Caneman kicked a well-worn toe of his boot
at the muddy surface of the shore. He was impatient. The hours
before he would have to leave for Rome to reconvene the papal
conclave were ticking by. "What makes you think this is the
most promising site?"

Dr. Neil Palmer's gaze did not waver from the screen of the
ground penetrating radar scope. The unit actually looked like a
large lawn mower. The screen Palmer watched so intently was
mounted on the two upright handles that allowed him to control
the direction and speed of the instrument as he and Caneman
walked it along the surface just beside a sandy ramp leading
from the hill's face down to the shore. Without moving his head
he said, "A number of things, David. First and foremost,
research. We had targeted this particular site three months ago
while we were still in New York. Everything about it fits. It is
near the ancient harbor of Formia. Though the new harbor where
the city now lies is actually three miles north. This area is right
on the seaward side of what used to be the main fishing landing
in ancient times." He stopped talking and halted their walk.

"Here, David. Look at this," Palmer pointed at the screen.
Caneman could see the shadows of the radar images of what was
beneath the ground under their feet. "You can see that darker
shadows open up to lighter ones, then white. The white is what
we are looking for. It means there is a cavern under there. Now
watch." Palmer turned the dial of the GPR unit, expanding the
depth at which it was looking and narrowing its field of view.
Then he took a few steps to the right.

"Do you see the straight line coming up from the cavern
floor and meeting another perpendicular line that runs along the
top? Those are structural joists. They support the ceiling down
there. Even in ancient times, the engineers used many of the
same mining techniques we do today. Besides, such perfectly
straight lines do not occur in nature. Those are man-made."

Caneman said, "So you have found the Treasure Vault of the Catholic Church," he declared with finality.

"We have found something, David. We won't know what it is until we excavate the entrance and get in there. Do not forget that there may be more than one vault here. It would make sense. Why put all of your eggs in a single basket? Entomb your treasure in several vaults. That way, if one is found and plundered, all is not lost."

Cardinal David Caneman was growing more frustrated at the academic's reluctance to commit to this discovery. Obviously it is the most promising site, he thought. He looked down the shoreline that curved around the crescent bay. They had spent most of last night unpacking the vans and setting up the site with tents, lighting for night work and erecting a cooking tent, sleeping tent and outdoor latrines for the workers. Caneman understood this was essential to expedite the real work once it finally began. It wasn't until after 9:00 am that they began running grid patterns with the ground penetrating radar unit. Since there were two different sites being worked within two miles of one another, they kept in touch by radio and cell phone.

For Caneman, watching the radar technicians trudging back and forth with the GPR unit across the grid was agonizing. Overhead the sun blazed after yesterday's storm, making the wet ground steam. At least we're on the coast, he thought. Even the prevailing breeze was hot. Still, its movement helped cool things off a bit. Caneman removed his wide-brimmed cotton hat with a back flap that fell down his neck to keep the sun off. He mopped the sweat from his brow. When he replaced the hat, he felt its sodden lining, now cool against his forehead.

"David, come over here," called Palmer from a spot down the beach hard against the rock wall next to where he had parked his GPR unit. "I want to show you something."

"What?" demanded Caneman, "have you found another entrance?"

"Maybe." The archeologist was reluctant to commit at such an early stage. "Our vertical GPR unit shows a large rectangular space behind what appears to be a hollow façade right here." He pointed to the orange spray painted outline he had drawn on the rock wall and the vegetation that had grown over its surface. Caneman thought it certainly did look solid enough. Blended perfectly with the surrounding cliff wall. If this was an opening to the vault they sought he could well understand how it had gone undetected over all these centuries.

"What now?" asked Caneman. "You will blast an opening, won't you?"

Palmer shook his head in shock. "No. Of course not. We do not know what is behind the façade. Blasting our way in could bring down the entire ceiling if it is not properly braced. Or it could destroy any number of priceless artifacts lying in the doorway. My professional archeologist has already called his colleague at the other dig and asked him to join us. He should be here in a few minutes. They will supervise drilling four pilot holes—one at each corner of the façade I have marked off. Then we will push through a small robotic camera and light to see—"

"To see the vast treasures of the Church," exclaimed Caneman finally releasing the impatience he felt consuming him as he stood in this very spot.

"To see," insisted Neil Palmer, "what we shall see. No more, no less."

Caneman waited along with the rest of the team. His arms were fidgety and his fingers snapped with impatience. He watched the diamond bit, high-speed electric masonry drill make short work of the sandstone cliff wall as it drilled its four holes. He noticed that these were not as small as he thought. They were large enough to shove a carry-on-sized case through. Finally, he saw the cart holding the snake-like miniature video camera on its cable and the cart holding its screen, recording system and battery to power the whole operation being wheeled into place. He quickly strode to the opening. The group of men gathered round parted to let him move to the front.

The archeologist who had been called from the other dig arrived in a cloud of sand and grit as his G550 skidded to a stop beside the site where they were working. The man leaped from

300

the Mercedes practically before it had stopped and ran to the doorway marked in orange spray paint.

The other professional archeologist nodded his head at his colleague's arrival. He carefully moved the camera, its lights and the small platform with little tank treads instead of wheels that it ran on into the lower opening in the sandstone wall. Caneman moved behind Palmer who stood facing the screen, waiting to see the inside of this cavern.

He kept watching. The screen remained black. "What is wrong?" Caneman asked Palmer.

One of the archeologists answered, "The light is dead. We can see only the faintest of shadows; no definition and not any color. Let's pull her out," he called to his colleague who stooped at the wall and guided the small camera trolley. "I'll change out the lighting. Won't take more than fifteen minutes," he said.

Caneman felt the vibration of his cell phone. He glanced at the screen and noticed it was Cardinal Angelo Chicarelli. Now of all times, he thought. What's the little twit want? But he said, "Hello, Your Eminence." Caneman's voice dripped with friendliness and goodwill. "To what do I owe this pleasant and most welcome distraction?"

"Your Eminence," replied a breathless Chicarelli, "I hope that I am not intruding too much on your busy schedule."

"Not at all, Angelo. You are never an intrusion. Quite the contrary. I am just admiring God's magnificent summer afternoon." Caneman shifted his gaze from the shimmering Mediterranean as it lapped at the white-hot sand to the lead archeologist and his technicians as they feverishly unscrewed the troublesome lighting unit from the camera trolley. "How may I serve you, Angelo?"

Chicarelli never stopped marveling at the way Cardinal Caneman could always make you feel at home and talking with your best friend. This man would make one of the best popes who ever commanded the 1.2 billion faithful around the world. Of that he was more certain than of anything in his life. Like so many others he had spoken with outside of conclave, he would follow this man into the gates of hell if that is what he required. He was dead certain that Cardinal David Caneman was the man to lead the Church away from the troubles into which its lesser-qualified chiefs had allowed it to stumble.

Chicarelli spoke up, "Your Eminence, I wanted to let you know that they have succeeded in locating Cardinal Laurent Monsengwo Pasinya from the Democratic Republic of Congo. He has boarded a military helicopter and is being airlifted out of the jungle. They estimate his travel to Rome will take approximately 36 hours."

Caneman stood stock still. There it was—the deadline. He had thought that he would have two more full days to excavate the vault opening, then remove the most valuable artifacts— including the special one that he knew must be there—and get back to Rome where he would reconvene conclave. Now a full half-day had been taken away from him.

Caneman swallowed the dry salt air and cleared his throat. He forced silkiness back into his voice. "Angelo that is excellent news. The best I have heard all day. Thirty-six hours you say?"

"That is correct, David. A day and a half and you can take the next step on this extraordinary journey that is your destiny."

"And how is His Eminence Alexandre José Maria dos Santos? Have his doctors cleared him to travel from Mozambique to Rome?"

Chicarelli said, "Oh, David, you know Father Alex. He may be 88 years old and his health may not be what it once was, but he can drink both of us under the table. He'll be here in Rome within the next 24 hours. Soon as he heard that his Cardinal Caneman needed him, he rallied and told his doctors that he had a higher calling to attend to. He's on his way now."

"That is wonderful news, Angelo. Wonderful," repeated Caneman. "Just 24 hours? Perhaps you could be my representative at the airport to meet him?"

Chicarelli was flattered beyond words. His Cardinal always seemed to say exactly the right thing. To personally request his service in this most important of Vatican State matters was

302

beyond comprehension. "Yes, yes David. Meeting Father Alex shall be my mission. I will not let you down."

"That is what I had hoped for, Angelo." Caneman looked at the archeologists and technicians surrounding the tiny camera trolley. They appeared to be finished and were making ready to reenter the pilot hole. "Ah, Angelo, could you possibly excuse me. There is a small matter of minor urgency that I must take care of. Will you excuse me?"

"Yes, David. Yes of course. I just wanted to keep you updated, my chief."

"Thank you, Angelo. God be with you. Ciao." Caneman cut off the call as he was striding to the wall with what he knew would be its most revealing pilot hole.

"David. You are just in time," said Palmer. We are ready to retry our first penetration. Come, stand beside me and watch what just could be the most historic three-meter trip for any robotic camera in history."

Caneman watched as the technicians carefully set the camera trolley with its twin lights now blazing atop short aluminum posts inside the hole. He peered at the video screen. They were all watching. Slowly the image began moving as the trolley rolled away from the hole and penetrated the vault. At first Caneman saw only indistinct shadows. This was a doorway, after all.

Jack sat beside the driver of the first Iveco Mastif. Finally the rain had abated. The sun had risen as they crested a hill and now looked down on the ancient town of Formia. Helen was still asleep. So was Sister Mary Pat. Smitty was wide awake and talking softly on his cell phone to his office in New York. Jack turned in his seat and looked back to see His Holiness also on his red cell phone. Their eyes met. The Pope raised one hand and put a single thumb up.

"You got it?" asked Jack softly to avoid awakening the others. "That fast? You got the satellite photos?"

"I just received them," whispered back the Pope in an equally gentle voice. "They are...amazing. Here take a look." The Pope passed the red Papal cell phone forward to Jack.

Jack turned the small phone sideways so he could see the landscape orientation. There before him was a color image of a wide area with the hills and valleys they had just traversed on one side and the Mediterranean ocean on the other. Jack traced the image first from the tiny screen, then to the outside landscape. From their vantage point at the top of the hills leading down valley to the ocean he could see the very road on which they traveled.

Jack flicked his finger across the screen for the next image. This one had zoomed in on the area. Obviously it was focused on a much smaller area hard up against the hills that fronted the seashore. But this one was not close to the harbor.

"May I see?" asked Sister Mary Pat. She was awake and trying to peer over Jack's shoulder from the back seat. He handed back the cell phone. "Take a look."

Sister Mary Pat studied the photo for a few minutes. Then she took out her maps and compared the satellite photos to where she had expected the most likely area to be for the vault. She flicked a finger across the screen to move to the next and then the next photos. She saw first what appeared to be two different digs. Each had three large SUVs parked near. One had both vans parked alongside as well.

"I see what Cardinal David Caneman is doing—"

"What's that?" asked Jack.

"He's hedging his bets, that's what he's doing. He isn't sure of his research. So he has selected his two most likely targets and is working both. He has enough men so that isn't a problem. When one seems more likely than the other to be the vault, he'll pull the other men off the dry hole and bring them over to the more likely candidate." She was startled when the Pope's little cell phone chirped with an incoming message.

"Oh, Your Holiness there's a message for you. May I?"

"Yes, Mary Pat," came the immediate answer. "Go ahead. I know who it's probably from."

She pressed a few buttons, read the message, then looked toward the Pope. You were expecting a video stream from the National Reconnaissance Office?"

Jack answered, "Of course, Sister. Doesn't everyone get videos from the NRO? Hold it up for all of us to see and run it." Jack felt Helen's hand cuff the back of his head. "*Please*, Sister. Would you *please* do that for us?"

"This is amazing," said the Pope as they watched the video streamed from space in real time. It showed a group of men gathered around a hillside that was right up against the seashore. The resolution was sufficient to show two of the men bending low on the ground and shoving something into a hole in the wall.

"That must be Caneman's expedition," said Sister Mary Pat. "Seems like they think they've found the vault. Probably putting in a robotic camera for a look. Better than risking damage by blasting their way in before knowing what lays inside. But they're looking in the wrong place."

"Really?" asked Helen. "How do you know that?"

Mary Pat tapped the northwestern edge of her map. "They are too far south. My research pegged the spot not far from where the modern port of Formia is today. It is the most logical place. The hills are about two kilometers off the shore and the ramp up from the sea is fairly level. That is what you want to haul in heavy objects. Where His Eminence is now has about a 15 percent uphill grade—pretty steep if you ask me. Besides, my target is much better protected from the ocean storms that are known to pummel this area in the wintertime. The soil will be harder, easier to compact and provide a much more stable platform for building a vault. David Caneman's site is on the seaward side and at least a kilometer outside the protection of Formia's crescent bay."

Jack continued watching the live video of Caneman's entry. "Looks like they're going to a lot of work just to hit a dry hole."

"They are," said Mary Pat. "With their expensive equipment and all that ground penetrating radar technology, you would think they had a better idea of where to dig. It would take us days and days to get as far as they have. But at least we would be digging in the right spot."

"So why not let them do our work for us?" asked Jack.

"Whatever do you mean?" said Mary Pat.

Jack sat there for a moment continuing to watch the video image on the Pope's cell phone. "Well, we have a birds-eye view of their operation. Why not lay out here unseen in the weeds observing them. When it appears they've finally got the right spot and have penetrated the vault, then we swoop in and take over."

Helen looked at her husband of just one year. She didn't doubt he was serious. Nor did she question that he could do just what he said. But she saw they were outnumbered at least four to one. "What? You want to fight your way into the confines of an ancient vault with just six men against more than 20?"

Sister Mary Pat followed right behind with her objection. "Then you take over? Is that what you propose?"

"Oh why don't you grow a pair."

"Your Holiness," exclaimed Sister Mary Pat at what her boss had just said. "Such language. Where did you ever learn that?"

Jack looked back and saw the Pope's jaw jutting defiantly outward. He didn't have to wait long for the Pontiff's reply.

"Sometimes you just have to take the initiative, Sister. Use force for the good against force for evil. It takes balls. I have watched Jack, Smitty and their operators. They understand the strategic use of force. We are outnumbered. True. But we have one weapon they do not."

Jack thought this was getting interesting.

"And what could that possibly be?" asked Sister Mary Pat.

Jack saw a broad smile engulf the Pontiff's face. "We have the full power of the Holy See."

"Oh wow," said Mary Pat in a mocking tone. "Now that's impressive. We're up against four times the armed men, ground penetrating radar and—"

Jack now saw the depth of their friendship. That a mere nun could mock the Pope and get away with it. Jack said, "And Sister, don't forget the explosives they have and the *Carabinieri* in their pocket. Seems to me we've got them right where we want them. What do you think, Smitty?"

"Roger that, boss. His Eminence won't know what hit him."

* * *

CHAPTER 30

Cardinal David Caneman stood there outside what he was certain was the treasure vault he sought. His eyes were transfixed on the screen linked to the robotic camera that Dr. Palmer had just sent into the bottom hole of the doorway. "Where is the treasure?" Caneman asked impatiently as the image on the screen showed nothing but dirt piled up around the entrance.

"Patience, Your Eminence," urged Palmer. "The science of archeology is inexact. Let me reorient the camera so its back is to the door." Caneman saw the picture swivel as the camera trolley spun on its treads. "There," said Palmer, "now we have the reinforced doorway to the cavern right before us. See the timbers running up the sides of the doorway and over the ceiling to keep it from falling in?"

"They look so ancient," complained Caneman, "they don't appear able to hold up anything of any weight."

Palmer lost himself for a moment. "Of course they're ancient. These timbers are centuries old. They have been in this sandstone tomb adjacent to the seashore with its wet environment for all of that time. What do you expect?"

Caneman did not back down for a second. Not with the world expecting him to resume conclave in less than two days now. "I expect for you to show me the rows of priceless artifacts, gems, precious metals, manuscripts and everything else that you promised was inside this vault."

Palmer turned back to his camera screen. "Alright then. Let's enter the vault and see what there is to see." They watched as the camera trolley lurched and crawled over the rocks and mounds of sand obstructing the entrance. They could see the gray earthen tones of the vault. Here and there was evidence of human presence. Palmer stopped the trolley and focused lights and camera on an ancient shovel with a broken handle. Beside it was a pole to which would have once been attached the dry reeds and kindling of a torch to light the way. Palmer pressed the joystick and the image moved on, deeper into the cavern. It

308

seemed the further it went inside, the more debris and obstructions it encountered. The camera stopped and focused on a single sandal lying on the dirt floor. Palmer panned the image up toward the ceiling.

"Ah, there David. Do you see how the ceiling joists at this point were not strong enough to hold up the fragile sandstone? The ceiling has collapsed right through them and into the cavern. At this point, the floor literally becomes the ceiling, making further passage impossible."

"It will take us days to excavate this cavern," said Caneman.

Palmer looked at his next Pope and said, "No, David, it won't. Because we're not going to waste any more time on this location. We have hit a dry hole. I have seen more than my share during a long and successful career. The old popes saw the same thing. They most certainly abandoned this location before actually using it as a depository. The worst thing we could do at this point would be to waste more precious time excavating dirt that holds nothing just to prove what I already know. Time to move on."

Jack peered at the Pope's iPhone. The screen showed what appeared to be a mass exodus of Caneman's workers from the site. "SMP, you might want to take a look at this," he said handing Sister Mary Pat the smart phone.

"Ah, see? There you are. Caneman understands his mistake. He is packing up his tents, breaking camp and preparing to move to a more likely location. Doubtless he has a number of promising places."

By this time all of Jack's small team had gathered at their lead Iveco Masif. "What about the other location?" asked Helen. "Are they still working that one?"

Sister Mary Pat slid her finger across the phone's screen to change video images until she found the most recent satellite feed she was looking for. "My, our Cardinal Caneman is an impatient one isn't he? His second team at the other location is striking camp as well. Within another hour they will be on their way to other locations. I can only hope that they consider the folly of their ways and head north instead of sticking to this southerly course. North takes them back to the port city of Formia to my first choice of locations."

The Pope said, "So you want to protect the riches of the Church from plundering by what amounts to nothing more than a modern day pirate?"

Jack smirked at that. "Naw, Your Holiness. What concerns me is something else you said a while back. You said that if you were Caneman you would be looking for an artifact. Something common, but with a provenance to prove its authenticity. You said this artifact could unite the 1.2 billion faithful behind this fundamentalist fanatic. You caught my attention when you likened such a group throwing themselves fully behind Caneman as the Taliban on steroids. With the speed of social media, modern communications and the billions in his war chest, His Eminence certainly seems someone to reckon with. It is not beyond the realm of possibility that such a man with the backing of that General Spider Marks and the military ordnance company he heads could resume the crusades of centuries ago and just roll right over any resistance. The world can't beat today's unskilled, untrained and under-funded Al Qaeda fighters. Imagine what someone with Caneman's resources could do as Pope.

"You're not the only one who knows his history," Jack continued, speaking to the Pope and to Sister Mary Pat. "Civilized society had a brief moment to stop the Taliban and Al Qaeda back in 1994 when the students banded together in Pakistan's conservative Muslim schools. But we didn't see it for what it was. Then just two years later, when the small but fanatical Taliban took over Kabul in Afghanistan we had another chance. Once again the world was too weak in the face of such a bully to lift a finger to stop them at a time when their size was still manageable. Not this time. This time we act. We will not seek consensus from the United Nations. We will not ask for permission to use deadly force from a Congress more interested in getting itself reelected than in doing its job." Jack turned to the Pope, "Your Holiness, I have known you for only a short time.

310

That's all the time I need. You have my respect and my trust. If you give the green light on this op, we go."

His Holiness stood there in the half light of the coming day. Outside the small port city of Formia, Italy he had made a decision that would save millions of lives and decades of strife if he was right about Caneman. He thrust his right hand into the center of the circle they had become. Jack put his hand on top of the Pope's. Then came Helen's, then Smitty's, then Sister Mary Pat's and the four other SEAL operators they had brought along. The Pope said, "I am making a conscious decision that will likely end in bloodshed. I do this with full knowledge that it is I alone who will bear this hideous responsibility. Jack, you have a green light from the Holy See. Let's roll."

Jack said to his team, "As soon as they decide on a place to stop, we'll move as well. I want our position to be on higher ground looking down on them. We need to be within a quarter mile of where Caneman and his people decide to resume their camp. When the time comes I want to strike them hard and fast so they cannot form any real resistance as we take over the dig."

* * *

CHAPTER 31

Cardinal David Caneman sat off to the side, out of the way of the workers on a camp stool that Palmer had provided for him. Surrounding the area were harsh pools of light against the encroaching night. It had taken them all day to locate and decide on this particular site. Now the sun had set. What light there was came from the light standards already erected around the camp. There was a steady hum from the electrical generators providing necessary power to the camp. Having been through the routine of setting up camp, running the ground penetrating radar over the grid area that Palmer's team believed most promising, David Caneman was still impatient. But this time, a little less so. He saw how Palmer's methodology was strict and identical with each dig. This was a process. It would take as long as it takes to find and excavate their way into the vault. Caneman looked down at his wristwatch. Now there were likely just twenty hours left before the last two straggling cardinals arrived in Rome and then he would have to reconvene conclave. He was not worried about failing to win election as the next Pope. However, the cardinal conclave had proven over the centuries to be a fickle lot. History held many surprises for the candidate seen as the frontrunner who either came in second or failed entirely to even make the first trial ballot.

No. Being elected Pope would certainly make this crusade toward a fundamentalist doctrine easier and faster, but it was not absolutely essential. However, the essential thing—the one thing that Caneman could not accomplish his goals without was the artifact—whatever it might turn out to be. Its unifying imagery would pull the faithful together as one from all corners of the globe. If Caneman did his job of marketing and public relations correctly—and he had proven his mastery over both time and again—the process of changing dogma to what he knew to be the one true path would occur naturally, quickly and as if it were truly the will of God. Which, he constantly told himself it was. Still, the hours ticked by to the reconvening of conclave.

"What's going on now?" asked Sister Mary Pat. The small caravan of just three Iveco Massifs had pulled off the road and tucked themselves behind the hills overlooking Formia's harbor and the crescent bay beyond. Everyone had left the vehicles to walk into the rocks so they could look down on Caneman's second attempt at an excavation and entry into what they all hoped to be the vault.

The Pope passed her the binoculars. The team had stopped once they were convinced that Caneman's expedition had decided on a location and was setting up their next encampment.

"It looks like they're proceeding with their initial penetration into the cavern," the Pope said. "They'll want to make sure that nothing valuable is blocking their way before they blast through the sandstone doorway into the vault. That must be why it looks like they have a robotic camera."

"Hmmm," exhaled SMP. "Jack picked a pretty good vantage point up here." They were sitting within a rock outcropping, surrounded by boulders that were still warm from the heat of the day to blur any thermal signature someone might be looking for. They were indeed about a quarter mile away from Caneman's dig. And they were looking down into his inviting pools of bright light.

"Do you think this is a more promising place?" the Pope asked.

Mary Pat said, "Why yes, of course it is. They moved directly north to within just a few hundred meters from the port of Formia. It is well protected from the winter storms. And the particular location they are working now with their GPR units is particularly promising. It has a flat area connecting the mountainside with the shoreline. Perfect for hauling heavy items from a beached boat into the vault. Yes, I believe this could be the one. Frankly, I identified the general area but must admit that I overlooked this particular sector. Caneman must have at least one professional archeologist on his team."

Jack picked his way through the warm boulders on this moonlit night toward them. "What have we got now?" he asked

313

them both in a softened voice. You never could tell just how sound would carry as it bounced off of rocks and the breeze carried it.

At first Caneman saw only shadows. Objects, yes. Man-made certainly since there were straight lines. He had been through this before on the first dig only to be disappointed. Now he was prepared as he watched the screen with its live feed from the little robotic camera on miniature tank treads that crawled its way into the cavern. Then his eyes took in what no man had seen in centuries but for which thousands had searched.

"Well bless my soul," said General Marc "Scorpion" Greggory, one of Caneman's inner circle of most trusted advisors. He had arrived at the dig with ten of his Ranger commandos to maintain security. As Chairman of General Ordnance Corp.—the world's largest manufacturer and seller of advanced military hardware—Marc Greggory and his people definitely had a place in Caneman's new Holy See. "I have never seen such opulence in all of my days. Not even when we invaded Sadam Hussein's palaces. Compared to this, Sadam was a punk and small-time piker at that."

Caneman watched Greggory trace his finger on the screen image, along the overhead piece of the entry ceiling. It shined even in the gloom lit only by the twin lights of the tiny camera robot. "Solid gold," Caneman exclaimed. "When can I gain entry." It was not a question.

Dr. Palmer sat watching the screen in stunned silence as the robotic camera panned the entryway, then rolled on its treads into the first treasure gallery. His fingers played the joystick and made the camera turn a slow 360 so he had a complete picture of the entire entry gallery and ten feet into the vault. He looked at his Pope-in-Waiting, "Now, David. Now is the time to seize your destiny. Within thirty minutes you will stand where no man has stood for centuries."

"But how will you knock down this wall?" asked Caneman. "It is solid rock."

314

Palmer nodded to the first row of onlookers. "General?"

"I figured you might need some demolitions capabilities," said Marc "Scorpion" Greggory. "I brought along two of my best men and all the high explosives they might need. Give us some room so we can get to work," he ordered. The crowd before the rock wall with an ancient door again outlined in orange spray paint parted to let the two demolitions experts through.

Caneman looked at his watch—a Patek Phillipe given to him by the Vatican Bank's CEO on his ordination into the priesthood just 15 years ago. The foolish man could not grasp that his protégé would oust him from his post in the coming years and send him to a tiny parish on the Egyptian border with Israel. Truly his assignment was the Church's equivalent of purgatory for one who had risen so high only to be caught with his own hand in the cookie jar. Even back then Caneman had suspected that Vatican Bank would require a thorough house cleaning. He also believed that he would be the one asked to do it. And so his journey had begun.

Now we are getting someplace, Caneman told himself. It had taken another day to locate the vault. Now we are on the verge of breaching its door. I can get what I need, leave the others to catalog the first tier treasure and get back to Rome to reconvene conclave. But he also realized it was none too soon. The last cardinal, His Eminence Alexandre José Maria dos Santos, would soon begin his journey from Mozambique to Rome now that his cardiologist had cleared him for travel. Once all the players were in place, Caneman knew the natives would be restless. He would not have any further excuse to delay reconvening conclave and elect the Church's new Pope. He needed to explore the vault contents and find the precious artifact, then get back to Rome.

"Fire in the hole," shouted one of the demolitions experts. "Clear out of here. I don't want anyone's holy butt blown off." The crowd surrounding the solid stone opening outlined in orange spray paint immediately pulled back. The door stood out on a promontory. There was a corner of the hill that the group receded to just behind where the explosion would breach the wall.

"How did you set it up?" asked Marc Greggory from his position around the corner from the anticipated blast along with the rest of the workers.

"General, I positioned the shaped charges in such a manner that they would concentrate their energy from the bore holes out into the rock wall. There will be no damage to the interior since no energy is going inward. We shouldn't see much wasted energy in a blowout either. The rock wall will simply crumble, folding in on itself."

Scorpion Greggory smiled. "Just the way I would have done it, gentlemen." Then he motioned for the excavation workers to stand by, ready to go into the breach and begin clearing a path inside once he gave the word after the explosion detonated.

"I see some action," said the Pope, offering the binoculars to Jack.

"Whatcha got?" asked Jack as he took the offered binoculars. He sat beside the Pope on the sandstone rocks that gave what people in the US would call a million dollar view of the oceanfront.

The Pope held up his little smartphone, "I have been watching the workers milling around what seems to be the doorway into the cavern. See it outlined in orange paint on the sandstone wall? I am certainly no expert but it would seem to me that they intend blowing a hole in the wall."

Jack held the binoculars to his eyes. Below, against the hillside right on the shoreline he saw Caneman's workers suddenly scurry out from in front of the painted door and scuttle around the wall. "Yep, Your Holiness. Looks like they're just about ready to blow a hole in what they think is the door to the vault." Jack lowered the binoculars. Time to execute his plan.

"Helen and Sister Mary Pat," Jack said. Both were right beside he and the Pope, securely hidden within the rocks.

"Right here, sweetie," said Helen.

"Good. Caneman is going to be inside that vault within an hour or so. That means we had better launch our attack on their security force and take over the dig—"

"How're you going to do that?" asked Sister Mary Pat. "We are outnumbered four to one."

"Don't worry about that. Smitty and I are experts at force projection."

Helen said, "That's the art of making the size of your force seem much larger to your enemy than it really is."

"In this case, I figure by a factor of ten should be about right. What do you think, Smitty?"

"Yeah, Boss. By at least a factor of ten."

Jack continued, "So when we have them running for the hills and once we've entered the vault we need to be organized. The four SEAL operators we brought along will provide cover security. His Holiness, SMP and Helen will enter the vault and video what's there. His Holiness will identify the object that would have united over a billion of the faithful behind Caneman and gotten him elected Pope. Smitty, while they're inside the vault, I want you to get us exfiltration transport from here to Rome."

"Roger that, Boss. I should be able to get some sort of chopper in here. I already checked—the nearest airport to Formia where a small plane could land is Naples International. That's 93 kilometers away. It would take too long to travel that far. Not to mention the risk of traveling by ground through Indian country. I imagine Caneman will be royally pissed off at us. He'll whistle up whatever armed support he might have with the *Carabinieri* and sic 'em on us. We need air transport from right here. Let me see what I can rustle up."

"But we're not the bad guys," exclaimed Sister Mary Pat.

Jack said, "That's not the way it will look to Caneman's armed supporters. He's the Vatican's representative and heir apparent to the papacy. He has every right to be here. We, on the other hand, do not. We are plunderers of the Vatican treasury. They will see their mission to stop us as something holy and virtuous. They will come after us with everything they have."

The Pope said, "If we fail in our mission of taking over the vault and securing the artifact, just imagine Caneman's mounting fundamentalist influence over the billion plus faithful worldwide. Domination by this hoard in every Catholic population center around the world will come astonishingly fast. They will be ruthless, well-armed and have all the funds they require to make freedom of religion or anything else a thing of the past. Like the Muslim fundamentalists, Caneman will start in the smaller third world countries. As his movement gathers strength he'll expand to larger and larger population centers, taking over entire governmental functions. The masses will see his movement as nothing short of heroic."

Jack said, "I can assure you Cardinal David Caneman is anything but heroic. Seems to me he's an opportunist taking advantage of a situation of his own making. See ya." Jack crept away from the rocks toward Smitty and the four operators to get ready for their strike.

* * *

CHAPTER 32

"Just a few more minutes," said Dr. David Palmer to Caneman. "The dust inside will choke you, even with a respirator. I've been in my share of freshly opened tombs, believe me. Just a few more minutes of patience while the dust settles and the men clear a path through the debris."

Caneman spent the time organizing his search party. There would be five of them on the initial penetration. He included Palmer and the General. Palmer was an expert and knew what they were looking for. General Spider Marks had earned a spot due not only to his past loyalty but for the resources he would provide once Caneman was elected Pope and his shift toward the strict fundamentalist doctrine began.

"We are ready, Your Eminence," said Neil Palmer. The distinguished academic and archeologist stood before the ragged hole in the mountain the demo guys had blasted. By now only a minor dust cloud issued from the opening. "Here, Your Eminence, better wear this." He held out a breathing mask for Caneman to put on. "There is no telling what buggies these ancient tombs contain."

Caneman grabbed his light torch and flicked its on-switch. It was the Wagman Mega Spot that all five of those entering the vault carried. Its bright LED beam bore through the dust and turned night into day wherever he pointed it. As the team entered, Caneman saw the torch beams flashing on the walls all around them. He led the small group of five. As they progressed into the vault the lights merged into one as all pointed their electric torches in the same direction. The dark pushed back to the outer edges of their circle of light. Within, it might as well have been high noon.

Caneman stopped before the first structural joists supporting the ceiling. This is what the robotic camera had shown them. Its golden surface seemed to glow back at them in the torchlight. He shined his light over its surface. The inscription was in Latin. The first line was: *Archivum Secretum Vaticaun.* Caneman said to himself as much as to the others in his small group, "Secret Archives of the Vatican." He read aloud the next line beneath it, " *'Treasure for the glory of God'*. It seems that the popes who serviced this vault by making so many priceless deposits over the centuries thought of it as their personal property."

"Well I'll be damned," said General Spider Marks walking beside Caneman. Looks like you found us a treasure vault, Dr. Palmer."

"Indeed, General. There was never a doubt we would find it. The only question was when." Palmer was smart enough to know that he had been extremely lucky to hit pay dirt on just the second penetration attempt. It rarely went so quickly. He thought of it as a sign of His Eminence Cardinal David Caneman's destiny to ascend to the Papacy.

As they slowly walked through the threshold, the natural sandstone cavern passageways branched out in different directions. Caneman played his torch down each. He saw things; wondrous things. There were wooden shelves floor-to-ceiling running the considerable distance of his light beam, stretching on into the darkness beyond. Each was laden with wooden boxes and crates doubtless containing gems and golden artifacts. Where the objects were too large to fit on the shelves, they stood on the floor. Caneman spotted two life-size horses in dusty gold leaf and beside them was the Roman chariot they pulled, also in gold.

"David, over here," called Neil Palmer. Caneman shined his torch down one of the branch corridors as he approached. Twenty feet in, Palmer stood before shelves and shelves of books. Caneman could see they were ancient by their old but still viable bindings and covers. "These must be the Pope's collection of books and manuscripts that were banned by the Bible. Can you imagine the wealth of knowledge stored in just this single place within the vault, David? It could keep a hundred graduate students fully committed for twenty years or more."

"That is nice, Dr. Palmer. But completely irrelevant to our mission. Stay focused and be of some use, please." Caneman marched on shining his torch and peering into every nook and cranny he came upon.

Down another corridor, Caneman spotted a torchlight that had stopped and was focused on something. He approached the General. "What have you found?" Caneman asked.

The General did not answer immediately but kept his torch steady on the ancient cloth laying in the box he had opened. "The box had Hebrew lettering. I opened it and this is what I found. What do you make of it?"

Caneman played his light over the cloth. There was a clear impression of a human face burnished into it over time. The face had a scraggly beard and a band around its head that appeared made of vines.

The General exclaimed, "I always thought the Shroud of Turin had been discovered and was being kept in the British Museum. They seem to have everything else worthwhile."

"Wrong on both accounts," corrected Caneman. "The artifact generally thought to be the Shroud of Turin—the shroud in which Jesus was buried after his violent crucifixion—has been studied with the most modern radio carbon dating procedures. That result along with chemical analysis of the fibers that compose the cloth have drawn into question its authenticity."

"So what do we have here?" asked the General.

Caneman ran his torchlight the entire 13-foot length of the burial shroud then said, "Probably the real shroud in which Jesus was buried. If it is here in this vault, my guess is that it's the real thing." Caneman stepped into the intersection of two corridors, not interested in the general's find. One corridor ran at an angle, straight back into the furthest reaches of the vault. He took it.

Jack spotted movement. "Smitty? See him?" Two clicks came through Jack's earpiece. The four others that Jack led continued their slow slithering on the ground, down the mountain toward the brightly lit camp below them. The guard Jack had pointed out was just one of twenty they had spotted. All were dressed in brand new black tactical battle dress. He could see that most of them carried the HK MP5 submachine gun. Smart, he thought. A fine close quarters weapon. The ambidextrous trigger group allowed the shooter on the fly selection of safe, single fire and full auto. He knew the weapon and was well aware of its threaded barrel to accommodate a silencer. "You're seeing the same things I'm seeing," Jack told his small but deadly team into his throat mike. "The latest weapons. But clean clothes and shiny boots. And they're standing in the light. Dumb move. They should be crawlin' around on their bellies like we are now."

"Well-trained kids who have never seen combat," came Smitty's soft voice. He was fifty yards off in the weeds to Jack's right. "They look bored. More interested in what's inside that vault their boss just entered rather than what's out here."

Each of Jack's men was assigned one of the Mercedes G-wagons. Jack and Smitty also took both of the Mercedes Step Vans. Rigging each vehicle with explosives took them only thirty seconds in and out and then they were back out of harm's way. Within an hour they had reassembled up in the rocks with Helen, Sister Mary Pat and the Pope.

After nightfall Jack had pre-positioned two remote controlled mortars each a hundred yards left and right of the target. Smitty had set up two more remote controlled .50 caliber machine guns at opposite angles to the vault door and the artifact sorting tables they had already set up.

Sister Mary Pat spoke softly to Jack over the com link, "Tell me how you're going to make our little brigade seem larger than His Eminence's twenty-man security force."

Jack nodded his head toward one of the rock outcroppings. "You can't see them but two of my snipers are out in the rocks armed with night scopes. We've intentionally spread out our ordnance, both manned and remote controlled. When the time comes, all hell will break loose down there, Sister. There will be so much firepower coming from so many directions it'll seem like an entire battalion swooped in and took control."

"People will die," observed Sister Mary Pat. It was a statement.

"Some, yes. Killing people is not our objective. I want to get their immediate attention and force them to surrender in the face of what appears to be overwhelming force. Their security people will be the first casualties. But they signed up for that possibility. The others will probably just turn around and let us zip-tie their hands behind their backs then rope all of them together so they can't escape. Then we get what we came for in the vault and leave."

"It sounds like a can't-miss plan, Mr. Schilling."

"Sounds like you are mocking me, Sister Mary Pat. Even so, I've learned never to be cocky. No plan survives contact with the enemy. Something will go wrong."

SMP nodded as if she had just heard some good advice. "When will you start your attack?" she asked.

"Patience. I want them to do as much of our work for us as possible. I'm happy just sitting up here watching for a while."

Back in the deepest part of the vault Caneman's torch seemed but a pin-point in a vast universe of darkness. He constantly moved its beam back and forth across the debris-strewn dirt floor to avoid stumbling. He could tell that this section was seldom used. The shelves and racks held few of the shiny gold and silver works of art. There were few books and no manuscripts that he had seen. Nothing of any intrinsic value caught his eye—exactly where he wanted to be.

He was talking to himself in the privacy of the vault's farthest reach. The others had stuck with the main corridors where the gold, gems and manuscripts were located. These were the items with the highest market value and could be readily sold, "Adding to the Church's coffers, to be sure," Caneman said aloud. "Still, they hold not one scintilla of the value to redirecting the road down which the old popes have allowed the faithful to stumble."

Cardinal David Caneman continued down the dark passage. He directed his torch at several wooden and metal objects sitting on the shelves. None were of interest. Neither were they marked in any way to describe what they were and why their significance—whatever it was—had earned them a place in the most secret and holy vault on earth.

"No," said Caneman into the darkness as the beam of his torch caught a well-worn leather switch. Such switches had been used for centuries to whip horses and donkeys into moving. However, with the internal combustion engine, the need for such implements had ceased. "A donkey switch would not resonate with the faithful," he said, "even if it had belonged to one of the biblical characters. For the masses to get excited they must identify in some way with the object. It must be something in use today, every day. It must have some provenance that proves who used it and when and its connection with Jesus." Caneman continued his walk through the artifacts that he was certain documented centuries of Church history.

Cardinal David Caneman was a confident man if nothing else. Before entering the vault he had ordered Neal Palmer to contact the Naples airport and charter a helicopter for a one-way flight from the dig directly to Leonardo da Vinci airport in Rome. He wanted to get his artifact—whatever it was—out of the countryside and into Rome as soon as he could. He told Palmer to have the chopper on the ground within 90 minutes. That should be enough time, he told himself.

"Ah, here we are," said Jack Schilling. He pulled the binoculars from his eyes and handed them to Sister Mary Pat. "See the long tables positioned outside the vault entrance? These are the best-lit areas in the camp. My guess is that those excavating the vault will pull out the most valuable artifacts and hand them over to the people manning those tables."

Sister Mary Pat said, "They're called archivists. And you are correct. Their job is to number each item, photograph it and record it in the dig's master catalog."

Jack understood, "It's a way of inventorying everything in the vault. That way they can keep track of where each priceless item is at all times. It's the same thing that a company does with its inventory of saleable goods." He took the binoculars SMP offered back to him. Sure enough, Jack could see the tables down the mountain at the site. He watched as workers took hold of golden calves, a silver crown studded with emeralds and four-foot long gold scepter with a cluster of diamonds on its pommel, ending with a large ruby on its end button. Those privileged few who were excavating the vault handed each item to an archivist standing at the vault entrance. The archivists walked the object to the sorting table where they handed it to another archivist who numbered and photographed it, then cataloged it. Jack watched as yet a third archivist took the now-recorded item from the sorting table and placed it on another table farther back. Two guards, armed with distinctive looking HK MP 5 submachine guns, stood beside the table. "Those artifacts aren't going anywhere," said Jack. "Then again, they don't have to. We're not interested in them." He handed the binoculars over to the Pope. "Your Holiness, take a look at their set-up down there and tell me how we can tell the object that Caneman is looking for."

The Pope scanned the well-lit area. He could feel his heart beating inside his chest. That was a new feeling that had occurred since his heart attack at the farmhouse. Twice he felt his heartbeat come off its regular rhythm. His cardiologist at the hospital had called it atrial fibrillation—A-fib for short. When that happened, the Pope could feel his heartbeat become irregular and disorganized. His breath became short and even the slightest exertion made him feel like passing out. Fortunately, he had experienced only two episodes of the A-fib. Each had lasted only a few minutes. He had laid down immediately and waited for his heart to regain its steady, regular beat. This time it wasn't A-fib. Instead, he reasoned, it was just the excitement of being so personally engaged in something so important.

The Pope held the binoculars to his eyes and commanded himself to relax and take big, deep clearing breaths. He did not want another episode of A-fib now but he still needed to control his excitement to hold the binoculars steady. With the binoculars screwed into his eye sockets he worked his way from the sandstone vault entrance with remnants of the orange spray paint around its borders to the sorting table and then to the storage table. He felt like now he was in control of his heart's steady beat. He intended to keep it that way. Back and forth he worked his scanning.

"Ah, here we are," said the Pope. "If I were David once I find whatever it is that I am looking for, I would not let it out of my sight, let alone my hands. I would hand-carry it myself from the vault to the sorting table. I would hold it there while it was numbered and photographed, then cataloged. Speed would be my priority. I would need to get back to Rome so I would be ready to reconvene the Papal conclave the instant the final two cardinals arrive." The Pope sat there on the warm boulders, calmly breathing his deep breaths in and out. He thought some more.

"Yes, if I were David I would actually want some time before conclave resumed to do some marketing of the artifact."

"Marketing?" asked Sister Mary Pat. "What does Caneman know about marketing?"

"Oh, my nun friend, quite a lot. He sold the entire Vatican on his qualifications to be named a cardinal even though he had only been Catholic for fifteen years and a newly ordained priest for less than six months. He marketed himself as a financial engineer whom the Church sorely needed to restore financial order, credibility and profitability to the Vatican Bank. He knew the cardinals and the man who was then Pope would see dollar signs before they saw caution. This object that I am sure he is searching for in the vault this moment will be a testament to David's fundamentalist ideals. Through a thoroughly professional campaign of mainstream media, social media and old-fashioned missionary boots on the ground he will solidify his doctrine first throughout the third world countries and then expand into Europe, Asia, Africa, South America and eventually North America. It won't take long before he holds over a billion Catholic faithful by their collective ecumenical collars.

"This is just the way Al Qaeda and the Taliban work. With David though, his unifying artifact, his ascent to the Papacy and the hundreds of billions at his disposal will greatly speed the global spread of his fundamentalist influence. Where Al Qaeda took over twenty years, plan on Caneman taking no more than ten years, probably half that time. His horde will cast a larger shadow around the world than every national government on earth save for China, the UK and America. And those countries will crumble from within before him. Why? Because millions of their own people will believe in David's own fundamentalist doctrine far more than that of their own governments. In those countries with a democratic system, David will run his own people for political office and get them elected into positions of vast influence. There will be fewer and fewer non-Caneman ideologues left to run things.

In those countries run by dictator it will be even easier. David's holy warriors will mount a coup and simply eliminate the opposition. They will step into power and immediately give the people what the old regime could not. He has the money to do that."

During the Pope's short lecture Jack had taken the binoculars back and now watched the opening to the vault intently. Sure enough, soon the unmistakable silhouette of Cardinal David Caneman emerged cradling two objects in his arms as if they were precious infants. Jack watched him refuse one of the archivist's offers to take the objects from him as he proceeded to the sorting tables.

Cardinal David Caneman was in the deepest part of vault. He was at the end of the last corridor. Except for the narrow beam cast by his torch, the interior in this section was blacker than any black he had ever seen. He continued casting his beam slowly across one length of shelves, then down to the next. He saw many things. All looked very old. He was constantly asking himself if anything evoked a flicker of the possibility that the Blessed One Himself had owned it or at leased used it. He carefully stepped forward so as to avoid stumbling over the debris in the corridor.

With not more than fifty feet until the corridor dead-ended into the side of the sandstone mountain his torch beam slewed across a shelf holding just one object. He stopped his progress and pulled the light back to it. Unlike the other objects jumbled one on top of another on each shelf, this one sat completely by itself. There were no other objects within five feet of it save for an old wooden box that lay right beside it. Touching it, actually.

Caneman stood upright and shone his torch on the piece. There was no mistaking what it was—an ancient broom, obviously. It had a long crooked handle—hickory, guessed Caneman. A woven twine fastened its straw bristles to the handle. Altogether, the broom measured maybe four feet in length. "Why would the priests add a common broom to this collection of priceless artifacts and memorabilia, he wondered. He stepped forward to the shelf on which it sat but did not touch it.

Instead, he inspected the box that lay to its side. Its outside was wood, so old that he could see under the torchlight it had turned gray in color. On its front was the faded and worn image of the cross depicted in the Church of the Holy Sepulchre. Any seminary graduate would immediately recognize its inwardly bowed arms three-quarters of the way up the staff. It had been carved into the box's top by someone using crude tools because the cross with its ragged edges was definitely not the work of a modern era artisan.

"Huh," said Caneman. "What have we here?" He wondered what secrets the box contained about the broom. Their deliberately close proximity to one another certainly indicated that they belonged together. Did the box contain some sort of provenance for the broom?

"We may as well see, then" Caneman set his torch on its base so it shown on the box. Way down the corridors he could hear the other members of his excavating team speaking to each other excitedly as they undoubtedly uncovered priceless pieces of incalculable value on the antiquities market. He returned his attention to the small wood box. He took both hands and pried the box open. Dust flew from its lid and hung in the beam of light from his torch. Caneman held the light close to better read

328

the box's contents. Inside he saw an ancient animal skin inscribed with a black ink that carried this scripture from the Book of Matthew 26 beginning at verse 17. This is what he saw:

On the first day of the Feast of Unleavened Bread, the disciples came to Jesus and asked, "Where do you want us to make preparations for you to eat the Passover?"

18 He replied, "Go into the city to a certain man and tell him, 'The Teacher says: My appointed time is near. I am going to celebrate the Passover with my disciples at your house.' "

19 So the disciples did as Jesus had directed them and prepared the Passover.

20 When evening came, the twelve disciples came to the appointed house. There they found Jesus, their Rabbi, at work sweeping the room with a broom made of straw. They watched as dust clouds flew around their teacher's sandaled feet.

Peter said unto Him, "Master why do you sweep the floor like a common servant?"

Jesus stopped his sweeping and leaned on the broom with both hands on top of its crooked hickory handle and with its stiff, straw bristles splaying against the floor, bearing his weight. Then he did hand the broom to Peter for him to hold. Jesus bent down and scooped the dust into his own hands, then tossed the dirt out the open door. He then did recover the broom from his disciple and resumed his sweeping. The Holy One sayeth, "Learn ye and never forget, there is honor in work for everyone. There is no man so high that he cannot sweep the floor of his host's home."

Jesus continued sweeping until the dust was no more. Only then, when his sweeping was done did he stand the broom in the corner and take his seat at the center of the table where he reclined with the Twelve.

21 And while they were eating, he said, "I tell you the truth, one of you will betray me."

Cardinal David Caneman stopped reading. He knew the Book of Mathew by heart. He also knew that Verse 20 as written on the skins in this box was a departure from any other text known to the Church. Never had he read of The Savior sweeping a room clean like a common servant. He stood there in the gloom and thought for a moment. He knew that the ancient popes had placed not only priceless artifacts in the Church's vaults, but things they did not wish disclosed to the public that might be contrary to their preferred version of historical events. Certainly it was not beyond possibility that some overreaching pope once rebelled at the thought of Jesus sweeping a room to rid it of dust like an ordinary man.

Caneman looked back at the broom with the straw bristles. It was a common object. Everyone had a broom. There was no one who had not used a broom at sometime in their life. They had done what He had done. Some do it every day. Finally, he said to himself, here is the bond that crosses the centuries from the Church's beginning to modern day. He flung himself to the ancient, dusty floor and gave thanks for his discovery. His private reverie did not last long. He got up and patted his khaki clothes down to rid them of the gray dust from the cavern's dirt floor.

Caneman looked back at the box containing what he guessed was actually the original book of Matthew as dictated by God or at least one of the disciples and written without editorializing. Radio carbon dating would prove the authenticity of the broom and the box containing the authentic scripture. Of that he was dead certain. Otherwise, why would the ancient priests have taken the trouble to place it here in this vault with accompanying scripture proving its provenance. He silently gave thanks to God for delivering these two items unto him. Cardinal David Caneman closed the box then gathered it and the blessed broom in his arms and hiked out of the vault behind the bright beam of his torchlight.

Jack watched as Caneman left the vault entrance. He spoke softly into his throat mike, "Saddle up boys. It's show time." He paused for a half minute, then, "let's begin our attack

330

on my 10-count." Jack began counting down from ten. He knew his five other operators already had fingers on launch buttons and had grabbed up their weapons. He was the only one left up on the hill. The others were already deployed to their stations at various points around the dig.

General Marc "Scorpion" Greggory was a combat soldier; had been for more than 40 years. He knew the sounds and the smells of the battlefield better than any man alive. As soon as the two .50 caliber machine guns opened up, firing toward the vault, he knew they were under attack. From his position in the vault—about 100 feet inside and in a corridor off to the left—it sounded like a muffled, pop-pop-pop. The three round bursts told him a professional soldier was on the trigger. An amateur would have just sprayed lead all over hoping to hit something. This guy was targeting, firing and moving on to his next target. All in controlled two and three-round bursts. Greggory dropped the priceless golden rope he was admiring and raced for the vault entrance.

He emerged into pandemonium. The archeologists Caneman had brought were running for cover. His commandos, on the other hand, were cool. They did not run. He saw that each of the twenty under his command had their weapons at the ready, pointed out into the darkness beyond the bright lights of the dig. They were not panicked into firing until they saw a target.

Greggory pulled his Smith & Wesson .45 caliber semi-automatic and took aim at the first of the three light stands. He fired a two-round volley and saw the bulbs explode in a torrent of sparks. He repeated his shooting at the two other light stands. When he was done the dig had plunged into total darkness.

But not for long. Suddenly the closest Mercedes G-Wagon detonated in a deafening explosion. The area within a hundred feet around it was immediately lit with the orange flames of the ensuing fire. Before the explosive concussion ceased reverberating off the hillside, the next G-Wagon detonated, followed by the other four, one after another. There was a pause of not more than five seconds after the last explosion before both

Mercedes Step-Vans blew up simultaneously and launched both vehicles a full ten feet in the air before coming down on their sides.

By the ambient light from the burning wreckage, Greggory's men could see into the night without being backlit by the intense lighting that served the dig. They picked out targets and began firing.

Jack's finger pressed the fire button on the remote control console. The mortar he had positioned earlier fired its first round. Just seconds later he heard the explosion it caused. Jack couldn't tell if the target area he had pre-aimed for held any of the armed guards. Jack turned the light enhancement knob on his night vision goggles to better see into the dark camp. He scanned back and forth. "You're there for sure and I am sitting up here watching you," he said to the commandos spread throughout the camp. Then he stopped scanning. A familiar face came up on his NVG screen. It was that of General Marc "Scorpion" Greggory. "I might have known," said Jack. "Of course Caneman would bring along his aide de camp. You're the only one with any military training."

"Jack, who're you talking to?" came Smitty's voice over the com link.

The question jerked Jack back to his current position. "Smitty, scan ten meters left of the sorting tables. There's a boulder. Wait for the head popping up every so often. Does that face look familiar to you?"

"Scanning. Wait for it. Gotcha," said Smitty. "You're Scorpion Greggory. I know this guy and his record. He's one mean son of a bitch. What's he doing here?"

Jack said, "I know him too. He serves as Caneman's chief of staff at Vatican Bank. If he had just cooperated with my audit request, we wouldn't be here. Instead I had to fly to Rome to meet with the Pope. That's how all this began. You really screwed the pooch on that one," Jack spoke as if Greggory were right in front of him.

"He's not anyone to dick around with," came Smitty's response. Jack was quiet for a moment. The General's men fired a few volleys every so often just to let Jack know he hadn't been forgotten. They could keep this up for as long as necessary. After all, their vehicles were destroyed so they couldn't leave.

That's got to be embarrassing, thought Jack. They weren't going anywhere soon. Then in the distance he heard the familiar thump-thump-thump of a helicopter. Its distinctive rotor sound bounced off the rocks around him so he couldn't tell its direction. "Smitty?"

"Got it boss." Smitty was positioned several hundred meters down the side of the mountain with his four men. He could hear the chopper rev its engine as it flared for a touchdown on a flat section a hundred meters from the sorting tables. "Apparently the pilot doesn't know he flew into a combat zone, Boss. He left his marker lights on."

The helo's mission suddenly dawned on Jack. It was here to pick up Caneman. The guy must have actually recovered the artifact the Pope says he came out here to get. "Time to move out boys," said Jack. "Smitty, everyone angle over toward the chopper. I want to stop it from taking off again. Let's move."

As soon as Jack moved down the mountain he drew fire from the commandos scattered throughout the camp. Bullets snapped around him, breaking rocks and slamming into the still-sodden earth. It made his progress slower than he wanted. That, and the fact that his bullet wound by now felt like a hot poker searing into his left side. Jack ignored the pain and kept moving. He knew the rest of his five men were also drawing fire. Jack stopped for a moment and pulled out his remote control firing console. He pressed three buttons simultaneously. In less than a second both .50 caliber Remington machine guns opened up, pouring lead into the camp. Then the mortar fired. Jack told himself that at least he was smart enough to direct all fire away from the sorting tables so he didn't destroy the priceless antiquities he knew would eventually be there.

"That stopped 'em for the moment, Boss," came Smitty's voice over the com link. "I guess they don't much appreciate being fired on either."

All six picked up the pace. But as they did, the fire they drew from Greggory's commandos escalated right with them. Bullets snapped overhead like angry wasps. Their ricochets buzzed off through the night. Jack and his small group of just six men struggled to make forward progress toward the chopper before Caneman boarded it and took off. Jack could see they were within 200 meters of the chopper. Its engine was still revved up and its rotors were spinning. Jack knew the pilot could lift off in just a few seconds—no need to wait while the engine ramped up and the rotors came up to speed. Behind them the commandos gained ground. Now they were within 150 meters of Jack and his group.

Jack said over the com link, "All this shooting is getting to be dangerous, boys. Somebody's going to get hurt. Time to put a stop to it. Circle the wagons."

And that's exactly what they did. Jack's group immediately stopped moving toward the helicopter. They formed a semicircle that allowed them to cover all 180 degrees of the advancing commandos. Each man chose his target and fired in short two or three round bursts. Jack guessed there were no more than twenty of the trained soldiers. Within a minute Jack saw six of Greggory's men go down. But the other fourteen were still up and by now royally pissed off. Jack kept his men moving to prevent them from becoming stationary targets.

They were no closer to the chopper. But Greggory's men had gained another fifty meters. Their numbers were now down to ten. Jack kept looking for Greggory himself. From his brief encounter with the man at Vatican Bank he knew that he would be the point man in any fight. Jack hoped that he would have the pleasure of putting him down himself.

"Give me the controls, please," said the Pope. He held out his hand insistently toward Sister Mary Pat. She handed the remote control console with its two joysticks and throttle controls. "You are wobbling the mini-drone. If we are going to fire its miniguns and its two missiles the platform needs stability." The Pope concentrated on the monitor in front of him showing the CIA's newest armed drone they had launched when they saw Jack and his team were in trouble.

"You got the hang of it pretty quickly, Your Holiness," said Helen. "You've done this before?"

"In a manner of speaking," he said and stopped talking while he threw the throttle lever forward and sent the drone on a beeline toward the ever-advancing commandos. "I sometimes spend late evenings down in the Vatican's IT department talking with the boys. They taught me. They have all the latest video games—Call of Duty, Max Payne, Grand Theft Auto. There I learned how to control the joystick and shoot. It is not much different here." The Pope watched as the small drone—no larger than two shoeboxes with wings and a propeller in back—silently swooped up behind the advancing commandos.

"May God forgive me," said the Pope.

"Helen said into the com link, "Jack and everyone else, stay put. His Holiness is going to launch a missile from the drone."

Jack spoke up, "You're kidding me, Hon. The Pope is flying the drone?"

"Yea, right," she answered. "But he is and he's pretty good at it. Stand by and don't move. I'm not sure about his aim."

The Pope lined up the crosshairs on the screen with the middle of the advancing soldiers. Without hesitation his finger pressed the blue button that fired a laser to paint the target. Immediately his finger moved to the green missile lock button. Now the two AGM—114D Hellfire missiles were locked on their target. The D designation indicated they were the tiny version designed for minidrone use and just five inches long with miniature fins to guide them. Without hesitation the Pontiff pressed the round, red button and fired the first Hellfire. "Fox One away," he said. After a count of three, he pressed the fire button again. "Fox Two away." He lined up the crosshairs on the screen and prepared to fire the miniguns in the event the missiles left anyone standing.

Jack watched as two tiny streaks of white lightning darted down from the sky. They hit, then exploded right in the middle of the advancing group of ten soldiers. Out of the left corner of his eye, Jack spotted a shadowy figure running from the vault entrance toward the chopper. He was carrying two items in his arms. Peachy, thought Jack. That's got to be Caneman. He's got his loot and it looks like he's going to catch his ride. They were still too far away to intercept Caneman.

"Helen, see if His Holiness can fly the drone over to that helo and keep it from taking off." Two clicks were his confirming answer.

Helen tapped the Pope on his shoulder, got his attention and pointed toward the chopper almost a quarter mile from where he had the drone orbiting looking for any survivors. "Jack wants you to keep that chopper from taking off."

The Pope nodded, then began working the joysticks and throttle controls. The image on the screen from the drone's nose camera swung up from the ground and turned toward the flashing strobe lights of the helicopter. The pilot still hadn't turned them off. The image quickly turned larger as the drone accelerated toward its new target.

Jack's attention was back on the two soldiers who had somehow survived the missile attack. One man put up his hands and dropped his submachine gun to the ground. Seeing this, the other leveled his own rifle at the man and sent a burst right into him. Jack watched as the force of the bullets threw the man to the ground. "The trigger man must be General Scorpion Greggory," He said over the com link. "This is one soldier who will go down fighting and trying to take as many of us with him as he can. Be careful, guys." As he finished, he heard the chopper's rotor spool up, biting into the air. He turned up the magnification on his night vision goggles to see Caneman jump into the side door of the aircraft just as it was lifting off. The door slammed shut and the helo accelerated up and toward the safety of the mountains.

336

"Can't you make it go any faster?" urged Sister Mary Pat

"This is just a small drone used for close-in air support," said the Pope. "It's like using a 4-cylinder Mini Cooper to catch a Bugatti Veyron."

"Then fire another missile," said Helen.

"It only carries two and I already fired them," said the Pope.

"How about the miniguns?" asked Sister Mary Pat.

The Pope raised the drone's nose to account for the fall of the rounds over the distance to his target and fired a long burst. Every fourth round was a tracer so he could see where his rounds landed. They all fell short of the chopper as it accelerated away through the valley and up into the mountains.

"Sorry, guys," said the Pope, "I couldn't catch them. However, all may not be lost. I have Plan B."

Jack watched as the chopper flew away. Guess His Holiness isn't the shit-hot drone pilot he thought he was. Then Jack turned back to the final member of Greggory's soldiers. He walked over to where his group of five surrounded the last man who was supine on the ground. He had been right. This was the General and he had not gone down without a fight. From the rattling sound of his breath Jack could tell he was mortally wounded. Greggory slowly turned his head toward Jack as he approached.

"So, the bean counter can shoot straight," he said. "Who…would'a … thought."

"General, you should have seen to it that Caneman took the time to answer my questions about that Letter of Credit. It would have taken less than five minutes. All this bloodshed could have been avoided. But no, you had to piss me off by calling me names and exercising your power." Jack heard another breath barely escape the dying man's lips. He knew the General had less than five breaths left. He spoke over the com link, "Helen get everyone packed up. We rally at the trucks in fifteen." He heard two definite clicks in response. Okay, Jack told himself, let's figure out a Plan B. But honestly he didn't have a clue.

* * *

CHAPTER 33

"Thanks be to God, David. You are finally here," called
Cardinal Michael Chicarelli from the tarmac.

Caneman looked down from the folding airstairs of the
Beechcraft Bonanza. The helicopter had quickly whisked him the
90 miles or so from the dig in Formia to the Naples airport.
There, his assistant had already chartered the twin engine
Bonanza on his orders. It was waiting with engines running when
the chopper touched down. The distance from Naples to Rome's
Leonardo da Vinci airport was well within the Bonanza's range.

"Thank you, Michael. It is good to be back and get on with
the important business we have to conduct, eh?" Caneman still
stood at the top of the stairs.

"Let's us not waste a moment, Your Eminence," suggested
the Cardinal.

"A moment, Michael. Please. I have something important in
the airplane's hold behind the cabin. If I might retrieve it before
we leave?"

The minor cardinal loved when Caneman spoke his
Christian name with the same easy familiarity used between
trusted friends. After all, he believed that Caneman would most
certainly be elected the next Pope. Even better that his assistant
had called from New York saying that Cardinal David Caneman
himself had requested him to meet him at the airport. "Yes, yes
of course, David. Where is it, please and I will get it for you."

Caneman held up a hand. "Do not trouble yourself, Michael.
It is behind the cabin. I won't be a moment and then we shall
leave. Please, get yourself comfortable in the limousine. I shall
return shortly." Caneman's voice had that syrupy sweetness he
reserved for the fools who ran his errands. He thought as he
always did when toying with the idiot Chicarelli that he could
not be trusted to pick up after the dogs. When he was Pope he
would cut the guy loose in a manner that would reflect back on
himself favorably but would still tell all that he suffered fools
only with great reluctance and not for very long. Like so many
others, he would dismiss Chicarelli as soon as he had sucked dry

339

the man's last ounce of utility to him and his cause. Caneman ducked back into the aircraft. When he emerged again, he carried two objects wrapped in brown butcher paper. One was long—about four feet in length and thin. The other was square and smaller. He bounded down the airstairs and quickly strode to the waiting limousine. He was a man on a mission.

Cardinal Chicarelli stood beside the open door as if he were Caneman's personal chauffeur. "What have you there, David? May I place them in the trunk for you?" The short, squat cardinal reached for the two objects Caneman carried without waiting for an answer.

Caneman stopped and turned his body, protecting his precious items from Chicarelli touching them. "No, Michael. It is alright. I would prefer keeping them with me inside. You cannot imagine the sacrifices that were made to obtain these."

Chicarelli looked inquiringly into Caneman's face. He wondered what on earth he was talking about. What were these two items that were so valuable and that had required his personal hero to sacrifice anything in obtaining them? "Of course, David. I was only trying to help. Let us proceed then to the Vatican and your date with destiny."

Caneman looked into the southern sky as the limousine sped out of Da Vinci airport toward Vatican City. He was searching for another aircraft that might contain that Jack Schilling who had tried stopping him. Caneman had watched as the tracer shells fired at his helicopter, fell to the ground as the increasing distance and gravity took their toll. He knew his worry was absurd. There was no way Schilling could have gotten his tiny retinue out of Formia by now, let alone to Rome. Besides, even if he had somehow accomplished that impossible feat, the man was beaten. Caneman expected he would be elected Pope within the first three rounds of voting. The first two would be for show to the world. He wanted the proceedings broadcast around the world to appear transparent. The inconclusive first two votes would add to the drama of his election. He would be the reluctant savior. The one who took the post not because he wanted to but because the throngs of faithful had demanded his help.

Then he would show the world what he had returned from Formia with. The simple but oh-so-meaningful broom and its accompanying holy provenance would change the Catholic world forever. These items and the video footage of the vault with its incredible riches still streaming to his smartphone would ensure anyone election to the papacy. But he was not just anyone. He was Cardinal David Caneman, the next Pope in waiting. More importantly, he was God's chosen emissary who would lead His church out of the darkness and into the light of strict fundamentalism. The time of reconstructing God's holy doctrine had come and he was its shepherd. He would accelerate it by using the technology of his own modern era. Insisting this conclave be broadcast around the world rather than be held in closed session exclusively for the cardinals' pleasure was his first step. He knew this gesture would be seen as a welcome departure from a centuries-old tradition.

Not only did he have the attention of the world, his broadcast of the conclave set the stage for the rest of his technological presentation. Even now the video streaming to his smartphone was also going to his IT department right here in Vatican City. Already he had ordered the computer geeks who once were loyal to the old Pope but who now had no choice but to do his bidding to edit the video into a dramatic tour of these newfound riches. He had also ordered a remote control be placed on the Chapel's dais where he would be conducting conclave. His intention was to control all imagery feeding to the two giant screens within the Sistine Chapel as well as what was fed directly to the Vatican News Service broadcast van outside that connected the rest of the world with the proceedings. His attention to detail had the good sense to order a huge jumbotron TV screen set up in St. Peter's Square that would show the assembled multitudes the very same imagery. He reasoned that these people would provide real-time cheering at his triumph. The crowd in the Square would generate a roar of approval that no audio engineer in the broadcast van could ignore. He would call it the voice of the faithful heard 'round the world.

Though the trip into Vatican City was not long, to Cardinal David Caneman it seemed to last an eternity. Finally, the limousine turned into St. Peter's Square and agonizingly crept its way through the throngs of people that occupied every square centimeter of the area. The Square was always mobbed like this during the pending election of a new Pope. Caneman's car was marked on the doors with the two flags with crossed keys of the Pope. He saw that as soon as people noticed the car with its insignias they immediately peered inside to see who the dignitary was. The entrance to the Sistine Chapel was still at least 50 meters away. But the people jammed cheek to jowl barred any progress as word spread of the car's occupant. They stood clapping and cheering, but not moving to let the car pass.

"Driver," said Caneman, "this will have to do. Stop here. I will walk the rest of the way." To Michael Chicarelli sitting beside him he said, "My fellow soldier in Christ, will you join me on this historic walk? Also, could I ask you to walk ahead of me, clearing the path?"

"Of course, David. I will consider it my personal mission." Chicarelli again reached for the two brown-paper-wrapped parcels. Again, Caneman snatched them out of reach.

"Your Eminence, I was just going to carry them for you. A man of your station should not have to bear anything but the burdens of his high office."

"No. I must be seen bringing these into the Chapel myself. Do not lose track of me. I need you parting the waters for me every step of the way."

"*Si, grazie,*" exclaimed the Cardinal. "Then it will be my honor to escort you into the place where you will be elected our next Pope."

As both men emerged from the limousine, another cheer went up from the crowd. Caneman felt the exhilaration of being recognized and loved by so many. He smiled at all and reached out to touch the extended hands. But his time of triumph must of

342

necessity be cut short. As he had observed back in Formia, the natives are restless. With the arrival in Rome of the two tardy cardinals, conclave must resume.

"What's our Plan B?" asked Helen. She had directed her question from the back in the third seat of the Iveco Massif forward to Jack who was riding shotgun while Smitty drove toward Rome. "Tell me again why you couldn't get us an airplane? Or maybe at least a fast helicopter? Caneman got himself a helicopter."

Jack turned in his front seat and gave his wife of just one year the stinky eye. He also noticed all eyes were on him, expecting an answer. Except for the Pope. Jack noticed his serene, unconcerned look. He simply stared out the window at the countryside as they bumped along the side road that would take about 14 hours now that the weather had cleared to get them to Rome.

Smitty provided cover for his boss. "Hon, Caneman has the *Carabinieri* in his pocket. I saw that on our way down to Formia when my old friends suddenly refused to provide me with any information about Caneman's expedition. By now they surely know it was us who tried stopping Caneman from leaving after he looted the vault. To them we are the criminals. Caneman is their new pope-elect. They have probably launched a manhunt by now for us. If we tried entering the airport property we all would be immediately arrested. Then where would we be?"

The Pope stirred from his gazing and said, "Mr. Smith does have a point." Then he returned to serenely staring out the window, a man deep in thought—or patiently waiting for something.

Helen said, "Is that why you're sticking to these awful back roads?"

"Yes it is", replied Jack. "The *Carabinieri* would expect us to attempt flying to Rome or at least take the main highway in a car. They have the manpower for that. They don't have the personnel to patrol the back roads too."

"What about a drone for surveillance?" asked Sister Mary Pat.

Jack and Smitty both looked at one another and laughed. Jack said, "The *Carabinieri* had but one camera drone. They lent it to us at the farmhouse. It didn't survive the attack. We're lucky to have made it out with the mini-predator drone."

Helen said, "We have been on the road now for six hours. By now Caneman is already in Rome and has probably reconvened conclave. He's probably just waiting for his election."

"You are part right, my dear," answered the Pope. He had now turned away from the window and reengaged with the conversation. His hand slid into his jeans pocket and pulled out his red papal iPhone. "Apple TV. They sent me the first prototype version two years ago. I told them they would have an uphill battle unseating the networks. What did I know? Anyway, I've been watching on and off the proceedings broadcast from the Sistine Chapel. Quite interesting."

Sister Mary Pat spoke up, "Your Holiness, doesn't it bother you that Caneman is about to take your seat?"

The Pope shrugged. "It would if I didn't have Plan B. Caneman's own vanity will be his undoing. He will engineer a few trial votes that end deadlocked and don't result in a valid election. His point is to ramp up the drama for the worldwide audience he now has. By the time his trial votes are run and they have several recesses because the cardinals find the whole proceedings so exhausting we will be in Rome."

"How long will that take?" asked Jack. He suspected the old guy would reveal what he had up his sleeve when he was ready.

"Hmmm. I would say that Caneman is a good six hours from holding the first election that will vote him into the Pope's seat."

"And that doesn't just gripe you?" exclaimed Sister Mary Pat. "How can you sit here contentedly chatting when—"

"When what, my nun friend? When we seem to be facing the global creation of a force potentially more destructive than Al Qaeda ever was?" The Pope peered at his red iPhone and typed

344

out a response to an incoming text message. "Mr. Smith, how about pulling off to the roadside please. Right here on this large, flat spot should do nicely. Right here, Mr. Smith please?"

Smitty did as the Pope requested. He didn't turn off the engine in order to keep the air conditioning running in central Italy's summer heat. Within a minute Jack heard the muffled, but still unmistakable steady thump-thump-thump of a Blackhawk helicopter. He and Smitty looked at one another in sudden comprehension, then both turned back to the Pope.

"Plan B, ladies and gentlemen," answered the Pontiff to their unspoken question. "How did I get such a marvelous machine? Is that what you wish to ask? Well, I will tell you. It seems that Jackson's godfather has a rather significant amount of influence. While you were packing up the little drone and getting us ready for travel I took the American President up on his kind offer of help whenever and wherever I needed it. After all, he did put his private telephone number on my speed dial. I explained our little problem of timing here and that Caneman had a significant head start. I simply asked him to level the playing field a bit. He was only too happy to oblige. Within five minutes I got a call from a Commander Jim Krause of the Helicopter Sea Combat Squadron 85. It seems they are conducting some training around the hills of Rome."

Both Jack and Smitty nodded to one another. They each knew the Firehawks. It was the Naval air branch that flew SEAL teams in and out of Indian country. Both men had experienced firsthand the best pilots in the world belonged to the Firehawks.

Suddenly, with no more than a loud whoosh and a cloud of dust, the modified noise dampened and stealthy Blackhawk swooped in over a ridge and straight down onto the flat dirt pad next to the Iveco Massif.

"Ah," said the Pope, "this must be our ride. After you, ladies."

During the two-hour chopper ride to Vatican City, the Pope was in his own world of technology. He worked feverishly on his laptop computer and spoke every few minutes on his red smart phone with various people.

* * *

CHAPTER 34

David Caneman stood alone on the raised dais looking out over the sea of cardinal red in the Sistine Chapel. He was resplendent in his specially-altered vestments. Yes, they were similar to that of every other cardinal. After all, he had reasoned, it would be presumptuous to separate himself too much from the rest of them before the first vote. Standing there, he was without a doubt just another servant of God. Still, he wanted them to see him as possessing an elevated station beyond their reach. So he wore the red vestments and red cape. Except his red cape was bordered in the cream-colored satin reserved for the popes. And on his head was the white satin *zuchetti* also reserved for the pope rather than the red all the cardinals before him wore.

He stood there knowing each noticed the departure from tradition in his vestments. He also knew that not one of them would say a word questioning the audacity of his choice. For they all knew he would be the next pope. To cross the pope—especially Pope David Caneman—meant almost certain retribution. He had heard the stories repeated about what had happened to the priests he had fired from the Vatican Bank. The gossip was that those who crossed or disappointed David Caneman might was well have suffered excommunication. They were dispatched to far distant parishes never to be heard from again. The stories were sometimes exaggerated. He deliberately did nothing to set the record straight.

Caneman took one step back from the dais and glanced at the table beside him. On it, in full view of the assemblage, sat the two still brown paper-wrapped packages he had carried from the vault in Formia. He had seen several of the cardinals speaking among themselves and pointing to the packages. It was just the curiosity he had intended. Having the large video screens set up on either side of the dais gave them some inkling that this was not to be an ordinary conclave. Oh no. In earlier sessions he had activated the screens from his remote control station right there on the podium. The cameras alternately had shown him speaking to the assembly and then panning the cardinals and locking on individuals with especially enthusiastic reactions to what he had said. The time had come. Caneman knew it. His cardinals knew it.

Caneman stepped to the microphone. In his deepest, most sincere voice he said the usual prayers that opened conclave. He considered this a mere administrative duty. Every *camerlengo* who oversaw conclave followed the tradition. Caneman, however, added the sense of theater for the masses watching on television around the world by stopping every so often between prayers to explain in English what these prayers were and the history behind them. Cardinal David Caneman had become the world's guide to the immense complexities and ancient traditions of all things conclave. This elevated him to the faithful's trusted leader, even at this early juncture. Perfect.

With this time-consuming foreplay now over, Cardinal David Caneman said, "Brothers, our Church is right now without a rudder like a ship set adrift in stormy seas with no way to navigate to safety. That is where we now find ourselves. With the tragic death of His Holiness we have the duty of electing a new pope. Whoever this new leader of our faith is, he will have large shoes to fill. Times have changed. Technology has vastly accelerated the speed of communications." With that, he punched a button on his console to activate a video the Vatican's IT people had prepared several days ago at his request. It showed a series of quick clips featuring the faithful from around the world in church, at play, in confession and various other activities. The video dissolved into a close-up of Caneman now on the dais. "It is the responsibility of all Church leaders from we here in the Vatican to those parish priests serving the faithful around the world to establish Catholic beliefs and disseminate the word, accurately, with humility and quickly so that we may all speak, behave and practice our faith as one.

"Yes, the time has come to elect a new pope. We will do that perhaps today, or tomorrow or the next day. But we *will* elect a new pope. However, before we get to such serious business, I have something to share with not only you cardinals assembled

348

here, but with everyone around the world watching these proceedings. I believe that you will enjoy and appreciate as much as I the importance of what we have discovered."

Caneman stepped from the microphone over to the brown-paper-wrapped objects. An acolyte appeared by his side to take the paper he was about to remove rather than just drop it on the carpet in an untidy mess. He waited a few seconds for the cameraman who operated the remote camera to step to the dais and position himself for the shot he had personally directed earlier.

Caneman flipped the on-button of his remote mike so he could be heard. "Brothers and everyone, I have a story to tell you. It is a very good story. I had to suspend conclave late last week while we awaited the arrival of our three cardinal brothers. Canon law states that all cardinals must be present to elect a new pope. So I had no choice but to suspend conclave until they arrived. I am happy to tell you now that His Eminence Antonios Naguib of Egypt has been released by the Taliban rebels. His Eminence Alexandre José Maria dos Santos of Mozambique is feeling much better. I spoke to Alex's cardiologist three days ago and was pleased to hear from him that he had finally cleared our Brother for travel. His Eminence Laurent Monsengwo Pasinya from the Democratic Republic of Congo has finally emerged from the jungle. All three are here with us today." Caneman stabbed at the console button that split the big screens in the Chapel, the jumbotron in St. Pete's Square and in the live feed going out to the production van and from there around the world. The three panels showed the three cardinals sitting in the audience smiling and waving. Caneman himself began clapping for the Brothers. Soon the entire assembly was on its feet as one clapping for the tardy three.

"Welcome, Brothers. It is so nice to have you with us for this extraordinary undertaking. While we awaited your arrival there was some activity. I don't know what you did with that time, but I finished a project I began eight years ago. May I tell you about my pet project?" Caneman paused, letting his rhetorical question hang in the supercharged air inside the Sistine

Chapel. The camera caught the cardinals nodding an enthusiastic, *yes*.

"Alright then. Here's my story. It begins in the 16th Century under the reign of Pope Alexander VI. This was a wise pope. He understood man's weaknesses. You may have heard rumors of a vast Vatican repository—a vault—that contained the treasure from contributions of the faithful over the centuries. History says that Pope Alex had seen the treasury. It was real. There was even a map to its secret location that the popes had passed on to one another over the centuries. Well, Pope Alex felt the responsibility of keeping the treasury's secret location was too much for one man to bear. So he split the stone tablet on which the map was carved into six pieces and gave five of them to each of his most trusted cardinals and kept one for the pope."

Caneman paused to gaze out at the cardinals. Not one was asleep as they were so often in these proceedings. Each sat with rapt attention and hung on his every word. Perfect, he thought. Caneman continued in his greatly simplified diction for the masses he knew were watching and listening. For it was their hearts and minds he ultimately was after.

"Over the centuries, the five tablet pieces given to the cardinals went missing. It became a little-known tradition between the popes to conduct a ceremony officially passing the sixth stone piece from the old pope to the new pope on the day he assumed his office. Except over time existence of a vast treasury of unimaginable wealth belonging to the Church turned from fact to rumor to just a humorous story." Cardinal David Caneman paused again to flash a 10-megawatt smile down the throat of the camera that was focused on him and him alone. To his audience, it was as if they were sharing a private moment with the youngest cardinal ever elected and the golden boy of the entire Church.

"Some of my friends know that my hobby is Church history. I love learning about what we Catholics have done over the centuries. When I heard about the supposed six tablets, I became curious. Now understand my friends, like you I doubted these

350

tablets even existed, let alone could lead to a secret vault containing unimaginable wealth. But I wanted to know. So I mounted a search for the tablets. Guess what." The smile flashed again. "I found one." He paused for dramatic effect, allowing the tension to build.

"Yes, I did. It took three years of research and reading everything I could about the tablet's history. But I found it. So I kept searching. The second one came more quickly—in just six months. Now that I knew how to search and just what I was searching for I could see things progressing. Eight years after finding the first stone tablet with the Church's treasury map carved on its face I discovered the sixth and final tablet. That was just two weeks ago. It took every bit of that time until last week to decode what the map was telling me. But I finally got it.

"So when I was forced to suspend conclave while we waited for our three lost brothers to join us I mounted an expedition to the location. Just to see if such a treasure vault even existed. For, like you, I was skeptical. It turns out the location carved into the six stone tablets so many centuries ago is not far from here. It is in Formia, just 500 miles or so down the coast from Rome. Would you like to see what I and the members of my expedition discovered?"

Jack Schilling felt the Blackhawk break left. His arm reached out to grab Helen so she didn't slam into the bulkhead next to her. He knew these Navy pilots could pivot their aircraft at what seemed 90 degree angles without slowing at all. He also knew they only did it when there was danger afoot. Jack glanced out the window. The chopper was now out over the Mediterranean Ocean. The pilot was jinking left and right as he was streaking for the safety of international waters. Jack could see the helicopters pursuing them. There were three. Each was a black Robinson Model R-44 Raven—manufactured in Torrance, California and easily the most popular light chopper in the world. All three had *Carabinieri* stenciled in white lettering on their black tail struts. Police departments the world over liked the R-44 for its ease of operation, modest maintenance expenses and

the fact that they could be configured for a variety of missions—
surveillance, ground support, and armed intervention. Jack
guessed his pilot had heard the irritating warble of a missile lock
through his headset.

Jack crab-walked across the jinking helo's deck and into the
cockpit. He tapped the pilot on the shoulder. "What do they
want?" Jack asked after plugging his own headset into the
console.

"Sir, it's the *Carabinieri*. They're saying something about
robbing the Church's treasury and are demanding we return to
land immediately or they will fire on us."

"You going to do it?" asked Jack.

"Sir, I have no choice. My orders are to protect the lives of
everyone aboard at all cost. There are three against one up here. I
can't outrun them. The R-44 is one fast SOB. And they've got us
surrounded. What would you do?"

Jack looked back at his passengers. He was responsible for
each. Then he looked at his watch. Maybe it won't take too long
to talk our way out of this and be on our way. "Okay, Captain.
Turn into them and stop jinking. Can you let me hear what they
have to say?"

"Blackhawk intruder, this is the *Carabinieri*. Follow our
lead aircraft. Remember we have two other armed helicopters on
your five and seven tail. They are armed and ready to resume
missile lock if you do not comply."

Jack said, "Roger that, lead R-44. Will comply. But guys,
we are just a sightseeing mission with some dignitaries out of
Leonardo da Vinci airport. Is there a way we can all proceed to
da Vinci and land there? We'll get this misunderstanding sorted
out on the ground without inconveniencing our VIPs."

There was a short silence, then in lightly Italian accented
English came, "Jack? Is that you Jack Schilling? I cannot believe
it."

Jack looked at Smitty who was by now standing beside him
and listening in on the exchange. "It's me alright. Who's this?
With the chopper noise I don't recognize the voice."

"Jack, it is me, Antonio Spinelli. We met when I was training in Coronado with you guys and learning to fly the Navy way."

Smitty cut in, "Tony, I'm here too. It's me—"

"Smitty? You too? Tell me please that you both are not giving tours of the Italian coast to VIPs in a Blackhawk gunship."

Jack shrugged at Smitty, giving him the control. "Tony, I cannot lie to you. That would be disrespectful. And I know you guys have two sparrow missiles each back there. If you escort us to da Vinci I can fill you in on our mission. Can you do that, Tony?"

"I am sorry, Smitty. That is not possible. My orders are to bring you down at Naples International. The *Carabinieri* has a district office there. Apparently there was an attempted looting of some tomb and they think the criminals escaped by car or boat or airplane. All traffic is stopped. Now please, we all will make a course change to 187 degrees and line up with Naples air traffic control. Please to follow me, gentlemen. Oh, this is priceless— bringing down the famous Jackson Schilling and his sidekick Mr. Smith for a chat."

Smitty snapped off the mike switch so he could speak with Jack. "Damn, Boss. Naples puts us even farther away from Rome. What do we do?"

"Let's bring up His Holiness and see what he can come up with." Jack pointed at the Pope and motioned for him to join them. As Jack raised his left hand to make the gesture he could feel the stitches that held his bullet wound closed pull dangerously taught.

"What is up?" asked the Holy Father. Jack could hear his breathing was shortened and his color was a bit on the ashen side.

"You okay there, Your Holiness?" he asked and placed an arm around his bony shoulder to steady him on the moving aircraft.

The Pope gave a short wheezing cough and waved any concern away with his hand. "Just a little too much excitement today, I'm afraid. I will be okay. Why are we turning back toward Naples?"

"The *Carabinieri* in front and behind us insist on it. How do you want to play this, Your Holiness?"

The Pope looked at his watch. He had been watching Apple TV and the conclave proceedings along with the rest of the world. "Well, we are running out of time. I estimate Cardinal Caneman's video demonstration of his archeological skills will take another 30 minutes." The Pope said this with tongue in cheek. He was growing impatient with Caneman pimping himself to the world. "Then, if I am correct about him having at least two trial votes before they have the real one electing him Pope, that will take another two hours." The Pope stood there in the cockpit doorway with Jack and Smitty. He looked out and could see the landing lights and terminal buildings at Naples International. "We will land in ten minutes or so. Give me that time to think, will you?"

"Sure," said Jack. "Take your time. We're only on a mission that will stop a new movement with ten times the power and influence of Al Qaeda from sprouting up."

"Would you like to see what I and my expedition discovered?" Caneman repeated the question. He heard every cardinal in the Chapel say an enthusiastic, *'yes'*. He imagined hearing the billions around the world say the same thing. He had them. He knew it and they knew it. Perfect.

"Alright then. For the first time in about five centuries, gaze with me on a site no man—or woman—has seen." Caneman stabbed at the button on his remote console. The video his expedition had made as it entered the vault and began looking around appeared on both screens in the Chapel. The same image streamed through cables, to the jumbotron in St. Pete's Square, into the control trailer outside and then out to the world.

The video camera in the vault paused and focused on Caneman himself. He was dressed in his expeditionary khakis and looked nothing like a future Pope or even the Cardinal that he is. Instead, he appeared as every common man. He spoke to the camera, "Hi, it's me David. We are in what appears to be the Catholic Church's treasury vault. Let's have a look inside and see what's in here." Caneman walked ahead of the camera, under the golden arch supports with their engraved writing. He didn't stop to read the words to his audience. He knew a video of the treasure would be far more impactful to the common man. Caneman walked through the dusty corridors, pointing out artifacts here and there. Then he stopped before one of the golden horses beside the Roman chariot it pulled with ropes of gold.

"My friends, our Church has been blessed that its members have collected priceless works of art through the ages and donated them to us. One such donation sits before us right here. For the first time in centuries, you are seeing objects that no one has viewed. Each is a priceless work of art. These happen to be from ancient Rome and I would guess are made of pure gold." He allowed the camera to pan over the golden horse, then zoom in on the golden ropes and run along its golden bridle to the reins that tethered it to the chariot. Caneman's image faced the video camera again, He said, "My friends, I have another mission inside this wondrous vault and must leave the video archiving to our archeologists. Ciao."

And so went Caneman's video of his discovery. He allowed it to run just another three minutes. It was enough time to prove his achievement, interest the masses as the camera stopped on piece after piece, each of unimaginable value. But he didn't allow the tape to run so long as to bore an audience he knew had a short attention span even for something so momentous as this.

"Now, my fellow faithful," he resumed his live oration from inside the Chapel, "I want to show you the real discovery. It is far more valuable than any of the gold and gemstones we found so far and are still discovering. Let me show you." Caneman turned toward his two objects still wrapped in their brown paper and sitting on the sacramental table beside the podium.

The Pope eyed Jack. If he hadn't been entirely sure Jack believed how a seismic shift to fundamentalist Catholic doctrine around the world could create a dangerous faction whose destructive power completely eclipsed that of Al Qaeda, he was now. During the few minutes they had before landing at the *Carabinieri* station at the Naples airport the Pope had instructed Jack and Smitty what he wanted them to do. The Pope had heard Jack radio his request to Captain Antonio Spinelli, the lead pilot in the Robinson ahead of them. As they descended, the Pope spotted several more Robinson helicopters on the runway apron along with a variety of fixed wing propeller aircraft and one shiny business jet with *Carabinieri* written in bold script along the fuselage. Perfect, the Pope thought.

The Blackhawk's skids hit the runway ramp where Spinelli had ordered them to land. It was right outside the *Carabinieri's* hangar. Jack and Smitty both jumped out of the aircraft and closed the door behind them. Spinelli had already landed and shut down his engine. Before his aircraft's rotors stopped he was already running toward the two men, arms outstretched and ready for a reuniting embrace with his old friends.

Inside the Blackhawk the Pope watched the reunion. He also observed three men exit from the hangar, striding toward them. The man in the lead was obviously the senior officer of the police force that had its roots in the Italian military. His black uniform was immaculate with its four-silver-button jacket and black pants sporting a bright red stripe down the side of each leg. His shoulder boards displayed two gold stars with silver filigree below and there were a number of gold medals on his breast. His hat bore the symbol the Pope had seen used by nearly all military constabularies—an exploding grenade. The Pope thought: only the famous Italian fashion house of Valentino could have designed such a garish uniform. Then he thought better of his criticism as he remembered his own regalia. Maybe we'll have to change some of that pretentiousness in the Church, he thought. The Pope consulted his watch again and glanced at his iPhone showing the proceedings inside the Sistine Chapel still rolling to what the Pope knew would be its inevitable election of Caneman as Pope if he wasn't stopped.

Outside the Blackhawk, Spinelli introduced Jack and Smitty to the *Carabinieri* chief of station. Their friend, Antonio Spinelli, worked hard to vouch for them and tried to smooth the way. Jack said, "Divisional General, it is not our intent to make your life difficult here. We're on a very special mission." Jack paused to be sure he had the Division General's attention. He wasn't sure how well he understood English.

The Division General said, "Mr. Schilling, I speak English as well as you do. Your reputation precedes you. If you say you are on a special mission, I am willing to hear you out. But understand, I have my orders. They come from…a very, very high source."

Jack was certain that Cardinal David Caneman had placed a call to the Commanding General of the entire *Carabinieri*. His orders to stop the looters had been filtered down to all divisions in and around Formia. "Division General, if you will join me inside my helo, all will be revealed." When Spinelli and the other two officers accompanying the Division General started toward the Blackhawk to join their boss, Jack said, "Sorry guys. This meeting will have to be with just the boss here." Turning to the General, "Sir, you will understand why in just a moment. Please…" Jack waved his arm indicating for the General to step forward. The door slipped open enough to admit him, Jack and Smitty, then Helen quickly closed it.

The General removed his sunglasses and allowed a moment for his eyes to adjust to the diminished light inside the Blackhawk. No one spoke as he scanned the two pilots standing at the cockpit entrance. He moved on to Helen, and paused for a half second. Maybe he recognizes her from her pictures in the *Times*, wondered Jack. Then he moved on and stopped on Sister Mary Pat. Everyone recognized SMP. With her job as Vatican News Service anchor reporter, she was the world's most famous nun in or out of her habit.

"Sister," the General said and touched a finger to his hat, now looking somewhat confused. When he focused on the Pope,

Jack saw his eyes grow wide. Then the man instantly dropped to his knees and removed his hat.

"Well, General, that is not the reaction I was hoping for," said the Pope.

"*Excuse, il Popo,*" stammered the police officer as if he had seen a ghost. In fact, to him the Pope was dead, had been killed by the bombing of Castel Gandolfo. He made the sign of the cross before him.

The Pope was out of his seat and trying to help the General to his feet. "It is alright, my son. They tell me that I am one of the most photographed people in the world. And after all, it's not everyday you see someone who was supposed to have been killed almost a week ago." He waited for the General to regain his composure. Then, "I am afraid we have only a limited amount of time. I must get to Rome and resume my duties. Do you understand, General?"

The General blinked his eyes, still in wonder at the man speaking to him. "*Si, prego.* Yes, Your Holiness I understand. But why...what happened?"

Jack spoke up, "General there's no time to explain right now. We need an executive jet. Can you help us, Sir?"

Jack knew what the man was thinking. Like all military or police personnel he had his clear orders—in his case they were to stop and detain anyone possibly linked with the activities at Formia. Instinct was to resist at all cost disobeying those orders. But Jack reasoned you didn't become a general by always following orders. Especially when the circumstances change as they obviously had now. Jack waited, allowing the General to figure it out for himself.

"Yes. Yes, Your Holiness. Of course, I will extend to you every available courtesy at my command. How may I assist?"

The Pope resumed command, "As Jack said, we must borrow your jet sitting over there." The Pope jerked a thumb over toward the sleek jet sitting empty on the tarmac. "We will fly directly from here to Leonardo da Vinci Airport. Then we will need one of your police vans to meet us there and take us immediately to the Sistine Chapel in Vatican City. We have no time to waste."

"Yes, Your Holiness. That is true. I have been watching Cardinal Caneman on the television along with the rest of the world."

"Then you know how urgent our mission is," piped up the Pope. "It would be best if I interrupted his conclave and stopped them from electing him Pope. Otherwise we would have two duly elected popes. That would not do, would it?"

"Certainly not," exclaimed the General. He spun on his heel, stuck just his head out of the door and shouted to his aide-de-camp, "Ready that jet for an emergency flight to Rome." When the Lieutenant did not move as fast as he wanted, the General said, "Do it before you take your next breath, you idiot." From inside the Blackhawk everyone watched as the young lieutenant sprinted for the hangar to spur the pilot and ground crew into action.

The Pope turned to the *Carabinieri* General, "And you, Sir, I am afraid we must ask you to accompany us. I do not want word of my presence to leak out before I am ready. And the addition of a Division General in the *Carabinieri* just might come in handy. Do you mind?"

The General said, "Your Holiness, it will be my sincerest honor to accompany you on your mission to retake the head of our blessed Church."

"Now that's what I'm talking about," said the Pope, pleased with himself.

* * *

CHAPTER 35

Cardinal David Caneman pulled the brown paper wrapper first from the ancient broom that sat on the sacramental table beside the podium. Then he did the same to the box containing the passage from the Bible that proved its authenticity. The camera followed his every move. The young acolyte standing behind and to the side of Caneman immediately grabbed the discarded paper and left the altar with it.

"My fellow faithful," he began, "what we have sitting on the table beside me are two objects that I retrieved from the treasure vault. As you can see," he gestured to the first object, "it is a common broom. We all have one. I do. And like you I have used it on many an occasion." Caneman paused for another few seconds of dramatic effect.

Caneman's folksy manner sped through the airwaves and around the world, "You are probably wondering why am I showing you a common broom when there are statues of gold, paintings by old masters and gemstones by the bucketsful in the vault. I understand your confusion. For I was just as confused when He showed me His broom. I can guarantee its value to we faithful is many times that of the most priceless object that will ever be discovered in the vault—and there are many. Allow me to show you."

Caneman turned from the broom to the ancient wooden box sitting beside it. He waited for a moment until the cameraman could move in for a close-up showing the cross inscribed on the box lid.

"When I was delivered to this single and remotest corner of the vault, I believe it was by divine directive. I am certain of it. For why would I, or anyone for that matter, deliberately go down the darkest and most inaccessible passageway that contained nothing of apparent value when there was so much more of far greater value and with far easier access? I believe that I was directed by the Holy One Himself to this common broom. For it is an object that will unite us all as one in the only true faith."

Caneman paused for a three count, allowing anticipation to crescendo for the money shot. He picked up the broom, cradling it in both arms to present to the cameras. "Jesus himself held this broom. Jesus himself used this broom to sweep the floor of the house in which he conducted the Last Supper. If there was ever

360

an object that provided irrefutable proof that Our Savior walked this same earth that we walk today, it is this not-so-common and far-from-ordinary broom."

Cardinal David Caneman pressed the button of his remote video control so that it scanned the faces of the cardinals seated before him. They suddenly knelt on the newly installed richly carpeted floor and prayed for thanks. Then Caneman released the remote button and allowed the camera to focus on him again.

"My friends, we are a faithful people. For that is the definition of faith: accepting something as truth without physical proof. However, the rest of the world is not so faithful. They require proof. Therefore, proof they shall have."

Caneman lifted the lid of the ancient wooden box. He motioned for the camera to focus on what was inside. "My friends, this box was sitting on that ancient shelf inside the treasure vault right beside the broom. It is clear that they go together. Inside you can see that it contains a script of animal skin. That was the medium used back then to write things. Indeed, our Holy Bible was first written on the same animal skin. You ask what is written on this animal skin that so obviously goes with the broom?

"I will tell you. It contains a partial book from the Old Testament. When I first read it, I knew immediately that it came from Matthew 26. It begins with verse 17. Caneman removed the animal skin with theatrical care and began reading aloud:

On the first day of the Feast of Unleavened Bread, the disciples came to Jesus and asked, "Where do you want us to make preparations for you to eat the Passover?"

He replied, "Go into the city to a certain man and tell him, 'The Teacher says: My appointed time is near. I am going to celebrate the Passover with my disciples at your house.' "

So the disciples did as Jesus had directed them and prepared the Passover.

Caneman stopped reading and looked into the camera once again. "This is straight from our modern Bible that each of us has

361

read many times." He paused and smiled, sharing the private joke that he knew, as everyone knew, not enough of the faithful spent sufficient time with the Bible. In that single moment the hundreds of millions around the world understood the man with this simple, humbling and-all knowing gesture. He had them. "But what is *not* from our modern Bible comes next. Let me continue reading this original script:

When evening came, the twelve disciples came to the appointed house. There they found Jesus, their Rabbi, at work sweeping the room with a broom made of straw. They watched as dust clouds flew around their Teacher's sandaled feet.

Peter said unto Him, "Master why do you sweep the floor like a common servant?"

Jesus stopped his sweeping and leaned on the broom with both hands on top of its crooked hickory handle and with its stiff, straw bristles splayed out against the floor, bearing his weight. Then he did hand the broom to Peter for him to hold. Jesus did bend down and scooped the dust into his own hands, then tossed the dirt out the open door. He then did recover the broom from his disciple and resumed his sweeping. The Holy One sayeth, "Learn ye and never forget, there is honor in work for everyone. There is no man so high that he cannot sweep the floor of his host's home."

Jesus continued sweeping until the dust was no more. Only then, when his sweeping was done did he stand the broom in the corner and take his seat at the center of the table where he reclined with the Twelve.

And while they were eating, he said, "I tell you the truth, one of you will betray me."

Cardinal David Caneman stopped reading and looked into the camera once again. "None of us has ever read of The Savior sweeping a room clean like a common servant in the Book of Matthew. This passage was removed by some overreaching pope who rebelled at the thought of Jesus sweeping a room to rid it of

362

dust like an ordinary man. Back then they had their own ideas of how to portray our Savior. Apparently it did not include common work. So they removed this original manuscript and replaced it with one more in keeping with their own ideas without regard to what the word of God had actually said. But even they could not discard entirely the original word of God. So they buried it in the Church's treasure vault."

Caneman oh so carefully put the animal skin manuscript back in its box and slowly closed its ancient lid. Then he turned to the broom, all the while minding the camera angle so as to keep both himself and the broom in the picture.

"My friends, this is not just any broom, this is *our* broom. It provides a solid link for each of us to Him. For each of us has used a broom at some time in our lives. Some of us do it every day. This was Jesus' way of saying to his disciples they need a clean sweep of their faith." Caneman repeated, "A clean sweep. We have all done such clean sweeps. Some do it publicly as I did at Vatican Bank two years ago. But all of us make clean sweeps from time to time. I hope that whomever the College of Cardinals sees fit to elect as the next Pope will make such a clean sweep. The next pope must rescue our Church from its harmful course and deliver it back to one closer to our Catholic fundamentals."

Caneman grabbed the box containing the original manuscript and offered it up to the camera as if giving the world a gift. Then he said, "This is the original book of Matthew. It was dictated by God or one of the disciples and written without editorializing. Radio carbon dating will prove the authenticity of the broom and the box containing the authentic scripture. That is what science will eventually tell us. What I have seen and what you have too is evidence of the broom and its provenance laying side by side in the vault I discovered. Praise be unto the Lord."

There was a moment of silence from the cardinals still kneeling. Then they rose as one cheering for Cardinal David Caneman and the miracle of his discovery.

After they landed at Leonardo da Vinci International Airport, a *Carabinieri* van sped Jack and his small group through the streets of Rome, into Saint Peter's Square and skidded to a stop *behind* the Sistine Chapel. The Pope had requested an anonymous entrance—one where the fewest people would be likely to see him. This was it.

As they all exited the van, Jack threw his worn worker's jacket of blue denim over the Pope's head just in case. To anyone watching, the group looked like six laborers of varying ages entering the back of the Chapel.

"Look," observed the Pope. He pointed to the roof of the Chapel. There, a simple chimney—a little taller than most—but not any more significant than the others belched a plume of black smoke. From back here they could hear throngs of people lining every inch of the front of Saint Pete's Square groan as one.

"Caneman's second trial election failed to elect a new pope," observed Sister Mary Pat, never missing a chance to give a lesson in Church lore. She continued as they rushed to the first door attended by a Swiss Guard. "The balloting conducted by the College of Cardinals sends out smoke signals: White when a new pope is elected and black as we see here when the ballot is inconclusive. Tradition requires all the ballot forms and any personal notes made by the cardinals to be burned—"

They stumbled to a stop before the Swiss Guard who held up a hand to halt their entry. Before the *Carabinieri* General could produce his badge, the Pope ducked out from under Jack's coat and held his head up, smiling at the guard. "Would you kindly admit me and my party?" he asked. The guard stood for a moment, dumbfounded and confused at whom he was seeing.

"It's the ears, isn't it?" said the Pope. "I knew the ears would give me away. Very hard not to be missed with these attached to both sides of my head. Well, what can a guy do?"

The Swiss Guard recovered from this unexpected shock. "Yes, Your Holiness. Yes, of course." He unlocked the old door made of stout wooden timbers and swung it open for them.

364

The Pope turned back to the guard, "Please join us. We don't want to spoil the surprise of my presence for Cardinal Caneman." So now the Pope's party included both a General in the *Carabinieri* and a Swiss guard. It would continue growing as the Pope knew it would.

"Where are we?" asked Sister Mary Pat. Even as a nun, she was unfamiliar with the Sistine's warren of back rooms. This was a section never seen by the public and seldom by anyone else but the museum's curators. It was poorly lit and smelled musty—completely unlike the world-famous Chapel.

"Where do you wish to go, Your Holiness?" asked the Swiss Guard. I know every inch of this place."

The Pope thought for a moment. They could hear the deep rumblings of the College of Cardinals as their deliberations, conversations and occasionally, Cardinal David Caneman's voice on the audio system reverberated throughout the ancient structure. He said to his posse that had grown to eight people, "I want to set up the timing just right for my entrance. I believe that I will get just one chance to establish my credibility with the Cardinals. I have been thinking of how best to do it." Then, to the Swiss Guard, "Take us quietly to the Chapel of St. Christopher, please."

Helen was looking at her map of the Sistine Chapel she had printed online before they had left Elkhart. It seemed a lifetime ago. "I don't see any St. Christopher Chapel," she said.

"Oh you won't, my dear," said the Pope, urging them all to quickly follow the Guard. "Few outside of the popes and their closest aids even know of its existence." They walked at such a pace that the Pope began coughing and he choked to catch his breath.

Just thirty yards into their trek, they turned a corner and ran into another Swiss Guard. This one was not so cooperative. He had heard the noise of their footfalls and was waiting with drawn gun as they rounded the corner. "Who goes there?" he commanded.

The first Swiss Guard stepped forward. "Lars, it's Kilian here. We are on a mission for the Pope."

"There is no Pope," said Lars, "that is the purpose of the conclave going on right now. They are about to conduct another vote—the third."

The Pope stepped from the back shadows into the light and said to Lars, "There are a few of us here, young man, who beg to differ with you."

Lars did a double-take and continued peering at the Pope. "It is a story I have yet to hear," said Kilian. "Lars, use your walkie-talkie to order the Pope's guards to assemble at St. Christopher Chapel. Do not tell them anything more than that on the Pope's orders. Do it now, please, Lars." Kilian motioned for the group—including Lars—to join them as they proceeded to St. Christopher's Chapel.

By now they were far enough into the Chapel complex that the noise from the conclave's proceedings was clearly audible. Jack made a note to keep his voice down. "You okay with this, Your Holiness?," he whispered to the Pope. "I can see you're tired. Want to stop and rest?"

The Pope was bent over at the waist with hands on his knees like a runner catching his breath. "No time, Jackson. I'll be okay in a minute. Let's press on."

"The Chapel of St. Christopher is just two minutes further," said the second Guard they had picked up.

The Pope had dropped to the back of their pack. Jack and the *Carabinieri* General met him back there. They positioned themselves on each side of the Pope, placed one shoulder under each arm and lifted. The Pope—who weighed in at just 150 pounds—suddenly rose off the rough, gray concrete floor in this part of the old building and virtually flew the rest of the way until they reached the locked door of the Chapel of St. Christopher.

Jack eyed the keyring the first Guard produced. He whispered, "Careful with those keys. If we can hear them this clearly, Caneman can hear us too." Jack watched as the soldier silently leafed through the keys until he found the one he was searching for. While they were waiting, another four Swiss Guards hurried to their location, summoned by the radio call.

Jack held one finger up to his lips and shook his head for them to be quiet. He heard the tumblers quietly slip into place and the heavy oak door to St. Christopher's Chapel opened. All of them slipped into the small room and softly closed the door behind them. By now they numbered 13.

"It is almost as if the conclave were right next door," Sister Mary Pat said in a hushed voice.

"It is," whispered Lars, the second guard they met. "This room is just around the corner from the entrance to the Chapel altar where Cardinal Caneman is speaking. He is within thirty meters of where we are standing right now."

Jack saw the Pope sitting in a chair, bent over. The old guy looked tired. He knew how he felt. Jack's bullet wound ached. He went over to the Pope and saw that he was actually bent over his iPad, typing away furiously with one hand and holding his iPhone in the other. Finally he finished and looked up at Jack.

"Done," the Pope said. "I was on the phone with the Vatican IT department. With the touch of that button there," he pointed to the *play* button appearing on the Pad's screen, "I take control over all the content on the Sistine Chapel's screens, the live feed going into St. Peter's Square and everything downstreamed to the Vatican News Service production van outside and out to the world. I have managed to cobble together quite an audio and video presentation that shows Cardinal Caneman as the man he actually is."

Helen was standing with them now. "I didn't see you recording or filming anything. How did you get that content."

The Pope held up the little red phone the American president had given him. "It seems that your National Security Agency does more than just spy on citizens foreign and domestic. I explained what I was interested in—assassination attempts, bombing of Castel Gandolfo—that sort of thing and asked for some help. I presume your president had but to place a single telephone call to set the wheels in motion. Within two days I had recordings of Cardinal Caneman convicting himself of all sorts of awful things—most of which were at my personal expense.

"Amen to that," said Sister Mary Pat.

"From there it was just a matter of fitting the puzzle pieces together into a credible format. That's where my friends in the IT department came in handy."

From the main Chapel next door they clearly heard the amplified voice of Cardinal David Caneman say, "Your Eminences...Your Eminences, would you please finish up your discussions and take your seats. I would like to conduct the third vote for Pope in the next few minutes. Take your seats, please. While you are doing so, a new video was just sent to me from the Church's Treasury Vault in Formia. I want to share with you the newest discoveries that will surely fund the Church's good works well into the next century. I will turn up the volume so you all can hear the archeologists describe what we discovered."

Had there been any doubt before as to who would be elected the next pope, there was none now. And when Cardinal David Caneman was elected Pope, there was equally no doubt that his wishes governing the Church's new direction—no matter how harsh—would become canon law.

The Pope turned to Jack, Helen, Smitty and Sister Mary Pat, "Show time, everyone." His serene smile said that he was right where he wanted to be at this very moment. He pressed the *Play* button on his iPad. "Give it a moment, then let's go—all of us—and join Cardinal Caneman on the altar."

Caneman's portrait filled the twin big screens. His voice was unmistakable. There was no doubt as to who the speaker was. "But the Pope was killed," Caneman's voice boomed insistently through the speakers and other devices carrying the papal conclave around the world.

"Probably," said the caller. "If he somehow survived the concussion of the blast, he was likely crushed as the building collapsed. In my business, a confirmed kill requires me to observe unequivocal proof of death—preferably a body with no vital signs of life. As you might surmise, the entire area is clogged with police, fire and rescue crews searching the ruins for survivors..."

Caneman's voice came over the Sistine Chapel's sound system again, then was piped out to the 100,000 lining St. Pete's Square and the millions more watching around the world, "But you think the Pope was killed?"

"Yes," answered the rough voice on the other end of the damning call. "Unless I hear otherwise, my contract has been executed as agreed."

At first there was stunned silence while Caneman's audio voice echoed inside the Sistine Chapel. Then the cardinals looked up at Caneman with questions in their eyes and began wildly chattering among themselves.

"Let us go," said the Pope. He handed his iPhone to Sister Mary Pat and directed her to walk ahead while videoing him as he made his way into the Chapel. The video feed from the papal smartphone immediately fed into the Chapel's system as the Vatican's IT department had made the switch. The two giant screens lit up with the Pope's image live as he walked. A hush came over those gathered in Saint Peter's Square awaiting news of the next pope's election. People stood in the square facing the giant screen and talking while excitedly gesturing at the beloved man they saw. Around the world, the Pope appeared—those unmistakable, magnificent ears affixed to his head as usual. Had he risen from the dead?

The world watched as the Pope—dressed as a common laborer in a red, white and black plaid shirt and blue denim pants with scuffed leather work boots—purposefully walked down the rough corridor that led from St. Christopher's Chapel to the Sistine Chapel's main altar. He was in no hurry. The stunned silence told him that he had not only Caneman's and the College of Cardinal's attention but also that of the entire world. The Pope had a huge smile on his face and gave a friendly wave to the smartphone-serving-as-TV-camera Sister Mary Pat held in front of him. Cardinal David Caneman was not the only one schooled in the theatrical delivery of a public message.

The Pope mounted the two steps leading onto the main altar. He saw David Caneman still standing at the speaker's podium beside the table that held the broom and the box containing the true manuscript of the Book Of Matthew. He noticed Caneman's cardinal red cape bordered in the papal white. Arrogance was a trait for which he especially had no patience. The Pope felt a surge of energy as he strode up to Caneman. He said, "I will take it from here, David. Please step aside." The Pope felt in his heart that the actions he was now taking were necessary and a significant part of the job to which he had been elected.

He said, "Do not be so surprised. My presence here is far from a miracle, I assure you. I had some help from these extraordinary people beside me." His arm raised and went out to include Jack, Helen, Sister Mary Pat and Smitty. "The recording you just heard with Cardinal Caneman conversing with the assassin he hired to kill me speaks for itself. He will be judged eventually. But we have more important matters to deal with."

Jack stood off to one side of David Caneman where he could keep a watchful eye on him. There was a Swiss Guard positioned at each elbow. He watched as the Pope moved to the middle of the podium and visibly relaxed. This has got to be mucho stressful on the old guy Jack thought. Hope his heart holds out.

"The actions that Cardinal Caneman took against me—while personally distressing—are not all that unusual. Throughout history several popes have died under mysterious circumstances. However, thankfully and as you can see I am not one of them. Before I interrupted, you were about to vote for the next Pope. As I was following your proceedings, it seems to me this third vote would likely have been the decisive one." The Pope stopped and smiled out at the cardinals and the world who were all watching in silence at this most astonishing event unrolling before their very eyes. "Well, if it is alright with you, I would like to throw my hat into the ring. I believe that I am qualified,

370

having been elected once already and actually working this job for the last five years."

A familiar voice piped up from the first row of cardinals. It was Cardinal Augustus Hall from the United States. "But Your Holiness, you are not dead. Thanks, God. You never vacated your office as Pope. I do not see why any vote is needed. I think you should shut down this conclave for it is unnecessary."

The Pope smiled from the raised altar at Cardinal Hall. "Thank you, Gus, for your suggestion. However, let us not forget that the world is watching. I have an obligation to conduct these proceedings in as transparent a manner as possible. I am not afraid of a vote." He turned toward Caneman who was standing between his keepers, stiff as a board. "Are you afraid, Cardinal Caneman?"

Not having heard an answer, the Pope turned back to his audience and said, "Perhaps he is. Anyway, the Cardinal is not saying much. So, perhaps we should just have our vote. As the world watches the voting, Sister Mary Pat—whom most of you know—will explain what is happening."

Mary Pat wasn't expecting to have a speaking part. To the best of her knowledge no female had ever addressed a papal conclave. Nevertheless, she didn't need a second invitation.

She smiled into the camera and spoke in the same calm voice the world knew and loved. "Hello dearies, and thank you, Your Holiness. I guess I can still call you that, can't I?"

From the side of the podium the Pope said, "Maybe soon Sister, maybe never again if the vote goes against me."

"Well anyway," SMP continued, "this is a never before seen opportunity to observe an historic vote by a papal conclave. Look down there as Johnnie, my cameraman, follows the process. "You can see that all non-cardinals—except for us workers—have now left the Chapel. This would normally be a secret vote to the world, but watch what happens next."

The camera followed each cardinal as they solemnly walked to the altar. They held their folded ballot up high and said aloud so the entire College of Cardinals could hear, "I call as my witness Christ the Lord who will be my judge, that my vote is given to the one who before God I think should be elected."

Sister Mary Pat let this process go on for three cardinals before explaining, "See dearies how they each place their ballot on the ceremonial plate from where it slides into the chalice that collects all the ballots." Since there were over one hundred cardinals, this elocution took over an hour. Mary Pat filled in the time by describing how the Pope had survived the three attempts on his life.

"Oh," she interrupted herself, "I see the last ballot was cast. Now watch carefully. The priest holding the chalice has shaken it to mix up the ballots to maintain their secrecy. Okay, now he is transferring the ballots to a new chalice. He will now count the number of ballots to be sure they correspond to the number of electors. We wouldn't want any of the cardinal's votes to be missed."

Jack Schilling was not watching the proceedings. He kept a close eye on Cardinal David Caneman. He did not like the loose-fitting robe the man wore. Never can tell what is under there, he thought. Jack wore his denim jacket loose for the same reason. Now his hand rested just inside, on the butt of the Sig P-226 hanging in the shoulder rig he was never without. He watched Caneman's face. It had turned red and there was sweat on his upper lip. Was it just the tension of being outted in front of the whole world, wondered Jack?

He was alerted by Caneman's eyes. They suddenly grew wide. It took less than a second for the CEO of Vatican Bank to yank a pistol from beneath his vestments. Jack was ahead of him by half. He had his gun out, leveled at his target and was squeezing the trigger before Caneman's arm could extend toward the Pope.

The startling concussion of Jack's two shots—one to the chest, the other to the head—stopped the three scrutineers examining each ballot with the last one calling out the name on the ballot. It stopped Sister Mary Pat from describing what the world was seeing. Cardinal David Caneman fell to the new red carpet of the Sistine Chapel's altar. He was dead before he hit the floor.

Jack held up four fingers for the Pope to see. The Pontiff nodded, understanding that this was the fourth attempt on his life. The Pope now did what he had been elected to do. He took control.

"Brothers, calm down, please. Cardinal Caneman had a pistol aimed at my head and surely would have shot me dead had Mr. Schilling not intervened. For that I am grateful. But even this unhappy event should not stop us from our mission. I ask that the conclave continue to its end. Sister will you please continue."

Sister Mary Pat stepped back to the microphone. The Swiss Guards had already removed Caneman's body. Her professional's voice was shaky for only a few words them calmed down. With her assurance, the cardinals' excited jabbering ceased as well.

Mary Pat said, "Election of a new pope requires two-thirds majority. Since these rules were not changed in this conclave, that is what will be used. This is a very deliberate vote counting. After the scrutineers have counted and read the votes, there are revisers who double-check the scrutineers' work. You can see that is what they are doing right now."

But their work was pure formality. Already everyone knew the result of the balloting. There had not been a single vote cast for anyone other than the Pope standing on the altar. There was no need for scrutineers or revisers.

"Now dearies, here is where the smoke signals come in. See how the paper ballots and any handwritten notes made by the cardinals are collected. Now that the votes are counted and we have elected a new pope, all this paper is burned immediately."

Sure enough, two of the priests were tossing all the ballots and notes into a stove. One shut the door to the stove. The other took a white cartridge containing potassium chlorate, lactose and chloroform resin. It is the chemicals in this cartridge that produce the white-colored smoke the world sees coming from the chimney atop the Sistine when conclave has voted. White smoke meant that a new pope had been elected. However, today the smoke just preserved tradition. Everyone around the world already knew the Pope had been reelected. Nevertheless, tradition is what the world's most successful institutions are built around.

* * *

CHAPTER 36

The President's desk phone softly chirped. It was distinctive from all his other lines. It was the critical line that he and Grace, his secretary, had agreed was the one line he would answer immediately no matter what. He stood from the chair at the head of the two low couches that faced one another with a coffee table separating them in the Oval Office. "Hold that thought," he asked his Secretary of the Treasury. "Gotta take this one."

"Yeah, Gracie what's up?"

"Mr. President, the SEALs are here again."

The President stopped short and wondered for a moment. They were just here last week. He quickly remembered the heart-wrenching luncheon he had thrown for them and all the lead they brought for him to store. "How many of them this time, Gracie?"

"The Marine standing post at the Northwest Appointments Gate says just four SEALS. But also Jack Schilling—both junior and senior—Helen, and a Mr. Smith from the SEC."

"What about Tucker? Is Tucker with them?"

"Just a second, sir, I'll find out."

The President saw his council of economic advisors, the Secretary of the Treasury and the Head of the Federal Reserve all looking his way. He knew they were impatient to show him their numbers for GDP and domestic growth, predictions of interest rates and what not.

"Mr. President, sorry for the delay. Yes, Tucker is with them too."

The President remembered with great respect the young lieutenant and his Belgian Malinois who was every bit a SEAL as any man who had earned the right to wear the Trident. "Okay, Gracie, invite them all in. Have a Marine honor guard escort them here into the Oval Office. And maybe ask the mess to bring up some fresh coffee and scones and a dish of water and some dog biscuits for Tucker."

"On their way, sir," said Gracie. "Except for the dog biscuits. I didn't know about Tucker. I'll call Chef again."

The President turned to the country's most senior economic experts. "Sorry, gentlemen, we're going to have to cut this conference short. There's a situation with the Navy that I have to see to right away. Ask Gracie to put you down for my next available slot."

The suits got up and left.

"Welcome," said the President. "Welcome to every one of you. And thanks for taking your time to come see me again. You are always welcome in this house." The President stopped talking and looked each man in the eye and shook hands with them. He spoke a few words of thanks for their service. He didn't forget Tucker, the war service dog. He bent to where Tucker was sitting beside his partner with two titanium legs.

"Tucker, atten-hut," said his partner.

The Malinois immediately stood stock still and looked up at the President.

"May I?" asked the President.

"Sure sir. What do you want him to do, I'll tell you the command."

"I have this one, son. The President was still kneeling at animal eye level. "Tucker, at ease," said the President.

The dog's butt instantly hit the Oval Office's richly carpeted floor and he raised his paw to shake with the President. After a shake, the President ruffled Tucker's neck fur, reached into his suit pocket and pulled out a dog biscuit. He offered it to Tucker who gently took it and lay down on the Oval Office carpet to enjoy his reward.

"Good to see you again, Jack," the President said as he straightened up. I see things went well for you in Italy."

"Yes, Sir. But we didn't come here to talk about Italy. Mr. President, these fine men began a tradition last week by giving you the lead taken from their bodies during service to their country." The talking had stopped among the small group of men. They pulled in tight around Jack and the President. This

376

was a private and very personal conversation that belonged to all of them.

Jack continued, "Sir, I for one would like to see that tradition continue. Whoever occupies this office needs to see in real life what sacrifice looks like. You can't learn it from a memo or hear it second hand from someone who never felt what it's like being shot or taking shrapnel—"

"That's a fine speech, Jack and those are great sentiments."

"Sir, with respect I'm not quite done yet. The part I've been looking forward to, the part I've carried around with me for some ten years now is coming." Jack reached into his leather satchel and pulled out five of the same plastic boxes the others had given the President last week. Four were marked with various places in the Middle East. The last one said, *Formia Italy.*

"Sir, these are my small contribution to your collection. They have no better place than in your care alongside the contributions of my SEALs. Proud to serve, Sir."

The President stood there for a quiet moment as he held the lead pulled from his Godson's body. He felt humble, surrounded by these fine men who had given so much.

Then he said, "Gentlemen, it may surprise you that I also have a contribution to make to the national lead collection." He walked over to the Resolute desk where he usually worked and reached inside its top right drawer.

"During the election then the reelection, my campaign manager thought we should make a big deal out of me being wounded when my Marines went into Iraq. I refused. Couldn't see the point. So outside my immediate family you are the only ones to know." The President placed his own plastic box with its smashed 7.62x39mm piece of lead beside Jack's.

"Where'd they hit you, Sir?" came the question from Tucker's partner.

"Right shoulder." The President reached back and tapped the spot. "Damn near took my arm off."

The wounded SEAL bent down to Tucker and gently spread apart the fur on his right haunch. "See here, Sir, this is where

Tuck got hit. Twice. As for me, well you can see they took both my legs."

Another SEAL stepped forward, and rolled up the sleeve of his shirt, "Sir, a piece of shrapnel the size of a half dollar sliced through my arm right here." The wound was white and still shiny after three surgeries. "When it gets cold outside, I can still feel that hot metal."

For the next few minutes the President and his warriors compared battle scars and swapped war stories. It is what soldiers do.

Jack said, "Sir, before we leave, the Pope asked me to deliver something." Jack pulled two more plastic boxes from his satchel. "You already have the first bullet that got his ear. Pretty big target if you ask me, Sir. Hard to miss. Now there are these other two. Technically, the Pope was not actually shot. However, he is the Pope so what am I going to say? He was *shot at* twice. One round hit the huge steel cross he liked to wear, the other hit the small bible he kept in his breast pocket. See?" he said holding up one box containing the damaged steel cross and the bullet-shredded bible. "You can see the dent where the round struck the cross. He thinks we saved his life. So he wants to make a contribution. Will you accept, Sir?"

The President examined the contents of the boxes. Yes, he could see the two dents in the cross. "Gentlemen, I think we should let the man speak for himself." The President winked at those gathered around him, one warrior to another. The President pulled his private cell phone from his coat pocket and pressed a few buttons, put it on speakerphone then waited. The men in the room looked at one another, not sure if he was actually calling the Pope himself and wondering if the connection would be made.

"His Holiness speaking. How may I serve?" came the answer from the speakerphone. His smile was evident in the happy tone of voice. "How are you, Mr. President?" The two leaders had developed a close friendship over the last few weeks since Jack and Helen had four times saved his life. Both men used their titles only in mockery of the formality when they were alone or with those they felt particularly comfortable with.

"I have you on speakerphone here in the Oval Office, Your Holiness. Did I catch you at a bad time?"

"It is never a bad time for you to catch me. I am the Pope. Every time is a great time. Just a second." Over the phone they could hear the shuffling of feet, then a muffled, "Go with God my Son, but before you do, how about giving me three Hail Maries and do the stations of the cross for me?"

"Mr. President? Are you still there? I just had to finish up with the last confession. I'm here in the Pope's private chapel. I hear the house staff's confessional when I'm in town. It's more convenient for them. That was the chef—he burned this morning's oatmeal and wanted absolution. What's up?"

"Your Holiness, Jack and Helen are here along with some of their SEAL buddies. They have some questions for you related to the cross and two slugs you want to contribute to our national memorial."

"Okay, shoot—perhaps that is not appropriate under the circumstances."

"Your Holiness, it's Jack. Accepting your lead places you among a very rare group of men. You literally become one of us. This is not something to be taken lightly." Jack looked at Helen. Pulling the Pope's leg was getting to be fun.

There was silence for a few seconds then, "Jack, this is one of your jokes, right? You know to whom I directly report, don't you?"

"I do, Your Holiness. But we're talking about the SEALs."

"I see," answered the Pope slowly, guessing he was being played. "I'm ascending into an altogether higher category?"

"None higher, Sir."

"Okay, ask your questions."

"First, are you a leader who is ready to lead?"

"The Pope leads 1.2 billion faithful. I guess it is not too much to say that I am a leader who is ready to lead."

Jack raised an eyebrow toward the group of warriors standing around him listening. They nodded their heads, accepting the Pope's answer. "Next question, Your Holiness. Are you ready to follow?"

"My son, every Pope is first a follower and second a guide for his people. So, yes, one might say I was a born follower who learned to lead."

More nodding heads.

"Last question—"

"I can't wait, Jackson."

"Will you ever quit?"

"Quit? Me? I had half my magnificent ear shot off. I had the house in which I was recuperating from the first attack blown out from under me by a bomb. I was shot at twice more by some hired gunman. And had it not been for you I would have been shot again right there in the Sistine Chapel during papal conclave. How am I doing so far in the not quitting department, Jack?" the Pope shot back.

Jackson Schilling was not one to squander a good opportunity. "Not bad, Your Holiness. But you did get lucky with that crucifix and bible blocking two rounds. You gotta admit—"

"Jackson—"

"So, Your Holiness, would it be fair to say that you are **Ready to Lead, Ready to Follow, and Never Quit?"**

The Pope replied, "Ah the SEAL motto. Yes, Jack. As Pope, I am never out of the fight. And I will endeavor to live up to that ideal."

"Well, gentlemen? Shall we let him in?"

From each man came a full-throated, "NO!"

"Whew. Sorry, Your Holiness, that was close. You shoulda heard the last one." Then Jack looked again at his fellow warriors, the President and Helen.

"Oorah," they shouted into the speakerphone as one and Tucker barked.

* * *

CHAPTER 37

The warm summer sun sank into Washington DC's skyline.

"What do you have in mind now?" asked Helen as they exited the Northwest Appointments Gate of the White House and she led them along Pennsylvania Avenue.

Jack would have liked to remove his suit coat in the humid heat. But he was still wearing the Sig P-226 in its shoulder rig. He didn't think it prudent to expose a firearm in the immediate area. So he suffered. "I'm due in New York tomorrow. I'm supposed to represent the SEC in its oversight of returning the Vatican Bank's $200 billion public offering money to its investors." Jack could see a small truck parked at the curb down the street.

"How long will you be in New York?"

"Just until I can delegate responsibility to one of Smitty's people. Then I'll return to Elkhart." Jack could see the truck was small and painted red. "Why?"

Helen said, "Don't forget who you really work for. I need your answer about what putting a bigger engine in Kaito's new sport truck will do to its profit numbers." She snaked her arm through Jack's and pulled him close to her side.

"That's where we began this escapade, isn't it?" Jack stopped. Through the crowd of admiring young men he could clearly see the truck. "Say, hon, that looks like a 1956 Ford half-ton pickup. I have one of those."

"Does yours have two-on-the-tree and a PowerFlight transmission?"

"You know it does."

"Well, the honest truth is that I had the guys back in Elkhart check out your truck. They did a little maintenance work on it to be sure it was road-worthy and shipped it out here to me." Helen fished in her pocket and tossed Jack the keys." I was hoping I could persuade you to drive me home. Make a road trip of it. You deserve a rest."

Jack stopped and stared at his truck. It was Kaito's flagship color—popping cherry red. Every inch of it gleamed in the late afternoon sun. He shrugged out of his suit coat, no longer caring what anyone thought of his shoulder holster. He opened the door and tossed his coat across the red and cream-colored leather bench seat. The engine turned over as easily as the day she rolled off of Ford's production line.

Helen said, "How about delegating the refund oversight to Audrey. I talked with her mom yesterday. She's completely recovered now. She wants to get back to work."

Jack stared at his wife of almost a year now. "Audrey, huh. That's just what I was thinking. Let's get her on the horn and tell her she has a new assignment and a promotion." Jack pressed the accelerator and the little red truck carrying two people to whom so many faithful owed so much rolled down Pennsylvania Avenue in the general direction of Elkhart, Indiana. "If we drive straight through we can be home in time to catch the ball game."

"That would be the Single-A minor league South Bend Silver Hawks at Coveleski Stadium?" asked Helen.

"The very same. It just so happens that I have four tickets for Saturday's game. After you call Audrey, let's call Brad at the plant and see if he and his son Bobby want to join us."

THE END.

ABOUT THE AUTHOR

Chris Malburg is a widely published writer. With over 4 million words in print scattered among 11 books and over 100 magazine articles, his work is consumed in most western countries. He writes on the subjects of management, business strategies, corporate finance, industrial terrorism (*DEADLY ACCELERATION*) and now the overthrow of the Catholic Church. Chris is a CPA and a recovering investment banker. He lives in Southern California with his wife where they are volunteer puppy raisers for Canine Companions for Independence (www.cci.org) and Guide Dogs for the Blind (http://www.guidedogs.com).

* * * *

CONNECT WITH ME ONLINE

Twitter: http://twitter.com/#!/ChrisMalburg
Facebook: http://facebook.com/chris.malburg
Linkedin: http://www.linkedin.com/in/chrismalburg
Smashwords:
http://www.smashwords.com/profile/view/ChrisMalburg

* * * *

A FINAL WORD FROM THE AUTHOR

It is my sincere hope that you have enjoyed *GOD'S BANKER*. I normally work in the world of non-fiction. Still, like most writers, I'm a reader. I've always thought that if I ever had the time, I'd like to write an action adventure novel--something breezy and fun that would entertain at the beach or when traveling. That time came when I was recovering from surgery due to an athletic injury (I'm an endurance athlete). Laying there with Carrie, our Labrador retriever, by my side I conceived of the idea for *God's Banker* and began the book. Over 130,000 words later you see the finished product.

I invite you to review the book on whatever platform you purchased it. Finally, my readers are generous with their emails and tweets. I always make time to answer since I never forget that my readers are actually my employers. If you wish to send me a note, you are welcome to send it to mailto:CRM@WritersResourceGroup.com

Best wishes,

Chris Malburg

* * * *

OTHER FICTION BY CHRIS MALBURG

Deadly Acceleration
What happens when a handful of leaders in one country set their sights on the total annihilation of another? Deadly Acceleration is first an extraordinarily gripping story with an intensely satisfying end. It is also an insightful look into how each of us--when facing unspeakable evil--can rise up to become something much more than we ever imagined. *Deadly Acceleration* is available at all eBook retailers including:
- ☐ Smashwords: Deadly Acceleration on Smashwords
- ☐ Amazon: Deadly Acceleration on Amazon

Vision Machine

Rachel Kinder is a lawyer. She is trained to be skeptical. She values cold, hard evidence over speculation and shaded nuance. During her latest routine trial of an alleged Nazi war criminal, the most extraordinary turn of events in all of legal history falls into her lap--Vision Machine. Suddenly Rachel has the tool to produce the hard evidence she needs to win her case. The question is will her shaky faith and doubting lawyer's training reject the gift given her? *Vision Machine* is available at all eBook retailers including:

- ☐ Smashwords: Vision Machine on Smashwords
- ☐ Amazon: Vision Machine on Amazon

8/19

30173382R10221

Made in the USA
Charleston, SC
08 June 2014